Journeys Beyond the Fantastical Horizon

JOURNEYS BEYOND THE FANTASTICAL HORIZON

A GALAXY'S EDGE ANTHOLOGY

Edited by Lezli Robyn

CAEZIK
SF & FANTASY

ARC MANOR
ROCKVILLE, MARYLAND

✳

SHAHID MAHMUD
PUBLISHER

www.caeziksf.com

"Introduction" copyright © 2024 by Lezli Robyn.

"The Measure of a Mother's Love" copyright © 2021 by Z.T. Bright. First published in *Galaxy's Edge* magazine, issue 53.

"Choice of the Conquered" copyright © 2020 by Alex Shvartsman. First published in *Galaxy's Edge* magazine, issue 45.

"The Right Reward" copyright © 2020 by Katharine Kerr. First published in *Galaxy's Edge* magazine, issue 45.

"The Bone Kite" copyright © 2020 by Errick A. Nunnally. First published in *Galaxy's Edge* magazine, issue 46.

"The Ecology of Broken Promises" copyright © 2020 by Andrea Stewart. First published in *Galaxy's Edge* magazine, issue 47.

"Duty and the Beast" copyright © 2022 by David Gerrold. First published in *Galaxy's Edge* magazine, issue 56.

"Night Folk" copyright © 2020 by Barb Galler-Smith. First published in *Galaxy's Edge* magazine, issue 47.

"Things That Shouldn't Exist" copyright © 2020 by Marina J. Lostetter. First published in *Galaxy's Edge* magazine, issue 46.

"Substitutions" copyright © 2007 by Kristine Kathryn Rusch. First published in *Places to Be, People to Kill*. Reprinted in *Galaxy's Edge* magazine, issue 53.

"Hive at the Dead Star" copyright © 2022 by Lucas Carroll-Garrett. First published in *Galaxy's Edge* magazine, issue 54.

"With Our Songs of Scars and Starlight" copyright © 2022 by J. R. Troughton. First published in *Galaxy's Edge* magazine, issue 55.

"Who Smiles Last" copyright © 2021 by Fulvio Gatti. First published in *Galaxy's Edge* magazine, issue 53.

"Tracks on the Moon" copyright © 2021 by Todd McCaffrey. First published in *Galaxy's Edge* magazine, issue 52.

"Pleasing the Parallels" copyright © 2020 by Alvaro Zinos-Amaro. First published in *Galaxy's Edge* magazine, issue 45.

"The Negotiator" copyright © 2021 by The Winner Twins. First published in *Galaxy's Edge* magazine, issue 50.

"Grave 657" copyright © 2021 by Mica Scotti Kole. First published in *Galaxy's Edge* magazine, issue 48.

"Against the Current" copyright © 2007 by Robert Silverberg. First published in *The Magazine of Fantasy & Science Fiction*, October/November 2007. Reprinted in *Galaxy's Edge* magazine, issue 52.

"Echoes of Gliese" copyright © 2022 by Christopher Henckel. First published in *Galaxy's Edge* magazine, issue 54.

"Timely Visitor" copyright © 2021 by Jack McDevitt. First published in *Galaxy's Edge* magazine, issue 50.

"How Does My Garden Grow?" copyright © 2021 by David Cleden. First published in *Galaxy's Edge* magazine, issue 51.

"Barnaby in Exile" copyright © 1994 by Mike Resnick. First published in *Asimov's* magazine, February 1994. Reprinted in *Galaxy's Edge* magazine, issue 50.

"Giant Mechs in the Distance, Forever Fighting" copyright © 2022 by ZZ Claybourne. First published in *Galaxy's Edge* magazine, issue 55.

"Worrywart" copyright © 2022 by Effie Seiberg. First published in *Galaxy's Edge* magazine, issue 54.

"The Color of Thunder" copyright © 2022 by Alicia Cay. First published in *Galaxy's Edge* magazine, issue 56.

"Men of Greywater Station" copyright © 1976 by George R.R. Martin & Howard Waldrop. First published in *Amazing Stories* magazine, March 1976. Reprinted in Galaxy's Edge magazine, issue 57.

"O$_2$ Arena" copyright © 2021 by Oghenechovwe Donald Ekpeki. First published in *Galaxy's Edge* magazine, issue 53

"For the Great and Immortal" copyright © 2024 by Daniel Burnbridge. First published in *Journeys Beyond the Fantastical Horizon*.

"The Space-Time Painter" copyright © 2022 by Hai Ya. Originally published in the Chinese edition of *Galaxy's Edge* magazine, April 2022. English translation copyright © 2024 by Roy Gilman. English translation first published in *Journeys Beyond the Fantastical Horizon*.

ISBN: 978-1-64710-117-6

First Edition. First Printing September 2024.
1 2 3 4 5 6 7 8 9 10

An imprint of Arc Manor LLC
www.CaezikSF.com

This book is dedicated to the new writers who feel like they will never succeed, receiving rejection slip after rejection slip.

Don't self reject. If you keep submitting, one day your story could be published alongside the greats in the writing industry—or *you* could become one of the headliners!

CONTENTS

Introduction

by Lezli Robyn

When the first editor of *Galaxy's Edge* magazine, Mike Resnick, passed away, I didn't have time to mourn. I had to prepare the next issue for publication, and that turned out to be the most cathartic experience. I soon realized how much this magazine impacted new writers—and myself, as editor—when I started buying stories. The joy authors felt to get their acceptance letters, contracts, edits, and then see their words in print for the first time, was so infectious, and their happiness spilled over, deeply affecting me. It helped soften the grief, and it also showed me how much I really do love editing.

Stepping into Mike's very big shoes felt daunting at first. He had been a mentor in my life, and then my collaborator and friend, and now I was being entrusted with one of his creations. While I had already edited novels for a few years, I was now being put in a position of editing a magazine that was known for the "Writer Children" it created.

After ten years of publication, we've now converted the magazine into an anthology format to increase its distribution, and *Journeys Beyond the Fantastical Horizon* is the first book in the series. As a tribute to a decade of publication, this anthology collects the best fiction from the issues I've edited. Once you read the caliber of the stories, you will understand why the words written by these authors inspire me.

Writers' first professional publications have appeared in *Galaxy's Edge*, and we've showcased stories by venerated legends of this field, such as George R.R. Martin, who has a reputation for paying-it-forward as much as the original editor of the magazine. The opening story, "A Measure of a Mother's Love" by Z.T. Bright, tells the poignant tale of a mother learning how to let go of not only her human son, but her alien one, rightfully winning the inaugural Mike Resnick Memorial Award for Best Science Fiction Story by a New Author. The most recent winner of the award, "For the Great and Immortal" by Daniel Burnbridge, is first published within these pages.

Another author making a huge splash in the beginning of their career is Oghenechovwe Donald Ekpeki. I was absolutely delighted to be the first to publish "O$_2$ Arena," about one man's fight to save a life in a future Nigeria where oxygen is the currency, and sexism and poverty are a constant battle. That novelette has well earnt its stripes, becoming a BSFA, Nommo, and Hugo finalist, winning the Nebula Award for Best Novelette!

To say that I am proud of our authors is an understatement. When Barb Galler-Smith was announced as an Aurora Award finalist for "Night Folk"—the first story I bought for the magazine to be nominated for an award—I didn't know who was more excited: the author or the editor. When I first read Christopher Henckel's "Echoes in Gliese," about a captain desperately trying to save the life of his organic spaceship's newborn baby, or Alicia Cay's "The Color of Thunder," about a daughter having to defy her dad to save the winged creature believed to have killed her brother, I was blown away by these authors' talent. I cannot wait to watch their careers soar.

One of my favorite pieces is "Duty and the Beast" by David Gerrold. Not only is he the writer of one of the most celebrated *Star Trek* scripts, and the author of a novel that was turned into the movie, *Martian Child*, but after an accomplished career decades long, he continues to put as much heart and effort into his stories as our newer authors. As does Katharine Kerr with her short story "The Right Reward," showing her deft touch in sculpting words. I can't wait to edit her science fiction novel later this year.

Whether it is a fantasy story bordering on horror, such as Andrea Stewart's "The Ecology of Broken Promises," depicting how people try to deal with their deceptions being represented physically on their bodies in the form of extra (lying) mouths, or a science fiction story bordering on the post-apocalyptic with ZZ Claybourne's hauntingly beautiful and melancholic "Giant Mechs in the Distance, Forever Fighting," about a man's ability to hold onto the small joys in a war-torn life, this anthology will show you the scope of what the speculative fiction field has to offer readers.

Closing out this book is the incredible novelette by Hai Ya, "The Space-Time Painter," which was first published in the Chinese edition of *Galaxy's Edge*, and won the Hugo Award *before* it was translated into English for this anthology. If you watched his acceptance speech at the Hugo Ceremony, the trials Hai Ya overcome to make his first fiction sale is nothing short of inspirational.

I could go on and on about the writers in this anthology—extolling the talents of The Winner Twins, or pointing out how rare it is for an author to be able to write laugh-out-loud humor *and* also manage to tug at our hearts in the same story, like Effie Seiberg does with her utterly charming "Worrywart"—but then this introduction would become an essay, and I think you would much prefer to read the wonderful fiction.

So, enjoy!

Read. Dream. Celebrate life.

I now have to notify five new "Writer Children" that they are the next finalists for The Mike Resnick Memorial Award, and yet I am the one who feels like the winner for being able to work with such talented people.

The Measure of a Mother's Love

by Z.T. Bright

My pod on the Chinese national orbiting station is decorated to look identical to my home back in Guangdong Province. The only exception is that the view from my window looks out over the entirety of China, rather than my garden and my late son's tomb. It's not really a window, actually, but a large video screen in disguise. It spins with the rest of the pod which provides the simulation of gravity without the dizzying effect of perspective. It's also not nearly as spacious. Just a small kitchen, a modular couch-bed, and a bathroom. But it's all that Zhu and I need.

Zhu, my extraterrestrial son, reclines on the windowsill in silence. He's similar in form to a mantis, but more round and about the size and color of an American football. He's not really a "he"—his kind don't have genders like we do—but he chose the name of my son, Zhuang, so I think of him that way. He stares at Earth, tracing its curvature with a pencil-like foreleg, tapping distractedly with the firm shell of his exoskeleton.

Tink. Tink, tink.

Every morning I sit with my notebook and pen, relics from my days on Earth, waiting for Zhu to say something. He always says such interesting things, mostly about how strange humans are, and I write as much of them down as I can. I wish I'd done that with my first son.

But today, Zhu is quiet. He's never this quiet. It worries me.

5

"Would you like to help me make qingtuan later?" I say, hoping to prompt him. He loves qingtuan.

He doesn't respond.

"You *are* going to come with me tomorrow, right? I can't believe it's been a whole year since our last trip."

The Global Reclamation Organization allows everyone one day on Earth per year. Part of the united global effort to reverse human damage to the planet and keep future human impact as low as possible. They say that in the future people may be able to live on-planet again. I, like many, take my one day during the festival of Qingming. Traditionally, we sweep the tombs of our loved ones, honor their memories, and burn incense.

Zhu still does not speak.

In an attempt to brush off my concern, I begin to prepare the qingtuan—a traditional Chinese dumpling eaten during Qingming—since it seems I won't get anything out of Zhu this morning. For a time, I hear only boiling water and the rhythm of my knife as I chop spinach.

Zhu speaks into my mind as I drop the spinach into the boiling water. "Yes, Mei. I will go with you to Earth."

Though I've raised him from a larva these last five years, and I think of him as my son, he still does not refer to me as his mother. I try not to let it bother me, but it does. I can tell that something about his tone seems off—I'm his mother, after all—but I force myself to be glad that he's finally said something. I strain the spinach and boil its vibrant green juice as I knead glutinous rice dough.

It will be good to celebrate the first day of Qingming at the tomb as a family.

Zhuang, my human son, was only fifteen when the government mandated construction of the orbitals. It wasn't a surprise. The effects of global warming on the planet were no longer debated. Sea levels rising had displaced millions. Those same warming waters set off a ripple effect of aquatic species extinction that had reduced the availability of a significant number of human and animal food sources. With hurricanes, wildfires, not to mention the inability to control carbon emissions and the massive spike in related mortality rates—how could we save both our species *and* our planet?

Most governments had already implemented reproductive limitations. Now Earth was to become a protected nature preserve of sorts in the hopes that the removal of humans from the global footprint could reverse at least some of the major damage over the next few generations—potentially save the planet before humanity had triggered a mass extinction event from which there would have been no return.

The nations of the world set a ten-year deadline to get their first ships into orbit, sparing no expenses. They wouldn't get everyone up within that time frame, but it would be a start, and it would continue on a schedule.

Ten years felt like a long time. Zhuang would still have time at home before university, and even then, he'd go to school close by. And surely it would take decades, or more, to get *everyone* to orbit. He'd be able to experience a normal childhood before everything changed.

But the day after the orbital announcement, I found him packing his bags.

"What do you think you are doing?" I asked.

"Mother, they need as much help as possible with the construction of the ships."

"You are only a child! You have school!" I am ashamed to say I did not control my temper very well.

"Are there not more important things than school?"

"Not for a fifteen-year-old boy!"

"Mother, we are talking about our *planet*."

I couldn't admit it at the time, but I remember thinking how mature he seemed in that moment. Kneeling next to a black duffel bag with a folded T-shirt in his hands, he stared at me without passion. Our argument had not riled him. He was completely confident in his decision.

Any further arguments about him being too young to leave died before they reached my lips. I tried emotional guilt. "So, you are going to leave me here? All alone?"

He stood, stepping over his bag, and enveloped me in his long, wiry arms. "What is it Father used to tell me? 'The measure of our sacrifice is the measure of our love?' I sacrifice for you. For China. For Earth," he said as I sobbed into his chest.

That would only be the first time he'd quote those words to me.

✧ ✧ ✧

As I prepare to leave my pod and head for the shuttle, I place Zhu in my travel bag. He still has not given me permission to tell anyone else about him. As far as I know, he's the only one of his kind on Earth. He thinks so too.

I strap the bag to my back and descend the ladder from the pod bay and into the zero-gravity corridor that leads to the shuttle bay. I grab one of the moving handles and it gently tows me down the corridor.

Zhu is still not as talkative as normal, but at least he'll answer my questions. I don't quite understand his explanation of how the intimate nature of conversing telepathically somehow impresses the meaning of his words into my mind, to translate them from his native tongue, but he assures me that I wouldn't be able to comprehend the squeaks and clicks he'd make if he spoke out loud.

While *he* can speak into my mind, *I* have to vocalize out loud to him. Since there is no one near us to hear, I feel comfortable speaking to him. No one wants to be called crazy for seemingly talking to themselves. "Are you excited, Zhu?"

"I'm nervous."

"Nervous? Have you ever been nervous to go to Earth?"

"No."

"Have you ever been nervous about anything?"

"No."

"Then what are you nervous about?"

He doesn't answer right away, and I can't press him as I've arrived at the shuttle. Attendants help me off the moving handle, slow my momentum, and bring me to a stop at the shuttle door. I use the handrails to guide myself inside and into a personal seat-pod. I secure my bag in the under-seat compartment, fasten my waist and chest straps, and pull the helmet down over my head.

After the hissing of the pressure regulation, Zhu speaks into my mind. "Mei, I'm nervous because I have started to build my cocoon."

My heart drops into my stomach, and not because the shuttle has started its descent. Zhu's cocoon will prepare him to travel spacetime in search of a new home for his species. I am about to lose another child.

Zhuang didn't visit often from Shenzhen where one of the orbitals was being constructed. He said they hardly had any time off at all, working about fourteen hours every day. But he did visit every Qingming.

We would prepare qingtuan together and visit his father's tomb. Then we would enjoy the pleasant spring weather together for a day, though the skies became grayer, more murky, each year. We would walk and talk, trying to fit a whole year of conversation into a single day. As much as I wished we weren't apart, these full days together were my fondest memories with him.

But on year nine, one year before the orbitals were to be completed, I noticed he was having trouble keeping up with me. At first, I was proud that I was so physically fit as I aged. Then I realized he was sick. We spent the rest of that day together in the hospital.

He was diagnosed with COPD, given a personal ventilator—they were becoming more and more common—and given the all-clear to return to work. I begged him to stay. He'd done honorable work on the ship for so long. He deserved to stay home and get healthy.

Of course, he would not think of it.

"The measure of our sacrifice is the measure of our love."

The bus taking us to my village is nearly empty, so I can speak quietly to Zhu. Vibrant afternoon sun shines through the windows. I hold the bag on my lap and open it, revealing Zhu. He's wrapped himself in a type of film, almost like the film of a gourd seed as it dries. He's told me about this process. About how this moment might someday come. But I had been hopeful he'd choose to stay. If not to summon more of his kind to Earth, then to stay with me for himself.

After all, with humanity moving to the orbitals, could there be a better location for an alien species to settle? From what Zhu had told me, his species developed their technology to work in harmony with nature, and they actively improve the conditions of any world they settle on. I had no doubt they could help humanity undo so much of the damage we'd done to our planet. Unfortunately, they only move to planets where the dominant species accepts them—and their interstellar secrets—without reservations.

Why won't he stay? Can't his people at least *try* to work with human leaders? Apparently I am not enough for him. Not a good enough mother to convince him to stay. Tears slide freely off my nose and chin.

"Please be careful with your tears, Mei. If the cocoon gets wet, I will need to begin the process over again. It may take days."

I sniffle, wipe my nose with my sleeve, and nod. "Okay. I'm sorry. It's just that I hoped you'd stay."

"I hoped I would too. This is not about you, Mei. It is about your planet. About your people. My kind will need to cohabitate with another intelligent species, as I have with you. We are not physically capable of surviving on our own, especially with the wildlife of Earth. Do you really think humanity would accept us? Nurture us? Be grateful for the truths about the universe we can share? Or would they use us? Subject us to tests? Fear that we would usurp them?"

He'd previously explained that he believed his previous foster species had been dying off quickly due to an incurable disease. He didn't remember everything after this jump through spacetime, but this was his mission: to test other planets and intelligent lifeforms. I wasn't chosen specifically. It was just random chance we found each other. Though, he does say they are drawn to strong emotion in a sentient species when they choose a new world. Something about it increasing the success of the future bond between the two species.

My grief must have been an emotional lodestone for him.

"Zhu, have I not cared for you? Nurtured you?"

"Of course you have. But your people are quick to anger. Quick to violence. They have a long history of not accepting those who are different from themselves."

I can't argue those points, but I want to. "We are trying to mend our ways. That must count for something. We've even created orbital living stations to protect the planet from future harm."

"After you nearly destroyed it."

"Don't talk to me about humanity as a whole. I'm human, and I treated you well!" I can feel heat rising under my collar and I cut my retort short, understanding that I'm making his point for him.

He doesn't respond. I zip up the bag to protect him from my tears. Aside from my sniffles, we spend the rest of the bus ride in silence.

Zhuang didn't visit for Qingming on the tenth year. He called me to say he'd be coming back in the summer with our boarding passes. He could barely get the words out between coughing fits. Each cough squeezed my heart in a vise.

When he finally came home, I thought I'd be happy to see him, but he looked worse than he sounded. He was too pale, too thin. I made him tea and spoiled him with drunken shrimp and har gow—his favorite foods—for days. Maybe he just needed some rest and a mother's loving care after ten hard years.

In fact, he seemed to improve. He needed to wear his ventilator nearly all of the time, but he did have more energy. It almost seemed as if a weight was lifted off his shoulders. I let him sleep as much as he needed.

After a week, it was time. We watched the orbital launch into space, each of the 157 segments of the orbital launching individually. The suspense was painful. If any of those pieces didn't make it, the whole attempt would have been a failure. Some countries had already experienced failures, most notably the United States.

But our Shenzhen ship, China's first, launched each segment successfully. I was just happy to have the suspense over with and let out a long sigh of relief. I looked to Zhuang, his eyes glued to the television, tears of joy streaming down his face and onto his respirator mask. I understood then, in a way I hadn't before, that this ship was his life. He'd put everything he had into it, literally sacrificing his health for it.

One month later, it was almost time to start boarding the first wave. There was a lottery for most, but those like Zhuang, who had worked on the ship for so long, were given passes. We were only allowed two bags each. It had taken me an entire week to decide what to bring. But an hour before we needed to leave, Zhuang's bags were not by the front door.

When I approached him about it, he held out an envelope with my boarding pass. "There's only one. I will not be joining you." He tried to say this without emotion, but I could tell his voice caught at the end.

I was speechless, too many questions flooding into my mind at the same time. Why wouldn't he be coming? Did he really think I would even consider going without him? Why hadn't he told me this before? What had happened?

He took off his mask to speak. "Mother. I left to work on the ship because I felt it was my duty. For ten years, all I thought about was getting you into orbit in time. Before you got sick like so many older people are. Or before pollution, or the hurricanes triggered by the climate changes, took our home. Or worse …. And I succeeded. You get to go. But the orbitals are for people like you: currently healthy, many years ahead of you. Not for those who it's already too late for. We don't have the resources to send sick people up. Eventually, the people aboard will get old and sick. That's normal, to make way for the new generation. *That* needs to be our focus. I can't go."

For a moment it was I who couldn't breathe. I would not go without him. But I suspected he would hate me for it.

I've become desensitized to the state of disrepair my village is in. I haven't entered my old home in years. It's too depressing. My garden is now just an overgrown tangle of weeds, effectively making it indistinguishable from the rest of the village.

But, in the shade of a Chinese fir, Zhuang's tomb is kept clear. Or as clear as something can be that is only swept once each year. I crouch before it and unzip my bag, removing a small hand broom, a rag, and a bottle of water.

Zhu's cocoon is more opaque than it was earlier. Gently, I remove him from the bag and place him at the foot of the tomb. The cocoon feels light and papery, and I am reminded of a wasp's nest. I try not to think of the loss that the cocoon will bring to me and begin to sweep the tomb.

"Mei …"

"Yes, Zhu?"

"Are you angry?"

I don't answer immediately, trying to accurately assess my emotions. "I am hurt. And confused. And yes, I think I am a little bit angry, though I know I shouldn't be."

"I am sorry, Mei. It was never my intention to cause you pain."

"Thank you. Are you sure you have to leave? You have seen the progress humanity has made here. What of our orbitals? Solar shields? Tectonic energy harvesting?"

"These are great strides. But would you admit they came rather late? You flirted with disaster for many, many years. The damage to your planet will take generations to fix, *if* your plan succeeds. And what happens if your Earth Climate Pact disintegrates? The nations of your people are too splintered."

"We agreed that the orbitals would not be weaponized. We've entered an age of peace the likes of which this planet has never known."

"Correction, the most peaceful period your *species* has ever known. Yet, you don't think each country has weapons stockpiled secretly on Earth? This is the *most peaceful period in the history of your species*, yet one wrong political move could mean unparalleled destruction. You just admitted to being angry with me. If the one person who should nurture me above all others can get angry with me, how can my kind expect to be welcomed here?"

He has me beaten. I cannot win this argument. Just as I could not have won the argument with Zhuang all those years ago. I begin to cry again and watch a tear fall onto my shoe, only inches away from Zhu's cocoon.

"I've hurt you again, Mei. I'm sorry. I hope you know this is not what I want. I wish I could stay. But my people pull me back to them, and it is time."

I've never considered this. That the decision to leave wasn't entirely up to him. Guilt washes over me for arguing with him about this in our last moments together. "You don't want to go?"

"Part of me … much of me, wants to stay with you forever."

"But not all of you …"

"Not all of me. There are parts of me, as I assume there are parts of you, that require me to make sacrifices for the whole of my species. But if I could stop this, I would. At least for a while longer. I've already been delaying for longer than appropriate."

"I'm sorry, Zhu. I didn't know." I collapse to my knees. I want to scoop him up, but I don't dare let my tears fall on the cocoon.

"I cannot stop the metamorphosis, Mei … but you can."

We argued for days, Zhuang and I. But it wasn't until I unpacked my bags that he seemed to understand how serious I was. I understood why he was upset. He'd spent what should have been the best years of his life working on something for me, and I wouldn't accept it.

But I was equally convicted. I would not give in. What kind of mother would I have been if I'd willingly left my son to die alone?

We argued on the couch in front of the muted television. "Being your mother is all I care about! The only thing in this world that I care about. I'm sorry, Zhuang, but there's nothing you can do to change my mind."

How wrong I was.

Zhuang stood, removed his ventilator mask, and wrapped me in a hug. I sobbed into his chest, exactly like I'd done ten years ago when he'd left me the first time. "I'm sorry, Mother. We shouldn't argue anymore. I love you."

He sat back down, and I went out to the garden to pick some vegetables for dinner. When I returned, my basket full of cabbage and cucumber, Zhuang wasn't there. I suspected he'd gone to take a nap, and I began preparing our meal.

Halfway through slicing a cucumber, panic struck me like a lightning bolt. Had Zhuang's ventilator been on the couch? I dropped the knife and ran, the blade clanging to the floor behind me.

I knew before I saw it that I had been right. The ventilator was on the couch, turned off. I ran to every room in the house looking for him. I screamed for him so hard I thought my throat was bleeding. He must have gone out the back. I ran out the back door, but when I couldn't see him anywhere, I realized I'd never find him in time. I called for paramedics. They could barely hear me, my voice gone from the screaming.

I ran back outside to look for him, with no luck. It was the police that found him hours later. He'd walked straight into the forest, seemingly aimlessly. He had collapsed a little over one mile from home.

Unable to sleep that night, I found a note he'd written on a torn notebook paper and left with his ventilator.

The measure of our sacrifice is the measure of our love.

He underscored the word "love" three times, as if to make sure I understood why he'd done it. He knew I'd have nothing to stay for. That I wouldn't let his sacrifice be for nothing.

The next morning, mostly numb, partially angry, I walked through the trees where Zhuang had been found. That's when I found Zhu. He spoke into my mind, asking for help. I already had failed to save one child. How could I say no to another being just as vulnerable?

There was no sense in staying. Being home would only remind me of Zhuang. I grieved by packing my bags again, too broken to mentally process that I had just found an alien, or even consider the importance of first contact. The next day, I picked up Zhuang's ashes and we boarded the last shuttle to the orbital.

"Zhu, you're not suggesting that I—"

"I don't know what to do, Mei. I don't completely want to go, but I don't completely want to stay. I will find peace in either destination."

It would be so easy. I know he can't halt his primal instinct to create his cocoon, but if I just get it a little bit wet each time it started to form, he'd stay forever. "Would you resent me?"

"Why would I resent you? I am giving you permission."

I think of Zhuang during his last days. "Won't part of you always wonder if you should have gone?"

"I suppose. But if I go, part of me will always wonder if I should have stayed."

I stand and resume sweeping the tomb. Out of splash radius of the cocoon, I dampen the rag with water and begin wiping the tomb. Is this really a decision I can make? Could a mother really choose to abandon her son?

But maybe I'm not *really* his mother. Maybe that's just a lie I'm telling myself. Something that makes it easier after losing Zhuang.

I place the water and the broom back in my bag. The sun is starting to set. I will need to get back to the shuttle soon. I remove the incense and the container I packed with qingtuan. After lighting the incense, I open the container and sit down next to Zhu.

"I think this is my best batch yet," I say, taking a bite of one of the soft, green dumplings. It is earthy and slightly sweet. "It's a shame you can't have one."

Zhu understands the implication. "So, you won't ..."

"No. I love you too much for that."

The measure of our sacrifice is the measure of our love.

"Thank you, Mother."

Every morning, I wake up early and write in my notebook. I think of things my sons said or did during their time with me. Today is Qingming, one year after my last day with Zhu. So, I write the lesson my sons did so well to teach me.

The measure of our sacrifice is the measure of our love.

Zhu had requested I leave him at the tomb, where he would finish his cocoon and travel through spacetime to find another planet. I told him I loved him and left him there. It was painful, but right.

Lately, the news has indicated that scientists and politicians believe they've made first contact with an intelligent alien species. That that species potentially has the technology to help us heal our world. They've not released any specifics yet, but I think I know what this means. I hope Zhu had some nice things to say about me.

Smiling as I think of him, I rise to pack my travel bag. I will prepare qingtuan before I go—enough for two. After all, today is the first day of Qingming, and I look forward to sweeping the tomb.

This time for both of my sons.

Choice of the Conquered

by Alex Shvartsman

We watched Javier's house crumble and burn on the big screen.

"This is how the world ends," said Cho. "Not with a whimper, but with a series of bloody bangs."

Nicholas gripped the metal railing, his knuckles white from the effort. "We're down, but it ain't over. The world hasn't ended."

Cho nodded toward Javier, who seemed so small from the vantage point of the metal seats encircling the stage, where the rest of the prisoners sat. "Tell that to him."

Javier stood under the floodlights in the center of the stage, a dozen cameras encircling him like a pack of jackals. He was staring into space, somewhere past the cameras, his gaze vacant, his left eye twitching.

James Beamon sidled up to Javier. He was wearing an expensive gray suit and an orange tie which matched the color of Javier's overalls. His graying slicked-back hair and thin mustache made him look like the giant rat that he was. There was a big fake grin plastered on his face. He held a gold-plated microphone in his hand.

"There you go, ladies and gentlemen. Another round of righteous retribution delivered against those who would jeopardize everyone's safety and well-being." The screen became split, showing the close-up of Beamon's face on one side and the smoldering ruins of the house on another. "The demolished tenement was Mr. Soto's childhood home.

17

He inherited it from his parents and resided there with his wife and children up until his arrest last month. Mr. Soto, do you feel that this sacrifice was an inroad toward your repaying your debt to society?" Beamon shoved the microphone in Javier's face.

The hardest part is making the choice, no doubt about that. But being forced to grovel afterward in front of this fat quisling, in front of millions of indifferent assholes who tune in to watch our suffering for entertainment, that's almost as difficult.

The way I figure, there are two possible scripts. You can play the remorseful, reformed criminal, stare into the cameras and renounce your beliefs, your core values. Most people do this; toward the end, they aren't even pretending anymore, not really. This is the option the producers like—you get preferential treatment, some extra food afterward. Who knows, maybe even a slightly less gut-wrenching choice next time.

It is also permissible to be the defiant villain. You can hold up your chin, glare at the host, curse at him, say you'd cut his throat with a dull butter knife given half the chance. You can say almost anything you want, so long as you don't somehow insinuate that you're the good guy. There's no reward for this, but this sort of thing keeps the viewers tuned in, so you don't get punished, either. Don't go off script, keep your head down, and you can survive this process physically, if not emotionally.

Javier focused on the microphone. He stared at it in silence for a good ten seconds. Just as Beamon was beginning to get impatient, Javier reached toward it slowly with both hands, but then he kept going, grabbing for Beamon's throat.

This wasn't Beamon's first rodeo. Lashing out at the host is common enough, despite the consequences. He stepped back deftly, slapping Javier's hands aside. Before Javier had a chance to try anything else, the guards tasered him. Javier collapsed on the spot, stunned by the electric shocks.

Beamon straightened out his jacket. "I suppose that answers my question," he said into the microphone. "We'll be back after these messages."

The smile washed off his face as soon as the cameras stopped rolling. He looked like he was about to kick Javier in the ribs or something, but he just stood there and watched the guards drag the prisoner away.

They have this down to a science. The third-worst thing you can do is go off script during the live show. Javier went off script. Poor bastard was in for it now: beatings, starvation, and a stint in solitary.

The second-worst thing you can do is refuse to make a choice. They don't punish you for that directly; they simply consider your answer to be *both*.

The worst possible thing you can do is kill yourself. We've all wanted to do this at one point or another, to take the easy way out, so we don't have to choose anymore. It's the ultimate way to go off script. They tell you right from the start: you kill yourself, they will hunt down everyone you've ever known, and they will make them suffer.

The new guy was up next. I heard his name was Arnold or something, but I hadn't interacted with him yet. He was only brought in the day before.

"The next convict to pay for his crimes is Arnie Swekel of Madison, Wisconsin," Beamon said into the microphone. "Mr. Swekel was driving drunk. His truck swerved onto the sidewalk and hit Mr. John Thornton, vice minister of production for the North America region. Mr. Thornton died instantly. Mr. Swekel has been sentenced to make five choices as part of his punishment, starting tonight."

"They're dragging drunk drivers in here now?" Nicholas crossed his arms. "He ain't even political."

"It's all the same to the quislings," said Cho.

At the center of the stage, Arnie stood impassively, his expression neutral. I figured the reality of what he was about to go through hadn't really sunk in yet.

"What do you have to say for yourself?" Beamon offered Arnie the microphone.

The new guy didn't move to take it. He leaned in slightly and said, "It was an accident." Then he just stood there, hands at his sides, waiting.

The rat must've expected Arnie to be more eloquent, but he just rolled with it. He pulled the microphone back and the cameras zeroed in on him.

"During the glory days of the Roman Empire, its citizens could walk unmolested half across the known world, protected by nothing but the fear of retribution. Everyone knew that, should any harm befall a citizen, Rome would dispatch the mightiest military in the world to decimate whatever town or village was thought responsible." Beamon paused, staring intensely into the camera. "Decimate, ladies and gentlemen, literally meant killing ten percent of the population. They would line up every man, woman, and child, and kill one in every ten as punishment. Surely most, or even all, of these people were innocent. But so great, so disproportionate was Rome's expected response that anyone would think long and hard before they dared to harm a single hair on the head of a citizen."

Beamon was good at his job, I'll give him that. His baritone was smooth and velvety and hypnotic. You couldn't help but listen.

"We live in a dangerous world, ladies and gentlemen. The heroes who work for the Office of Planetary Security are the only ones standing between us and the total annihilation of Earth. Surely, they deserve as much or more protection from the terrorists and malcontents than the Roman citizens ever had.

"Mr. Swekel here," Beamon pointed at Arnie, "may believe he's innocent, but he's not. He chose to drink and get behind the wheel of his truck. And he killed a hero, a gifted administrator at the OPS, who could have made a tangible difference between the North American region meeting its tribute quotas and an annihilation of a city, perhaps even his own hometown of Madison. And for this, Mr. Swekel must pay."

Beamon's voice began to crescendo. "He must make a series of impossible choices, very painful choices that will prove to be more retribution than justice. Some innocent people whose only sin is their association with the convict will suffer greatly. But this is necessary, for it will make any insurrectionist think twice, keep the OPS personnel safe, and by extension keep all of *us* safe and secure, ladies and gentlemen."

Beamon turned to Arnie again. "Are you ready to make your first choice, Mr. Swekel?"

Arnie just looked at the rat, his expression still neutral.

On the screen next to Beamon, a photograph of an old woman appeared.

"This is Mr. Swekel's great-aunt Betty Connors. She is suffering from a late-stage stomach cancer and, according to her doctors, has only a few more weeks to live. She is currently in hospice care and her pain is somewhat mitigated by morphine drip."

The photo of the old lady was replaced by that of a man in his early twenties.

"This is Mr. Swekel's nephew Robert Tibbs, a promising young man who just earned an engineering degree from the University of Chicago."

The cameras focused on Beamon and Arnie again.

"Your choice is as follows: either Mrs. Connors will be denied her morphine and forced to suffer her last few days in unbearable agony, or Mr. Tibbs will be denied any engineering jobs—or, in fact, any non-menial job that pays more than minimum wage—for the rest of his life."

Beamon paused to let the implications sink in. "A relatively quick but extremely painful end for one relative, or a long life of mediocrity for another. You must now decide—who will pay for your crime?"

I didn't know this Arnie guy, but I was certain the choice wasn't an easy one. They do an extensive background check on all of us to make sure of that. The real punishment isn't so much making the choices, but having to live with them afterward.

Arnie once again refused to take the microphone. He said, "Robert Tibbs." His facial expression never even changed.

"He's a cold one," said Nicholas.

"I don't know," said Cho. "He's resisting in the only way possible—by denying them a good show. Who knows what he's actually thinking or feeling?"

I nodded. "I wish I had the poker face to do that."

On stage, Beamon kept babbling something about justice and retribution, but I wasn't listening. I studied Arnie's face, trying and failing to catch a glimpse of what was hidden behind the façade.

I was a junior in high school, filling out college applications, when the aliens came and the world changed.

Their ships circled the globe in high orbit, nearly halfway to the moon and too far for our missiles to reach. Their only communication was a twenty-four-hour warning: they would obliterate Orlando, Wellington, and Dubai in lieu of a greeting.

The governments did their best to get everyone out—even those who refused to believe the threats. We packed frantically, trying to decide what to take from our old family house in Baldwin Park, what treasures accumulated by three generations of my family to squeeze into the one-backpack-per-person limit mandated by the feds. I watched soldiers break down the door of our neighbor's home. They dragged the old man out screaming, cursing, shouting at the top of his lungs how this was all a government plot …

The three cities were destroyed on schedule, mere hours after we left, and whoever had managed to stay behind died.

Only then did the aliens respond to our hails.

They demanded unconditional surrender. They'd demonstrated their ability and their willingness to annihilate us, having chosen cities that, according to their calculations, would have relatively low impact on the planet's manufacturing capacity and infrastructure.

My father laughed bitterly when he heard that on the news. "They're making a statement," he said.

"What statement is that?" I asked.

"They blew up Disney World, son. They're telling us: no more fun and games."

The aliens claimed they were embroiled in an interstellar war, and they needed to shorten their supply lines. From precious metals to manufacturing complex chemicals, they would not only rob Earth at gunpoint, but force us to work like the prisoners in a gulag.

They provided detailed demands that would strain the planet's economy and manufacturing capacity. Any failure to deliver the decreed quota would result in destruction of another city in that part of the world.

World leaders held a summit in Italy, searching for a solution. In order to meet these quotas the very nature of the world's economy had to change.

After the weeklong summit, the Milan Accords were signed birthing the Office of Planetary Security—an organization granted extraordinary powers in order to enact this change, to protect humanity by acting as the aliens' overseers and enforcers.

By the time I got into college, OPS mandated that, like so many others, I switch my major. The new world order had little use for historians, but it badly needed more engineers.

Arnie was beginning to acclimate to what passed for a life in this place. I saw him chatting with some of the inmates: the conversations were always brief, always one-on-one. It was as though a feral dog was learning to be around humans again.

He tapped gently on the doorless frame when Cho, my cellmate, was out. I looked up from the dog-eared copy of *1984*.

"I saw what you were reading and couldn't help but comment on the irony," he said, leaning against the wall. "I'm Arnie, by the way."

"Richard. And yes, reading Orwell in here seems appropriate. The fact that the prison library stocks it either proves the quislings incapable of understanding irony, or it's a psychological mind fuck, like everything else about this place."

Arnie sat on the other bunk without waiting for an invitation. "How do you mean?"

I put the book down.

"You've noticed how this is not like your average prison, right?"

"I'm afraid I have no basis for comparison," said Arnie.

I counted off on my fingers: "Prisoners can mill around and socialize during the day, there are no work shifts, and there are no cameras in here. There's a library and even a decent infirmary. This place is quite tolerable, when they're not torturing you on live TV."

"So what, you're saying the quislings are being nice to us?"

"Not in the slightest. They just don't want to damage the merchandise. They don't want any of us breaking when the cameras aren't rolling. Hence this small measure of privacy and autonomy."

Arnie leaned forward slightly, his palms gripping the metal side of the bed frame. "I never actually read Orwell. My college sweetheart, Tina Perelli, she couldn't get enough of it. She kept quoting *Animal Farm* and *1984* and even some non-fiction essays or something that he wrote. True fan, you know? Me, I never understood the appeal of reading about dystopias. The world was a crappy enough place in real life, and that's *before* the invasion."

"I suppose there's some comfort to be found in reading about people and places that have it even worse than we do," I said.

Arnie was about to reply when Cho came back in. Arnie gave each of us this weird little nod, then squeezed past Cho and left without another word. I wasn't sure at the time if he had social anxiety or just didn't like Cho for some reason, or another thing entirely. We all become damaged in this place, even if we weren't before. I figured Arnie would come back and talk some more if he wanted to.

23

We didn't speak again until after the following week's torture session.

Arnie was called up to make a choice again. He looked Beamon straight in the eye as he elected to have some ex-girlfriend of his forced to move from Detroit to Vladivostok. Beamon said she was a copy editor by trade and didn't speak a word of Russian, but he couldn't elicit any sort of reaction from the stone-faced Arnie. Who knows, maybe that relationship didn't end so well and Arnie didn't mind seeing her suffer, but then quislings usually researched choices better than that to make certain every one of them really hurt.

A few hours after the show ended, Arnie pulled me aside in the corridor. "Can you and Cho meet me in the library at midnight?"

I stared at him, surprised. "What in the world for?"

Arnie leaned in close and whispered a single word into my ear. "Cicero."

I met Jen on the second day of college. We were both freshmen, and were both forced to study engineering instead of the liberal arts majors we had intended to pursue before the aliens arrived. We liked each other instantly and were already sleeping together a few days later. We made adjusting to new college life far more tolerable for each other than it might have been otherwise.

It was several weeks later when Jen told me she'd decided to join a resistance cell.

"You're out of your mind," I said. "Resist how? What do you think a bunch of hotheaded kids are going to accomplish?"

"I don't know," Jen said. "Things looked pretty gloomy for the French republicans and for the American revolutionaries at some points, right? If people hadn't joined those movements, we'd still be singing 'God Save the Queen.'"

"Yeah, well, that's what OPS is for," I said. "Let them deal with the aliens. They've got the resources and the worldwide support."

"Bunch of bureaucrats," she said. "All they seem interested in is filling the quotas and doing the invaders' bidding."

"What would you have them do?" I asked. "Slingshot themselves into orbit and slap the aliens?"

"This isn't funny," she said. "The world is changing around us. We've got to fight for what we have, or it will slip through our fingers and it will be too late."

I stretched and yawned. "This is way too philosophical for this early in the morning. Let's get some coffee."

She frowned, then scrawled an address on a piece of paper. "We're meeting here at seven tonight. If you change your mind, the passcode to get in is 'Cicero.'"

I laughed. "A passcode?"

"We're taking this seriously," said Jen. "You should, too."

"Okay, I'll bite. Why Cicero?"

"Weren't you going to study history? Cicero is, like, the inspiration for Adams and the other Founding Fathers. He pretty much invented the modern concept of liberty." She paused, momentarily lost in thought. "I wonder what he'd think about this alien invasion."

"All I remember is, he was the dude who just *let* the soldiers cut off his head when they came for him," I said. "I don't think he makes a great poster boy for the resistance."

"Whatever," said Jen. "That took more courage than fighting. Anyway, I've got to go, or I'll be late for Calculus."

There's technically a 10:00 p.m. curfew, but it isn't strictly enforced. Inmates gather in rooms to play cards or talk late into the night. As long as no one causes a ruckus, the administration will look the other way. They will, however, use the curfew as an excuse to add on an extra choice to one's sentence, if they want to punish that prisoner for some perceived offense during the game show. Some of us don't want to take any chances and obey the curfew, others are willing to take the risk; anything to make their time here fractionally more bearable.

Cho and I both tend to be careful, but Arnie's password was enough to prompt both of us to navigate the empty corridors. At night the library is a favorite spot for trysts among those men so inclined, as it is in a far-off corner of the building and the books that line its walls act as a natural sound suppressor.

Cho and I squeezed into the library. It was a cramped space the size of a teenager's bedroom and it was packed to capacity that night.

There was Arnie, and Javier, and half a dozen others leaning against bookshelves.

"I believe that's everyone," said Arnie after he nodded briefly to me and Cho. "Thank you all for coming."

"Who are you, really? What's this all about?" Cho wasn't a patient man and he got straight to the point.

"I gathered you here because each of you is an active member of the resistance," said Arnie.

There was a murmur among the gathered. I knew that Cho and Javier were members of the Engineers but I couldn't vouch for the others. They must've felt the same way. Everyone studied each other warily.

"You are members of several different groups. The Engineers, the Ethicists, and the Decemberists. Each group independent and effective within the resistance, but all of them coordinating their efforts under the leadership of the Washington Six."

He looked around the room. "I am one of the Six."

Everyone seemed to speak at once, the murmur rising to a crescendo of voices. The Washington Six were legendary—a group of ex-CIA, NSA and other government operatives charged with nothing less than restoring the sovereignty of the United States from aliens and the OPS alike. The name referred to the number of clandestine services banded together to form the organization, not the number of individuals involved, which must've been considerably higher. Even so, I didn't know of anyone who met one of the Six in person. Claiming to be one of them while inside these walls was just about the most dangerous thing I could conceive of.

Arnie held up his hand, silencing the crowd. "I know what all of you must be thinking," he said. "It's a big claim. A dangerous claim, even. I can substantiate it for all of you, with names of your superiors, passcodes, and other information the OPS agents don't know, else they would have already used it against you in their sick game. But before I can tell you more, there's a problem we must take care of. There is a traitor among us."

The murmurs returned, everyone casting glances around the room.

"I've spoken privately with each of you since I got here, and during the course of those conversations I revealed the name of my college sweetheart. Except I gave each of you a different name: all women who are involved in the OPS in some way."

Arnie took a step toward Dave Fisher, a gregarious, bearded man I've chatted with once or twice in my time here.

"Guess which name Beamon used against me this afternoon."

His back against a shelf, Dave moved sideways toward the door, but before he could take a second step, Arnie punched him in the solar plexus.

Dave doubled over and Arnie hit him again, sending the smaller man onto the floor.

"All of you have been forced to make terrible choices in here, a crime OPS will surely pay for, but this man made the most appalling choice of all." Arnie tapped Dave's body with his boot. "He elected to snitch on the rest of us to the OPS in exchange for a reduced sentence."

Arnie reached under one of the shelves and produced a chain of towels tied together. He placed the noose around Dave's neck.

"The punishment for treason is death."

Dave began to whimper, but Arnie held him down with little effort. He glanced up, challenging any of us to disagree, to try and save Dave, but no one moved.

"They'll investigate this," said Javier. "You're creating an even bigger problem."

"I've had some experience at making such things look like suicide," said Arnie.

"Please," Dave whispered. "I have a family. You know what the quislings will do to them if they think I killed myself."

"That is the risk you took when you chose to become an informant," said Arnie. "Their suffering is on you."

Dave tried to scream, but Arnie yanked the noose, tightening it quickly around Dave's throat, so only a brief squeal got out. He pinned Dave's head to the floor with his boot and pulled on the noose until Dave's body stopped moving. Then he turned toward us as he wiped beads of sweat off his brow. "Now then, we have much to discuss."

We may have been prisoners, but witnessing a murder was a new experience for most of us. Even so, no one dared to question Arnie.

"We're getting ready to move against the OPS," he said.

That got everyone's mind off of Dave.

Arnie went on, "They've taken their mission statement of streamlining things and protecting us from the aliens and corrupted it, usurping power from world governments and growing wealthy in the process. The aliens pose a threat, but it's the OPS agents that torture and kill their fellow human beings."

No one in the library could disagree with that.

"The Six created the Arnie Swekel persona, and everything about me is a lie. Every choice they present me with, every individual they torture had their records altered by our hackers; in fact, they are related to the quislings, or somehow complicit in their crimes. I've been furnished with enough sacrificial lambs to feed to the OPS while I set things up on the inside."

When OPS was still in the process of taking the power away from planetary governments, the United States managed to funnel a tremendous amount of money, weapons, and other resources to the Six. The core group was all lifers, experienced undercover operatives who managed to survive for years despite the unrelenting pressure from the OPS. Long after the presidency and the Congress have been eliminated, pretty much everyone opposed to the OPS recognized them as the last remaining agency of the U.S. government and accepted their authority.

"What are you going to do?" asked Nicholas.

"*We*," said Arnie. "We're going to fire the first shot in the coming revolution."

I couldn't help but think back to Jen's words as I traveled home for a brief visit after having completed my freshman year.

During those nine months the U.S. government was disbanded, its power was absorbed by the OPS with seemingly little resistance or struggle. The voices that spoke out against this change were silenced with the sort of vicious efficiency Americans had never experienced before.

People were disappearing in earnest and suddenly no one was much inclined to speak out. Halfway through the year, Jen left for class and never returned.

I went to the police to file a missing persons report, but they retained me for questioning instead. The woman who interviewed me wore an OPS uniform. I'd never been to any of the resistance meetings, and I assume my interrogator knew that, because she took it relatively easy on me. She let me go with an admonition not to look for Jen anymore, and not to ask too many questions.

My parents had remained in temporary housing, ever since we had to leave Orlando. It was basically a huge trailer park on the outskirts of Ocala. The government made a lot of noise about relocating every-one to affordable housing that wasn't on wheels soon, but after OPS took over, no one was even talking about that happening anymore. So when I got off the bus, I walked for about twenty minutes, making my way past the maze of overpopulated trailers with clotheslines hung across them, drying sheets flapping in the Florida sun.

Dad was sitting in front of our trailer with a bottle of Jack in hand, sauced out of his mind.

"Dad?" I rushed to his side. "What are you doing with that? You've been sober for twenty years."

My old man looked up, his eyes watery and unfocused. "Ricky? Welcome home, boy."

"When did you start drinking again?"

I didn't dare ask why.

My kid brother Daniel poked his head out of the trailer. "Rick!" He rushed out and hugged me.

Daniel was sixteen. Mom wrote that he had been assigned to vo-cation school. No college for him; they needed factory workers and mechanics more than they needed engineers now.

"Ever since we lost the Cold War," Dad said.

"Huh?"

"You asked when I started drinking again, boy."

"We didn't lose the Cold War," I said.

"Yeah? We got central planning, a dictator in charge, good people taken away in the night for speakin' out and placed in labor camps. You wanna tell me how this is different from the Russkies?"

"He always gets like this half a bottle in," Daniel said. "No use arguing with him 'til he sobers up. Come say hi to Mom!"

I reluctantly followed him inside. Dad rambled on, oblivious to the fact that he had lost his audience.

Mom hugged me and asked a million questions about college. I answered the best I could, not wanting to spoil her mood. When she finally slowed down, I asked about Dad.

"He's talking politics again?" She gave Daniel a withering look. "I told you, any time he starts doing that, drag his drunk ass inside the house. We don't need the trouble of his nonsense landing on unkind ears."

29

Daniel peeked outside again. "He went off."

"Well, go get him then! I'll get some dinner going. Ricky must be famished after his trip."

Daniel muttered under his breath and left in search of Dad. It was the last time I ever saw my brother alive.

Today was the day, and I was nervous. Scratch that—I was scared as hell, and so were the rest of us.

The Washington Six had devised the most elaborate operation yet. Arnie, or whatever his real name was, infiltrated the world's most notorious political prison, taking out a high-ranking OPS official in the process. The Six had people standing by to whisk away our relatives and friends, anyone the OPS might choose to retaliate against. It was the only way to ensure our cooperation. All of it was in preparation for this day.

Today was the day Oscar van Vliet, chairman of the Office of Planetary Security, was going to attend the recording of our twisted reality show.

Today we were going to kill him on live television.

The nine of us took seats as close to the guards as we could without arousing suspicion. For many of us this meant sitting in the front row. While attendance is mandatory, most of the inmates don't care to sit too close to the action, and I don't blame them.

The word "Retribution" in fat golden letters filled the large screen. The dots above each of the i's were drawn as the two plates of a scale, like the one the blind goddess of justice is meant to hold. The outline of the scale itself was sketched out in black on the blood-red background of the show's logo.

Justice and retribution. Today would be our turn to balance the scale, and to have both.

We stood a chance. The guards weren't all that careful and the prison wasn't all that secure. Since the beginning of this program the thing that had kept us docile, had kept us willing to accept whatever cruelty they chose to mete out, was fear. Fear not for ourselves, but for our loved ones who would take our place should we stand out of line. But with the Six ready to move, to hide them from the wrath of the OPS, we were men with nothing to lose and plenty of hatred in our hearts. Also, Arnie said that he had an ace up his sleeve. He wouldn't offer details, but he told us to wait for the signal. He told us we'd know when it was time to act.

The bright lights flooded the stage and James Beamon strolled toward the center, a wide smile plastered on his rat face.

He spoke into the golden microphone. "Ladies and gentlemen, welcome to this week's episode of *Retribution.*"

The pre-recorded trumpets or trombones or whatever the hell they used for such things performed the show's iconic two-second sound effect. It reminded me of the *Law & Order* shows I saw as a kid.

Beamon carried on. "This is the only show where you can watch the criminals get what's coming to them. Live!" He shouted that last part with orgasmic joy.

They didn't have to make this show live. They could have taped it, censored out things they didn't like. But it was the prisoners going off script, the chance of an outburst, the drama of a human soul being destroyed in real time that brought in the ratings. Today we were going to make them regret it.

"We have a unique treat for you tonight, ladies and gentlemen, in that I'm joined by some very special guests."

This was it, it was really happening. I tensed up watching the commotion by the entrance. Several security agents walked in first.

"Please join me in welcoming Chairman of the Office of Planetary Security, the man who has done so much to keep all of us safe and comfortable, Mr. Oscar van Vliet."

The spotlight on him, van Vliet walked up to Beamon. He was in his sixties, tall and thin, with a few wisps of gray hair on a balding head. The two shook hands and exchanged a few words of banter, but I wasn't paying close attention. In a few minutes, van Vliet would be dead. I would probably be dead, too, but it would be worth it. He was Hitler and Pol Pot rolled into one, the man who had used an alien invasion to usurp an unprecedented amount of power. The world's first global dictator.

A section of seats was cordoned off from the prisoners and surrounded by security men. Van Vliet headed over there after his chat with Beamon, who raised his microphone again.

"That's not all, ladies in gentlemen. Also joining us today, in an extremely rare Earth-side appearance, is Fleet Commander Er'Grah of the K'a Protectorate, and his three adjoining broodlings!"

I swallowed a lump in my throat and exchanged glances with some of the other men. This wasn't part of the plan. The aliens seldom came to Earth, and certainly never before to a place like this. Did the Six know about this? And if so, why hadn't Arnie said anything? Arnie didn't turn around. He stared at the group of aliens surrounded by human guards, walking toward the podium.

They looked like a less exaggerated version of the alien Grays. The Fleet Commander was a bit over five feet tall, his skin tone somewhat gray and his head and eyes larger than a human's but not by as much as old cartoons would suggest. He could pass for a human from a distance, but up close his complexion as well as his smaller ears and almost non-existent nose marked him as truly alien. He wore a poncho-like tunic over what looked pretty similar to human pants and shoes. The trio of similarly dressed smaller aliens, ranging in size from three to five feet tall, followed him. Alien or not, who brings *kids* to a prison?

I glanced at Arnie again, wondering if the plan was still on. Attacking the aliens was not the same as attacking van Vliet. They would rain fire and death upon our cities. It was not what I had signed on for. On the other hand, this Fleet Commander was the true villain, the one who had destroyed our world by forcing us to reshape it. When would such an opportunity to strike back ever present itself again? Arnie turned his head slightly, making eye contact with a few of us in turn, and made a barely perceptible nod.

When Daniel found Dad that day, Dad was in the process of getting arrested by an OPS cop. Daniel tried to intervene, to plead with the cop. When that didn't work, my stupid hothead brother cursed the cop out.

The cop put two bullets in Daniel's heart.

I wanted to do something, but the memory of what had happened the last time I walked into a police station held me back. Later I found out that the cop reported it as Daniel questioning his authority and the authority of the OPS. He didn't even get in trouble for killing a kid, and few people were willing to risk attending Daniel's funeral so as not to be flagged as dissidents.

The rest of the summer flew by with me doing as best I could to keep the family going. Dad got sober and stayed sober, but he was never the same man again. Mom suffered a nervous breakdown. She was on all kinds of prescription meds, a shadow of her former self. I kept it together by dreaming of the things I'd love to do to that cop as I tried to fall asleep each night, but I was too much of a coward to try any of them.

Then the summer ended and I had no choice but to go back to college. OPS mandate: dropping out wasn't an option.

A few days after I returned to school, Kying-sun Cho, a junior I'd seen around the campus before, approached me on the street.

"You're Richard, right? Jen's boyfriend?"

I stared at him, surprised. No one had mentioned Jen to me ever since they made her disappear. "That's me."

"I heard about what happened to your brother. Sorry, man," he said. "Jen always had good things to say about you. It's a pity you never joined us. I was wondering if I may be able to change your mind."

He didn't have to work all that hard to recruit me.

The aliens made their way up to Beamon and he launched into another round of pompous introductions. Meantime, I saw one of the prison guards was laser-focused on Arnie.

Did he suspect something? The guard looked nervous, his hands tightly gripping an MP5 submachine gun.

Then Arnie looked right at the guard, their eyes locking, and nodded again.

The guard turned his gun on van Vliet's security men and started firing.

"Now!" Arnie roared, and all hell broke loose.

I lunged at the nearest guard, using the distraction to close the distance before he could react, and grabbing for his weapon. I couldn't see the others, but I was certain my co-conspirators were all doing the same thing.

Arnie knew the OPS censors would immediately cut the broadcast, but the Six had ensured that camera feeds would continue broadcasting online. The world would get to see what we did that day.

The guard and I struggled on the ground. There were bursts of gunfire and screams, and people running, but we focused on each other, punching and clawing, and choking. He was stronger and had me pinned me down, but my resistance kept him from using the MP5 strapped to his torso. Then the guard's body suddenly went limp and he collapsed on top of me. Standing above him was a prisoner whose name I didn't know; he wasn't a part of our plot. He had kicked the guard in the temple hard enough to knock him out, and he was smiling.

I liberated the MP5 and turned to face the stage. Although my struggle against the guard felt like an eternity, only a few seconds had passed. Many of the security personnel and many of the prisoners were down. The guard who fired first lay dead, his body riddled with bullets.

With so many extra security men there because of the aliens' visit, our plot would have surely failed had it not been for the other prisoners joining the fight, jumping at the chance for some retribution of their own. A number of them rushed the security men unarmed, buying the rest of us extra time. It seemed all the pressure built up in our prison had finally found a valve, and there was no stopping it.

I watched as some of the prisoners shot at the aliens, the bullets deflected by some sort of force shield. The aliens scattered in different directions, while the Fleet Commander shouted something into a communication device in his alien tongue.

Van Vliet and Beamon must've known something because they, along with the broodlings, raced toward the Fleet Commander and kept close to him. There was a flash of light and suddenly all of them, including the security guards who stood close enough, were gone, teleported away by some sort of alien tech.

It took only a few more seconds to finish off the remaining OPS security personnel and prison guards. Then the gunfire ceased and it was just the prisoners, hyperventilating over what we had just done ….
Except that wasn't quite right. Standing in the middle of the room, seemingly paralyzed into inaction, was the smallest of the aliens.

The silence didn't last long. "Get him!" one of the prisoners said, and advanced on the Gray.

"Stop!" shouted Arnie. He walked up to the alien, stared down at him, then turned to face the rest of us. "It's just a broodling. We don't attack children."

The crowd murmured, their mood dark.

"The alien bastards make no such distinction," said someone. The susurrus grew louder.

Javier joined Arnie, but the rest of the conspirators remained with the crowd. I was one of the handful of people in the room who had a gun. I had the power to make the unilateral decision, the opportunity to avenge Jen and Daniel that might never come again in my lifetime.

I looked at the alien kid. Whatever the differences between our species, it was clear that he looked very scared. The scales of justice and retribution danced in my mind.

Cho looked up from where he crouched over Nicholas's dead body. "We've failed, Arnie," he said, his voice cracking. "Van Vliet is gone. But the cameras are still rolling. We can still strike back at the aliens, for the sake of everyone on the planet. After all they've done, after they've treated us like cattle, it's worth doing, whatever retribution they mount."

Men around me nodded in approval. The crowd edged closer to Arnie and the alien.

"They don't treat us like cattle," said Arnie. "They treat us like bees." He pushed the broodling gently behind him, keeping himself between the alien and the bulk of the men.

"They're beekeepers. So long as we produce honey, they'll leave us alone. Maybe even protect us from whatever other threats exist in the universe. But if we sting, if we start acting like wasps, they might be inclined to fumigate the hive."

"Bees may sound prettier, but that still makes us slaves," said Cho.

"Yes," said Arnie. "And it sucks. But we can't afford to do anything about that, not for now. We need to deal with the more immediate threat of the OPS—the *humans* that betrayed us. They're the ones killing people, they're the ones setting up labor camps and profiting from everyone's misery in what they deem as the best interests of the aliens. We need to make the aliens understand that we can meet their quota, contribute to their war effort better without these leeches. Perhaps even gain their cooperation in eradicating the OPS, or at least ensure that they won't stop our revolution, as long as we keep producing.

"We can't afford to antagonize them. But none of those things matter. The real reason is that if we hurt this child, then we're no better than OPS and no better than the aliens. If we're just like them, then why the hell are we even fighting?"

Cho grudgingly lowered his gun. "All right. Let's show them we aren't wasps."

I understood Arnie's reasoning, but logic and need to act rarely go hand in hand. I gritted my teeth.

Out of the corner of my eye I noticed another prisoner with a gun edge his way to the side of the room where he had a clear shot at the alien. Arnie, who was focused on the angry mob of prisoners in front of him, didn't even see him. There was no time for a warning.

I was a veteran of many terrible choices that were forced upon me, one at a time, and now I faced what seemed like the easiest choice yet. The man with the gun had absolved me of the responsibility, saved me from having to make the decision myself. All I had to do was stand there, to merely let events take their course. Let someone else be responsible.

I looked into the oversized eyes of the broodling, peering around Arnie's thigh. Then I raised the MP5 and fired a single shot at the man with the gun.

He screamed and went down, clutching at the shoulder wound. I was glad that I did not kill him, even though I'd aimed for the heart. I'm not a marksman.

I stepped forward and turned to face the crowd alongside Arnie and Javier, aware this scene, this stark reality, was still streaming around the world.

"He's in charge." I pointed at Arnie with my free hand, my gun leveled at the crowd. "We do things his way."

No one was happy with this turn of events, least of all me. Some of the men tended to the guy I'd shot. Many of the others looked like they were summoning up courage to attack us unarmed, like they had the OPS men. Even our fellow conspirators seemed undecided, not moving against us, but not joining us in facing off against the crowd, either.

It was a long, difficult standoff pregnant with anger and uncertainty. I'm not sure what would have happened had the aliens not shown up.

They arrived in a flash of light, two dozen of them teleporting into the room. They all had strange-looking guns and wore body armor.

"Stand down. Do not shoot!" Arnie raised his hands above his head. "Put down your weapons, people."

With the alien guns trained on us, I made a show of very slowly resting my MP5 on the ground. Cho and Javier discarded their weapons too. The crowd surged back, away from the armed aliens.

"Step back," Arnie said quietly. Javier and Cho and I did as we were told, joining the crowd.

Arnie stood there unarmed, next to the broodling. He gently ushered the little alien toward his people. The broodling seemed too traumatized to move. It wasn't until one of the aliens came over and took it by hand that it followed, leaving Arnie alone in the center of the room.

"Take me along," he said. "I wish to speak to Fleet Commander Er'Grah."

The alien who came over to retrieve the broodling stopped, considered Arnie.

"I'm the one responsible for what happened here," said Arnie. "Not these men. He may want to punish me, or he may want to hear me out. Either way, you won't get in trouble for bringing me along."

The alien seemed to consider it. I couldn't tell what he was thinking, but then there was another flash and the aliens were gone, and Arnie was gone along with them.

The men around me sighed with relief, as did I. I'd expected the alien soldiers to shoot us all down. Not that I was optimistic about what came next. The OPS SWAT teams were surely gathering at the prison by now. *Those* bastards, those traitors, I didn't mind shooting. We were all dead men, but we'd take as many of them with us as we could on the way out.

I wasn't afraid to die, not after everything I've been through already. Instead, my thoughts were with Arnie. For all I knew, the aliens might be peeling his skin layer by layer already. But I had to believe that they weren't so different from us that they would not see the value in what he had done.

Arnie had made the difficult choice to stand against his own people in order to protect the alien child. It was out there, for the world to see, because the cameras had never stopped rolling.

He was the sort of leader humanity deserved.

He was also the sort of leader the aliens might choose to work with. After all, why deal with the angry bees when you can placate them and get the results you want instead? Surely our conquerors would see it this way.

I picked up the gun and waited for the OPS goons.

37

The Right Reward

by Katharine Kerr

"**M**a, I gave you the damn credit card 'cause I wanted you to use it." Over the phone Jimmy's voice sounds just slightly exasperated. "It's been months, and you haven't charged a thing."

"Well, there's nothing I need, really," Mrs. Walker says.

"It's not for things you need. It's for things you want. Something for fun. New clothes, you know? CDs—I mean, records. Fun stuff."

"Oh. Oh well."

Mrs. Walker is sitting in her beige vinyl recliner while she talks on the phone to Jimmy, her clever son, the one who's the computer programmer up north of San Jose. From this chair she can see about two-thirds of the mobile home into which she moved when Jimmy's dad died. In the front end by the windows stand the maple chairs and the loveseat with the white upholstery printed with parrots (there wasn't room for the matching sofa and the little hassocks with the contrast ruffles).

"Ma," Jimmy says. "You can even go out to dinner on it."

"Oh, oh well, I don't know about charging food. It seems so wasteful."

"Ma. Jeez."

"I know! Lorena's kids need—"

"Nothing, Ma. My nieces are spoiled little princesses already. Buying them stuff isn't going to change that."

38

Spoiled and thoroughly nasty to their grandmother as well, is what Jimmy means. Mrs. Walker has to admit it, though she refuses to say it aloud.

"Well, maybe something for your nephew then. A baseball glove?"

"Ma, Jason is a little geek in training. Books, if anything. Comics."

"Disney?"

"No, Ma. Superheroes."

He might as well have spoken in another language.

"Um, well," she says. "Let me think."

Between her and the living room stands the big simulated cherry-wood TV on the top of the room-divider bookcase filled with magazines, stacked neatly on their sides. After that comes the built-in pale pink formica dinette designed around the view window opposite the niche for her recliner. Her back is to the bathroom, and the all-formica kitchenette with the built-in appliances stands between her and the little bedroom area at the far end.

"Ma, there must be something you want."

Mrs. Walker is afraid to tell him that she would love a bus ticket from Santa Regina, down in the Salinas Valley, which is where she lives, north to San Jose, so that she could visit him and meet his new fancy friends and see his brand-new condominium. She is pretty sure he'll find a polite and cheerful way to say no to that proposed way of spending his money. Neither of her children has wanted to visit or be visited for nearly a year now. She embarrasses them, she supposes, with her mumus and old lady comfy shoes and lack of smart conversation.

"Tell you what," she says instead. "Tonight I'm going to watch the home shopping channel."

"Now that sounds great. I bet you'll find something there. Call you again soon, Mom. Bye."

Mrs. Walker hangs up the pale pink Princess touch-tone phone. Jimmy gave her an iPhone for her birthday. It sits in its box on her dresser top. Outside the view window she can see a ten-foot-wide strip of lawn, some spindly trees in tubs, each tub wrapped in astro-turf for a rustic appearance, and the gray aluminum siding of Mrs. Gonzales' trailer in the next hook-up over. Even though the sun is still shining in the cool of a summer evening, she picks up the remote and turns on the TV. A few clicks brings her one of the several home shopping shows available from the Santa Regina basic cable.

She nearly changes the channel immediately, because the current program features pieces of one-of-a-kind jewelry. The only jewelry she wears these days is her wedding ring set. What catches her interest is a brooch so ugly that she wonders who would have made such a thing, much less worn it. A two-headed worm made out of gold curls around an insect with only one head but two necks and torn wings made of silver. Oddly shaped red stones stick out of the worm at random intervals. Bit of green glass stud the insect. The skinny blonde women who holds up the items for sale stares at it and fails to smile.

"Sure is different," Mrs. Walker says.

It is ours. The voice in her head sounds as real as Jimmy's had. *Please, someone help us! We must get it back, or all is lost.*

"Well," Mrs. Walker says, "it's been marked down. You could just order it."

She can hear us! The voice in her head turns into many voices, all babbling together in some odd language. The original voice snarls a word that seems to mean "shut up," because they fall silent. It continues in English. *Please please help us!*

Maybe she is going crazy. Suddenly hearing voices? I've been alone too much. Yet they seem so real! "Why don't you just buy it?"

We are not of this earth. We come from the stars. Thus, our shipping has no address.

Aliens? "You're pretending. Aren't you? Something you saw on TV?"

Please, no, this is the truth! You seem like such a kind lady.

"How come you know English?"

We don't, silly. This is telepathy. Also in one of your Earth movies .... I know I know—we will reward you. Anything you want that we can give!

"I don't suppose you could get my kids to visit."

A hard one, that. Our spawn are just as ungrateful as those of your species. But we can try.

The TV screen no longer displays the golden worm-thing, but Mrs. Walker remembers the item number. She hesitates, then realizes that if nothing else, she can tell Jimmy she bought something. Her purse, with the credit card in an inner pocket, sits at her feet.

"Oh, all right," she says. "It's only fifty bucks."

The sound of rejoicing aliens fills her mind.

"Shut up! I've got to make the phone call."

Since Mrs. Walker splurged and also paid for express delivery, the package from the home shopping channel arrives two days later. They certainly pack things well, in yards of big plastic bubbles as well as certified archival tissue paper. She takes the gaudy plaque out with both hands. From the sheer weight of the thing, she can assume that it's pure gold and jewels masquerading as something Dollar Store cheap. Until that moment, Mrs. Walker has convinced herself that she imagined the alien voices, but looking at the gleaming worm-thing wrapped around the half-headed bug-thing convinces her that only aliens could have made it.

No human had such bad taste, surely.

Further proof arrives that night with the aliens themselves. Three upright beings wrapped in garments more or less like hood-ed sweatshirts and big baggy pants knock on her door about two hours after sunset.

We have brought you your fifty bucks. And a tribute.

"Well, thank you. Come in."

In the soft electric light of the living room she can see that their faces inside the hoods match the worm thing, not the bug thing. They have two eyes, they have a slit of a mouth, and their moist skin is a dark yellow, much like gold. They also have hands with three fingers each. One of them lays a package wrapped in some sort of green leaves onto the end table and quirks his? Her? Its? Mouth in an imitation smile.

You are a hero of the Zargoth Empire. We salute you. You have returned the Narg of Plinsk!

Another alien chimes in: *open it open it open it.*

Hush! Don't be rude to the hero of the Zargoth Empire! One of the shrouded figures turns toward her. *My spawn lacks manners. Some things appear to be universal.*

"Well, I guess so. What is this? Some kind of memorial?"

Yes, to a great victory. Without it, the new emperor cannot be cloned.

Mrs. Walker has heard about cloning on the news. "How interesting."

She smiles. They bow from the waist. She opens the package and finds two things. The first is a circular plaque made of silver with a reproduction of the piece of jewelry in the middle. All around it lies a design that looks like it might be lettering. The second is a framed piece of paper with someone's attempt at writing English.

The translation.

"Thank you."

The statement, We hereby declare Mrs. Pamela Walker a hero of the Zargoth Empire, is mostly misspelled in clumsy purple printing, but clear enough.

"Well, that's real nice. Real nice indeed."

They bow, they smile. She smiles back. One reaches into the sweat-shirt-like garment and brings out two twenties and a ten. He/she/it lays it on the end table.

Reaching your children are a problem. We cannot get into any of their minds. They are not like you. But if you think of anything else you want, please call to us.

"Well, I guess they just aren't. I was kind of afraid of that." She allows herself one deep sigh. "There's really nothing else I need."

More bows, more regrets, and at last they leave, taking the Narg with them. Mrs. Walker looks at the reproduction of the plaque and decides that no, she won't cry about the children's lack of visits. She really hadn't expected anything different.

Jimmy calls her the next day. Her purchase has shown up on his credit card statement.

"I'm glad you got yourself something." His voice sounds genuinely happy. "Jewelry, it says. Ma, if you would only use that iPhone, you could send me a picture of it."

Mrs. Walker has to think fast. He is not going to believe one word about the Zargoth Empire.

"It's not exactly jewelry. It's a weird little thing. It made me curious, that's all. A plaque. Like you hang on the wall."

"That's good, too. Something kind of cheerful? Kittens? Flowers?"

"Not exactly. Um, it's kind of strange."

"If I can get away, I'll come down and take a look at it. One week-end, maybe."

Mrs. Walker has heard that "one weekend, maybe" before. She smiles, not that he can see it, and says, "That would be real nice."

Later than evening, while she drinks her usual cup of bedtime Postum, something odd occurs to her. Maybe she can figure out how to use that phone Jimmy gave her. After all, isn't she a hero of the Zargoth Empire? And Jimmy did print out very careful instructions on how to use it. In simple language.

It takes her most of the next day, but in the end she does charge the phone, take a picture of the plaque, and send it off to Jimmy. Although she doubts that she did it right, he calls her about five minutes later.

"Uh, Ma, what in hell is that thing?"

"I told you it was kind of strange. I just thought it was interesting."

"It is that, all right. Uh, Ma, I was thinking maybe I'd come down Saturday. See if you're all right."

"What? You think I'm getting senile or something?" She puts a little laugh into her voice.

"Course not! I know we all leave you alone too much, that's all. I thought I'd stop by Lorena's and pick up the kids, too."

"The girls won't come, but it'll be nice to see Jason."

Her prediction turns out wrong. When Jimmy's big SUV pulls up on Saturday afternoon, all three kids get out and come running to the door. Lorena and Jimmy, her two spawn, as she has started to think of them, walk up more decorously. There are hugs and chatter, and everyone settles down to eating the pie she made with the ice cream Lorena brought. No one, however, mentions the plaque. Finally, once the pie's gone, the chatter has died, and the two girls are watching cartoons on the TV, Mrs. Walker can stand it no longer. She smiles at Jimmy and Lorena.

"Don't you want to see what I bought?"

"I do," Jason says. "The picture looked cool."

"You saw the picture?"

"Uncle Jimmy sent it to Mom."

Lorena looks so embarrassed that Mrs. Walker can guess that the spawn were worried about her, all right. Oddly enough, she rather likes the way this makes her feel.

"It's okay, Ma." Jimmy speaks so fast that she knows she's right about the worry. "What counts is that *you* like it."

"I want to see it."

"Jason, don't be rude to your grandmother."

Who is, Mrs. Walker thinks, *a hero of the Zargoth Empire.*

"I'll show you, Jason. I've got it down at the other end of the trailer."

43

"I'll just wash these dishes up," Lorena said. "No need for you to do it, Mom."

Drawn by the TV, Jimmy joins the girls on the floor of the little living room. Jason follows Mrs. Walker when she goes into the bedroom area. In her top dresser drawer, she keeps the plaque wrapped in the leaves that came with it. Although they've dried to a pleasant yellow, they are still flexible.

When she unwraps it, Jason whistles under his breath. "Grandma, that is so cool."

"I thought so, too."

"It looks like it comes from some alien race. Y'know, like Star Wars."

"It does."

"The movies?"

"No. it's real. It's called the Narg of Plinsk."

Jason spots the framed translation. "Some alien wrote this, right?"

"Right."

"Oh cool!"

"Don't tell your mom, all right? She'll think I'm just getting old and strange."

"Yeah, that's what she said. Uh, I mean …" He blushes scarlet. "I wasn't supposed to tell."

"I figured it out anyway. But they were real aliens. I promise."

Jason studies the plaque for a minute or two, strokes the leaves, reads the translation again.

"It's too bad we can't visit their planet."

Mrs. Walker is about to voice one of those soothing platitudes that adults use to squash children's dreams. Instead she smiles at her only grandson. "Well, I don't know. Maybe we can. I could ask. I can't promise."

"I know!"

"All right. And then we'll have to plan some way your mom and uncle won't miss us while we're gone."

"There's gotta be a way."

"We could just tell them the truth, I suppose."

"Grandma." Jason pulls a long face. "Like they'd believe us! We need a secret identity."

"Ah." Her memory bestirs itself. "Like Superman."

For some minutes they study the plaque in silence. Jason looks up with a grin. "Yeah," he says. "I know. We'll just tell them we're making it all up. A game."

"Now that's the best idea yet. And that's what we'll do."

They are shaking hands on it when Lorena comes bustling back to join them. Mrs. Walker slips the translation under a convenient pile of underwear. Lorena reaches for the plaque, but draws her hand back fast.

"Oh Mom! It's so ugly."

"Yes. I'd never seen anything like it before, that's all. Lorrie, I've been meaning to ask you. Now that school's out, I was wondering if you wanted Jason to come stay with me some week. Just to give you and the girls a little special time together."

"I'd like that, but honey—" she turns to Jason, "would your feelings be hurt?"

"Nope. I like hanging out with Grandma."

"All right then. Phone me, Mom, and we'll work it out."

With one last shudder at the plaque Lorena hurries away.

Yes, Mrs. Walker thinks, *this could work out just fine. I'll call out to them tonight—how do I do that, exactly?—and see if we can visit. And if not, I've already got the reward I really wanted.*

"Hero of the Zargoth Empire," she says. "That sounds real nice."

The Bone Kite

by Errick A. Nunnally

Jessica rolled over, half asleep. Her elbow struck something solid, where her husband should have been. She massaged her elbow and rolled over. Her hands swept along a warm, smooth surface. She frowned.

Dinner had been good, the wine had been great, and once their daughter had gone to sleep, the sex had been magic. All of this culminated in a sleep so deep that now she felt as if she were clawing to wakefulness through a veil of cotton.

"What the hell?" She swore under her breath and reached to turn on her light. Its glow barely penetrated the fog.

Fog?

She turned back to her husband's side of the bed. He lay enveloped within a clear rhomboid-like prism, similar to Lucite. She recoiled, her heart slamming in her ribcage. She slowly reached out, hesitant to touch the invasive material, and ran her hands over the warm surface again.

Her stomach turned and convulsed, her skin went cold. She worked her jaw until she ground out, "Jeff," and slammed her palm against the unyielding substance. "Jeff!"

Jessica stared at her husband, suspended, motionless …. Wait—not motionless. His chest rose and fell. She could make that out, at least, through the clear prison encasing him. She laid an ear on the rhomboid, listening past the blood thundering through her own body. Jeff's strange prison felt warm against her ear.

There's a heartbeat.

Relief tingled across her body and her shoulders relaxed. This madness felt like a nightmare. Something so surreal it was as if she'd stepped into one of Jeff's stories, an author's bizarre imagination spilled across reality. Nothing in her accounting background had prepared her for this. The corrupted world around her required an effort to process.

"Alive," she sighed, "but ..."

Her daughter's name speared her thoughts, *Allana.*

Pulse hammering again, Jessica swung her legs over the side of the bed, freezing just before her feet touched the cotton-like substance she'd mistaken for fog.

"What the hell is this?"

Her eyes took in the room. Everything was different, sketchy. *Literally* sketched. It was as if the room was roughly drawn, like thick pencil on paper. The walls, the windows, nightstands—everything but the bed had a surreal quality to its form. Even the space between objects seemed wrong. Fearing for her sanity, she struggled with her desire to look up, to verify there was a ceiling. When she did, she saw the same cotton-like substance hovering overhead and a feeling of vertigo made her sway.

Beneath her dangling feet, she could make out objects in the thick fog. She reached down and felt resistance against her hand before her fingers met the floor underneath the fog.

I have to do this, she thought and heaved herself out of bed. Her bare feet made little noise as she made her way out of her room and down the hallway to their daughter's bedroom, moving as fast as the clouded environment would allow. A night-light served as the sole illumination. It had been transformed into a warm, glowing orb, suspended just above the fog and snug against the wall. As she made her way to the doorway, the fog dragged against her skin, a bizarre resistance akin to slogging through thick mud under water.

She leaned through her daughter's door and felt the emotional punch of loss, a hole driven through her core. Allana wasn't there ...

The bathroom.

Jessica spun and high-stepped to the bathroom, evading the pull of the fog.

Empty.

Fear and sorrow pulled at her heart, the scream she felt in her throat came out as a whimper. "Allana?" she called out. No reply.

Sounds drifted in from outside. A warbling voice echoed, sometimes singing, sometimes talking, all incoherent. She felt the icy tendrils of shock creeping through her body and the walls began to dim, shadows pulled closer.

The walls.

"Why is this familiar?" She sniffed, denying any premature grief, and traced a finger along the sketched, paper walls. Then she ran her palm roughly under her eyes, smearing tears, remembering her daughter's drawings. From the corner of her eye she saw vague, sketched footprints. Childlike renderings of feet traced a path from Allana's bed, circled the room, went up the wall, and to the window.

Jessica scrambled over and peered out. Suspended in the air, like bits of paper frozen in the wind, footprints stepped down to the street below. All around her, the neighborhood was vague in definition. The streetlights were mere sticks with glowing dots on top, the pitched roofs a jagged repetition of angles. Cutting the night sky, a massive rainbow, impossible and flat, bent to the horizon. Movement caught her eye and she watched with growing horror as a figure came into view. It skipped and danced, singing to itself as its impossible, stick-like legs carried it along. Jessica watched and listened, her hands covering her mouth. It was a sort of potato shape and color, its face taking up more than half of its lumpy upper body. Two gelatinous orbs twitched in place of eyes. As it sang, a terrifying caricature of joy spread across its face beneath sparse and wiry hair. It stopped with a jerk and turned to look up at the window.

Jessica ducked and shuffled backward before creeping forward to peek. The thing looked at the house for long seconds. Then it returned to singing its song. As it skipped away, Jessica recognized the word it was crooning over and over: "Allaaaaaaaahnaaaaa!"

A nagging realization pushed her back to her bedroom where she circled the bed to open her husband's nightstand. He still lay there, trapped. She touched the substance entrapping him again before focusing on the task at hand and rooting through the top drawer. Inside, she found Jeff's Moleskin. Full of notes and sketches, it was something that Jeff always had at hand and scribbled in at odd moments.

Jessica had gotten used to the behavior early in their marriage, an unsurprising price to pay for marrying an artist.

Flipping through the pages, she found the note she was looking for. Jeff kept notes on his own creative ideas, as well as some of the more interesting things their daughter had said when she was much younger. The one she was looking at was from age five. Jeff had written a couple of words, "Eliot, portrait, 5." Next to it, Allana had drawn a pencil sketch of her childhood friend, a grotesque interpretation from her mind using awkward hands. It looked like the creature that Jessica had seen on the street. Other pages contained portraits of her and Jeff, recognizable only by the wiry interpretation of her loc'd hair.

She tossed the book on the bed and began pulling on clothes. Manic adrenaline drove her twitchy movements. She chose athletic gear and tried to remember the last time she'd needed to run with purpose. Snatching up the book, she shoved a small flashlight into her sweatshirt, along with the notebook. Her gaze shifted to her phone. She scooped it up, but it turned out to be nothing but a high-tech paperweight. No signal, just a bright screen of incoherent shapes. A bit of dull metal caught her eye. Jeff carried a folding knife and it sat with the other things he typically stowed in his pockets. She grabbed the knife and took a final look at her immobilized husband. It was time to find their daughter—she had no other options.

"I'll find her, Jeff. And I'll be back."

At the end of the hall, she found the stairs were flat, like a sheet of paper with lines drawn on it to represent stairs. Testing it with one foot, she didn't feel safe sliding down the paper. Jessica tensed in frustration and went back into Allana's room. The floating footprints remained. The window, she now realized, was nothing, just an empty space in the wall, a child's conception of glass. Despite that, there was a cool surface barring her way. She struggled with the geometry of grabbing the bottom of the window frame and managed to slide it up and open. She ducked, stuck one leg out, and paused, terrified. Love and trust guided her foot to the first, tiny floating footprint.

Better this than falling through paper stairs to God-knows-what.

The footprint sagged a bit, but sprang back when she took her weight off. Jessica looked down at the lawn.

"It's only fifteen feet or so," she told herself. "C'mon, Jess." Her scalp tightened at the thought of falling even a relatively short drop.

She tested it again, feeling the resistance, and levered herself farther out the window to trace her daughter's footsteps. Her back struggled with the effort to balance on the sketchy sole cutouts, and she fought back feelings of vertigo. At the bottom, the lawn, she realized, was actually a set-piece of oversized Easter grass. Everything had the surreal appearance of diorama objects hundreds of times their normal size. The footprints went into the street and pointed the direction the potato-head thing had gone.

The prints were so small. Jessica placed her foot next to one, knowing it was her daughter's, but trying to understand why it was so much smaller. Allana wore the same size shoes as Jessica now. Whenever Jessica dreamed of her daughter, however, Allana was small, still a young child. She'd grown so much since then. In the present, waking world, Allana tested her autonomy, worked to get her bearings as a twelve-year-old.

Far down the street, Jessica heard the thing singing again, warbling Allana's name. With one hand to steady the book, she jogged in the same direction, an absurd idea forming in her mind. The creature came into sight and she slowed to a fast walk, being careful not to make too much noise. She grasped the knife in her pocket and called out, "Elliot!"

The creature stopped on a dime and turned. "Yes?" Its voice sounded so young and slurred the "s" sound, making it into an approximation of "sh." The same way Elliot used to do. It trotted toward her.

Jessica clutched the knife and suppressed a shiver despite the very comfortable temperature. This world smelled like plastic, sugar, milk, and occasionally cinnamon. As "Elliot" approached, however, the smell turned to something akin to the collective scent of a daycare. Fresh diapers and lotion, juice boxes and dried snacks. And its appearance—*his* appearance—made the smallest, most primitive part of her brain scream with terror. It was a physical configuration that was impossible for anything alive, as all child-drawn stick figures were.

"Hi!" it yelled gleefully. "Hi, Miss Jessica!"

Jessica choked back her rising bile. "Hello … Elliot, how are you?"

"Good." He fidgeted, tracing one stick-foot on the ground.

"Elliot, I need to ask you, where's Allana?"

He hopped up and down on impossibly skinny legs, an excited grin splitting his lumpy head. "She's down here. I'm lookin' for her to play!" He pointed in the direction her prints indicated she had gone.

Jessica's skin crawled whenever Elliot moved, and the misshapen thing wouldn't stop moving. The boy was nothing but a drawing, a child's illustration given form and substance and life. Though she was now immersed in a world of such impossibility, Jessica shuddered with revulsion at the overwhelming evidence. The horror she felt at the sight of this childish interpretation brought to life paled in comparison to her desire to be reunited with her daughter.

"Would it be okay if I walked with you, Elliot?" she asked, pushing aside her fear and tattered sanity.

"Okay!" He started off again, singing his Allana song, bright and happy.

Under the scritching sounds Elliot's legs made as they bounded off the asphalt, Jessica could hear something else. Static? No. More like a million echoes of Elliot's footfalls.

The air had congealed into something sweet and familiar. She could smell grape jam and peanut butter. Elliot stopped, but began dancing from one leg to the other. He wanted to go forward, but something appeared to be making him nervous. Jessica shuddered. She held the folded knife in clenched fingers as different sounds came closer, surrounding them. The cloying sweet smell raked the inside of her nose and she felt something scuttle across her toe.

Elliot screamed.

The jump was instinctual, as was the yelp. Jessica twitched back a step as her spine tingled with Elliot's childlike screams of pain and terror. His voice clawed at her ears, set her instincts on fire, but the ants were everywhere on him. They scrambled up Jessica's legs, the size of pine cones, leaving sticky trails of sweetness. Jet black, the creatures were secreting the fermented sweetness of a peanut butter and jelly sandwich forgotten in the bottom of a backpack, soggy and molded. The ants pinched at her clothes, her skin.

Jessica brushed at her legs, pushing the ants off in rapid sweeps. "Elliot, brush them off, run!"

"No, no, no!" Elliot wailed and turned, stumbling, his skin inflamed and splotchy. The ants crawled into his huge maw and he tumbled to the ground.

The gurgling sounds coming from Elliot's throat pushed Jessica to the edge of panic. The boy was allergic to peanuts—the real Elliot, out in the real world. She glanced back at her home, then forward, at the little footprints marching off into the distance.

Without much more thought, she sprinted, her feet alternating between sliding on the viscous death of crushed ants or sticking in the aftermath of their passage. She ran until she couldn't hear the Elliot-thing anymore and her breath came in heaving gasps. Her husband's Moleskin notebook, still tucked into her sweatshirt, pressed into her side, scraping at her until she finally came to a halt, breathing hard, choking back her panic.

She fished the notebook out and began flipping through the pages. Throughout the front half, Jeff's scribblings had been supplemented by Allana's drawings and her own incomplete concepts. The little girl had a jarring, free form imagination, no doubt fueled by her father's interests. Her interpretations of his fantastical ideas had found their way into Jeff's notebook.

Above Jessica, the sky remained a flowing, indigo bisected by the massive rainbow. In the notebook, there were a few words and a sketch showing "the rainbow clam." A crustacean who emitted a rainbow while its shell was open.

"Jesus fucking Christ," Jessica muttered, her adrenaline-charged fingers pinched on a page with a single, hastily scrawled quote: *Ants are peanut butter jelly!* She flipped through a few more pages, trying to get familiar with the imaginings before continuing.

At the very end of the street, a copse of pine and maple trees separated the neighborhood from a private school campus. The trees were now impossibly tall, stretching straight up to the "sky" and striated. The trunks weren't closely packed and the forest floor was as flat as fresh concrete, but soft with pine needles. All of the branches above were entangled, with none appearing to dangle below their towering tops. Allana's penciled footprints led through the trees, and so Jessica followed.

As a family, they'd walked this way with Allana more than a few times to visit the bakery just beyond the campus. The small patch of forest was larger and darker than she remembered. Midway through, she spotted a collection of branches jutting out lower than any of the others. Entangled within them was an object composed of stick-like ribs in the shape of a diamond. A kite made of bones with a tail beneath it. Bright white, it hung above Allana's footsteps. Her little girl had apparently circled the tree a few times before moving on.

Jessica walked past the bone kite, getting a closer look, and saw that its tail was a string of vertebrae.

A quiet voice spoke, seeming to come from nowhere. "You must be Jessica."

She spun around, scanning the gloom. "Who's there? How do you know my name?"

"Allana told me. She said you might come looking for her."

Jessica stared at the kite. It had no face, nothing to articulate with, but it spoke.

"Where's my daughter?" Fire burned in her gut—she'd tear this thing to pieces if she had to.

"I'm not entirely certain where she is at this moment, but we can follow the footsteps."

"You spoke with her. Where's she going?"

"I can't be entirely sure …"

"Tell me where she's going or—"

"Or what? You'll take me from this tree? Because that's what I want."

Jessica stared at the thing for precious seconds before making her decision.

The kite called after her, "Wait! Wait …"

Jessica stopped walking.

"She went to the Rainbow Clam."

Jessica looked through the trees, toward the horizon where the rainbow dipped. "How do you know that?"

"That's where I told her to go."

"Why?"

"To help me. Only the clam knows how to help me fly again. I've been stuck here forever." The kite paused. "Allana couldn't reach to take me down, so I sent her to get help."

There was a time, Jessica remembered, when Allana had been dangerously naive. She wanted everyone to be happy, always wanted to help, no matter the cost. It worried Jessica to no end that someone might easily convince her daughter to stray. It had taken years to get through to her, to get her to be more cautious. The girl she was now, at twelve, was very different, but that little girl was the one Jessica most often remembered in her dreams. This thing had taken advantage of her little girl's trust.

"I see you met the ants," the kite said, breaking her from her thoughts. "Had I been there, I could've warned you, guided you through safe passage."

"Allana got past."

"She's a clever girl. Let me help you avoid dangers. Take me down."

Jessica pulled the notebook from her pocket and flipped through it. One of the last entries during Allana's preschool years was a simple, diamond-shaped drawing with the words "bone kite" beneath it. Jeff's only annotation was a line of question marks. She looked at the frame of thin bones, trapped in a tree. "Fine." Jessica sighed, reached up, and plucked the bone kite from the tree. It was extremely light, felt dry and brittle. "We're following her tracks, right?"

"Absolutely."

Jessica tucked the kite under her arm and started walking. Soon, they cleared the stand of trees and a vast expanse of the Easter grass lay before them, the low chain-link fences breaking up the space in intermittent planes. Dotting the grass were massive, cabbage-like growths. Dozens of heart-shaped, colorful faces floated above the field. Beyond them lay the bizarre brick buildings of the private school. A stink like hot garbage hung in the air.

"This field—never mind all this weird stuff in it—it's way too big, more than I remember."

"It is as Allana saw it, Jessica."

Allana's tiny footprints could be seen heading into the grass and beyond. A large dinosaur-like creature, the same hue as the grass, swam through the field and leapt over one of the fences, briefly scattering Allana's paper footprints. Its long green body twirled in the air, flippers tucked close, before it splashed down on the other side.

"Oh my God, is that thing dangerous?"

"The pliosaur? Not at all. It's the brain cabbage that you need to be wary of."

She looked at the gnarled shapes. "What do they do?"

"Think. Very hard. At you, into you. They'll destroy you from the inside out. Allana's mind is all soft angles and magic. She's safe."

Jessica glanced at the kite, then looked at the line of her daughter's footprints and clenched her teeth. Allana had been through here. She took a step to follow.

"Wait," the bone kite said.

"For what? My daughter is—"

"For *her*. Look carefully."

In the middle distance, the approximation of a girl danced. She had a deathly pale pallor, paperlike, and graceful. Her legs ended in little round stumps slipped into ballet shoes. She wore a pink leotard and tutu to match her shoes.

"Who's that?"

"Ecnad, The Little Ballet. You can follow her safely through, but you'll need to get her attention."

"How?"

"Try calling her?"

Frustration tensed Jessica's jaw, but she took a deep breath and shouted the dancer's name. The figure didn't react, simply kept twirling and hopping, bending at two-dimensional angles.

"She can't hear me from here."

"You'll have to get closer."

"But you said—"

"I know, but you'll never make it all the way across the field without her. The cabbage will make your brain their own. Your mind will become one of theirs and you, well, you'll be *gone*, just a lumpy green thing in a field. There's no other way."

Jessica swallowed her fear and wondered, *Why not go around?* She looked to the left and right of the field only to be met with the unsettling sight of nothing. The edges dropped away in hard angles marred only by the strange "fog" she'd wandered through to get here. She remembered seeing a ballet dancer in the notebook so she pulled it out and started flipping through the pages. *There.* Jeff had transcribed a story along with some pasted-in clippings of Allana's drawings. The story, titled "Ecnad," recounted the tale of a ballet dancer whose classmates trick her into dancing by herself all day. It ended with Ecnad impressing the teacher with her dedication; she goes home to her mother, triumphant with the teacher's highest praise.

"Won't those things affect you too?"

"Don't be foolish, I'm a kite made of bones."

Jessica swore under her breath and eased into the field, trying to move at an angle that would intersect with the twirling Ecnad. She hoped there was something in the story that could help her through this. She passed the first brain cabbage, moving through the grass with a wary step.

The first cruciferous obstacle, about waist high, glistened a pale green. It shivered and Jessica froze. Her throat tightened and she swallowed the lump before moving on. The brain-cabbages grew larger toward the middle of the field. She glanced and saw Ecnad ahead. A tingling fear crept up her spine, tightening her scalp. A sense of confusion swept over her. *How could this world exist? Where did it begin and end?* She frowned, memories sifting through her mind. Her daughter, over the years, the scares along the way. A broken arm, when she was seven. A misdiagnosed infection that kept her in the hospital for a week. The desperate effort to understand her child's wants and needs as she got older. The transition to—

"Jessica."

She blinked. Within arm's reach stood one of the cabbages. A huge one, easily two feet taller than she was. They were in the center of the field, though she didn't even remember walking here.

"Call to Ecnad. Jessica, don't lose yourself."

Jessica gulped and stepped back from the plant, took a deep breath and called to the dancer.

The Little Ballet froze in mid-twirl, twisting like paper, searching for the source of the voice. Jessica wanted this to be over, wanted to see her daughter again, to bring her back home and free her husband from the prism. None of this made sense. Her daughter's magical flight, the ants, Elliot, this strange world, the kite—

"Jessica!"

She turned on her belly in the fake grass, the dry edges tickling her face. Her mind had drifted again and this time she caught herself crawling toward one of the cabbages. Ecnad bent at an impossible angle to look in Jessica's eyes.

"Help, please, I have to find my daughter," she said to The Little Ballet.

The paper girl looked at the kite, then helped Jessica to her feet and began leading her back to the forest.

"No, Ecnad—the other way, please," Jessica said.

Together, they stumbled to the edge of the field where Ecnad released Jessica's hand and gave her a gentle push. The Little Ballet waved and twirled back to the field, resuming her dance.

Jessica sagged, struggling with an aggressive headache. Sweat and tears soaked her skin just from the fight to keep concentrating. "Oh, God ..."

"As I said," the bone kite said.

"Shut up. Which way now?"

The kite held silent under Jessica's arm.

"I said 'which way,' damn it." She felt how brittle the kite was and imagined breaking its bones.

"Follow the rainbow."

She sighed and looked up at the unchanging, indigo sky. The rainbow remained, bifurcating the expanse. It flickered, the colors dimming and coming back to full volume. "What was that?"

"What?"

"The rainbow. It flickered. Why?"

"I don't know."

"You don't—you said the rainbow came from the clam." Jessica tracked the arc down to the ground. It no longer appeared to land across the horizon, but somewhere more like a half-dozen blocks away. "That the Rainbow Clam is where Allana is." She started walking around the impossible geometry of the private school.

"Yes. That's where she *should* be."

"What's she supposed to do there?" Jessica picked up her pace, ignoring the fatigue in her legs and the ache in her forehead.

"She went to query the clam about getting me back into the air where I belong. To help me. I tried to tell you earlier ..."

Jogging now, she asked, "Why'd the rainbow flicker? Does that mean it's closing or something?"

"I didn't see it flicker. There's no need to rush. Allana is perfectly safe with the Rainbow Clam. She's safe here, with us."

Jessica didn't answer, just focused on her pace, keeping her breath even and her thoughts to herself. The kite was part of this senseless world and she wasn't sure what to trust. The city was a distorted vista of windows and street. Cars had frozen in mid-air with oblong wheels and tiny cabs, two-dimensional people wandered here and there, staring with blank, happy faces. She avoided them as best she could.

As she drew closer to the end of the rainbow, her lungs and legs burned. The kite, light as it was, felt awkward to hold with so little substance to it. Its dry surface clung to the sweat on her skin. She rounded the final turn and came upon a stone structure in her path. No, not stone—they were pillows. A gigantic pillow fort. The walls of the fort stretched from the nothing of one side to the other. At the center, there was a doorway, half her height.

"What's this place?"

"The market. You have to go through it."

"Is this dangerous?"

"Not to me."

Jessica tossed the kite a nasty look. The light shifted again, but she held her tongue on the matter. To enter the fort, she had to duck down and shimmy through the doorway. It was not an unfamiliar experience. Allana loved to build forts. Inside, a line of people stood waiting at a single cash register. Jessica remembered when they'd bought the toy register for Christmas one year, a bright red-and-blue affair that made a ding sound whenever it opened and closed.

None of the people in line had anything to purchase. It appeared that they were getting items for sale from behind the counter before proceeding to the back of the pillow fort. The people in line clutched bright yellow coins and blue-tinted paper money.

"What am I supposed to do?" Jessica asked the kite.

"I don't know. Kites don't need to buy things."

Jessica ground her teeth and moved around the line. The people in line were sketchy outlines with rudimentary faces. They were hard to look at, difficult to perceive. She needed to find the exit on the other side of the structure.

When she began to move around the counter, her trajectory making it clear she intended to bypass the entire affair, the cashier would have none of it.

The vague figure appeared in front of Jessica. "You need to buy something. We're very busy."

Jessica huffed and made her way to the back of the line. The figure resumed selling. She stood, moving forward a step as others took their place behind her. Her daughter was somewhere beyond this place, waiting, in danger, safe, not safe …. The thoughts nagged at Jessica and frustration drove her to push forward, shoving her way past the paper-like figures. She didn't hear their protests until she got to the front of the line.

"I need to get through here."

"You have to wait in line," they all said.

"No." Jessica hopped over the counter, only to find herself back on the other side. After a moment of shock, she hopped the counter again, surging forward to find herself back where she had started. "Please," she shouted, "I have to find my daughter, I have to get to Allana!"

"You have to wait in—" The chorus cut off and every paper face in line turned toward Jessica. "Allana is your daughter?"

She nodded to the queue, her eyes burning. A delicate touch shifted Jessica's attention. A bouquet of paper hands held out plastic coins and paper money. Jessica took a bit from each hand offered. They gestured to the cashier and she stepped up to the front of the line. On the table were a cornucopia of items, some of which were familiar, most lost to memory. She recognized the game: choose something, pay, and be on your way. She chose a small blue figure of a dolphin. It had a keychain embedded where its blowhole should have been. She handed over the money.

The cashier lifted the gate on the counter and waited until she'd passed. "Allana gave us commerce, we give her you."

"Thank you. All of you." Jessica moved on through the back and into the strange air beneath the strange sky before wiping her grateful tears away. The rainbow remained in place.

"Well done," the kite said.

"Shut up," Jessica replied, exhausted.

The kite said nothing more.

Jessica put one foot in front of the other. It was all she could do at the moment. Ahead, a sparkling blue river flowed beneath a pink bridge. She felt sticky; the air clung to her skin and hair. She wished she could take a moment to rinse off in the river, but taking time for herself was out of the question.

She reached the foot of the bridge and saw movement in the water. Undulating bodies sluiced by, a strange appendage on their heads. Her desire to bathe in the river dissipated.

"What is *this* now?" she said under her breath.

The kite remained silent.

Testing the bridge with one foot, she felt confident that the crayon-pink wood could hold her weight. Regardless, this was where her daughter's footprints led. Her own steps sounded heavy on the bridge and she heard a splash over the steady rush of the river. When she glanced to her left, a wet slap knocked her to the boards. Startled, she hit hard, scraping her hands and elbows, jarring her shoulder. Next to her, an eel flopped and rolled. The brown creature had an umbrella-like canopy growing from its head that flapped and folded as it managed to fall back into the water.

She reached up to where the eel had glanced off her head and her fingers came away covered in slime. Her temple throbbed.

"Damn it. Why didn't you warn me about these stupid things?"

"You told me to shut up," the kite said.

"Oh, *now* you follow my orders?" Jessica hauled herself up by the railing and ducked as another eel sailed past. It was soon followed by another and yet another. She started to scramble forward when a massive arm twisted over the railing ahead of her, hauling the bulk of a misshapen beast behind it. Its eyes were the size of dinner plates, black and unblinking like a fish. Between the staring orbs was a nose the size of her torso, and beneath that nose, the downward curve of a mouth with block-like teeth jutting between thin lips. Lank hair hung from its head, curled like kelp and as green and brackish as anything she'd ever seen or smelled. It vomited gallons of water onto the bridge before it spoke.

"Clip-clop, clip-clop, who's come knocking 'pon my bridge?"

"Oh my God ..."

The beast looked through Jessica and began pawing at the bridge. "I said, who's come knockin' 'pon my bridge?"

Another eel sailed over Jessica's head. Something was both familiar and ... what? There felt a nagging realization at the back of her mind, an elusive fact that—

"You should answer him," the kite said.

The beast's head snapped around, locked in Jessica's direction.

She glared at the kite, realizing that the creature was blind or very close to it. She put one finger to pursed lips and leaned against the railing. More eels thumped onto the bridge, confusing their bellowing obstacle.

"Bone Kite? I heared ye, trespassers. Bring me a little morsel, a tasty treat. Who goes there?" It bellowed at the last, taking a step forward.

Jessica remained frozen, hoping to slip past the brute. He bent at the waist and started pawing at the bridge, so huge that he covered every square inch as he moved forward.

Frantic, she managed to make no sound and forced herself to think. She had to cross this bridge, Allana was on the other side. Even now, her daughter's paper footprints fluttered under the giant's sweeping paws, settling back into place once he'd passed. Jessica ducked a flying eel. Seeing no other options, she swept one leg over the rail, then the other, clinging precariously, her feet barely keeping purchase on the edge of the bridge. The smell of the ponderous roadblock became stifling as he closed on her position. She began edging forward along the railing, holding the kite awkwardly under one arm. An eel slapped into her back with a meaty thud. It felt like being hit with a rubber bat. The impact, she knew, was going to leave a bruise. Another sailed into her shoulder, turning in midair to slap onto the bridge, where it undulated until the troll swept it back into the water.

Wait—a troll! That story, the billy goats. She loved that story—

Her hand came down on a smear of slime on the outside of the rail and her weight shifted dramatically as she lost purchase. The kite came loose and screamed. She snagged it before it could tumble into the water.

The troll had passed, but now twisted its two-dimensional shape to look—or rather face—her way. Jessica tossed the squealing kite onto the bridge, vaulted the rail, and picked it up. The troll lumbered toward her and she sprinted, dodging the occasional eel. Her quick footsteps slapped an odd counter beat to the troll's slower pace and longer stride.

Her lungs burned, breath coming short, and the kite wailed about drowning. Ahead, she saw a thick, broad puddle of the eel-slime and vaulted it. The troll's huffing threats, hot on her back, propelled her legs. She felt a sharp pain in her right calf and heard a thunderous thud that rattled the bridge.

She didn't look back.

The air felt heavy in her nose with the syrupy smell of cotton candy. The ground had given way from the Easter grass to a sparkling sugar sand. Hedges made of pink fluff dotted with fat pearls lined the path and overhead, the sky remained bifurcated by the striking rainbow. Only … instead of six hard colors, it had been reduced to four. Light shifted at the corners of her eyes. It appeared that they were closing in on their destination. The arc of the diminished rainbow touched land just ahead. The kite had been quiet since the incident at the bridge.

"We seem to be getting close," Jessica said.

"Yes," the kite replied.

"You've been quiet."

"You shushed me on the bridge."

Jessica rolled her eyes. "You wanted me to talk to that thing. It could only hear us if we talked."

"And you were going to throw me into the river."

She sighed. "You can't swim?"

"Have you ever known a kite that could? I'd've sunk to the bottom and that would be that. If you'd spoken with Bumblebutt—"

"Okay, seriously, shut up. You knew that thing on the bridge? Don't answer that. I don't care. I should toss your bone-ass into a bush."

The kite didn't reply. Jessica knew there was a connection between the kite and Allana, that her daughter might be cheered and more willing to go home if she saw the kite down from the tree. She kept it tucked under her arm until a gigantic mound came into view.

Not a mound, the clam. It was as large as a king-size bed and lay on a nest of pockmarked black rocks. The rainbow gleamed from its partially opened maw and she could see that the angle of its top half cut off some of the colors. *Was it closing?* She began to jog, ignoring her aching limbs, and called for Allana. She didn't hear her daughter's voice and now that she was close enough, it was clear why.

Inside the clam, curled up in its felt-like tongue, lay her daughter, sleeping. She twitched at her mother's voice, but didn't wake.

"Allana! Wake up sweetheart, it's me, Mama …" Jessica dropped the kite.

"See there? See? She's safe, don't wake her," the kite said.

Jessica felt her heart clench at the sight of her little girl, so small, plucked directly from the past. From an age when she needed her parents for almost everything. "Allana, sweetie …" She reached into the clam and touched Allana's face.

"Mama," her little girl murmured.

Jessica remembered how hard it was to wake her daughter, how she could be dragged from car to bed, undressed, and tucked in without waking. Kids slept hard, when they slept. She crept up the piled stones, wrapped one hand around Allana's upper arm, and pulled. The clam convulsed, its tongue wrapping tightly around the little girl.

A surge of anger flared inside Jessica and she addressed the kite. "Why the hell won't this thing let her go?"

"She's where she's supposed to be, right now. Let the Rainbow Clam finish it."

Fuck this, she thought and unfolded the knife from her pocket.

"Jessica, don't," the kite said.

Jessica reached into the clam with her right hand, the knife poised to cut from her left, and the shell snapped shut on her wrist. A shock of pain wrenched a guttural shout from her throat. Blood flowed slowly down her wrist.

"I told you not to do that," the kite said. "She's with the clam. We're all here now, we're all where we're supposed to be. The clam will fix everything."

"Fuck off!" Sweat poured from Jessica's brow, her skin felt slick and worn. She ached all over, on the edge of exhaustion. Her fingers burned at the end of her trapped hand. She could wiggle them; her wrist wasn't broken. She could feel the warm surface of the tongue and wrapped her fingers in it, making a fist.

The kite said, "Once I have Allana's skin, I'll be able to fly again, all will be right in the world. That's the deal."

Jessica felt her stomach turn. She glared at the clam as bile crawled up her throat and she sobbed. Gulping back tears, she turned her wrist, an agonizing lever.

"You can't escape the clam, Jessica. Let this happen, it was meant to be."

The clam's shell inched up a bit, but the agonizing pressure remained steady. There had to be enough room to try. She pushed her other hand in, holding the knife, and started cutting. The creature convulsed again, curling its tongue tighter, but it only served to move against the knife's edge.

"No," the kite said.

Jessica pushed harder, cutting deeper, slashing along the length, both of her wrists raw.

The kite shouted, "No, stop!"

She fought the oversized mollusk, pulling at the tongue, slashing at it, and seeing the edges of its shredded pink coming through the mouth of the shell. It snapped open and Jessica snatched Allana free. They both tumbled into the sugary sand.

"I was promised! We had a deal—you don't know what you've done!"

The rainbow flickered in earnest as the clam thrashed, unable to move, other than to twist its tongue and snap its shell.

Jessica focused on Allana, but the girl only stirred slightly. Her mind turned cartwheels as she struggled to her feet, pulling her daughter up. "Baby, wake up—please, wake up." She tried to remember how she ever managed to get Allana going on those early mornings, during the first days of school, or when they traveled.

Our trip to Florida.

"Honey, we have to get Daddy. We have to wake Daddy up! C'mon, sweetheart!" She gently shook her girl.

Allana stirred and said, "Dada?"

"Yes, sweetie, we have to wake Daddy up. I need your help."

"Okay, Mama." Allana took her own weight and glanced around.

"Allana," said the kite, voice edged with desperation, "you have to get back in the clam. It's important. You have to help me, my dear."

"Bone Kite, I have to go with Mama now. I'm glad you're out of the tree."

"Let's go, honey," Jessica said, taking her daughter's hand. "We don't want to be late."

"No, stop! Allana, give me your skin! I *need* it!"

The sky cracked.

"Oh, God. Let's go, sweetie. Let's go, we need to go home." Jessica guided Allana away while keeping an eye on the incensed kite and its collaborator.

The clam spasmed again and colors in the rainbow shattered, throwing bits of light into the dull sky. Behind them, the world crumpled, folding like a cardboard diorama, the backing pulling away, exposing the raw materials of a nightmare. A void swirled beyond the artifice of this world, a maw of nothingness.

"Mama, you're so sticky and dirty and sweaty," Allana said as her mother stepped up their pace.

"We have to get out of here, honey, come on. I don't know ..." She thought back through all the obstacles and the distance between them and safety. "Oh, it's so far, honey. It's so far." Panic set in. She had to save Allana. Had to get her out of—

"Mama, this way," Allana pulled.

"But we have to go back. This is the way we—"

She shouted, "It's *this* way, Mama!"

Jessica stood, dumbfounded, unsure, as the world crumpled behind them. She looked at her daughter, really looked at her, seeing the wild run of imagination that had brought them here. All of this had sprung from her little girl, all of this was a part of the unfathomable ticking of her young brain. Maybe ...

"Okay, let's go," Jessica said.

Allana tore off, running up the sugar sand path until it turned green. Her bare feet flung behind her, carefree, afropuffs bobbing with each step. She wore her favorite pink nightgown with an oversized-cartoon print, and Jessica followed and watched, appreciating her every step, loving her little girl. Then Allana veered off, moving parallel to the strange river. The papery grass shook in waves from the destruction that followed closely behind. The little girl hit the edge of the world and started feeling with her hands until she found purchase and pulled with both hands. A seam appeared, tearing in some places as the edge peeled away.

"Here, Mama!"

"You first, honey."

Allana nodded and paused. Jessica followed her gaze, over the river, where the pillow fort lay in the distance. Hordes of figures stood in the foreground. She could see Ecnad, The Little Ballet, and crowds of paper people. They waved and Allana waved back before ducking through the tear in the paper. Jessica followed and—

✧ ✧ ✧

She awoke in her bed, startled. Allana had been right in front of her. Her body ached, fatigue hummed along the edges of her sight. The room looked normal. Jeff looked normal.

Jessica reached for her husband and her skin burned where the clam had bitten her arm. Bloody and gummy, coated with sweat, dried slime pulled at her every move. "Jeff," she shouted and launched herself from the bed.

Jeff jerked and said, "What is it?", only to see his wife scrambling from the room. He glanced at the filth in the bed, the blood stains, and bolted after her. "Jessica, are you hurt?"

She turned into her daughter's room only to find the bed empty. "No, no, no," she sobbed. Jeff's hands grabbed her shoulders and she looked at him. He said something, but she missed it. She surged forward and pushed past him, into the hallway, toward the long shadow in the rising sunlight. She turned the corner to the stairs and there was Allana, standing by the window, watching the sun rise.

"I'm sorry, Mama," she said, her eyes watering. "I'm sorry, I didn't mean to—"

Jessica crushed her teenaged daughter into a hug. "I'm just glad you're okay, honey. If we never work out what happened last night, I don't care." All she felt was the rush of sheer relief.

"You always said I had a vivid imagination, but I—" Allana hiccupped, glancing up at her mom with wide eyes. "There's just so much stuff I'd made up and forgotten. Were you really in my dream?" Allana's hand hovered over her mother's raw wrist and she glanced at the dirt and scrapes.

Jessica pulled back, wiped the tears from her daughter's cheeks, and smiled wryly. "Your father kept your ideas, even if you forgot. He always talked about it. Where else would those things live but in your dreams? What else can explain it?"

Jeff took in their disheveled appearance, and marveled at their hints of a shared nightmare. A stream of questions spilled from him. Questions that had no answers.

Jessica pulled Jeff's notebook and knife from her pocket and handed it to him. "One thing is certain, you and your father need to come up with stories that have less of this weird stuff and *happier* ideas. Much, *much* happier ideas."

Jeff, holding his notebook, stood utterly confused, but relieved his family was otherwise okay.

Jessica sighed heavily, her arms wrapped around her daughter, the sound of her baby's laughter echoing in her memories.

The Ecology of Broken Promises

by Andrea Stewart

The undressing is always the hardest part. Lisa makes sure that it happens in the dark, but even so, no matter how much she contorts and evades, a stray brush of his finger reveals her secrets.

The man stops, and in that moment, she can't breathe or even remember his name. All she feels is fear, white and electric as a lightning bolt. His fingers brush the place on her ribs again, lingering over the threads she used to bind the tiny mouth shut. Flesh-colored thread, of course, not that he can see in the dark.

"Is this the only one?" Jason whispers. That's right; his name is Jason. His breath tickles her cheek. It smells like mint and alcohol.

She knows without looking, without touching, that he is blemish-free—just from the way he says those words. He's young, she supposes. It makes sense.

"There's another," Lisa says. She guides his hand to a second set of stitches on the opposite hip. And one more, though she doesn't add that aloud. That one, the result of her infidelities, her broken vows, lies on the bottom of her right foot. He doesn't need to know about it. "Does it bother you?"

Now she wishes it wasn't dark, so she could see the expression on his face.

"No," he says. "At least you know better now. At least you know what not to ask of other people. What's too much, too far."

He leaves the rest unspoken—that she knows not to ask too much of *him*—and kisses the juncture between her neck and shoulder. For a moment she hesitates, because she's accustomed to more. She wants more. But then she leans into his chest, guiding his hands so they do not touch the mouths on her hip and ribs.

One step, and another, and then they fall onto the bed together, their mouths, the real ones, pressed lip to lip.

He doesn't call her back.

Lisa stows the secret phone back between mattress and box spring. The screen showed only the time, nothing more. She should have known the mouths would bother Jason. Maybe he's talking to his friends right now about sleeping with her, about how it was a one-time thing.

"She had two extra mouths," he might say.

"That's nothing," a friend would reply, "I once fucked a girl with *five*."

The mattress squeaks as Lisa's husband shifts beside her. She glances over, but he's still asleep. When they bought this bed, they joked about the sexual gymnastics they'd undertake on its wide surface. Now that surface feels like an ocean, his slumping shoulder the mountain of some other continent.

One mouth mars his shoulder, and Michael never bothered to sew it shut. Its lips probe the empty air, like a baby searching for a teat. He told her, on their twelfth date, how he earned it: a promise to his mother that he'd become a doctor.

He'd tried, of course, and he'd wept when his MCAT scores were too low, and he told Lisa of the itching and the dread as the mouth grew on his shoulder—a red, patchy rash expanding into a hole to signify his failure; his broken promise.

Lisa rolls onto her back, staring at the blank expanse of the ceiling, wishing that were her skin. She never told Michael about her mouths, and even when the third one appeared on her foot, he didn't ask.

It's private.

The silence in the car presses on her eardrums, making her tap her foot on the brakes. The tapping fills the air, and Michael sighs. He rests his head against the window, his breath fogging the glass. "Do you have to do that?"

She stops, reaching for the radio instead. As soon as she turns it on, it blares, the strumming of a guitar magnified a thousand-fold.

"Fuck, that's loud!" Michael covers his ears and glances at her, and she reads it on his face: *Can't you do anything right?*

Her chest tightens as she mutters an apology, and she dials the volume down to an acceptable level. She checks his expression the way she checks her mirrors. His lips are pressed together, and she can see the vein throbbing at his temple.

"Should I turn it off?" she asks.

He says, just as quickly, "Does it matter what I want?"

"It matters to me."

His gaze goes out the window again. "Really? Are you sure?"

That shuts her up. She doesn't know what to say, what to do, to assuage his anger. She's not sure what caused it in the first place. He couldn't possibly know about her infidelity; she's never left a sign. He would never know the reason for the mouth on the sole of her foot.

When they married, she wouldn't have dreamed of going outside their marriage, of breaking her vows. Things have changed. Every time they talk, it seems to lead to more fighting. It's exhausting, and she needs some sort of release. Sometimes, when they're yelling at one another, Lisa imagines just digging her fingers into his scalp, peeling back skin and flesh and bone to reveal the thoughts beneath.

She could use that sort of insight.

"At least your flight is on time," she says, lamely. It's all she can manage.

Michael just grunts a reply.

When they pull up to the airport, she watches him visibly brightening. He lifts his head, his hands passing over his shirt, his tie. He straightens in his seat; he clears his throat.

It's just a business trip, Lisa reminds herself, for what feels like the hundredth time. But she sees his colleague waiting for him just inside the sliding glass doors—her long, supple legs, her white-toothed smile, the perfectly coiffed hair that Lisa smelled in passing once: all ocean breeze and lavender. She'd bet that woman has skin as smooth as a cultured pearl. She'd bet that woman has only ever made small promises, easily kept.

There haven't been any new mouths on Michael's skin; she's checked. But it won't be long, Lisa can feel it. Maybe this time Michael will return with an angry welt on his chest—a welt that grows into a pair of lips, a tongue, a gaping orifice that cannot be filled.

"Have a good trip," Lisa says as her husband reaches for his bag. "Love you." *Promise you'll think of me while you're away.* But she doesn't say it.

"Love you too," he says. He doesn't kiss her or even meet her eyes. The words are hollow, the rote repetition of a parrot.

As Lisa watches her husband greet his colleague with a smile, all of her mouths ache at once and she feels them straining at their stitches.

In the next breath, they're quiet once more.

She stops by a bar on the way home. Sure, it's only two p.m., but the whole drive and drop-off has her anxiety levels through the roof. Michael would never hit her, would never call her names. But when they're alone, she feels the tension between them and it's somehow worse.

She almost wishes he'd hit her, just to clear the air. Just to give her a good reason.

Smoke fills the inside of the building; it stinks of beer and tobacco. The soles of her shoes stick to the hardwood floors as she walks. It's not any place she's been before. "A Bud Light, please," she says as she sits on one of the barstools. A couple of regulars occupy other seats. They glance at her and then their gazes stray back to the television. The bartender, a middle-aged woman, nods and grabs a bottle from the fridge.

"Troubles got you down?" a voice says from behind her.

Lisa turns and does her best not to gape. A young woman stands behind her, one hand on the back of Lisa's barstool. She's lanky and borderline hollow, like a greyhound that's seen one too many races around the track. Her chestnut hair is pulled into a messy bun, and she's wearing a cropped black tank top and jean shorts that reveal not one, not two, but *eight* mouths. None are sewn shut. The one on the woman's left shoulder opens, a small pink tongue lolling out. A musky scent hangs around her, like moist soil and rotting wood.

It's *grotesque.*

"It's rude to stare, y'know," the woman says. "Just wanted to know why you're here. Never seen you here before."

The bartender slides the Bud Light in front of Lisa, and she grips it, the coolness of the glass bringing some clarity to her thoughts. She gathers herself. "Sorry. I didn't mean to stare."

"Troubles got you down?" the young woman says again.

Normally, Lisa would just shrug, or tell the young woman it was none of her business, but everything about this encounter has her off balance. "Husband problems," she says. She takes a swig from the bottle.

The young woman sits in the barstool next to Lisa. "Imogene," she says. "That's my name."

"Lisa."

"I know all about husband problems," Imogene says. She points to the mouth on her shoulder, and then to the one next to her belly button. "Two divorces."

"You *chose* to get married again?" Lisa says. She picks at the corner of the bottle label. "You'd think once would be enough." A lot of people don't get married at all, but the two Lisa knows who've divorced have vowed to never marry again. It's just not worth the risk.

Imogene shrugs. Despite her disheveled appearance, her cat-eye eyeliner is perfectly applied. "My mom and dad were married thirty-five years before he kicked it. They were so fucking in love—every day. Always wanted what they had. Always kept hoping for it." She laughs. "Still hoping for it, really."

Lisa doesn't ask about the other mouths, but Imogene answers anyway. Their lips strain for her finger as she points at them. "Swore I'd be friends with someone forever. Promised to be nice to my homophobic coworker. Made a pact with myself that I would never, ever be so stupid again …" Imogene lets out a long breath, her shoulders caving in on themselves.

Lisa wraps both hands around the bottle. The scratched surface of the bar chafes her elbows. "Three," she says.

Imogene only nods. "Can't be avoided."

"I mean, it can," Lisa says. "You just have to avoid making promises in the first place."

"Sure," Imogene says, but Lisa feels her sidelong glance. "That's not worked well for you, it seems."

Why is she letting this stranger get under her skin? She shrugs. "Knowing what I have to do and doing them are two different things. I never should have gotten married."

"And I never should have lent money to Natalie 'cause she bailed and now I'm short for this upcoming week's rent. High hopes. We've got them. Clink." Imogene touches an imaginary bottle to Lisa's. "Life's a bitch."

Lisa smiles for the first time today. Misery *does* love company. "Sounds like Natalie's the bitch."

Imogene laughs—a husky, throaty sound. "Damn right."

"Let me buy you a drink," Lisa says, even as she wonders if Imogene gets drinks by latching onto people, or if Imogene is an alcoholic. But the bartender is standing in front of them and it's too late to worry about enabling.

"Same as what she's having," Imogene says.

"Are you sure this is okay?" Imogene grips the doorframe as though it's the only thing holding her upright. Maybe it is.

"Yes, yes." Lisa waves her in. The hallway swims before her eyes. Two beers, three shots, some horrible bar food and a cab ride later, it's nine p.m. She'll have to go back for the car tomorrow. "Michael's gone for five days, anyway. Another business trip with his beautiful, perfect coworker." More bitterness leaks into the words than she intended. It's the alcohol.

"But you don't even know me." Imogene's voice sounds plaintive.

"You've got two sisters and a brother," Lisa says. "You like Thai food and pizza, and you fucking *hate* Natalie."

"Sure do." Imogene pushes off from the doorframe and swaggers into Lisa's apartment. She swings an arm around Lisa's shoulders, and Lisa doesn't even mind when the mouth on Imogene's wrist probes her skin. Imogene's words slur together. "Michael doesn't goddamned deserve you, you know that? You're *so* pretty, like a princess. But not a stuck-up one. Like, a warrior princess." Her eyes widen. "Like, you're fucking Xena."

"I'm not really interested in fucking Xena."

Imogene throws her head back so hard when she laughs that Lisa loses her balance. They stumble together into the wall. "Owwww," Imogene says.

"You okay?"

Imogene disentangles from Lisa. "Yeah. Just the mouths. They make everything more sensitive."

Lisa takes Imogene's elbow and guides her to an armchair. "You could sew them shut, you know."

Imogene sinks into the plush cushions. "I did, once. But it hurt too much. Couldn't be bothered." She reaches for the bowl of pistachios on the coffee table, shells one, and pops it into the mouth on her shoulder.

"You *feed* them?" Lisa collapses onto the couch.

"Sometimes," Imogene says, her voice small.

"Well, what happens to the—that is," Lisa circles a hand in the air, "you know."

"It's not a full separate being like you or me," Imogene says, "so it just, sort of … comes back out later." Lisa's disgust must have shown on her face, because Imogene scowls at her from beneath dark brows. "Yeah? Well, what do you do? Just pretend they're not there? Pretend you never made those promises in the first place?"

Lisa thinks of Jason's lips on hers, his hands hot against her skin. "Sometimes." She still remembers her first affair—Caleb. He plied her with compliments, with caresses, with the sort of sweet attentions that Michael no longer seemed interested in giving. When they fell into bed together she thought, *This is real*, and she hadn't even minded the mouth that grew on the bottom of her foot.

But no. Reality was three months later, when Caleb met a tattooed barista named Adira and lost Lisa's number. After that, what had it mattered? She was already scarred.

"Should I leave him?" Lisa wonders aloud.

"You're asking the wrong person," Imogene says. She reaches back and pulls out the pins holding her bun in place. Her hair falls in waves about her face, softening the angles. "Can't anyone make that decision but you."

"Is that what someone told you about your two husbands?" Lisa can't help the sharpness in her words.

Imogene gives her a wry smile. "Nobody told me nothing. My mom passed soon after my dad, and I'm the eldest child. I didn't have anyone to give me advice. But my heart said 'stay,' and my head said 'go,' and between the two of them, my head's always been the smarter one."

"And you'd marry again?"

"If I found the right guy, yeah."

Lisa blinks, trying to keep the room from spinning. "I don't think I would. This marriage—this is my one and only chance to get things right."

"There's always another chance."

"And how many chances for you until you're covered with the consequences?"

Imogene makes a sound halfway between a cough and a sob. "That's kinda mean, don't you think? I know what I am, what I have on my skin. I think about it all the time." She presses a hand into her forehead, like a headache has started there.

"I'm sorry," Lisa says quickly. She pushes herself to her feet. "Let me get you some water."

When she comes back with the glass of water, Imogene is lying across the couch, her knees up, one arm over her eyes. She doesn't reach for the glass. When she speaks, it's an imposition into the silence. "Well, you must have gotten married for a reason. If you could go back, would you do things differently?"

Freedom, a chance to begin anew. "Yes." Lisa stands over the couch, watching the way her shadow creeps up the side of Imogene's cheek. The mouths across her body are still. "You?"

"No," Imogene says. "I made these choices. I'll suffer for them, one way or another." Her lips press together. "It's my lot in life."

"It sounds like a miserable way to live."

Imogene peeks at Lisa from beneath her forearm. "Who are you, my shrink?"

Lisa kneels and runs a hand over Imogene's hair, spilling over the couch cushions. She weaves her fingers into the silky strands. "No. Just a friend."

"Oh," is all Imogene says.

Lisa watches the way her throat moves as she swallows. There's power in this—a power she doesn't have as a wife, when she can't do anything right. She flicks her gaze to Imogene's. The ends of Imogene's cat-eye makeup smudge into her eyelids. Deliberately, Lisa curls her fingertips at the base of Imogene's neck and tugs.

Imogene gasps.

Without a thought for the consequences, Lisa leans over and kisses her. Imogene's lips give way before hers, Imogene's hands seize the front of Lisa's shirt. Lisa's heartbeat races; it pounds in her ears. She climbs atop the other woman and runs a hand up her thigh. All of Imogene's mouths fumble at Lisa's skin, leaving wet trails in their wake.

Imogene pulls back for a moment, her shadowed eyes troubled. "I don't really know you," she says. "I don't really know you at all." But then she hooks her fingers around Lisa's ears and drags her back down.

Their limbs tangle together. Clothes become obstacles, things to be discarded in haste. Lisa grabs the bottom of her shirt and pulls it up over her head. It catches at her shoulders, and as she struggles to wriggle free, something on her hip tears.

It burns. Imogene tugs the shirt off, and they both look down. The stitches on Lisa's hip have torn, freeing the mouth beneath. Scars and frayed thread mark the circumference. A tongue emerges, hesitantly, swiping across the upper lip, licking away little pinpricks of blood.

Lisa presses a hand to the mouth. "It hurts," she moans.

"I know," Imogene says. "Shh … I know." She rests her palms on Lisa's waist and kisses her hand. "Here. Let me." When Lisa slowly draws her hand away, Imogene presses her lips to the mouth.

The world swims. Lisa can't be sure what she sees, but she thinks the mouth on her hip kisses Imogene back. She thinks she can *feel* it—the mouth of a broken promise, Imogene's mouth, tongues twining together.

"Imogene," Lisa whispers.

Imogene opens her arms. "Come here, love."

Light falls through the blinds in horizontal slats. Lisa cracks an eye open. Her mouth feels as though she's swallowed cobwebs. The back of her throat still tastes like the Jack Daniels she drank the night before.

She tries to stretch and finds her neck sore from spending the night on the couch, propped on an armrest. For a moment she thinks Imogene is gone, but then she hears humming from the kitchen and the scrape of a spatula against a pan.

As Lisa rises to her feet and dresses, the stretching and pulling makes the mouth on her hip sting. It hangs open, the skin around it loose, as if years of being sewn shut means it can't close on its own anymore. Lisa gropes beneath the couch and finds the metal tin she

76

keeps her sewing supplies in. The needles and buttons rattle as she brings it to her lap.

Her fingers move with a learned repetition. She has to replace the stitches every so often as they dissolve. She threads the needle, ties a knot at the end, grits her teeth, and begins. The scar tissue shields her from the worst pain. Each loop pulls the lips together, getting her closer to some semblance of normal.

Imogene emerges from the kitchen, the spatula in hand. She watches the process for a moment as something pops on the pan behind her. "Looks like it hurts."

"Yes," Lisa says. She pinches the skin and pierces both sides with the needle.

"You're not perfect, you know. Anyone who expects you to be is spouting bullshit." Imogene punctuates her words with a thrust of the spatula.

Lisa runs out of thread and ties the end. She's managed to do half, so far. "Doesn't mean I should stop trying."

Imogene shrugs and turns back to the kitchen. "It's too late. You do this for Michael? Why torture yourself for him?"

Not for Michael, not anymore—for all the others. With shaking fingers, Lisa unspools more thread. No matter how hard she tries, she can't seem to thread the needle. Frustrated, she throws everything back in the tin. Her phone, the non-secret one, catches her eye from the side table. When she picks it up and hits the button at the bottom, she finds her screen blank.

No new messages. No calls.

Two years ago, when Michael first began traveling for work, he texted her several times a day and never ended a night without a call. After a year it was just a phone call at night, and now she gets nothing. She still remembers the day she met him, playing Frisbee on the campus greens, his hair wild, eyes bright. The Frisbee hit her as she was on her way to class, and she remembers his hand at her forehead—as if touch and concern could stop a bruise from forming. She had the uncontrollable urge to kiss him, right then, and though she refrained, she had another chance at it two days later, on their first date.

Back then she had no concept of "forever."

On an impulse, Lisa sends a text to Michael: "Thinking of you. I miss you. Wish you were here."

Imogene walks into the living room with two plates and Lisa drops the phone. "Figured the least I could do was make you breakfast."

They eat scrambled eggs and pancakes in silence, as though they both used up all their words the night before. As soon as they're finished, Imogene gets up, her eyes darting to the clock on the wall. "I should go. Got work in a few hours."

Lisa reaches out, her fingers grazing the mouth on Imogene's wrist. "Stay," she says. "I have the day off."

"I don't think that's a good idea."

"Can I at least get your number?"

The mouth on Imogene's wrist finds Lisa's index finger, lips latching onto the end. Imogene gently pulls away. "I don't think that's a good idea either."

Lisa's heart feels heavy as a stone. "Did I do something wrong?"

Imogene smiles, leans down, and kisses her. Her warm breath gusts past Lisa's cheek. "Thanks for letting me stay the night." And then, without a backward glance, she picks up her purse and goes to the door.

The click of the latch echoes across the hardwood floors, and all of Lisa's mouths feel hungry and hollow, empty as her apartment.

She doesn't finish sewing up the mouth, not for the entire day and the day after. At work, the freed half nips at her blouse each time it flutters close enough. She pulls up the waistband of her pants to cover it.

When Lisa gets home, she sits on the bed and kicks off her heels, delighting in the feel of the rug beneath her sore toes. She reaches between the mattress and the box spring and removes her hidden phone.

There's a message. In an instant, her heartbeat quickens. For a moment she thinks, impossibly, that it must be Imogene, but then she reads the name. Jason.

"Sorry I haven't called," it reads. "Can I see you?"

He never promised to call; she didn't expect it of him. She texts back that he can come over now, that her husband is gone, that she's alone. As soon as she presses "send," she remembers the mouth.

Hastily, she goes to the living room, grabs the sewing kit, and starts to bind the rest of the mouth shut. She wants it to be smooth, seamless but for the soft, downy feel of thread. It's hard and painful work. She barely has time to wipe the sweat from her brow when a knock sounds.

Lisa shoves the sewing kit back beneath the couch and answers the door.

Jason stands there, still wearing his work suit, his jacket unbuttoned, his hands in his pockets. He smiles when he sees her, and his dark eyes fix on hers. "Hope I'm not bothering you."

She stands to the side to let him in. "Come in." As soon as she shuts the door he presses up against her, hands tangling in her hair, the stubble on his chin grazing her cheek.

"I've missed you," he says, but the words mean nothing.

Reaching up, she takes his hands and removes them from her hair. She wants to put his fingertips to her scarred, sewn-up mouths, to force him to acknowledge what she is, what she's done. But she just holds them in front of her, not quite able to meet his eyes.

"Lisa?"

She starts to unbutton his shirt, just to give herself time to think. With each button, she backs him up a step. He gives way, his chest heaving. Once she has him up against the couch she removes the cufflinks from his shirt and sets them on the side table, then moves to his jacket.

"If you had to break a promise," she says quickly, "what would it be?"

"Babe," he says, "if I had to make a promise, it would be to you." He reaches for her, but she sidesteps his grasp.

"And then you'd break it."

A frown mars his face, his single, only mouth. "Come on, what's the deal? Why does it matter?"

"It matters to me."

Jason closes a hand over her wrist, moves it up her arm, fingertips caressing her skin. "Let it go."

She feels the words on the tip of her tongue: *promise me*. But she lets him draw her in, lets him cover her mouth with his, lets the words drown. As his hands find their way beneath her shirt she can't help but notice—he never touches the mouths.

Lisa wakes to the sound of a car pulling up to the sidewalk outside. The engine idles, never turning off, and a spike of dread worms its way into her heart. She throws the blankets off, disturbing a murmuring Jason, shrugs on her robe, and goes to the window.

The streetlamps illuminate a taxicab at the curb. The door opens and a man steps out. Michael. He reaches back inside for his suitcase. "Jason," Lisa hisses. "Jason, get up."

He moans, so she stalks back to the bed and pulls the rest of the blankets off of him.

"What the hell?" he says, his voice sleepy.

"My husband is here," she says. "He's back early."

For a moment, he says nothing, and then, *"Shit."*

The room becomes a whirlwind as he explodes out of the bed. Lisa tosses him his pants and his belt; she kneels to feel around on the rug for his socks. Jason reaches for the lamp, but she stops him. "Are you *crazy?*" she whispers. "He'll see."

He diverts the movement into pulling on his shirt, grabbing his jacket from the back of a chair. "Why'd you tell me it was okay to come over?"

"Because it *was* okay," she bites back. "Go out the fire escape. Quickly."

His shoes in hand, he darts out of the room and to the back of the apartment. Lisa has to help him lift the window; it sticks a little once it's open halfway.

A key turns in the lock.

"Go go go," Lisa says.

Jason shakes his head a little, and she knows this time he won't be calling her back. She finds she no longer cares. And then he's gone, just as Michael steps inside.

Lisa takes a deep breath, as though she's taking in the night air. "You're home early."

"It's dark in here." Michael flips on a switch. "Couldn't sleep?"

"No," she says. She leans on the top of the window to shut it. Below, in the alley, Jason is hopping as he puts on his shoes. She turns to face her husband.

He sets his rolling case on its base and pushes the handle to retract it. Just as he pivots to hang his jacket on the hook by the door, Lisa notices Jason's cufflinks on the side table. Bright silver against dark brown. Her breath catches. But then Michael looks at her and she snaps her gaze away.

"I got your text," he says. "I've been thinking about you too."

He has? A memory pops into her head—of the time Michael's mother dropped a not-so-subtle hint about his MCAT scores, about

80

how little she thought of his current profession. And Lisa felt the blood rising to her cheeks, the pounding of her pulse in her neck as she called his mother—his *mother*—a bitchy nag. Michael worked damned hard for a living, thank you very much. He was good at it too. And if his mother couldn't recognize that, then she should keep her mouth shut.

She remembers the way Michael kissed her later that night and told her how fiercely he loved her. There are so many memories like this one; they clutter her mind.

Michael's expression hardens. "You haven't texted me in ages," he says. He marches into the living room. "What's the deal? What do you want?"

"I just wanted to tell you I was thinking of you." Imogene. The mouths.

"Bull*shit*," he spits out. "It was manipulative. You knew I was busy. You wish I was here?" He spreads his arms. "Well, I'm here. You might as well just say whatever's on your mind."

Speaking against his anger is like swimming upriver. If she shouts back, they'll fight again and then they'll stop talking and nothing will be solved. She turns her head, as if that will give her the chance to breathe. Lisa's gaze slips once again to the cufflinks. Michael doesn't seem to notice; he's too fixated on her.

What if he notices? What if he finds out?

She realizes then: it doesn't matter. She doesn't want this anymore. Doesn't want the fighting, the silences, the marriage. An itch starts between her shoulder blades. "I don't want a divorce," she blurts. The cufflinks blur in her vision as her eyes fill with tears. Her throat aches; her mouths ache.

Michael sighs, and he seems to deflate. "I don't want a divorce either." His feet scuff against the floor as he shuffles closer. He sinks into the armchair that Imogene sat in only two nights before.

"Maybe," Lisa says, her voice trembling, "maybe we can go back to the beginning. Make things right between us?"

He sags, leaning his head into his hand. "I don't know you anymore, Lisa."

"You could get to know me again." It's pointless, useless, but she tries anyway.

Michael straightens, untucks his shirt, and lifts it. A welt marks the soft flesh just below his ribs. "I love her," he says, and Lisa knows he's not referring to his wife. The words cut, even though Michael hasn't loved her for a long time. "We don't have to get divorced," he tells her. "We could just carry on as usual. Dani doesn't want to get married."

The itch sharpens. Another mouth if she gets divorced. Four of them. Carrying on as usual would be easy, simple. She could keep just the three mouths. Not perfection, but closer to it. She could live without making any more promises, without hoping for better.

The thought is smothering.

Lisa unties the belt of her robe, letting it fall to the floor. She stands in front of Michael, leans down, and takes his hand.

"Lisa," he says, his voice choked, "don't—"

She presses his hand to the stitches on her hip. The first time he touched her there, he did not pull away or hesitate. There's so much shared history between them, and too much left unsaid. "This one," she says, her voice low, "is for the promise I made to my brother, to always protect him." Michael stills at the touch, his gaze on the stitches. She guides his hand to her ribs. "This one is for the promise I made to a friend, to always listen." She lifts her foot and the ache in her mouths ease, though the ache in her throat does not. "And this one is for the promise I made to you."

Her duffel bag weighs on one shoulder as she steps into the night. Michael listened as she spilled her secrets, and wept at the last mouth, the one on the bottom of her foot. He hadn't the right to tears, but then, neither had she.

Lisa doesn't need to look at the itch between her shoulder blades to know it's now a welt. She told Michael she wanted a divorce, and she meant it. The welt will grow a pair of lips when she sends him the papers; it will grow a tongue when they finalize it. Another mouth to mar her skin, to broadcast the failure of her hopes.

As she strides down the sidewalk, the air cool against her neck, she recalls that day, nine years ago, when Michael took her hands in his, his smile a little lopsided. She could smell the sweet roses from the flower arrangements, and she remembers the cold, heavy feeling of the ring on her finger. Michael's voice trembled only a little when he spoke his vows, and he looked down at her with a surety that made her heart pound as he promised to be with her to the end. To love her forever.

She concentrates on putting one foot in front of the other. Maybe someday she'll sew this new mouth shut. But for now, she'll let it be.

Like her, it needs a chance to breathe.

Duty and the Beast

by David Gerrold

They all made it out before the portal closed.

I didn't go.

You gotta do what you gotta do.

So I did. I made sure they got out.

I didn't follow. There were no more travel pods. But that wasn't the reason.

After they were across, after the channel was clean, I did what I had to do.

The portal shut down. It severed the connection and shut down completely. It wiped its calibrations, then emptied its circuitry. Incapable of powering up, no connection of any kind could be established again.

But just to be certain, I vaporized the station.

It was a total break. Downline was gone. Irretrievable. No one else was going home.

But I wasn't done yet.

I picked up my gear and headed northwest. The day was bright and I made good time. The sun wouldn't be overhead for hours. If I couldn't reach forest before noon, I'd put up the tent to avoid the heat. I had food for three days and I knew where to refill my canteens. Not the easiest trek, but not impossible either.

It would be a long day crossing the big valley. I'd have to circle the high grass where the predators lurked. It'd be safer. Mostly. I'd have to go slow.

The sun was touching the western horizon when I reached the rocky jumbles. Up here, I'd have to watch out for the dark catters; they were vicious and always hungry. I'd printed up a swarm of disposable flutterbys. They circled above me like insects, so I had an umbrella. It should give warning, but the catters could camouflage, even muting their heat signatures, so I'd have to monitor closely. I had a shrill-frequency emitter which would annoy the most likely hunters, but it would also give me away to any human observers. The stay-behinds were going to be the real problem.

I made it to the top of the ridge without seeing any troublemakers, but the worst of them wouldn't be out hunting until after dark.

Twilight brought a dry evening wind. I refreshed the umbrella and took shelter near a break where three enormous boulders clustered together. I put out a ring of night-eyes, had half a ration for dinner—more than enough—watched the sun creep slowly into the horizon, watched all three moons tumbling through the dark, admired the sparkling ribbon across the sky. I never got tired of that view, but finally as the temperature dropped toward freezing, I curled up in my cocoon.

I slept fitfully. Occasional strange noises came echoing across the hills; howls and barks, grunts and whistles, but nothing close enough to set off an alarm. But that wasn't the reason for my discomfort. I didn't like this whole job, but there wasn't anyone else who could do it.

The second day, travel was slower. I'd expected it. The terrain was rougher here, broken by gullies and arroyos and even a sharp canyon. I had to climb down one side, cross a rushing stream, then back up the other. I paused only to refill my canteens.

A storm in the north promised a flash flood. The air already smelled wet. When the rain finally came, I hunkered down beneath a sharp cliff where I'd be out of the scouring wind and water. The worst of the storm stayed far to the north and east, but the fringe was bad enough. I sheltered in place for hours. After the clouds passed, the ground dried quickly—the land was thirsty here. Rivulets found the path of least resistance, trickles turned into streams, and I followed them down.

By early afternoon, I had reached the broad savannah. Distant herds spotted the range and that meant there would be predators here, the biggest ones. The distant forest was still a line of dark blue on the horizon—it would be a long trek. I kept telling myself that once I got deep enough into the shelter of the trees, I should be fine. I just had to keep putting one foot in front of the other. I'd get there. It would be okay.

The rex almost caught me by surprise.

The ground shook and the beast came rising up out of the high grass ahead of me. The flutterbys had missed it. The monster had been lying torpid in a rill, soaking up the heat of the day, invisible to their sensors while it slowly digested its most recent meal. I had come too close. My footsteps, light as they were, had disturbed it.

It grunted, blinking, looking for something to focus on. I yipped in surprise, suddenly aware that I was in the middle of a large open space with no place to hide and the distant trees too far to run to.

I could freeze where I was and hope it wouldn't recognize me as prey. Or if it looked away, I could drop to the ground. I had weapons, but they weren't designed to stop a creature that large. The animal had a stretched-out body, a long flat snout, and teeth as long as my legs. A rex usually ambled on four legs, but when it was searching for prey, it stood up on its thicker and taller hind-limbs. This one was standing up now.

I had one advantage: I could scramble around it faster than it could turn to follow. That kind of a contest would be decided by my endurance against the animal's own frustration.

The rex moved.

It swung its wide head, first to one side, then to the other, regarding me with its right eye, then the left. Whatever thought processes sparkled in its tiny brain, it really had only three choices: eat, fight, or fuck. The first was always eat.

The beast dropped back to all four legs and lumbered toward me. It didn't look fast, but that was an illusion—the thing was huge, a walking mountain of meat and bone. I had to make up my mind whether to dodge to the right or the left. My choice was impossible. It could lunge either way.

I did the smart-stupid thing. When it lunged, I flattened to the ground. Its jaws passed over me as I scrambled straight ahead, ducking beneath its long neck and between its tree-trunk legs and into the dark shadows beneath its wide belly, all the way to the high space between its rear legs. If I could stay underneath the monster, I could confuse it. In its eyes, I would have disappeared. I'd be safe for the moment—unless it suddenly decided to lie down again. Then I'd have to move fast. But if it looked around and couldn't find me, lost interest and gave up—if it ambled off into the distance, I could flatten and wait. Or, if it turned around and spotted me again, we could start all over. These creatures weren't stupid.

The creature grunted. Confused? Maybe. I don't speak rex. It lifted up one front leg, then the other. It lowered its head and sniffed the ground in great shuddering inhalations. Not a good sign. It turned around slowly; I moved to stay beneath its hind legs. It was dangerous, but I could tell which way it was going to move by the way its tail was swinging and by the way it shifted its weight.

Now it roared in annoyance and started to step sideways, I jumped and dodged. Maybe it knew where I was. It turned around, it started forward—I moved with it, barely fast enough.

Not good.

It could amble at thirty klicks, or it could charge at fifty. I could barely do twelve, even in this lighter gravity. If it started forward, I could be exposed. A rex rarely walks in a straight line, it moves in a deliberate zig-zag pattern, swinging its head in a constant search for any prey that might have gone to ground.

I ducked beneath its swinging tail. I was out of its shadow and into the bright sun again. My one hope was to flatten out and scramble toward the distant trees. Or I could just run for it. Neither was a good option. If the rex saw me, no matter what I did I would still die tired.

The rex turned and saw me—

—and exploded!

A bright red flash hit the wall of the rex's neck, gouts of flame splattered outward, and the beast staggered left, collapsed sideways, and disappeared in a flower of smoke and flame. The shockwave flung me back across the grass, flattening it beneath me as I slid.

For a long, confused moment, I wasn't sure who I was, where I was, or what had happened—but the sky was a beautiful shade of blue.

Or was it Cyan? Turquoise? Green? Whatever. It was nice. I could lie here forever—

A dark shape hulked above me. "You gonna get up?" it asked.

I didn't answer. Instead, I rolled sideways, got my arms and legs under me and managed to stand. Turned and looked. I might have wobbled. The world was still ringing.

My eyes blurry, watering. I looked. Something large and scowling. Very large. It blocked the sun. Four meters tall, probably two and a half wide. Hard to tell under all that gear, which was mostly armor and weapons and whatnots. Obviously it was large. Larger than large. One of the largest of its kind. Impressive.

I stepped sideways and looked around him. Pieces of rex were still pattering down from the sky, bits of skin and bone and fragments of flesh. The stink was horrific.

Carrion eaters would feast easy today. They wouldn't be long in arriving—as soon as the wind spread the smell of raw meat. There wouldn't be a lot of snarling competition around the carcass, what was left of it. There was more than enough here for all of them. Large chunks of the rex had splattered everywhere across the savannah.

"You're welcome," said the hulk, as if that was sufficient. He stepped away, moving from one chunk of carcass to the next, looking for the right one. Finally, he pulled out a huge knife and began slicing at a larger chunk of meat. "Dinner," he said.

"Yours. Not mine," I said. I turned and headed toward the trees. Wanted to get away before the local equivalents of jackals arrived. Life is vicious everywhere. A pack of them would be even more dangerous than the rex.

The hulk shrugged and caught up with me.

"Don't want company," I said.

He pointed forward. "I'm going in this direction. You go wherever you want." He waved left and right.

Wasn't ready to argue. Not yet. Still too annoyed, mostly at myself for being caught by surprise. For needing to be rescued. Embarrassing. Had it been it a grief reaction? Loss fugue? Or just exhaustion? Whatever it was, it almost killed me. Reminded me to stay awake. Can't depend on my stalker to be there next time.

He grunted. "My name is Constant."

Didn't answer, headed toward the trees. Mebbe we should settle this in the shade.

I wasn't the only person who'd stayed behind. But I had a job to do. The rest of 'em—not the kind of people I wanted to be on the same planet with.

Peak population here had barely reached half a million. The evacuation had started eighteen months ago and even with long trains of pods coming from farther out on the portal lines. The stretch to the frontier goes out quite a way from some places, not here, only a few more stops to the last one. But enough. For a while pods from our up-line were coming through twice a day, all of them adding to the evac from here. Less than four hundred thousand from this rock had gone downline. And the rest? That's their choice.

With the downline portal down, there would be no possible connection to any of the other hundred worlds. This was permanent isolation (some people wanted that. No way to know how many), since evacuation meant a long journey downline through multiple portals till they found a stopping place, maybe even a new home, but evacuees would be refugees. They'd scatter across multiple worlds, wherever they could find opportunities. All their separate communities would disappear, ultimately forgotten.

So some people thought that staying behind was a better option. I'd met enough of them to know that I didn't want to be here for that. Ornery, stubborn, cruel, and stupid. I could accept ornery and stubborn—I was mostly that myself. But cruel and stupid—? Just bad news.

This hulk lumbering beside me? Stubborn, yes. The other things? I didn't know yet. I didn't want to have to kill him. Not impossible, but probably difficult. Strong risk of injury.

I reached the trees by early afternoon. Found a shadowed place that looked safe enough to sit. He sat opposite, settling his enormous bulk onto the web of twisty roots that circled a gnarly tree. The limbs curved around his weight like a personally designed chair. He took out a ration bar, broke it in half. "Hungry?"

Okay, maybe not cruel.

I took the half-bar. Flavored sawdust, but better to eat his rations than mine. Drank a capful of water, didn't offer him the canteen. Finally cleared my throat, looked across at him. "What do you want?"

"What do you have?"

"Don't play games on me. You been following me—stalking—since the portal collapsed."

"Good thing for you."

"Mebbe. But you're not very good. I've had eyes on you the whole time."

"Really?" He reached into his pocket and pulled out a handful of crushed flutterbys. He held them out for me to see.

"Yes, really." I reached into my own pocket, pulled out what looked like dust—a small cloud of skeeter-bots. I flung them in his direction. "These are harder to catch."

"I knew about those. Didn't mind 'em much. Let you think you knew something."

"I knew something. I spotted you a month before I headed south."

"Been tracking you longer than that."

"You were hiding in the noise. Too much chatter to filter out. But not well enough. You're too big. You stuck out. Didn't know you were tracking me then, coz of the evacuation, but this last month? Sure. So answer the question. What do you want?"

"You needed my help," he said. "Might even need it again."

I could have argued that, but it would have sounded stupid. I'd gotten too close to that rex and I was probably going to spend a few long nights rehearsing and examining that mistake.

"My turn," he said. "You were tracking me, why?"

"Because you were tracking me. Again—why?"

He scratched himself. Possibly wondering if he should answer. Apparently not. "I'm going to sleep now," he said. He settled himself on the gnarly branches and closed his eyes.

I wasn't going to waste daylight. As quietly as I could, I gathered my gear and headed north. I wanted to get through the thickest part of the woods while I still had daylight.

Three hours later, he caught up with me. Didn't say anything, just plodded along beside me. I could feel the weight of every step he took. Probably easier to have him beside me than behind me.

But that would mean we'd have to talk. Even if neither of us wanted to.

We got to the hills above Bias Station in late afternoon, not yet twilight. We stopped below the crest, dropped down flat and crawled just far enough forward to peer through the grass. The dome had scorch marks and even a few gouges where something had attacked it. Whoever or whatever, they hadn't gotten in.

I backed down to the nearest cluster of gnarlies. He followed.

"You stay here," I said.

"You think someone inside?"

"Five. Two large, three small."

He didn't ask how I knew. Instead, "You have plan?"

"My plan is you stay here." I unbuckled my gear, pulled off my boots. Peeled off jacket, shirt, body armor, unders, kilt, trousers. Stripped naked, I smeared dirt all over my body, unbound my hair and finger-brushed it all askew.

Constant watched, possibly skeptical, possibly bemused. "You … very small," he said.

"You just notice that?"

"Your armor, your jacket, your boots, all the rest of your gear—make you look larger."

"Might say the same about you." I tossed my amulets aside. Now it was just my bare skin and a ragged blanket, the leftover threads of a poncho.

"That's your plan?"

I looked at him, a tower of muscles and armament, three meters high. "You think they open door for you, even without your gear? No. So you stay here."

I staggered down the hill, tripping and falling and finally tumbling clumsily to the bottom of the slope. When I got back up, slowly and painfully, I limped to the dome, clutching my side, wailing. Circling the dome, looking for the door—I finally found it and began crying and pounding, all in low-country accent, un-educated. "'Eelp mae! 'Eelp! Anyone? You 'afta be there! 'Eelp mae, pleese! Pleese!" I kept it up for the longest time. Long enough to be a nuisance.

At last, the outer door slid part way open. Just enough for a glimpse of a gaunt face. "Go away."

"Pleese! Almost night! Freeze out here. 'Eelp me! An' I 'eelp yah! Know things, I do. Let mae in, pleese?"

"No." The outer door slid shut.

Right. I resumed pounding, wailing, shrieking. "Monser affer mae! 'Eelp mae! Pleese!"

The door opened again, this time a little further, still not far enough. "Who you?"

"Noddy. Nodding. Missed alla portal. Got nodding, no one. Looka mae. Can't 'urt you. Just need a warm place for a night, or mebbe two. Can 'eelp, reelly."

"Wait—" The door closed again. This time a lot longer. I started pounding again. "Gedding colder, pleese?"

Finally, the outer door opened and two skinnies stepped out, a large and a small. The door slid shut behind them. Squatters. Both looked haggard. Thin. Dirty. Not eating well. The large handed me a blanket, not much better than the one I wore. I clutched it, fumbled it around my shoulders. "Tankily, much tankily."

"No food you," the small said. "Ain't none."

"Just a warm place for sleep? Be gone morning?"

They looked at each other. The small shook her head. The large said, "Can't." He pointed. "You go now. Go."

Thought about crying. Decided not to. Wouldn't work on these two—selfish. I'd have to take them down.

But the door was closed behind them. Problematic. I really needed to get in.

And then Constant rose up. Up from the grass. Covered with mud and leaves, looking like something out of a marshy swamp. But the railgun was real. Red dots glowed on both of the squatters. He stepped up beside me.

"You folks, inside!" he called, his voice amplified, booming like thunder. "All you out now. Or I kill these two."

"Won't work," the skinny large said.

Constant ignored them. "Everybody out and nobody gets hurt. Sacred promise." And then, still aiming with his left arm, he held up his right—a gleaming token, a badge, perched in his beefy hand. "Portal authority!"

"Portal down," said the small. "Authority meaningless now."

"Not to me." He raised his voice again. "Everybody out or the station goes down. I can do it. Thirty seconds. Don't think. Don't talk. Out now."

I didn't expect it to work, but the doors of the dome, both outer and inner, slid open. One large, two small—they came out slowly, raising their hands to show they were weaponless.

"Alla smart," Constant gestured with the weapon. "Line up here."

The second large grumbled into place. "Told yah. Shouldna opened. Now we're dead."

"No one's dead," Constant said. "You listen, you live. Just want—something." He looked to me. "You know where it is?"

Nodded.

"Go get it."

"I go with," said the grumbling large. "Make sure, no steal."

Constant snorted. "Squatters, alla you! No voice, no argue!"

"No, it's okay," I said, abandoning my low-country accent. "Let 'em see. Just want one thing, then we go. Right?"

"You sure?"

Nodded.

"Okay, go." He pointed to the large. "You be good. No good, I get mad. Everybody die. Especially you. Very painfully. Long time too."

The grumbly one followed me into the dome. It was a mess inside. Not like I remembered. Trash everywhere. Things broken, piled high. And it smelled bad too. Unwashed and sick. Bad cess. I wasn't going to stay anyway. Just grab and go.

Grumbly followed, all the way around to the service bay. Wires were hanging loose, everything powered down. I expected that. Whatever happened here, not good.

"What you want anyway?" Grumbly asked.

I ignored him, pushed some wires out of the way, counted squares on the panel behind. Three down, two over. I put my hand on the square, waited. Nothing happened. Took my hand away, then put it back. Waited longer. Still nothing. Hmm.

I slapped the square hard. Once, twice, three times. The third time, something behind the wall clicked. The square popped open, a drawer slid out.

I reached in, felt around.

Yes. Found it. A wooden box. Just big enough to fill my hand. Something heavy inside.

"What you got there?! Give me!" Grumbly grabbed my arm—

I let him live.

I picked up the box from the floor. It didn't look damaged. Sealed tight, fancy designs all over.

Grumbly was still rolling around on the floor clutching his stomach and moaning. "Why you do that. Just wanta see."

"Not yours, no look. Big mistake. Now you get up. We go out."

Grumbly pulled himself up with his one good arm. The other hung limp, broken. He stumbled outside where the air was a lot fresher. I followed, carefully carrying the box.

Constant looked at Grumbly, looked to me, noted the box, then looked back to Grumbly. "He give you bad time?"

"No. He just stupid. Station a mess. Stinks inside."

Constant scratched his neck, thinking. "Want me kill him?"

"Let them go. I have what I want."

"Don't like skinnies," he said. "And you—" he pointed at Grumbly, holding his broken arm. "I see you try something. Make me very mad."

"No, pleese! No kill—"

Constant shook his head. "No kill. Shut!" He waited till they fell silent again. "But I gone blow this station. Alla you go."

He pointed again to Grumbly and the two smalls who came out with him. "You go that way. Go fast and no get hurt. No come back." He pointed to the other two, the large and small who came out first. "And you go other way. Same thing. Go fast. No get hurt. Go far." He motioned with the railgun. "Go now! Go!"

They all looked at each other, realized he was serious, then broke for the trees. Grumbly started to curse, looked at me, thought better of it, clutched his arm and limped away in pain, the two smalls helping him.

Constant lowered his rifle. "You good?"

Nodded. "You gone blow this station really?"

"Nah. Just lock it up good. They come back, they don't get in." He tapped at his badge. "Big mess inside?"

"Very."

He tapped some more. "Okay. Repair bots online. They fix. Power first, then repairs. Synthesizers too. Month from now—maybe two, three—good as new. You come back then, eh?"

"Don't think so."

"Eh?"

"Gotta do what I gotta do." I turned and headed back up the hill. Constant put his badge away and followed.

By the time I finished cleaning off the worst of the dirt and pulled my clothes back on, darkness had fallen. Not safe to travel at night. Not easy either. Constant built a fire and put the slice of rex on a spit. We sat opposite each other, watching the embers rise through the smoke.

"Think they'll come back?" he asked.

I finished tugging on my boots. "Probbly. Squatters. That what they do."

He pointed at the engraved box next to me. "Why that important? Can I ask?"

"Ask. I won't answer."

"Okay." He stirred the fire with a stick. "You wanna talk anything else?"

"No."

"I do gotta ask this. Why you walk. Why not a flyer?"

Shrug. "If I fly, you not follow."

"You want me follow?"

"Easier to kill you if I know where you are. I mean, if I have to."

"Still think that?"

"Mebbe. Now my turn to ask. Why are you here?"

"Following you."

"No. Not that. Why you stay? Portal open long time. Why no go?"

"Same thing you. Gotta do what gotta do."

"What that?"

He pointed at me. "You. Gotta do you."

"Don't need you."

"Gotta dead rex that says other. And those skinnies too. You mebbe good, but you alone."

I didn't answer that.

"I'm right, aren't I?"

Didn't answer that either.

Long silence. Finally, "They called you Duty. That your real name?"

"Who's they? They who hired you?"

"Not hired. Assigned." He tapped his chest, indicating his badge. Portal Authority. "Coulda said no. Coulda gone."

"But ...?"

"No place to go. All I know is here. Why you?"

"You already know. I gotta do what I gotta do."

"You closed the portal."

"Somebody had to."

"You know why?"

"Complicated."

"We got time. Meat ain't done yet."

Too much to explain. And not to him. Not yet. Mebbe never. His language doesn't have the words for it. Not even the grammar.

I don't do portal mechanics anyway. I know only what everyone knows: set the coordinates out to the umptillionth digital of pi, resolution fine enough to measure the circumference of the universe out to the width of a quantum particle. But there's still an infinity of irrationalities beyond that … so every time the techs open a new portal, no matter how carefully calibrated, it's always a gamble. Sometimes the portal opens to vacuum, sometimes to the core of a planet, or worse—a star. So when you find a barren rock, like a vacant moon or a large asteroid, any good place to stand, you use it. You go through and set up shop where playing portal roulette won't accidentally destroy half a continent. You keep doing it until you find a home-like world, then lay tracks, send pods, and the portal tree grows another branch upline. Expensive and time-consuming, but the reward-to-risk ratio is compelling. A whole new planet, right?

Between here and anywhere, this world and all the worlds downline, there are a lot of barren asteroids serving as spacers, with tracks running out of one hole in space and into another, linking a good place with the next good place upline—each asteroid a connecting link in the branch. Mostly safe, but not this time. The asteroid between here and the rest of downline—they say it's about to get vaporized by an expanding red giant. This branch of the line and everything upline from here will be broken off. Isolated.

There are several worlds upline from here—only a few, none very well settled, most still getting explored, so no big investment there, not much population to lose. Less than a million. But this place—? It's sorta settled. Find enough ornery, stubborn people—they'll stay in spite.

It was just too much to explain, and I don't like to talk anyway. But he wanted an answer, so I said, "If you really Authority, you already know."

"It ain't the truth." He didn't explain. "Want some rex?" He cut off a thick slice, bigger than three of me could eat, and held it out, stuck on the end of his knife.

I took it carefully. Still hot. Not bad. I could save the rest for later.

"Ever have chicken?" he asked.

"No."

"Tastes like rex." He added, "But everything tastes like rex. Everything here."

"You been elsewhere?"

He shook his head. "No need."

And that was as much conversation as either of us had. Constant kicked out the fire and we bedded down for the night. Him on his side, me on mine.

In the morning we headed west.

We had to detour around the trailing members of a herd of grassbeasts. A pack of stalkers followed the herd and an outlier came sniffing, but the rest ignored us. Caution slowed us down. Proceed carefully, stay safe. Remember the rex.

By midday, we could smell the ocean, an hour later we reached the shore. The tide was out, so we walked on wet sand, easier than pushing across the dunes. In the distance, a jumble of cliffs stretched sideways, pointing further north and west. We'd go up there, turn inland.

That was where they ambushed us. The skinnies. The two larges from Bias Station and fourteen more. They'd been hiding in the marsh where the flutterbys and skeeter-bots couldn't detect them. Smart. Dangerously smart.

They outnumbered us. Seven surrounded us with spears and rifles. Nine more in a larger circle around them. They looked hungry and gaunt. Hard times. We might take out three or four, maybe more, but not all. Not with some behind us.

Standoff.

Grumbly, his arm tied up now, studied us. "You no kill. We no kill. Honor, yes? What in box? Give."

"It won't do you any good," I said.

"Important to you? Important to me. Give."

Looked to Constant. A question. What do we do?

He leaned toward me. "What he wants—is it worth dying for?"

"Truth? No."

"Then give."

That surprised me. "Don't want to fight?"

"Don't want to die."

"Not a good day for it," I agreed.

Turned back to Grumbly. "Okay. I give." Took box out slowly. Placed it on the ground between us, stepped back.

Grumbly picked up the box, shook it, held it to his ear, listened. "Heavy," he said. He tried to pull it open, tried to twist it open, eyed it angrily.

"That won't work," I said.

"Why?"

"It has to be opened the right way."

"Tell me."

"Can't. No have words."

He didn't like that answer, but he accepted it. He put the box back down. He pointed at it. "You open." Then he backed away. All of them took a few steps back.

Glanced to Constant. He nodded. I stepped forward and bent to the ground. The box wasn't locked, but the top had to be twisted around until all the top and bottom symbols matched, meshed, and clicked—then twisted once more to unlock. I pulled the top open and stepped back. Way back. Constant too.

Grumbly approached suspiciously.

He peered into the box. Frowned. Reached slowly. Touched. Grabbed. Lifted. All the skinnies leaned forward to look. Constant too.

A gray metallic disk—no, not a disk—a roll of shining ribbon. Inscribed with square markings. He frowned at it. "What this?" He held it out to me, accusing. "Explain!"

"It's a message," I said. "For a machine. A bot."

"What it say?"

"Don't know. Don't know what it says."

"Important, yes?"

"Must be, yes."

"Trade for money? Food?"

"Probbly. If you can get it to—" I looked to Constant. "Should I tell him?" He nodded. Back to Grumbly. "Blue Tower. You know Blue Tower? Up where the ice glows?"

He grunted. "East. Long walk east."

"Very long walk. Okay, you no go. Give back?"

Grumbly snorted. "I keep." He started to tuck the shining roll into his jacket.

"Don't you want the box?"

He kicked it away. "Ugly thing. Can't open it." He pointed to Constant. "You have food, yes? Give now. Then go. Both."

"He wants the rest of the rex."

"I spent a long time smoking that meat."

"Is it worth dying for?"

"Truth? No."

"Then give."

He unloaded the slab of meat and laid it on the sand. The skinnies grabbed it and vanished into the bushes as fast as they had appeared.

Constant looked at me. "Now what?"

I scooped up the box, closed it and tucked it into my coat. "We go on."

"Really?"

"Gotta do what I gotta do."

"Without the spool?"

"Annoying. Not fatal."

"Explain?"

"No."

We headed inland, away from the ocean now. Skinnies had to be watching, following until we were well away from their land.

We didn't stop until hunger stopped us. Ration bars, barely enough. We pushed on until evening, made camp in the rain forest. Wet winds came in hard, bringing damp smells and fog. We climbed into the higher branches and strung hammocks. Fell asleep listening for prowlers and weezils—especially weezils. They can ooze right up next to you without a sound. Hammocks have alarms, loud: shake awake like a quake. Most weezils shriek and drop. Most. So slept with gun.

We stayed wrapped long after dawn, waiting for morning to warm. Climbed down, found a shower tree, and stripped off. I hadn't washed since Bias Station; still felt dirty. Constant stripped down too.

Shower trees are convenient. The midnight rains pool up in the leaves, water trickling down until the broadest leaves at the bottom hold great reservoirs. They fill, they overflow. Stand under the right branch, you get a shower. Scrub for a bit, then stand under the next and rinse. Repeat until clean. Or until tree is dry. The mud around the tree can be deep, but there are usually pools to wash my feet.

I stood naked in the sun to dry off. Constant too. The big hulk stood apart, looking at me. Didn't look back. Didn't want to know. But he watched me.

Finally, I turned to him. "What?"

"Nothing. Just looking."

"Why?"

"Never seen a small naked."

"Now you have. Stop looking."

"Make you nervous?"

"No."

Constant hesitated. "Duty?"

"What?!"

"You ever do it with a large?"

"Never done it with anyone. Turned it off before it started." A thought occurred to me. "You?"

Constant looked away for a moment, then back. "Yes. Have three babies. Two mine, one contract. All went downline. I promise to follow. But—" He stopped.

Long silence.

I looked over. "Am I supposed to say sorry now?"

"Only if you mean it."

"It was your choice to stay."

"No one else could. No—that's not right. No one else was—"

"What?"

Constant cleared his throat. *"Do you speak interlingua?"*

Huh?

Interlingua? The portal engineers' language? Stared at him. This large was not what I thought he was. He stared back, waiting for me to reply.

"You already know that. Or assumed."

"This is what I know. When they asked me to stay—when they said I should stay—I said I would stay only if they told me the truth. So they did. And it doesn't matter if I tell you now because the portal's gone. The story they told everyone about the evacuation? It's a lie. The real reason—there's something wrong about this place, it does something to us. It changes us, every generation. That's why some of us breed large and others breed small and too many are skinny. And some are other things too. It affects us up here—" He tapped his fingers on the side of his head.

Kept my face still. Had to consider this. Maybe. Not impossible. But— *"It's all theories and chatter, yes? Symbiotic evolution. Mutable genetics. Ecological reflection. Nobody knows."*

"Yes. No—maybe. Nobody knows. Synergistic interaction probably. But whatever, it doesn't just change bodies. It changes brains too. Especially the skinnies—they're not people anymore. We don't think like downliners, none of us. That's why downline ordered the portal closed. They don't want us spreading down."

"But then, why the evacuation—?"

"Yeah, that. All those people gone downline—all into permanent quarantine. A dead-end world. All those pods went on a one-way trip. Whatever it is, downline wants to contain it, study it, take it apart and maybe find out how to control it. So they can design specific forms of ... of whatever we are. The large ones—like me. Not just to adapt to other worlds, but to invade them. Now you know why I stayed. You understand?"

I didn't answer. If Portal Authority had lied to all the evacuees, they would just as easily lie to Constant. But I didn't say that.

"And you? Why did you stay?"

"Because I'm Duty—"

And stopped there.

Didn't finish the sentence. Didn't finish the thought. I was not ready to talk about it. I hiked back to where I'd hung my clothes to dry, shook them out, and dressed in silence. A moment later, Constant followed. "You okay?"

"No."

"Should I say I'm sorry?"

"Why?" I pulled on my jacket. Looked up and up. Looked to his eyes. "When you asked if I'd done it, I thought we were going to have the conversation about you and I doing it. The conversation we did have—that wasn't the conversation I expected. Or wanted to have. It changes things. Mebbe things between us."

"Is that what you wanted? That conversation?"

"No. I dunno. Woulda said no. Gotta think this out. No more talk now."

We were only half a day from the end. We filled our canteens and headed north and west to Green Valley where the grass was taller than Constant. A good place to be caught by a prowler. We stayed in the foothills, above the highest.

The north end of the valley narrowed to a high rocky canyon, not quite a dead end, but not an easy passage either. No matter. We weren't going the distance. Halfway up, we came to an old wooden shack tucked in the space between two huge boulders and the cliff wall. The door squeaked, then fell open. Inside, a chair, a fallen table, some left-over parts of broken things.

"This is it?" asked Constant.

"This is it," I said.

He looked around, frowning. "Don't see why."

I shrugged out of my gear, dropping it all to the floor. "Now we wait."

"For what?"

"For me to decide."

"Decide what?"

"If I have to kill you."

"Doubt you could."

"Hard, yes. Not impossible. Things you don't know. Things they didn't tell you. Gonna sleep now." I looked around, found a place less dirty, spread hammock as a rug, stretched out on the floor. Stared at the ceiling. Thick webs, looking like veils, hung from the rafters. Just as dead as the rest of the cabin.

"Duty?"

"What?"

"What's to keep me from killing you? While you sleep?"

"You could. But then you'd never know why we're here. Or what I know." I turned off and slept.

Darkness woke me. And cold too. I sat up and looked around.

Constant was gone. All the tracking bots were negative.

Probably had enough of me. Fair choice. Easier without him.

I boiled water for tea. Drank slowly. Waited for dawn. Finally stepped outside to pee and looked around, walked out into the canyon. Up and down. No Constant. Not even footprints.

Sat down to think.

Constant couldn't have known everything. But he had to know more than he had already said. Or he wouldn't have stayed with me. Protected me. So he knew something … more. I just didn't know what.

But he left for a reason. So why? What did that mean? That I didn't need him anymore? Or that he had gotten what he wanted—this location. Even if he didn't know why.

So if this was what he wanted to know, he'd be back.

And probably not friendly. I should have killed him when I had the chance.

Too many mysteries. Too much to think about. Most of it un-necessary. I'd been given a task, been given a tight focus—so tight that I'd missed the rex. So tight that I'd missed why Constant was here. Assigned to me, yes—by who? Protection because—? Too many questions. Distracting. But I knew one thing now. They shouldn't have focused me so tightly.

Time to go. I gathered my gear from the cabin, strapped up, checked myself—confidence was high, everything green—and head-ed down the canyon.

The sounds of flyers stopped me, seven of them dropping down from the sky. An entire combat team, Constant in the lead.

I dropped my gear and waited. Put my hands on top of my head. "Surrender," I said. "I surrender."

"Why?" said Constant.

"You brought troops."

"Thought you might need them."

"Oh." I put my hands down. Picked up my gear.

He fumbled in his robe. "Thought you might need this." He held up the roll of shining metal ribbon, then he tucked it away.

"Did you kill them?"

"Only the one. Didn't like him anyway. He took my meat."

"Not his fault. Didn't know better. Hungry. Desperate."

"Well, not anymore." Constant pointed to the other larges behind him. "These are my brothers."

"Obvious."

Constant said, "Talk honest, you and I?" He pointed down the canyon. I followed. After a bit, after he was sure we were out of ear-shot, he stopped. He looked to me, an accusation in his eyes. *"You know things."*

"Most of them hurt."

"Most of life is hurt."

"You don't know what things are true."

"Do you?"

"Probbly not."

Constant frowned. *"Tell me what you know. We'll think it together."*

Fair enough. *"Agree. Ask."*

"Why the rex?"

"Wanted to pass it. Wanted you to wake it."

"Wanted it to kill me?"

"Mebbe. Didn't know who you were."

"Why Bias Station?"

"I had to hide it somewhere safe until retrieval. Bias was closest."

"It's important?"

"It's useful. It lets me leave."

"Leave to where?"

"Upline."

Constant registered shock. *"Not possible. Upline portal shut down months ago."*

"There's another upline. Unauthorized."

"Not possible. Portal Authority would have detected—"

"Yes, they knew. The stress field disturbance couldn't be hidden. But location could be. Made them crazy."

Constant stopped, confused. His expression collapsed, became unreadable. He looked like he wanted to say something. Or do something. Instead, he turned around and howled at the sky. A long moan of frustration and rage. Did his brothers hear him? Would they come now?

When he finally came back, he must have seen the question on my face. He said, *"No fear. We howl in private. It's our way."*

"I didn't know that."

"I trusted you. I showed you my pain. Now you trust me. Tell me everything. I have no more howl."

I thought about it. Didn't matter anymore. Why not? *"Portal Authority lies. Portal Authority has big secrets. But others have bigger."*

"Do they lie too? The others?"

"Probbly. Secrets hide behind lies. Bigger secrets hide behind bigger lies."

"You know these secrets?"

"Only the smallest part."

Constant held out a corner of his robe, as if it was more than a robe. *"Unraveling starts with a single thread."*

"Depends on where you pull. So pull here. Portal Authority—that story they told you? About the unknown genetic shift? Was that a lie on top of a lie? Nobody knows. But think this. Mebbe they don't want larges downline. Larges are the biggest change of all. You be a threat, just by existing."

"We don't fit downline. Not go."

"Convenient."

"Was not expecting portal to close. Not what we were told."

"More lies, more secrets."

"What was Portal Authority hiding? Do you know."

"Only guesses. Portal Authority couldn't find this upline. Too well hidden. So probably dangerous. How far does this upline extend? Who's up there? Big unknown. Mebbe invasion? Mebbe monsters? Mebbe disease? Much to fear. They were even more afraid when their agents disappeared. Portal Authority isn't just this world. It's the whole branch. They couldn't find upline. So they had to close downline to cut off the whole branch."

Constant's expression darkened. For a long moment he looked dangerous. But he'd asked for the truth— *"How can I know you're not lying?"*

"Mebbe it's all lies. Mebbe there's some truth. Mebbe we can't know. There's only this ... I did what I gotta do. So did you. We both been used. We were useful. Now we're not."

"Used. Yes."

"Now, your turn, Constant. Tell me. Why were you following me for so long?"

"Assignment. They said you were going to illegal upline. I was to follow you, find the station, destroy it, and kill you. But then downline shut down. So Portal Authority is over. Nothing else to do, so I follow anyway. Now I know. Is this the upline I have to close? But why now, if downline gone? Very confusing. Do I still have to destroy it?"

"You don't have to. I'm going to. After I go through. Unless you kill me first. Then you can destroy it. If you find it."

"Hmp. Thought you were logical."

"Could say the same about you. So here we are. Used and useless. Lies and secrets over. Nothing left. Still want to kill me? Want to try?"

"Haven't seen upline station yet. Will decide then. Are there larges up there?"

"Yes. Everyone who disappeared. All the missing. Even larges. All recruited. Yes."

"Recruited?"

"Yes."

"So my brothers and I can be useful again?"

"Yes."

Constant turned and lumbered away. He headed off to talk with his brothers. He was gone a long time. I wondered if he'd forgotten me. Or if they were talking about leaving. But before the sun had moved too far, he came back.

"Question. Recruit us? Me, my brothers too? Can you?"

"Will you take the oath? It is an oath more binding than any you have ever sworn before."

"Tell me."

"Will you do what you gotta do? That's the oath. The rest is details."

"Hmp. Too easy."

"You think so. Do you swear?"

"I swear. I will do what I gotta do."

"And your brothers?"

"They will swear it too."

"I'll hold you to that. Because once we get upline, this portal will be vaporized too. This world will be cut off forever."

"Leave it to the skinnies then."

"Skinnies have feelings."

He didn't want to hear that. "They don't have feelings for people who aren't skinnies."

"Maybe one day they'll figure that out. Maybe not. Go talk to your brothers. Tell them everything. If they want to come, I'll take you. All or none."

He came back. "They don't believe there's a portal."

"But will they come?"

"Prove you can open it, they'll come."

"Follow me."

"If there's no portal, they'll kill you."

"If there's no portal, they should. Follow me."

We went back up to the cabin, crowded now with all those larges inside. I faced the back wall where it leaned up against the cliff. Constant held out the ribbon. "Need this?"

"Nope. Just a decoy. Just in case." I pulled the box out of my jacket, twisted the top around so a different set of symbols lined up. Pressed the box against a ragged splotch of gray.

Nothing happened.

"Nothing's happening."

"Wait."

"If something doesn't happen—"

"Wait!"

Behind us, the larges were restless. Muttering.

I turned and faced them. "What do you want? The portal or my corpse? Choose now. Do it or shut up and wait!" Turned to Constant. "Tell them!"

He grunted something in a language I didn't recognize. But the intent was clear. The others fell silent.

I pushed past them to the chair, plopped myself down. "These things take time. Safety scan. Identity check. Then power up. Energize. Handshake. Synchronization. All that, then more. Then, when confidence get high enough, then mebbe things happen."

"How long?"

"Long as it takes. Day or two or three, mebbe. You brought food?"

"Three days," the largest one said. "Three days. If not three days, you die, we go."

"If not open in three days, I kill myself. You won't have to."

"No," he insisted. "My job. My pleasure."

But it wasn't three days. Only two and a half.

It began with a queasy sensation, then a deep note that got bigger until the whole canyon was rumbling. The walls of the cabin opened, flattening outward. The boulders that sheltered it rolled back with a great grinding sound. The cliff face cracked, slid open, revealing a deep cavern.

Inside, more great doors. Huge. And a rack of travel pods, just waiting to roll down to the tracks. One by one, they clicked to life, their lights gleaming blue.

Constant moved forward in cautious awe. His brothers followed slowly, looking up and around as if they'd never seen a portal lock before.

I came up beside him. "Believe me now?"

He turned around, towering over me. "Believe you now." He leaned down to ask quietly. "A question, Duty. What up there?"

"A whole new world."

"You want me to follow you?"

"Do you want to?"

"We good for each other, yes?"

Looked up at him. Up and up. Finally smiled. "Yes."

That startled him, but he recovered. All business again. "World harder than this one?"

"Much harder. It'll hurt."

"Good." He straightened and waved to his brothers. "Let's go!"

Night Folk

by Barb Galler-Smith

Bonnie loved the quiet dark with her friends, but tonight she felt unsettled. The games area of Sunnyside Acres Assisted Living was deliciously deserted.

Magnolia stared out the window at the new crescent moon, her face a sad mask. Helen drummed her fingers on the table for the thousandth annoying time, and Abigail still pondered what was trump. Bonnie dropped her cards on the table and stood up.

"I'm tired and I'm hungry. Who wants to go out to get something to eat? It seems like days since I had anything filling. One simply can't live on green beans and veggie stew forever."

"Count me in," said Abigail and Helen together.

"I'm not feeling well," said Magnolia. "I think I'll stay here. I'm really … I'm just so tired of it all." She looked forlorn. "I'm done," she whispered to Bonnie. "My time is short."

Bonnie pulled her to her feet. "Nonsense! You just need a decent meal. Let's go get something."

Magnolia reluctantly followed as the others passed Kyle, night receptionist and handyman.

"We're going out for a walk," said Bonnie.

Kyle didn't look up from his comic. "Okay," he said, and then what seemed an afterthought, "Stay safe."

✧ ✧ ✧

108

Pete tossed the brochure for Sunnyside Acres on a coffee table already littered with advertisements from other assisted-living homes. "It's only for women! It was so perfect, but no married couples. No exceptions."

Ellie choked back a sob. "My blindness is getting worse. Soon I won't be able to do anything for myself."

Pete understood. Ellie's macular degeneration was debilitating for them both. "Sure you will. And I'll help you. We'll be all right." He gingerly rose from his chair in front of the fire, stretched and shook vigorously to loosen his joints. He took her hands in his, as he had for all of their fifty-three years of marriage. "We knew retirement wasn't going to be easy." He couldn't bear to see her so sad. "Our hunting days are over, my dear. It's time to relax and do other things." They would find a place to move to, and Ellie would be safe.

He transformed into his preferred shape—a German Shepherd-husky mix. He was large enough to wage battle and could take down and hold all but the strongest prey. With Ellie's talons helping, they could eliminate most others. But now, modern life had driven so many night creatures underground and those left in the world were fitting in as they never had before. Pete had to face it—they needed to retire. They were just not strong or fast enough anymore.

"Let's get out of here," she said. "One last flight as Night Folk."

He padded to the apartment door. She stuffed a change of clothes and shoes for them in the small pack he carried across his back. She stepped into the moonlight, then closed and locked the door behind them. He looked around to make sure no neighbor was watching. He woofed softly.

Ellie transformed and spread her wings.

Pete watched her soar then bank toward the river. He followed at a trot.

At the end of the block Bonnie and her friends turned into the park and kept close to the few streetlamps. It wasn't much of a park, but it had enough trees and shrubs to make it friendly to any who didn't want to be seen doing what they weren't supposed to be doing.

They took it slow, walking two by two, arms linked, and engrossed in quiet conversation. In their bright, baggy cardigans, using four-footed walking canes, Bonnie thought they looked like a multicolored twelve-legged caterpillar as they shuffled along the darkening path.

They pretended not to see the two guys creeping parallel to them.

"Careful," whispered Bonnie. "Keep walking."

They kept walking, eyes on each other, never letting their gaze linger on the men.

Then the men leapt from the near bushes. One grabbed at Bonnie's purse and pushed her hard against a large tree trunk.

Bonnie wheeled, elbowed him in the face, and threw him to the ground. Magnolia sat on his chest with her knees pinning his shoulders. He bucked and thrashed in an effort to dislodge her. Bonnie sat on his legs.

He yelped in pain. "Get off!"

The other man grappled with Helen. She jabbed him in the groin with the end of her cane. He fell to his knees, and Abigail kicked him flat and held him with a foot on his back.

The men struggled and swore, but were unable to extricate themselves.

"You shouldn't be here," Bonnie said. "There are consequences to being bad boys."

"Let me go, you old hag," cried the one under Abigail's foot. He nearly wiggled free, and she secured him with the tips of her cane pressing hard into the back of his knee.

"Let go!" he howled.

"This will hurt a smidgen," Magnolia said to the man she sat on. She leaned over and bit him hard on the side of the neck. "Ick!" she said, recoiling and spitting the blood to the ground. "This guy is full of drugs."

Bonnie had a stronger stomach than Magnolia. She quickly maneuvered to his neck, bit hard, and took a long drink. She winced at the taste. Whatever he was on, it was nothing she couldn't quickly overcome. His blood was the main thing. She drank until he stopped struggling. She nudged him. He wasn't dead but would be weak for a few days. She'd stopped short of killing him, or worse, turning him.

Magnolia stepped to the other man. "May I try that one?"

He stopped struggling for an instant. "Don't kill me," he said, his eyes wide.

Magnolia stroked his cheek. "Not my style," she said. She bent close and nibbled delicately on his neck. "No drugs," she murmured and sank her teeth deep.

The tasty man groaned. He didn't resist her—she had a flair for soothing her prey and they rarely struggled. She drank her fill. Her curly white hair grew bloody on the ends that draped over his neck. A glistening darkness dribbled down her chin. He stared up at her.

Both Abigail and Helen had a taste. Not enough to satiate them, but a decent snack.

Tasty's gaze never left Magnolia's face.

Bonnie recognized the look in his eyes. Hate rather than fear. They'd either have to kill him or let him go soon. If he were turned, he'd be a danger to everyone. Especially Magnolia.

High Guy scuttled backward as fast as he could. He grabbed his friend by the coat and tugged him a short way. When his friend didn't move quick enough, he ran.

Something growled behind them.

A massive dog knocked Magnolia to the ground. Abigail and Helen rushed to her rescue. Helen held her cane up to fend off the dog.

She was strong, but the dog was stronger. It grabbed her by the arm.

A silent, pale form dove at Bonnie with talons open. She jumped, swung a fist wildly and knocked an enormous owl to the ground. The dog immediately abandoned Magnolia and ran to the fallen bird.

"Hunters!" Bonnie cried. "Run!"

"Ellie!"

Pete transformed from his dog shape and knelt beside his wife, no longer an owl. A lump was forming on her forehead just above her left eye. Ellie opened her eyes, blinked and shook her head. "Oh gods, Pete, I can't see at all now!" Tears streamed down her face. "What am I going to do?"

Pete growled. He looked for the blood-eaters but they were long gone. If his Ellie was permanently damaged, there would be payback.

The clash with the Hunters seemed to take the spirit out of Magnolia. About a week after the incident in the park, she said she was ready to go. They pretended she was moving to Florida to live with family. She packed away all her belongings and Sunnyside Acres held a party for her.

Kyle gave a short speech. "Being a night person let me meet one of the best ladies in the place. I'll miss you, Magnolia."

They would all miss her.

Just before her last dawn, she bid her friends pleasant dreams and stepped into the cloistered garden. Bonnie and the others watched her through the blinds of Bonnie's heavily shaded room. As the sun rose, Magnolia waved to them, and then turned toward the rising sun with a smile.

Life wasn't the same without Magnolia.

No one felt much like going out, and had it not been for Bonnie's urging, the other two might have followed Magnolia into the sun. Bonnie kept herself occupied by discovering the lair that the two thugs used. The ladies worked harder at night to keep other hoodlums from returning to the park at dusk. As a result, neighbors started gravitating to their little green belt. Families gathered and children played during the day. At night young couples walked hand in hand without fear. Kyle said the park felt protected. That cheered her.

Bonnie sat with the others playing three-handed Whist. Three-handed was all right, but they really needed a fourth.

"Hey, Kyle!" called Bonnie. "Wanna play Whist?"

"Thanks for thinking of me," he said, putting down his ever present superhero comic, "but I need to greet our new resident in a few minutes. She's a night owl, just like you ladies."

Probably not quite, Bonnie thought with a smile, *but maybe she played cards.* The sight of the newcomer at the door with a white cane and a guide dog squelched that idea.

It took half an hour to settle the paperwork, and then the movers began unloading their truck. The woman and her dog didn't have much and within an hour all was unloaded. The men spent another two hours unpacking boxes. The woman and her dog disappeared into

Night Folk

her room, but after the movers left, Bonnie was sure she heard a man's voice coming from the small apartment.

She didn't want to be seen prying, but the hairs on the back of her neck prickled. She moved closer to the apartment's door and almost bumped into Kyle.

He grinned at her then knocked. "Ellie, I've got those last papers for you to sign right now." The door opened and he closed it behind him.

The scent of Hunters washed over Bonnie. She stepped back in panic and struggled to remain calm. A blind woman and her dog. But not just any dog. It was the dog from the park.

She gritted her teeth. The dog had nearly killed Magnolia. In a way, it *had* killed her.

Bonnie hurried back to the table.

"Well?" said Helen.

"Hunters."

Abigail shivered and put her head in her hands. "Oh no! I'm not ready to move on. I like it here, and this is where … where Magnolia was. I don't want to leave."

With Hunters so near, it meant life or death for her and the others to remain where they were at Sunnyside Acres. They tried not to kill and only drank what they needed to survive. Hunters had no such principles. Hunters killed *all* of their kind.

She snarled. "We'll just have to take them out. Divide and conquer."

The couple emerged from their room with Kyle and walked across to his desk. The dog was the largest Bonnie had ever seen, and he was by far the more dangerous of the two. The woman beside him must be the owl Bonnie had struck down.

In her human form, the woman was truly blind. She walked with one hand extended slightly, the other clutched the dog's harness handle. The dog had eyes only for her. Seeing a Hunter become such a frail figure somewhat saddened Bonnie. It was an emotion she could not afford to nurture. As soon as the dog turned his head toward her, he sniffed and his ears pricked. Then his hackles rose, and a low growl washed across the room. He had recognized her.

"Pete!" said the woman softly. "Not now."

The dog settled but he raised his lip to Bonnie in a promise of a more private meeting.

After they signed the last of the paperwork, Kyle led the woman to Bonnie and the others.

"Hey, ladies. This is Ellie and her dog, Pete. Ellie, these are my night-owl Sunnysiders—Bonnie, Abigail, and Helen."

"Welcome," said Abigail. She gave the woman a melancholy smile. "You're the spitting image of a friend who recently left us." She started to cry. "I hope you'll be very happy here." With that, she hurried away to her room.

Abigail was right. Ellie resembled Magnolia. They had the same height and build, and her hair fell in white curls around a heart-shaped face with a wistful smile. It was unsettling.

Ellie held out her hand to shake but withdrew it the instant Bonnie touched her. She shivered, as if ruffling feathers.

A grumbling threat came from the dog and he moved in front of Ellie.

"Pete! Back!" she whispered. "How do you do?" she added stiffly.

Bonnie stepped back. They all knew, but they couldn't allow Kyle to know anything was wrong. The Hunters also seemed to be keeping a low profile.

She watched the dog for a moment, and then smiled as if she meant it. "I think you will love Sunnyside. It's been our home for five years. It's very private and nobody pries. Turnaround is slow, so there is time to make new friends, but I think everyone who was here before us has moved on—some to more care and some ..."

Helen sobbed. "And some just died."

Ellie looked surprised. Kyle looked stricken.

"Our fourth musketeer, if you will," Helen said. After an awkward silence, she added, "She was in Florida."

Kyle wiped at the tears pooling in his eyes.

Ellie opened her mouth to say something. Pete gave a small whine.

Ellie scratched the dog behind his ears. "I best take Pete for a walk. We both need to get a good feel for the area. Is there a park nearby?"

"Yes, just a short block away. Do you need help with doggie things?" Kyle asked.

"Oh no," said Ellie, "I see just well enough out of the corner of my eyes to find and bag anything Pete might leave behind."

Bonnie and Helen watched as Kyle escorted the pair to the door and touched the automatic door opener. He'd just plopped into his chair and picked up his comic when a loud crash outside sent every-one hurrying to the front doors.

Two cars had collided in front of the building, barely ten feet from the entrance. One car had rammed another from the rear. The SUV had a crumpled back end, but the sedan was crushed in the front and smoke came from the engine. A bewildered and frightened woman jumped from her SUV and ran to Kyle. Two men escaped their dis-abled car and paused, looking around.

Bonnie recognized the hoodlums from the park.

Tasty pointed directly at Ellie. "It's her! One of the bitches who bit me!" He stepped toward her just as Bonnie stepped toward him.

The sound of approaching police sirens stirred them all to action.

Pete hesitated between Tasty and Bonnie.

The man grabbed Ellie.

Pete was too late. He lunged but a well-placed kick knocked him back just long enough for the man to force Ellie into the SUV and slam the door. Pete jumped onto the hood snarling but couldn't hold on as the SUV jolted away. He hit the roadway dazed. Kyle picked him up and laid him beside the stunned woman.

Two police cruisers passed with sirens blaring and lights flashing.

Pete cut off Bonnie's path to help the woman from the SUV. He snarled and made it clear she would not be allowed near the bleed-ing woman.

She ignored his bared teeth. "Move it, dog-boy. That woman is more important than either of us right now."

He slowly backed away, making it clear that any wrong move from Bonnie and she'd have the beast at her throat.

Abigail pushed both Pete and Bonnie aside. "I used to be a nurse, so let me see. We'll take care of her and call paramedics," she said.

The woman seemed all right except for a shallow cut on her fore-head that bled profusely. It reminded Bonnie she was hungry. Kyle handed Abigail a cold compress from the first aid kit then dialed 911 for an ambulance and the fire department.

Bonnie watched the police cruiser's taillights disappear down the road. She knew the neighborhood well, and she knew who the culprits were and where they lived.

Abigail led the injured woman and Kyle inside.

Bonnie nudged Helen. "Come on. Ellie might be a hunter, but she's at risk and I'm pretty sure I know where they're going. Let's get those bastards."

The dog stood still, looked long and hard at Kyle, and made a decision. He transformed into a man wearing a too-tight guide dog harness and nothing else.

Kyle gasped, then collapsed as his knees buckled.

"I got him too," said Abigail from the doorway.

"Where are they going?" said Pete, murder in his eyes. "I don't trust you. She's my wife and *I'll* go get her."

"Not alone, Pete. Look, we all want to live here—*need* to live here. To do that we'll have to form some kind of truce. I can see your wife's not much of a hunter now"—Bonnie put her hand up to stall his protests—"and we're not the predators you think we are."

"Why would you help her?" Suspicion laced his tone.

Bonnie shrugged. "She's a Sunnysider now, so that makes her one of ours." Bonnie started running, Helen beside her.

Transforming back to his dog shape, Pete followed. For a couple of old ladies, they were impossibly fast. For blood-eaters, it was to be expected. In the old days, he could have run them down. Now, he was barely able to keep up. He felt what was going to be a very big bruise across his belly where the man had kicked him, and it slowed him down even more.

He wondered if age slowed the undead down the same way it had slowed him.

They arrived at a four-car police blockade. He caught the flicker of a movement and saw Bonnie and Helen skirt the cruisers, keeping to the shadows. He followed them along the side of the building until they hurried through the darkened entryway before the police noticed them. Pete had to chance doing the same thing, hoping he'd be mistaken for a police K-9 on the job. Regardless, he was on the job. Someone would pay dearly if Ellie was harmed.

Stairs greeted him on the other side of the doorway. He bounded up to the landing on the second floor where the blood-eaters waited. The landing divided into three hallways. They sniffed the air.

"Helen, can you tell which way?" Bonnie asked.

Helen took a deep breath. "Not sure. Should we split up?"

Pete stepped between them and took some satisfaction in seeing both blood-eaters jump back a couple of paces. He put his nose to the filthy floor. A decade of traffic left lingering molecules of filth, sweat, and decay. He wrinkled his nose and fought the urge to roll in it. And there, in the third hallway, the fresh and unmistakable scent of his Ellie. And the stench of his prey. Their prey.

He growled.

"Ah," said Bonnie. "Softly now."

Pete didn't wait. The click of his nails on the floor was a giveaway, but he hoped the men who held Ellie knew the difference between a dog and a man.

Bonnie laid a hand on the back of his neck. "Wait. Let me look," she whispered an inch from his ear. She flattened herself on the floor and peered under the ill-fitting door with one eye.

She sat up. "Ellie looks okay," she whispered. "She's against the far wall, sitting on the floor. The two others are loading firearms right now. It'll be a shoot-out if we don't get in there before the cops. Ellie might get hurt. We go through the door together—Pete go left, Helen go right. I'll go up and over. If we're fast enough, they'll aim at the door and miss. Their bullets won't harm us, Pete, but what about you?"

Worth the risk, he thought. He licked his lips and snarled.

"Right."

Bonnie kicked the door open. Helen dove right, and Pete rushed left as a hail of bullets from an automatic pistol sprayed the door.

He was hit—right flank grazed—but his momentum kept him going. He slid into Ellie.

"I'm okay. Get them," she said.

Pete spun, jumped on the nearest man and knocked the pistol out of his hands. Bonnie followed with a sharp blow that sent him to the ground.

Helen didn't fare as well. Her prey was stronger and fought hard to free himself from her grasp. Pete left the first man to Bonnie and jumped onto the other man's chest. He missed biting into the man's neck but chomped hard on his shoulder.

Helen took the opportunity to sink her teeth into the man's jugular, and in three strong pulls she'd taken enough blood to make him pass out.

Pete heard the cops on the floor below. They'd be here soon—they'd know what floor the shots came from.

He transformed to his man shape, untied Ellie while Bonnie dragged the thug to lie beside his unconscious partner. Helen stepped on the thug to keep him from wiggling away.

Pete needed help to get Ellie out of the house. "They must not find her," he said. "Please."

"We can get out the window, but we can't carry her."

Ellie moved toward them—her hands outstretched. "You can carry me if I'm an owl."

"No! You can't see! It's too dangerous."

"We'll guide her," said Bonnie.

They had just enough time. Pete changed back into his dog form and stood guard over both the criminals. Ellie transformed into her owl shape. Helen carried Ellie on her arm until Bonnie had climbed through the window, then she passed Ellie through. Helen made it out just as the police reached the doorway.

It took a few minutes for the police to come in, recognize Pete wore a harness that visibly marked him as a service dog, and arrest both men. The druggie walked out on his own, but the other, drained and weak, needed help to go down the stairs. When an officer tried to coax Pete to follow her and grab his harness, he rushed past her, down the stairs and into the dark embrace of the night.

Bonnie and Helen stood with their backs to the wall on a narrow ledge that led nowhere.

Ellie's talons bit deep into Bonnie's arm and then she leapt into the night. She hooted once. Bonnie watched her fly up and to the right.

"You're about six feet from the roof, Ellie. A little higher and you can touch the edge. We'll join you up there."

It had been a long time since they'd needed to climb. She dug her fingers into the crevices between the old bricks and took only a second to hoist herself up to the roof, stretching to ease the ache in her old bones. Helen followed.

Ellie perched on the building's edge, facing the city. She didn't move but hooted excitedly.

"I think if we get to that other roof, we can escape down the drain-pipe," said Helen.

Bonnie held out the bundle of Ellie's clothes.

Ellie transformed from owl to human and held out her hand but didn't take the clothing. "Thanks for coming after me," she said. Her eyes filled with tears.

Bonnie paused. "You okay? Can you walk?"

Ellie nodded. "I'm okay. In fact, it's probably better if I fly."

Helen tugged on Bonnie's sleeve. "We gotta go. Ellie, if you can fly from the ledge to your left, out a few wing beats, and then circle slowly down about sixty feet, you'll land on the grass. Or, if you wait for us to get down and call, you can also home in on us and land safely."

They waited just long enough for Ellie to change and fly before heading to the other roof and climbing down the pipe.

By the time they reached a small patch of abandoned yard on the side of the building, Ellie was circling above, and Pete joined them below.

With her husband there, also guiding her in, Ellie landed without mishap, and Pete rushed to her side as she resumed human shape.

"Pete!" she exclaimed, her eyes bright. "When I transformed into an owl, I saw the city lights. And I could make you out! As an owl I can still see—well, not the best, but good enough to get myself around. It's going to be all right."

The couple embraced. Ellie put her clothes on, and Pete changed once more into a dog—even Ellie wasn't happy about him walking her home while he was naked.

The four made their way back to Sunnyside without speaking.

The assisted-living care facility was brightly lit and most of the residents were sitting in the dining room in their bathrobes and fuzzy no-slip slippers. They were abuzz with excitement. The police investigators were just leaving, after declining tea and cookies more than once. An ambulance had taken the injured woman away. Kyle and Abigail were encouraging everyone to go back to bed—the thrill was over—but the residents would have none of that. They remained in their small groups, whispering eagerly.

Abigail checked Ellie out, and Helen sat with Kyle, explaining how shock can sometimes make people see things that aren't there. Bonnie knew from the look on his face he wasn't buying any of it. Still, he hadn't told the police what he'd seen, so maybe that bode well for the future.

Pete led Ellie to the sofa across from Kyle and sat at her knee. Helen settled on one side of Kyle while Abigail stayed on his right. Bonnie relaxed in the easy chair beside the sofa.

Pete growled at them.

Ellie put her hand on his head and he quieted. "I lost what was left of my sight the night we fought in the park. My sight was going anyway, but being able to see more tonight as an owl is a blessing I didn't expect."

Kyle leaned forward. "I knew it! I *did* see your dog become a man!" He whipped out his phone and pointed it toward Pete to get a photo. "This is going to go viral for sure!"

Bonnie leaned into him. "No, Kyle, it's not," she said, her voice soft and menacing.

His eyes widened, but he continued with all the exuberance of youth. "It's news, Bonnie! *Big* news. Guide dog is really a man."

"Save it for *The Onion*," said Abigail. "No one will believe you anyway."

Pete stood, shook himself, and looked around. He loped to Ellie's room, disappeared for a moment and returned wearing a pair of jeans and a T-shirt. No one remained in the hall but them. He sat beside Ellie on the sofa.

Kyle was ecstatic and held up his phone. "Just one photo?"

"No," they all said in unison.

Pete glared at Bonnie. "Going to kill him next for knowing the truth? Isn't that what you bloodsuckers do?"

"We have never killed anyone," said Abigail, "unlike you Hunters, who have killed a lot of us."

He moved toward Abigail, but Ellie took his hand and held him back. "We want to retire. You were our last," she said.

Kyle was recording anyway. Bonnie took the phone away from him and started deleting things.

"Hey!"

"Kyle, do you want to live?"

He suddenly looked uncomfortable. "Uhm, yes?"

"We like to keep our neighborhood quiet," said Abigail. "Can you keep secrets?"

He looked down at the stack of comics on a nearby table. "Like secret-identity secrets? Hell yeah!" He suddenly frowned. "Except this place only takes women. No married couples. Sorry, Pete."

Pete took Ellie's hand. "Not even crime-fighting dogs?"

Kyle smiled. "Service dogs are allowed, and husbands can visit as often as they want, you know. And maybe we can get the owner to change the policy." His expression wrinkled with distaste. "The owner turned against marriage after her husband emptied their bank account. It might be hard to get her to change her mind."

Bonnie smiled—she smelled a challenge she was well-suited for. "Everyone has something to hide, and maybe a trio of vampires, a blind owl, and a guide dog are just the ones to convince the owner that one happily married couple would be just fine."

Helen clapped with obvious joy. "Pete, can you play Whist?"

He scowled. "Hate it."

"He was never much for cards," said Ellie.

Helen's grin drooped away, but Bonnie had a weirder idea. "Since we aren't going to play Whist, maybe we can partner in a different way."

Ellie squinted. "Just what do you mean?"

Kyle retrieved his phone and grimaced at the absence of his photos. "I had selfies from Comic-Con on there," he muttered. When Bonnie frowned at him, he put the phone in his pocket.

"I propose a permanent truce," Bonnie said. "I propose we find out just what we need to make sure Pete can move here officially with Ellie. Then …"

"Then what?" asked Pete. "Partners in some crime to blackmail the owner of this place? We can find somewhere else."

Kyle looked up from his phone. "But you're a Sunnysider! Why would you want to go anywhere else?"

"I don't want to move! Besides, a little larceny so we can stay here is fine by me," said Ellie.

Pete looked at Ellie with surprise.

Bonnie waited. "Pete?"

He raised his lip in a snarl, but she could tell his heart wasn't in it. "So, this makes us partners in crime?"

"After you move in here with Ellie, we can work to keep our neighborhood safe at night for everyone."

Helen laughed. "Maybe think of it as partners in crime-*fighting*."

"Right," said Bonnie. "We may not be as fast as we once were, but we are every bit as treacherous, and dedicated to cleaning up the neighborhood and keeping it that way."

Pete looked at Ellie, then at the other eager faces. At last he nodded and grunted. "Truce."

It was almost time for sunrise, and so time for bed. Abigail and Kyle searched online for surplus police radios. Helen tapped a jaunty rhythm with her fingers on the arm of the plush sofa. Ellie put her head on Pete's shoulder, and Pete sighed.

This beat playing Whist while waiting for the sunrise. Bonnie put her feet up on the footstool. It felt comfortable. She was content to remain among her night-folk for a while longer.

Things That Shouldn't Exist

by Marina J. Lostetter

I t's 2185.

We can travel to the far reaches of the galaxy overnight.

But we can't fucking eradicate cancer.

I'm going to a place that shouldn't exist. The last place I would've thought of going three years ago. It's the last place I *want* to be.

The Face.

Oh, you don't know about The Face?

Funny.

I'd have thought ...

Anyway: if you happened to be on Earth, in the southern hemisphere, on a clear night, you could easily look up and find the constellations Sagittarius, Serpens Cauda, and Aquila. Between them is another dinky constellation, made up of not especially bright stars, called Scutum. In the center of that constellation, past the Sonnet nebula, astronomers found a face. Just a face.

Lilac purple, smooth and glossy, with pits for eyes and a strong nose and wide lips. About the diameter of Betelgeuse from chin to forehead. An effigy. *A face the size of a star.*

The back of The Face is concave, but only slightly. Here *slightly* means a depth of two light-minutes. The whole thing has a pressed-flat look about it, like a mask that won't really fit. One made for hanging on the wall instead of wearing to fancy masquerade parties.

I can't remember the last time someone wanted me at a fancy party.

That's my fault, really. I wasn't easy to live with before I left. They were making it too easy, so I had to make it hard. Everyone was so damn *accommodating*—like the word *terminal* changed who I was, who they were.

I'd ask and they'd provide. *Yes, yes, yes*—all the damn time. You'd think it'd be great. But it's … it's devastating. Because they tell you *yes* now because before they thought they'd have years and years to tell you *no*.

I hated it, so I kept pushing, asking for more and more ridiculous things, hoping they'd crack, hoping they'd say no, hoping they'd treat me like they did *before*.

It was like they thought their tolerance was a final gift to me, their acquiescence to my every whim a beautiful treasure instead of wholly dehumanizing.

Eventually I couldn't take it anymore, knew it was as bad for them as it was for me. I'd been lashing out, controlling them in the hopes of controlling something—*anything*—in my life. It wasn't fair of me. But I still needed … still *need*.

Control. The end I can control.

So I'm going. Am gone. Whatever.

I found a vessel making its pilgrimage to The Face of God (ha), paid my fare (who needs earthly possessions when you won't be around to appreciate them?), and left everyone I've ever known (Mom, Dad, Leroy). Because that's what you do when you're about to die painfully—do the wildest thing you can think of in an attempt to die not-so-painfully.

The Face makes no sense, which you've probably figured out on your own. It doesn't have any seams. No rivets, no soldering lines, no mortar, no superglue. It looks to be a solid structure, molded or carved. Scientists think it's metal. It looks and feels and acts like metal. But it's violet, and all the atoms are wrong or something like that.

It's *all* wrong.

It's as big as a big-ass star, like I said, but gravity is barely two thirds of a g at the surface.

And it cries. Two colossal rivers flow from its eyes, its tears liquid mercury instead of briny water. As the rivers flow, they slowly evaporate into the cosmos, leaving not a drop to drip from its perfect purple chin.

Thing is, everything else that flows down the rivers evaporates too.

They sent probe after probe down the rivers in the early years, and as the little machines made their journeys they got lighter, thinner. They disappeared slowly, molecule by molecule. At the top it was a fully functioning, high-end space-exploration appliance. At the bottom, nothing but dust and star stuff.

The probes couldn't even detect what was happening to them. They broadcast no helpful data, no special clue.

We don't even know where the mercury comes from, how it is replenished. There are no reservoirs, and the mercury appears to percolate out of the bottom of the eyes like water through the dirt floor of a well.

This is why The Face makes no sense.

Oh, and also because it's a *giant fucking face* in space.

We have no theories about The Face. Not real ones, anyway. Most people of any faith just slap divinity on it and go about their business. Scientists say ancient aliens built it while usually using some handwavium to explain why it looks human. My two favorite (least favorite?) explanations are *convergent evolution* and *mental matrixing*. That last one there implies it's not really a face, and that it just *looks* like a face to us because we're used to seeing faces everywhere. On Mars, on the moon, in your bowl of sludge-soup after the latest chemo treatment.

But they don't know. No one knows. There aren't any real clues, no leads, no evidence.

There's nothing else like it in the galaxy. No hands, no feet, no giant neck for it to sit upon. All we've found is The Face.

Why, what, who? All mysteries. What is it for? What does it do?

Does it matter what its original purpose was, now that we've assigned it our own?

It's beautiful, though. I saw it with my own eyes for the first time today. The surrounding nebula sends pinkish-orange rainbows over its contours. Starlight reflects more strongly off its surface than the surrounding ships—and there are hundreds of those. Some are just visiting, some are conservationists stationed to protect The Face—protect it from *what*, I don't know. Some are temples permanently in orbit.

The pilgrims who ferried me here told me to pick my last meal from the Trees of Life they grow in the ship's belly—a giant conservatorium, a special bio-dome, with arching windows that look out into the stars. Lights in the ceiling cross the expanse on tracks, back and forth, a strange strobe show. The kind of light the trees need, chaotic and unnerving.

Their trunks are bone-white. Because that's what they are: bone. Engineered to grow like plants, with marrowy sap and meaty fruit.

These bones are nothing like my bones, but there's still a sense of wrongness in them. Only their wrongness is a gift, and mine … my bones … well …

Meat. I picked an orange from a tree, unpeeled its hide, and a ball of hamburger fell out.

We can grow this shit, but we can't fucking cure my cancer.

But I'm grateful for the food. Something like this would have made me puke a week ago. But my stomach doesn't have long enough to reject what I put in it. The meat has grown well-seasoned on the tree. Spicy, tactile. Warm and juicy.

After, they fit me in my space suit, and we leave the reverent fleet to make for the tears.

Truth is, these things shouldn't exist. This too-human face, divorced from physics as we know it; these trees that feed me as though by a chef's hand; this shuttle with its willing priests, who will drop me in the river of tears and fly away again; this cancer eating my bones, distorting my marrow and taking over my blood. None of it should exist.

But it does.

They lower me down, like an acrobat or sky dancer, on a length of silk the same color as The Face. When I reach the river, I lay down and cross my arms over my chest like I'm a kid at the water park. It's just a slide. A long, long slide.

But I don't let go of the silk.

There's a priest on the other end. My guide. Holding tight.

I'm buoyant on the mercury. I can feel its pressure against my suit, rippling here and there, but I can't tell if it's hot or cold or any temperature at all. The current pulls me, and the silk is taut in my glove.

"Are you ready?" my guide asks over my helmet's comms. The shuttle won't leave until I let go. Even then, they'll scoop me out if I say so. My guide will even take me back to Earth if I've changed my mind.

But I haven't. I want this.

"I'm ready," I say, and feel my own tears welling in my eyes. They're tears of grief and tears of relief and tears of happiness all at once.

He makes the sign of his religion from where he leans out of the shuttle, his own suit masking his expression. I try not to laugh as he moves his hand—it looks like he's drawing a smiley face of old.

He doesn't push or pull.

I let go, and he lets go, and the silk falls across my body.

The current is fast, but I feel no great *whoosh*. Here I am, exposed to all the universe, to all of these ships and these people. They are too far away to see me with the naked eye, but I can feel their gazes on me, hot and proud.

They are proud of all the people who take the plunge.

I hope my family is proud too.

Or, at least, I hope they understand.

Space is lain out before me. The sensation isn't quite like flopping down in the grass on a summer night; the stars are clearer, and there are the ships all around, noses pointed at me like arrows. The ships make me feel like I'm looking out instead of up. Like I'm slowly slipping feet-first down a waterfall instead of meandering down a river.

I am alone on The Face's cheek, surrounded by quicksilver, rushing, rushing, through, away, beyond.

I feel light. The continuous background pains of my body rearranging and strangling itself abate.

I could pitch forward—upward—just a bit and float free into the void. Leave the surface of The Face. But I'm heading toward something now. There's an echo in my mind, like the howl of a distant wind, and it feels like a call, like I need to get closer to make out the words.

So much space. So much universe. The tall ridgeline of the nose is on my left. Distant and gigantic. I'm here already. That means I've been in the river for days. It doesn't feel like days. It's been seconds.

Nothing looks like it's changed—the ships haven't moved. The universe holds fast.

But has it always been this bright? Always been these colors?

Lighter, lighter still. I feel fuzzy, like my head is a balloon. And it's a wonder—these points, speckled space. So many colors spread out before me, each a globe, like I can see every single planet at once.

And the voice. It's gentle.

It's you, isn't it?

So much wonder and I don't know what it means. But I think when I reach the bottom I will.

The voice is many voices. The voice is all voices, even voices that don't use sounds. What is this place? What am I knowing, what am I seeing?

I'm elsewhere, but still on the river. The Face cries for me, grieves over the loss of me.

There is loss, but that is all entropy.

I can see the edge, the chin approaching beneath … not my feet. I have no feet. I don't know how I can see the end when there's so little of me left. But the vastness is forming to swallow me. I don't need my body anymore.

This was right. This is a good death.

Can you still hear me? Are you even real? Are the voices those of the others who have gone, or others who have yet to be?

And then I'm there.

I'm here.

I'm over the edge.

Nothing but dust and star stuff. That's all I ever was. Part of a star that walked, and breathed, and felt for a while.

A thing that shouldn't exist.

Substitutions

by Kristine Kathryn Rusch

Silas sat at the blackjack table, a plastic glass of whiskey in his left hand, and a small pile of hundred-dollar chips in his right. His banjo rested against his boot, the embroidered strap wrapped around his calf. He had a pair of aces to the dealer's six, so he split them—a thousand dollars riding on each—and watched as she covered them with the expected tens.

He couldn't lose. He'd been trying to all night.

The casino was empty except for five gambling addicts hunkered over the blackjack table, one old woman playing slots with the rhythm of an assembly worker, and one young man in black leather who was getting drunk at the casino's sorry excuse for a bar. The employees showed no sign of holiday cheer: no happy holiday pins, no little Santa hats, only the stark black and white of their uniforms against the casino's fading glitter.

He had chosen the Paradise because it was one of the few remaining fifties-style casinos in Nevada, still thick with flocked wallpaper and cigarette smoke, craps tables worn by dice and elbows, and the roulette wheel creaking with age. It was also only a few hours from Reno, and in thirty hours, he would have to make the tortuous drive up there. Along the way, he would visit an old man who had a bad heart; a young girl who would cross the road at the wrong time and meet an on-coming semi; and a baby boy who was born with his lungs not yet fully formed. Silas also suspected a few surprises along the way; nothing was ever as it seemed any longer. Life was moving too fast, even for him.

But he had Christmas Eve and Christmas Day off, the two days he had chosen when he had been picked to work Nevada 150 years before. In those days, he would go home for Christmas, see his friends, spend time with his family. His parents welcomed him, even though they didn't see him for most of the year. He felt like a boy again, like someone cherished and loved, instead of the drifter he had become.

All of that stopped in 1878. December 26, 1878. He wasn't yet sophisticated enough to know that the day was a holiday in England. Boxing Day. Not quite appropriate, but close.

He had to take his father that day. The old man had looked pale and tired throughout the holiday, but no one thought it serious. When he took to his bed Christmas night, everyone had simply thought him tired from the festivities.

It was only after midnight, when Silas got his orders, that he knew what was coming next. He begged off—something he had never tried before (he wasn't even sure who he had been begging with)—but had received the feeling (that was all he ever got: a firm feeling, so strong he couldn't avoid it) that if he didn't do it, death would come another way—from Idaho or California or New Mexico. It would come another way, his father would be in agony for days, and the end, when it came, would be uglier than it had to be.

Silas had taken his banjo to the old man's room. His mother slept on her side, like she always had, her back to his father. His father's eyes had opened, and he knew. Somehow he knew.

They always did.

Silas couldn't remember what he said. Something—a bit of an apology, maybe, or just an explanation: *You always wanted to know what I did.* And then, the moment. First he touched his father's forehead, clammy with the illness that would claim him, and then Silas said, "You wanted to know why I carry the banjo," and strummed.

But the sound did not soothe his father like it had so many before him. As his spirit rose, his body struggled to hold it, and he looked at Silas with such a mix of fear and betrayal that Silas still saw it whenever he thought of his father.

The old man died, but not quickly and not easily, and Silas tried to resign, only to get sent to the place that passed for headquarters, a small shack that resembled an out-of-the-way railroad terminal. There, a man who looked no more than thirty but who had to be three hundred or more, told him the more that he complained, the longer his service would last.

Silas never complained again, and he had been on the job for 150 years. Almost 55,000 days spent in the service of Death, with only Christmas Eve and Christmas off, tainted holidays for a man in a tainted position.

He scooped up his winnings, piled them on his already-high stack of chips, and then placed his next bet. The dealer had just given him a queen and a jack when a boy sat down beside him.

"Boy" wasn't entirely accurate. He was old enough to get into the casino. But he had rain on his cheap jacket, and hair that hadn't been cut in a long time. IPod headphones stuck out of his breast pocket, and he had a cell phone against his hip the way that old sheriffs used to wear their guns.

His hands were callused and the nails had dirt beneath them. He looked tired, and a little frightened.

He watched as the dealer busted, then set chips in front of Silas and the four remaining players. Silas swept the chips into his stack, grabbed five of the hundred-dollar chips, and placed the bet.

The dealer swept her hand along the semi-circle, silently asking the players to place their bets.

"You Silas?" the boy asked. He hadn't put any money on the table or placed any chips before him.

Silas sighed. Only once before had someone interrupted his Christmas festivities—if festivities was what the last century plus could be called.

The dealer peered at the boy. "You gonna play?"

The boy looked at her, startled. He didn't seem to know what to say.

"I got it." Silas put twenty dollars in chips in front of the boy.

"I don't know ..."

"Just do what I tell you," Silas said.

The woman dealt, face-up. Silas got an ace. The boy, an eight. The woman dealt herself a ten. Then she went around again. Silas got his twenty-one—his weird holiday luck holding—but the boy got another eight.

"Split them," Silas said.

The boy looked at him, his fear almost palpable.

Silas sighed again, then grabbed another twenty in chips, and placed it next to the boy's first twenty.

"Jeez, mister, that's a lot of money," the boy whispered.

"Splitting," Silas said to the dealer.

She separated the cards and placed the bets behind them. Then she dealt the boy two cards—a ten and another eight.

The boy looked at Silas. Looked like the boy had peculiar luck as well.

"Split again," Silas said, more to the dealer than to the boy. He added the bet, let her separate the cards, and watched as she dealt the boy two more tens. Three eighteens. Not quite as good as Silas's twenties to twenty-ones, but just as statistically uncomfortable.

The dealer finished her round, then dealt herself a three, then a nine, busting again. She paid in order. When she reached the boy, she set sixty dollars in chips before him, each in its own twenty-dollar pile.

"Take it," Silas said.

"It's yours," the boy said, barely speaking above a whisper.

"I gave it to you."

"I don't gamble," the boy said.

"Well, for someone who doesn't gamble, you did pretty well. Take your winnings."

The boy looked at them as if they'd bite him. "I ..."

"Are you leaving them for the next round?" the dealer asked.

The boy's eyes widened. He was clearly horrified at the very thought. With shaking fingers, he collected the chips, then leaned into Silas. The boy smelled of sweat and wet wool.

"Can I talk to you?" he whispered.

Silas nodded, then cashed in his chips. He'd racked up ten-thousand dollars in three hours. He wasn't even having fun at it any more. He liked losing, felt that it was appropriate—part of the game, part of his life—but the losses had become fewer and farther between the more he played.

The more he lived. A hundred years ago, there were women and a few adopted children. But watching them grow old, helping three of them die, had taken the desire out of that too.

"Mr. Silas," the boy whispered.

"If you're not going to bet," the dealer said, "please move so some-one can have your seats."

People had gathered behind Silas, and he hadn't even noticed. He really didn't care tonight. Normally, he would have noticed anyone around him—noticed who they were, how and when they would die.

"Come on," he said, gathering the bills the dealer had given him. The boy's eyes went to the money like a hungry man's went to food. His one-hundred-and-twenty dollars remained on the table, and Silas had to remind him to pick it up.

The boy used a forefinger and a thumb to carry it, as if it would burn him.

"At least put it in your pocket," Silas snapped.

"But it's yours," the boy said.

"It's a damn gift. Appreciate it."

The boy blinked, then stuffed the money into the front of his un-washed jeans. Silas led him around banks and banks of slot machines, all pinging and ponging and making little musical come-ons, to the steakhouse in the back.

The steakhouse was the reason Silas came back year after year. The place opened at five, closed at three a.m., and served the best steaks in Vegas. They weren't arty or too small. One big slab of meat, expensive cut, charred on the outside and red as Christmas on the inside. Beside the steak they served french-fried onions, and sides that no self-re-specting Strip restaurant would prepare—creamed corn, au gratin po-tatoes, popovers—the kind of stuff that Silas always associated with the modern Las Vegas—modern, to him, meaning 1950s-1960s Vegas. Sin city. A place for grown-ups to gamble and smoke and drink and have affairs. The Vegas of Sinatra and the mob, not the Vegas of Steve Wynn and his ilk, who prettified everything and made it all seem up-scale and oh-so-right.

Silas still worked Vegas a lot more than any other Nevada city, which made sense, considering how many millions of people lived there now, but millions of people lived all over. Even sparsely popu-lated Nevada, one of the least populated states in the Union, had ten full-time Death employees. They tried to unionize a few years ago, but Silas, with the most seniority, refused to join. Then they tried to limit the routes—one would get Reno, another Sparks, another Elko and that region, and a few would split Vegas—but Silas wouldn't agree to that either.

He loved the travel part of the job. It was the only part he still liked, the ability to go from place to place to place, see the changes, understand how time affected everything.

Everything except him.

The maître d' sat them in the back, probably because of the boy. Even in this modern era, where people wore blue jeans to funerals, this steakhouse preferred its customers in a suit and tie.

The booth was made of wood and rose so high that Silas couldn't see anything but the boy and the table across from them. A single lamp reflected against the wall, revealing cloth napkins and real silver utensils.

The boy stared at them with the same kind of fear he had shown at the blackjack table. "I can't—."

The maître d' gave them leather-bound menus, said something about a special, and then handed Silas a wine list. Silas ordered a bottle of Burgundy. He didn't know a lot about wines, just that the more expensive ones tasted a lot better than the rest of them. So he ordered the most expensive burgundy on the menu.

The maître d' nodded crisply, almost militarily, and then left. The boy leaned forward.

"I can't stay. I'm your substitute."

Silas smiled. A waiter came by with a bread basket—hard rolls, still warm—and relish trays filled with sliced carrots, celery, and radishes, and candied beats, things people now would call old-fashioned.

Modern, to him. Just as modern as always.

The boy squirmed, his jeans squeaking on the leather booth.

"I know," Silas said. "You'll be fine."

"I got—"

"A big one, probably," Silas said. "It's Christmas Eve. Traffic, right? A shooting in a church? Too many suicides?"

"No," the boy said, distressed. "Not like that."

"When's it scheduled for?" Silas asked. He really wanted his dinner, and he didn't mind sharing it. The boy looked like he needed a good meal.

"Tonight," the boy said. "No specific time. See?"

He put a crumpled piece of paper between them, but Silas didn't pick it up.

"Means you have until midnight," Silas said. "It's only seven. You can eat."

"They said at orientation—

Silas had forgotten; they all got orientation now. The expectations of generations. He'd been thrown into the pool feet first, fumbling his way for six months before someone told him that he could actually ask questions.

"—the longer you wait, the more they suffer."

Silas glanced at the paper. "If it's big, it's a surprise. They won't suffer. They'll just finish when you get there. That's all."

The boy bit his lip. "How do you know?"

Because he'd had big. He'd had grisly. He'd had disgusting. He'd overseen more deaths than the boy could imagine.

The head waiter arrived, took Silas's order, and then turned to the boy.

"I don't got money," the boy said.

"You have one-hundred-and-twenty dollars," Silas said. "But I'm buying, so don't worry."

The boy opened the menu, saw the prices, and closed it again. He shook his head.

The waiter started to leave when Silas stopped him. "Give him what I'm having. Medium well."

Since the kid didn't look like he ate many steaks, he wouldn't like his rare. Rare was an acquired taste, just like burgundy wine and the cigar that Silas wished he could light up. Not everything in the modern era was an improvement.

"You don't have to keep paying for me," the kid said.

Silas waved the waiter away, then leaned back. The back of the booth, made of wood, was rigid against his spine. "After a while in this business," he said, "money is all you have."

The kid bit his lower lip. "Look at the paper. Make sure I'm not screwing up. Please."

But Silas didn't look.

"You're supposed to handle all of this on your own," Silas said gently.

"I know," the boy said. "I know. But this one, he's scary. And I don't think anything I do will make it right."

After he finished his steak and had his first sip of coffee, about the time he would have lit up his cigar, Silas picked up the paper. The boy had devoured the steak like he hadn't eaten in weeks. He ate all the bread and everything from his relish tray.

He was very, very new.

Silas wondered how someone that young had gotten into the death business, but he was determined not to ask. It would be some variation on his own story. Silas had begged for the life of his wife who should have died in the delivery of their second child. Begged, and begged, and begged, and somehow, in his befogged state, he actually saw the woman whom he then called the Angel of Death.

Now he knew better—none of them were angels, just working stiffs waiting for retirement—but then, she had seemed perfect and terrifying, all at the same time.

He'd asked for his wife, saying he didn't want to raise his daughters alone.

The angel had tilted her head. "Would you die for her?"

"Of course," Silas said.

"Leaving her to raise the children alone?" the angel asked.

His breath caught. "Is that my only choice?"

She shrugged, as if she didn't care. Later, when he reflected, he realized she didn't know.

"Yes," he said into her silence. "She would raise better people than I will. She's good. I'm … not."

He wasn't bad, he later realized, just lost, as so many were. His wife had been a god-fearing woman with strict ideas about morality. She had raised two marvelous girls, who became two strong women, mothers of large broods who all went on to do good works.

In that, he hadn't been wrong.

But his wife hadn't remarried either, and she had cried for him for the rest of her days.

They had lived in Texas. He had made his bargain, got assigned Nevada, and had to swear never to head east, not while his wife and children lived. His parents saw him, but they couldn't tell anyone. They thought he ran out on his wife and children, and oddly, they had supported him in it.

Remnants of his family still lived. Great-grandchildren generations removed. He still couldn't head east, and he no longer wanted to.

Silas touched the paper and it burned his fingers. A sign, a warn-ing, a remembrance that he wasn't supposed to work these two days.

Two days out of an entire year.

He slid the paper back to the boy. "I can't open it. I'm not allowed. You tell me."

So the boy did.

And Silas, in wonderment that they had sent a rookie into a sit-uation a veteran might not be able to handle, settled his tab, took the boy by the arm, and led him into the night.

Every city has pockets of evil. Vegas had fewer than most, despite the things the television lied about. So many people worked in law enforcement or security, so many others were bonded so that they could work in casinos or high-end jewelry stores or banks that Vegas's serious crime was lower than most comparable cities of its size.

Silas appreciated that. Most of the time, it meant that the deaths he attended in Vegas were natural or easy or just plain silly. He got a lot of silly deaths in that city. Some he even found time to laugh over.

But not this one.

As they drove from the very edge of town, past the rows and rows of similar houses, past the stink and desperation of complete poverty, he finally asked, "How long've you been doing this?"

"Six months," the boy said softly, as if that were forever.

Silas looked at him, looked at the young face reflecting the Christmas lights that filled the neighborhood, and shook his head. "All substitutes?"

The boy shrugged. "They didn't have any open routes."

"What about the guy you replaced?"

"He'd been subbing, waiting to retire. They say you could retire too, but you show no signs of it. Working too hard, even for a younger man."

He wasn't older. He was the same age he had been when his wife struggled with her labor—a breach birth that would be no problem in 2006, but had been deadly if not handled right in 1856. The midwife's hands hadn't been clean—not that anyone knew better in those days—and the infection had started even before the baby got turned.

He shuddered, that night alive in him. The night he'd made his bargain.

"I don't work hard," he said. "I work less than I did when I started."

The boy looked at him, surprised. "Why don't you retire?"

"And do what?" Silas asked. He hadn't planned to speak up. He normally shrugged off that question.

"I dunno," the boy said. "Relax. Live off your savings. Have a family again."

They could all have families again when they retired. Families and a good, rich life, albeit short. Silas would age when he retired. He would age and have no special powers. He would watch a new wife die in childbirth and not be able to see his former colleague sitting beside the bed. He would watch his children squirm after a car accident, blood on their faces, knowing that they would live poorly if they lived at all, and not be able to find out the future from the death dealer hovering near the scene.

Better to continue. Better to keep this half-life, this half-future, time without end.

"Families are overrated," Silas said. They look at you with betrayal and loss when you do what was right.

But the boy didn't know that yet. He didn't know a lot.

"You ever get scared?" the boy asked.

"Of what?" Silas asked. Then gave the standard answer. "They can't kill you. They can't harm you. You just move from place to place, doing your job. There's nothing to be scared of."

The boy grunted, sighed, and looked out the window.

Silas knew what he had asked, and hadn't answered it. Of course he got scared. All the time. And not of dying—even though he still wasn't sure what happened to the souls he freed. He wasn't scared of that, or of the people he occasionally faced down, the drug addicts with their knives, the gangsters with their guns, the wanna-be outlaws with blood all over their hands.

No, the boy had asked about the one thing to be afraid of, the one thing they couldn't change.

Was he scared of being alone? Of remaining alone, for the rest of his days? Was he scared of being unknown and nearly invisible, having no ties and no dreams?

It was too late to be scared of that.

He'd lived it. He lived it every single day.

The house was one of those square adobe things that filled Vegas. It was probably pink in the sunlight. In the half-light that passed for nighttime in this perpetually alive city, it looked gray and foreboding.

The bars on the windows—standard in this neighborhood—didn't help.

Places like this always astounded him. They seemed so normal, so incorruptible, just another building on another street, like all the other buildings on all the other streets. Sometimes he got to go into those buildings. Very few of them were different from what he expected. Oh, the art changed or the furniture. The smells differed—sometimes unwashed diapers, sometimes perfume, sometimes the heavy scent of meals eaten long ago—but the rest remained the same: the television in the main room, the kitchen with its square table (sometimes decorated with flowers, sometimes nothing but trash), the double bed in the second bedroom down the hall, the one with its own shower and toilet. The room across from the main bathroom was sometimes an office, sometimes a den, sometimes a child's bedroom. If it was a child's bedroom, there were pictures on the wall, studio portraits from the local mall, done up in cheap frames, showing the passing years. The pictures were never straight, and always dusty, except for the most recent, hung with pride in the only remaining empty space.

He had a hunch this house would have none of those things. If anything, it would have an overly neat interior. The television would be in the kitchen or the bedroom or both. The front room would have a sofa set designed for looks, not for comfort. And one of the rooms would be blocked off, maybe even marked private, and in it, he would find (if he looked) trophies of a kind that made even his cast-iron stomach turn.

These houses had no attic. Most didn't have a basement. So the scene would be the garage. The car would be parked outside of it, blocking the door, and the neighbors would assume that the garage was simply a workspace—not that far off, if the truth be told.

He'd been to places like this before. More times than he wanted to think about, especially in the smaller communities out in the desert, the communities that had no names, or once had a name and did no longer. The communities sometimes made up of cheap trailers and empty storefronts, with a whorehouse a few miles off the main highway, and a casino in the center of town, a casino so old it made

139

the one that the boy found him in look like it had been built just the week before.

He hated these jobs. He wasn't sure what made him come with the boy. A moment of compassion? The prospect of yet another long Christmas Eve with nothing to punctuate it except the bong-bong of nearby slots?

He couldn't go to church anymore. It didn't feel right, with as many lives as he had taken. He couldn't go to church or listen to the singing or look at the families and wonder which of them he'd be standing beside in thirty years.

Maybe he belonged here more than the boy did. Maybe he belonged here more than anyone else.

They parked a block away, not because anyone would see their car—if asked, hours later, the neighbors would deny seeing anything to do with Silas or the boy. Maybe they never saw, maybe their memories vanished. Silas had never been clear on that either.

As they got out, Silas asked, "What do you use?"

The boy reached into the breast pocket. For a moment, Silas thought he'd remove the iPod, and Silas wasn't sure how a device that used headphones would work. Then the boy removed a harmonica—expensive, the kind sold at high-end music stores.

"You play that before all this?" Silas asked.

The boy nodded. "They got me a better one, though."

Silas's banjo had been all his own. They'd let him take it, and nothing else. The banjo, the clothes he wore that night, his hat.

He had different clothes now. He never wore a hat. But his banjo was the same as it had always been—new and pure with a sound that he still loved.

It was in the trunk. He doubted it could get stolen, but he took precautions just in case.

He couldn't bring it on this job. This wasn't his job. He'd learned the hard way that the banjo didn't work except in assigned cases. When he'd wanted to help, to put someone out of their misery, to step in where another death dealer had failed, he couldn't. He could only watch, like normal people did, and hope that things got better, even though he knew it wouldn't.

The boy clutched the harmonica in his right hand. The dry desert air was cold. Silas could see his breath. The tourists down on the Strip, with their short skirts and short sleeves, probably felt betrayed by the normal winter chill. He wished he were there with them, instead of walking through this quiet neighborhood, filled with dark houses, dirt-ridden yards, and silence.

So much silence. You'd think there'd be at least one barking dog.

When they reached the house, the boy headed to the garage, just like Silas expected. A car was parked on the road—a 1980s sedan that looked like it had seen better days. In the driveway, a brand-new van with tinted windows, custom-made for bad deeds.

In spite of himself, Silas shuddered.

The boy stopped outside and steeled himself, then he looked at Silas with sadness in his eyes. Silas nodded. The boy extended a hand—Silas couldn't get in without the boy's momentary magic—and then they were inside, near the stench of old gasoline, urine, and fear.

The kids sat in a dimly lit corner, chained together like the slaves on ships in the nineteenth century. The windows were covered with dirty cardboard, the concrete floor was empty except for stains as old as time. It felt bad in here, a recognizable bad, one Silas had encountered before.

The boy was shaking. He wasn't out of place here, his old wool jacket and his dirty jeans making him a cousin to the kids on the floor. Silas had a momentary flash: they were homeless. Runaways, lost, children without borders, without someone looking for them.

"You've been here before," Silas whispered to the boy and the boy's eyes filled with tears.

Been here, negotiated here, moved on here—didn't quite die, but no longer quite lived—and for who? A group of kids like this one? A group that had somehow escaped, but hadn't reported what had happened?

Then he felt the chill grow worse. Of course they hadn't reported it. Who would believe them? A neat homeowner kidnaps a group of homeless kids for his own personal playthings, and the cops believe the kids? Kids who steal and sell drugs and themselves just for survival.

People like the one who owned this house were cautious. They were smart. They rarely got caught unless they went public with letters or phone calls or both.

They had to prepare for contingencies like losing a plaything now and then. They probably had all the answers planned.

A side door opened. It was attached to the house. The man who came in was everything Silas had expected—white, thin, balding, a bit too intense.

What surprised Silas was the look the man gave him. Measuring, calculating.

Pleased.

The man wasn't supposed to see Silas or the boy. Not until the last moment.

Not until the end.

Silas had heard that some of these creatures could see the death dealers. A few of Silas's colleagues speculated that these men continued to kill so that they could continue to see death in all its forms, collecting images the way they collected trophies.

After seeing the momentary victory in that man's eyes, Silas believed it.

The man picked up the kid at the end of the chain. Too weak to stand, the kid staggered a bit, then had to lean into the man.

"You have to beat me," the man said to Silas. "I slice her first, and you have to leave."

The boy was still shivering. The man hadn't noticed him. The man thought Silas was here for him, not the boy. Silas had no powers, except the ones that humans normally had—not on this night, and not in this way.

If he were here alone, he'd start playing, and praying he'd get the right one. If there was a right one. He couldn't tell. They all seemed to have the mark of death over them.

No wonder the boy needed him.

It was a fluid situation, one that could go in any direction.

"Start playing," Silas said under his breath.

But the man heard him, not the boy. The man pulled the kid's head back, exposing a smooth white throat with the heartbeat visible in a vein.

"Play!" Silas shouted, and ran forward, shoving the man aside, hoping that would be enough.

It saved the girl's neck, for a moment anyway. She fell, and landed on the other kid next to her. The kid moved away, as if proximity to her would cause the kid to die.

The boy started blowing on his harmonica. The notes were faint, barely notes, more like bleats of terror.

The man laughed. He saw the boy now. "So you're back to rob me again," he said.

The boy's playing grew wispier.

"Ignore him," Silas said to the boy.

"Who're you? His coach?" The man approached him. "I know your rules. I destroy you, I get to take your place."

The steak rolled in Silas's stomach. The man was half right. He destroyed Silas, and he would get a chance to take the job. He destroyed both of them, and he would get the job, by old magic, not new. Silas had forgotten this danger. No wonder these creatures liked to see death—what better for them than to be the facilitator for the hundreds of people who died in Nevada every day.

The man brandished his knife. "Lessee," he said. "What do I do? Destroy the instrument, deface the man. Right? And send him to hell."

Get him fired, Silas fought. It wasn't really hell, although it seemed like it. He became a ghost, existing forever, but not allowed to interact with anything. He was fired. He lost the right to die.

The man reached for the harmonica. Silas shoved again.

"Play!" Silas shouted.

And miraculously, the boy played. "Home on the Range," a silly song for these circumstances, but probably the first tune the boy had ever learned. He played it with spirit as he backed away from the fight.

But the kids weren't rebelling. They sat on the cold concrete floor, already half dead, probably tortured into submission. If they didn't rise up and kill this monster, no one would.

Silas looked at the boy. Tears streamed down his face, and he nodded toward the kids. Souls hovered above them, as if they couldn't decide whether or not to leave.

Damn the ones in charge: they'd sent the kid here as his final test. Could he take the kind of lives he had given his life for? Was he that strong?

The man reached for the harmonica again, and this time Silas grabbed his knife. It was heavier than Silas expected. He had never wielded a real instrument of death. His banjo eased people into forever. It didn't force them out of their lives a moment too early.

The boy kept playing and the man—the creature—laughed. One of the kids looked up, and Silas thought the kid was staring straight at the boy.

Only a moment, then. Only a moment to decide.

Silas shoved the knife into the man's belly. It went in deep, and the man let out an oof of pain. He stumbled, reached for the knife, and then glared at Silas.

Silas hadn't killed him, maybe hadn't even mortally wounded him. No soul appeared above him, and even these creatures had souls—dark and tainted as they were.

The boy's playing broke in places as if he were trying to catch his breath. The kid at the end of the chain, the girl, managed to get up. She looked at the knife, then at the man, then around the room. She couldn't see Silas or the boy.

Which was good.

The man was pulling on the knife. He would get it free in a moment. He would use it, would destroy these children, the ones no one cared about except the boy who was here to take their souls.

The girl kicked the kid beside her. "Stand up," she said.

The kid looked at her, bleary. Silas couldn't tell if these kids were male or female. He wasn't sure it mattered.

"Stand up," the girl said again.

In a rattle of chains, the kid did. The man didn't notice. He was working the knife, grunting as he tried to dislodge it. Silas stepped back, wondering if he had already interfered too much.

The music got louder, more intense, almost violent. The girl stood beside the man and stared at him for a moment.

He raised his head, saw her, and grinned.

Then she reached down with that chain, wrapped it around his neck and pulled. "Help me," she said to the others. "Help me."

The music became a live thing, wrapping them all, filling the smelly garage, and reaching deep, deep into the darkness. The soul did rise up—half a soul, broken and burned. It looked at Silas, then flared at the boy, who—bless him—didn't stop playing.

Then the soul floated toward the growing darkness in the corner, a blackness Silas had seen only a handful of times before, a blackness that felt as cold and dark as any empty desert night, and somehow much more permanent.

The music faded. The girl kept pulling, until another kid, farther down the line, convinced her to let go.

"We have to find the key," the other kid—a boy—said.

"On the wall," a third kid said. "Behind the electric box."

They shuffled as a group toward the box. They walked through Silas, and he felt them, alive and vibrant. For a moment, he worried that he had been fired, but he knew he had too many years for that. Too many years of perfect service—and he hadn't killed the man. He had just injured him, took away the threat to the boy.

That was allowed, just barely.

No wonder the boy had brought him. No wonder the boy had asked him if he was scared. Not of being alone or being lonely. But of certain jobs, of the things now asked of them as the no-longer-quite-human beings that they were.

Silas turned to the boy. His face was shiny with tears, but his eyes were clear. He stuffed the harmonica back into his breast pocket.

"You knew he'd beat you without me," Silas said.

The boy nodded.

"You knew this wasn't a substitution. You would have had this job, even without me."

"It's not cheating to bring in help," the boy said.

"But it's nearly impossible to find it," Silas said. "How did you find me?"

"It's Christmas Eve," the boy said. "Everyone knows where you'd be."

Everyone. His colleagues. People on the job. The only folks who even knew his name any more.

Silas sighed. The boy reached out with his stubby dirty hand. Silas took it, and then, suddenly, they were out of that fetid garage. They stood next to the van and watched as the cardboard came off one of the windows, as glass shattered outward.

Kids, homeless kids, injured and alone, poured out of that window like water.

"Thanks," the boy said. "I can't tell you how much it means."

But Silas knew. The boy didn't yet, but Silas did. When he retired—no longer if. When—this boy would see him again. This boy would take him, gently and with some kind of majestic harmonica music, to a beyond Silas could not imagine.

The boy waved at him, and joined the kids, heading into the dark Vegas night. Those kids couldn't see him, but they had to know he was there, like a guardian angel, saving them from horrors that would haunt their dreams for the rest of their lives.

Silas watched them go. Then he headed in the opposite direction, toward his car. What had those kids seen? The man—the creature— with his knife out, raving at nothing. Then stumbling backward, once, twice, the second time with a knife in his belly. They'd think that he tripped, that he stabbed himself. None of them had seen Silas or the boy.

They wouldn't for another sixty years.

If they were lucky.

The neighborhood remained dark, although a dog barked in the distance. His car was cold. Cold and empty.

He let himself in, started it, warmed his fingers against the still-hot air blowing out of the vents. Only a few minutes gone. A few minutes to take away a nasty, horrible lifetime. He wondered what was in the rest of these houses, and hoped he'd never have to find out.

The clock on the dash read 10:45. As he drove out of the neighborhood, he passed a small adobe church. Outside, candles burned in candleholders made of baked sand. Almost like the churches of his childhood.

Almost, but not quite.

He watched the people thread inside. They wore fancy clothing— dresses on the women, suits on the men, the children dressing like their parents, faces alive with anticipation.

They believed in something.

They had hope.

He wondered if hope was something a man could recapture, if it came with time, relaxation, and the slow inevitable march toward death.

He wondered, if he retired, whether he could spend his Christmas Eves inside, smelling the mix of incense and candle wax, the evergreen bows, and the light dusting of ladies' perfume.

He wondered …

Then shook his head.

And drove back to the casino, to spend the rest of his time off in peace.

Hive at the Dead Star

by Lucas Carroll-Garrett

T he last light in the universe clicked off. Squib turned away from
their pointless hobby at the Hive's only observation lens and back
to the gray segments of their designated pod. The plasticized alloy
could bend and endure for several hundred billion years without even
a fold or blemish. Without even changing at all. Really, it wasn't much
different from staring out into the empty universe, hoping to see
the glimmer of a star, something new amongst the black. But Squib
couldn't quite believe that all such change was truly dead.

"Sqμ-18. Report in."

The Director's voice de-abstractor formed the words in Squib's
central nervous system. Sending actual vibrations to other sapients
cost unnecessary energy, and with only the spinning ergosphere
of the Hive's black hole to act as a source, every shift in valence
had to be managed carefully. "Your scheduled global transmission
begins with the next rotation. Are you prepared to present your …
plan?" The data that the de-abstractor unpackaged into Squib's
mind did a good job of capturing the Director's pregnant pause,
loaded with disdain.

Not surprising. But they needed this venture. The Hive needed
it to outlast their gradually slowing source of rotational energy. And
Squib needed it to escape the crushing sameness of their existence.
Sapients couldn't even leave the walls of their pods. The perfect sphere

147

of gray looped around them a mere millimeter away, broken only by the pinkish strands of neural tendons.

"The details of the expansion vessel's launch procedure are all encoded for your transmitting pleasure," Squib sent back. A little twinge in the neural tendon showed the Director's confirmation. There was no data to unpack this time, but they were sure even that gesture was begrudged. No matter. If Squib could convince the Hive, soon they would both be rid of each other.

Enduring the itching sensation, they regrew the atrophied cells in the tendon that branched off to the Hive's central communications network. The nutrients required to fill out the myeline tube depended on the Director's approval, but now Squib was once again connected to the entire Hive. A faint buzz of neural activity and errant, fragmented thought greeted them.

They had no throat to clear and the sapient's redesigned circulation pump was too well-regulated by the Algorithm to race as hearts once did. All the same, Squib felt nervous as the Director announced the end of the annual rotation and the beginning of the presentation.

"Fellow sapients of the Hive," Squib announced to the network. "I, the eighteenth natural-born head of Wing Mu, subset SQ, request your attention and cooperation." Sparks of displeasure arced up and down the network, though they were quickly suppressed. The Mu Wing was often maligned for their archaic practice of creating new life rather than transferring an already existing consciousness pattern to a clone. The others believed it made sapients like Squib irrational. Squib preferred the word "interesting."

"The expansion vessel's prototype is finally complete. Launch procedures have been sent to the head of each wing by the Director, pending your deliberation and approval. Fellow sapients, this represents sixteen generations of Mu Wing's expansion efforts." Squib used a bit of their precious time allotment to pause for effect. An unfocused silence spread along the network. It was not the stable energy of rapt attention, but rather cold quiet of dispassion.

Squib pressed on. "We are at the cusp, fellow sapients. Launching this vessel to set up a turbine at the nearest detected ergosphere is not simply a fail safe for when—not if—our own black hole begins to run dry. But more than that, our expansion is also a moment of progress, of forward change, perhaps the last chance to retake our dead universe.

The sooner we launch, the sooner we can act upon such an opportunity." Squib kept the rest of their thinking off the network: the sooner it launches, the sooner I can get out of here, the sooner I can see something new, for science's sake .... In the end, they could not resist adding the last bitter dreg of the thought. "And, since it requires a pilot, the sooner you will be rid of me."

The network buzzed indistinctly as the Hive considered the message.

"How much energy do you propose for launch?" Asked $Dg\beta$-01, the perennial head of the Beta Wing. "Our research and development simulator can spare a bit, but ..."

"It will take 4.6 terajoules to fire the vessel."

Outrage flared through the network, though the need to conserve energy kept them all quiet. "$Sq\mu$-18," the Director said slowly, "that amount of energy equates to the entire Hive's surplus for the next hundred billion years. If we transfer that now, we will have none left over for repairs, let alone the other wings. Please perform your calculations again."

"I have been using my wing's surplus energy allotment for the past thirty-seven rotations to double-check the calculations. They are correct. That amount of energy ensures the vessel can reach the nearest source of Hawking Radiation and set up a transmission system, no matter the size of the dead star's ergosphere. It is a guaranteed success."

"Guaranteed!?" Beta Wing burst out, the de-abstractor blaring their shock into everyone's minds like a sudden and harsh light. "It only reaches the closest source! And we haven't even confirmed that singularity is still rotating. You're asking us to bet a hundred billion years on one expedition."

"$Dg\beta$-01." The Director's voice held the dark weight of warning. "Wait until confirmation before sending a global transmission. As for you, $Sq\mu$-18 ... you've made your argument clear but understand that this proposal is asking a great deal. Is there a reason it cannot be postponed while your wing accumulates energy? That would allow us a response in the event of a malfunction and allow the other wings to continue their own projects in the meantime."

There was a pause. Then Beta Wing added, "Like a probe, for example. We could confirm this singularity of yours first."

The Hive was right, of course. Rationality dictated the cautious approach with the highest long-term probability of success. But rationality dictated everything in the Hive, from the ever-prevailing dark to the stationary spin around the central turbine, the constant press of centripetal force squishing the sapients' shapeless bodies down even tighter into their pods. It dictated that, while the Hive deliberated and double-checked, Squib would whittle away life unmoving and unchanging. Squib had grown tired of rationality.

"I would like to take this opportunity to remind my fellow sapients," they sent out, trying to keep their frustration off the network, "that my Wing's plan to set up a new Hive is not a vanity project but a vital step for our future. Your future. We dedicate ourselves to expansion as per the original plans for the Hive which, I remind all of you, was not intended as a permanent hole for us to hide in but a stopgap measure until we can find a way to circumvent entropy. The Hive does not run on infinite energy. You all can clone yourselves for trillions of years, but eventually the dead star will slow down. Extract all the rotational energy and you all will die, just as my ancestors did."

"We are aware," came the transmission from the Director. "The allotted time for debate has ended, Sqμ-18. Please refrain from any more hysterics."

Squib sat fuming while the Hive ignored them. Votes for the new probe plan piled in and Alpha Wing announced the expected outcome: "We have reached a decision regarding the timeline of Mu Wing's proposed expansion effort. We agree that while it may be a worthwhile venture, the proposed energy consumption is not sustainable. We sanction Beta Wing's proposal for a probe and will amend energy flow to allow Mu Wing increased storage rate. The Algorithm projects 768 billion years of accretion sufficient to allow other wings to continue their projects. Thank you."

Buα-01, the spokesapient of the administrators, prattled on about the details. Squib stayed silent. Seven-hundred and sixty-eight billion years. Almost a quarter of the Hive's projected time remaining, and twice over the time Squib's cellular components had before irreparable degradation. They would die in this black pocket before anything could change. Perhaps this would spare them, keep them from finding out that this was all pointless, that the new hive would fail and nothing would ever change again.

Anger blazed up and down the synapses wired throughout Squib's body, exciting the cytoplasm until it grew uncomfortably hot. They were ignoring the problem. No, they had forgotten. An eternity of lifeless monotony had dulled the fear of death.

But not in Squib. Mu Wing remembered.

They focused on that cold, creeping dread, the impossibility of a thinking being coming to terms with the cessation of thinking. Gathering it up and packaging it into data, Squib waited for the Director to clear their connection for Mu Wing's closing report. Then they transmitted the dread to the entire Hive.

Dead silence froze over the network. It was not the same static-like silence as the sapients' existence between transmissions, but a new, chilling variety. Or, at least, a variety that hadn't been felt in a very long time.

Satisfied for a brief moment, Squib let the Hive savor the primeval fear they had all fought so hard to forget. The fear that only Mu Wing had kept alive with their "irrational" life cycles. He could feel the pressure building as they all processed an emotion they had presumed extinct, fighting with themselves not to waste energy over it. But they didn't have the experience necessary for control. Soon the network exploded with voices.

"What *is* this data?"

"No, the Beta Wing *will* find a solution to the energy crisis ..."

"How dare you threaten the Hive!"

"Don't forget it was your wing that vetoed the digitization process. We could all be safe in our databanks to live out eternity like the other species. If not for you!"

"Make it stop, just make it stop—"

More and more voices, an echo chamber of terror. The network flickered under the unaccustomed weight of emotionality, which only added fear to the fire. Then the Director had no choice. They torched the network. The flashing, splitting pain shot through everyone, unpackaged directly into their mind by the Algorithm, pain their bodies had not been able to experience for trillions of years. It shut everyone up. Everyone except for Squib.

They cried out over the sustained pulse, taking the only opportunity they had. "This is no threat but a reminder! I only want to save us, preserve us all at another dead star. Please ..."

The Director dialed up the intensity and the pain became too great for Squib to speak. Finally the network fell silent. "I regret the necessary use of force." Everyone received the Director's broadcast in a haze. "But we must remain civil. Remember that any energy used fighting amongst ourselves is energy wasted. Energy we cannot afford. We will now close down the network to assess damage."

Black silence returned to Squib, once again with nothing to focus on but the walls of the pod, threatening to close in around them. When they shook off the pain, Squib discovered that the vast majority of their neural tendons had been severed.

"That was foolish, Squ-18." The Director contacted them through the emergency tendon, one of the few left intact. "I cannot express how disappointing such a stunt is, considering you are the head of a wing."

"It was necessary to reverse the Hive's decision. You're all waiting too long—"

"Enough. You have lost the right to engage in debate. Effective immediately, sapient Squ-18 is to be cut off from all non-emergency transmissions except those pertaining to their duties in managing Mu Wing and their surplus energy allotment is forfeit." There was no sadness in the unpackaging, and Squib wondered if the Hive was glad they were finally rid of the dissenting voice. "Now I must return to assessing the damage you caused. I trust you know I will use the torch again if you break quarantine."

And then it was deep into the empty quiet. Life, or what was left of it, settled into a dull circle. Receive energy and nutrient rations from Phi Wing. Allocate accordingly. Oversee progress on Mu Wing's project, the expansion vessel. Follow the pink threads snaking around the pod until they webbed back to Squib's own outer membrane. Receive resources again and watch the circle go around and around, unbroken even by a petty complaint from the other wings.

The madness crept in.

The only change Squib had to occupy themselves was watching their projected lifespan tick down second by second, millennium by millennium. Another blip in the mitochondrial DNA. Seventy more before an irreparable mutation. The Algorithm whirred with concern and added another artificial telomere cap. Forty-six thousand left. Forty-five thousand nine hundred ninety-nine. Ninety-eight.

Squib started to grow fidgety, made mistakes in simple calculations. They needed something else, something more, something new. There was nothing new.

But Squib did have a new idea, or at least one that the Director hadn't thought of. Control of their nutrients usually just meant following the Algorithm's suggestions to maintain lifespan, but each sapient could technically direct the materials where they wished.

Picking a private neural tendon to experiment with, their personal connection to the Hive's database, Squib started reallocating carbon to regrow the connection and filled it with ions that were rather desperately needed in their central nervous system. Exhaustion quickly slipped into Squib's being, and the pod began to sway around them unsteadily, tendons and gray panels bleeding together.

Cold panic momentarily seized Squib's attention when the Algorithm detected the change, but all it did was allocate them more emergency nutrients. As the bliss of simple sugars rushed through Squib's system, excitement rode the flood of energy. A few more cycles and the tendon sparked to life, granting access to a sunrise of information. No longer constrained to Mu Wing's dry diagrams and launch simulations, Squib tore through the files to find something that would take the edge off their ravenous boredom. The records were far from new, but they could at least relive past excitement. Especially if they found the right ones. The ones that recorded change.

The Algorithm took its time, but Squib found the right information. An excited pulse through the neural tendon stopped the endless sifting of data when it reached the point where history began.

Squib opened up the files pertaining to Ea-$0^{19}1$, the first recorded planet. There were trillions of them. Squib had the algorithm sort out the thousand or so that would give them the best balance between narrative and cursory understanding before downloading the information to their cortex.

The first section was brief despite the four billion years it covered. A spinning disk of gas, a smattering of planets, a collision to form a moon. So far, so typical. Then Squib found how the planet had produced so much data. Life formed, not just the mindless self-replicating carbon engines found on so many other planets, but complex life. Matter that could grow, breathe, think. Matter that could make things change.

Squib slowed down one file, experiencing the moment along with the dirty, filament-covered creature as it squatted below the stars. Suddenly their sheer vast beauty sparked something in the organism's simple mind, latent until that moment. The creature's messy, inefficient carbon computing system captured something. No, it captured everything. The endless number of stars that once filled the sky were condensed and contained, impossibly, into a single mind, a single idea. After that, there was no turning back.

Squib sped the drop back into a stream and immersed themselves in it. Even if the journey had ended, they could still relive its twists and turns.

The creatures changed subtly, but the world shook under their new understanding. A million years swept by as they moved, pressed, and stretched out into the world, seeping into every crack and fold in the planet's crust. One day, the satisfaction of being full and safe was not enough. They pushed harder, farther. Squib watched in amazement and terror as the creatures, these proto-sapients, took hunks of stone and lengths of carbohydrate and reshaped their planet. They kept crossing the vast puddles of dihydrogen-oxide that covered their world, despite the roughly three percent success rate of the voyages. They took other organisms and shaped them to their will or wiped them out as they saw fit. Even other proto-sapients, just as clever as they were. Gone, swept under the pull of the current, all in the name of reaching more.

That chilled Squib the most, yet excited them just a bit at the same time. These creatures would never stop. It wasn't that they didn't want to stagnate or that they were merely driven to explore. They were incapable of stopping. A twist of DNA always left just enough members of the species to push and probe outward no matter the cost. Then, one day, they pushed through all the way. An aluminum tube exploded off their planet, taking these creatures to the stars, finally touching the infinity they had lived under for so long.

That was where Squib stopped. Not because they knew the rest of the story—the whole journey was common knowledge—but because they knew how it ended. They were living the ending. It was cold and dark.

A strange pain stole over the sapient, not harsh like the torch but aching and hollow. The algorithm reported no biological problems, only a temporary neurotransmitter imbalance. Another problem it wasn't prepared for. No matter. Squib knew what had to be done. The probe was not enough. The knowledge of eventual success was not enough. Squib took the pain and nursed it, fed on it, grew accustomed to it. And that gave the creature an idea. A new idea.

Starving themselves, Squib regrew tendons, slowly and carefully. One for a public channel, not to speak and give away their scheme, but just to listen for news on the probe's launch. The timing had to be right. The second aimed for a more direct connection to the expansion vessel built under Squib's pod, hiding all the excess energy their wing could muster in the engine. Another tendon grew its way into the mainframe of the Hive's energy network, using Squib's authority as head of a wing to convince the Algorithm nothing was out of the ordinary enough to notify the Director. If they caught on, repercussions would be swift and brutal. But that was the purpose of the last energy expenditure.

As often as they could endure, Squib replayed the stored sensation of pain that the Director had used to torch the network. It was terrifying, almost maddening at first. But it was necessary. The more accustomed their mind became to the sensation, the less power the Director would have over them. So Squib forced the pain into their mind until the Algorithm shut it off for fear of damage. But over time, that length of sustainable agony grew and grew.

Fifty-seven billion years passed until the next blackout.

The announcement was brief but cordial, as always. "Hello, fellow sapients. This is the Director with the final reminder that Beta Wing's Hawking probe will be launched at the end of the year. It will require a blackout to ensure stability of the network, so make preparations. Thank you for your understanding."

Squib had made preparations. At this point, they could barely contain their preparedness. Just before the network winked out, Squib tucked the launch data and construction subroutines into the vessel. The matter needed to create the ergospheric turbine and Hawking Radiation absorption array slid into the vessel's sleek flanks without a sound. Squib's pod would attach to the other side, providing the slight imbalance that would start the vessel spinning when edged into the pull of the black hole. Perfectly calculated. Mu Wing had even developed a line of code that would trick the Algorithm into overloading the distribution system. Only the energy remained.

Squib took a moment to steady their nerves. Growing the final neural tendon to connect the Beta Wing's probe and the expansion vessel required delicacy. And after that, everything had to happen at once.

Reshuffling nutrients, Squib broke down sections of their vital organs and fed them into the neural tendon's matrix. It made what was left of the sapient's body queasy, though that might have been the excitement bubbling against their membranes. It was happening. Finally, something was happening. A jolt shot through the tendon. Connection.

The Director noticed immediately but wasted time on an emergency transmission. Squib did not respond to their query to identify the problem. The Director would figure that out quickly enough on their own. Instead, Squib sent routines to the Algorithm's branches in energy storage and Beta Wing. The probe was currently launching, taking a massive amount of energy from the Hive's turbine to propel it out into the empty space. Using the authority of the mainframe, Squib redirected the energy. The Algorithm would not be launching the probe. It would be launching the expansion vessel.

Using a bit of the energy, Squib lowered their pod into place within the vessel. The craft had been built directly below their place in the Hive, which was adjacent to one of the ports for launching matter into the vacuum. This had all been planned generations before Squib, and the docking process was automated. Vibrations jiggled through Squib's cytoplasm as it began. They lacked the nerve endings to feel it precisely, but the jostling of their already bruised internal organs was vaguely unpleasant. Squib didn't care. The feeling was new.

The final transmission had a simple task as well, albeit a more dangerous one. The energy storage center was only prepared to give up enough energy for the small probe, not the entire prototype Squib had in mind. So they sent the line of code, timing it just as the energy transfer was supposed to stop. Power started flowing in, more and more until the vessel had all of the surplus energy available. That was when the Director took action.

The torch seared into Squib's being. They pushed through it, for the moment. They now had the probe's energy, the extra energy from the Hive, and everything Mu Wing had stored. Endure until launch and they would be free. Squib ran a few final calculations. The Director dialed up the torch's intensity to paralytic levels.

Insufficient.

Mind clouded by agony, Squib had a moment of elation, thinking that the Algorithm calculated the pain would not be enough. They had become immune to the Director's power.

But the message came from the vessel, not from their biological diagnostics. The vessel did not launch. There was not enough energy. That was the signal the Algorithm was trying to push through the pounding haze. The deficiency was not in the Director's power but in the engine's.

Squib no longer had the ability to feel cold, but that didn't stop the chill from passing through them. Somewhere, a calculation had been off. Maybe a single number. But that was enough. The ship wasn't launching.

The torch grew even hotter, pressing Squib into the borders of their consciousness. There, they found one last decision. The neural tendon in the mainframe was still active. They could tap into the Hive's emergency power, steal just enough, and blast away. If something went wrong, anything at all, the ship wouldn't launch, or the Hive would collapse, or the torch would burn Squib's nervous system to dust. But it was that or going back to the crushing sameness of the Hive. Squib prepared the transfer.

Then a strange thing happened. The pressure of the torch cut off. A voice de-abstracted into Squib's mind, full of emotion and intonation, like a symphony after so long without any contact.

"Squ-18. I am asking you, personally, to stop this. Please, as a fellow member of the Hive." It was the Director's voice, but it sounded strange. Gone was the cold assumption of obedience. Now the voice trembled with so many little emotions, always carefully filtered out of transmission. They were begging, Squib realized.

"No. I'm leaving. I'm making something new."

"What you are making is a mistake! Have you run an analysis of this betrayal of yours? Do you even know what it could cost the Hive? Squ-18, you are risking our very survival for this one expedition."

"An analysis?" Squib almost sent a laugh down the tendon, but paused a moment to gather their thoughts after the torch had scattered them. "No, I haven't had the luxury of analysis. Every bit of energy I had went into this escape. I'm not stopping on account of the sapients that rejected me."

The tendon prickled with the Director's suppressed fury. "We did not mean to reject you. We only meant to move toward the best probability of success." The prickling died down, leaving a hollow, sucking sensation. Regret? Sadness? "You are not well, Sqμ-18. Your vitals are unstable. Please return the energy before the Hive is endangered. This scheme of yours has such a low success rate that it's not worth risking your life on it."

Everything was ready by this point, only awaiting Squib's command. But they were curious in spite of themselves. "My life is my decision, Director. But I do want to minimize risk to the Hive. What are the projections from your analysis? The chance that nothing goes wrong?"

The answer came through with a somber twinge.

"Three percent."

Something snapped in Squib. It made no noise, caused no damage, but it broke all the same. The odds were terrible, impossible. And that excited them. The Director saw this and sent a desperate new flood of pain into their system. Gripping to the plan for dear life, Squib sent their last coherent thought to the network: *launch*. Then the torch silenced their mind.

It was several millennia before Squib recovered enough to think. By then, their vessel was far away from the Hive. The sapients would still be close enough to observe Squib's progress, if they had kept enough energy. But Squib's theft crippled the entire Hive, plunging the structure into still darkness for billions of years. The network couldn't fire, the observation lens couldn't send out photons, and degraded matter in the turbine couldn't be reorganized. All they could do was wait.

Squib could not see the Hive shutting down behind them. Their vessel lacked the right kind of sensors. It didn't have access to the network's databases or the other sapients, only programed to reestablish contact when the turbine was established. There wasn't even energy to review the setup procedures. As Squib sailed through the void, only excitement sustained them. The millennia drifted by, unchanging, but the hope of discovery never relaxed its grip.

With Our Songs of Scars and Starlight

by J.R. Troughton

S tories are told about my daughter and the day she vanished into the ocean. On my trips to the mainland I hear them; tales of the violent storm she called down on our island and the lightning that came, fierce enough to split the ocean in two and burn the sky black for a month and a day. These stories don't mention the details of her disappearance; not the curses she screamed until her throat ran red, nor the torrents of starlight that burst from her pores as she became one with the white foam of the sea.

If she is still out there, in whole or in part, I hope I can find her and tell her it is okay. That it was never her fault and that I should have been kinder, and wiser, and, perhaps, less ambitious. If she is still alive, I want to apologize. It should never have been her.

I simply chose the wrong daughter.

I lean over the railing of the lighthouse, shielding my eyes from the ferocious blue of the sky, and watch the summer gulls dance above the surf as the tide rolls in. The ice in my glass rattles as I shakily raise it to my lips and sip the whiskey; I roll it around my mouth and savor the familiar smoky taste, then the hints of vanilla and toffee that follow. Jagged rocks reach out of the water below like wild claws, desperately searching for purchase. Each evening I return here, hitch my skirt up above my knees, and weakly climb the spiraling steps, my bones brittle, legs ironcast. Then I wait.

Each evening, my heart brims with hope once more.

Not a day goes by that I don't miss my daughters, both. It has been too many years to bear. Perhaps even a decade already? The years appear like an amateurish watercolor; out of focus and unclear. Individual memories blend together, almost beyond recognition.

Icante, then

In the distance, cutting through the crystal water, is a pearl-white schooner. White as the swans of the lake at the center of our island. Yet it's even more graceful, carving a wide arc around the island at impressive speed. I narrow my eyes; there are several figures on the boat. They come no closer than a hundred meters from the shore before the schooner turns and heads back in the direction of the mainland. I watch until it vanishes into the horizon, then turn my attention back to the gulls.

Boats come most days, though none ever make landfall. Icante is a dead island now; a curio for those brave enough to still set sail in these waters, or rich enough to think themselves beyond danger. Nobody else is left but me.

Not that anyone knows that for sure.

Nobody but my children.

I taught the twins to sing to the wind when they were six and to the rain when they were ten. Only simple songs, melodies their young minds could remember and repeat.

It was a few days after their tenth birthday, and a burning hot summer's eve, when we stood at the top of our lighthouse—Isla, Caitlin and I—and sang to the sky together. High above the rolling green hills of the island, the clouds bulked, grew bulbous and dark, then burst over the town and drenched the townsfolk. We cried with laughter and the children rolled around my feet like drunks, cackling and whooping; I had always enjoyed a joke, and they did too.

They'd taken on all my best qualities, and a handful of my worst. What more could a mother dream of than for her daughters to be better than she was?

The governor of the time was a man so thin it was as if he were built of twigs, with a round head like an egg and a most unfortunate haircut—the style of the time, I gathered, though I thought it left him looking like a battered crow (and remarked as such to raucous guffawing from the girls). He sent soldiers to speak to me, and they spoke most unkindly, demanding I show him the appropriate respect and turn the weather at their beck and call. So each day I carved the weather into unkind shapes with my tongue and spat it at them angrily. I gave them a month of floods and blistering winds; apologies came after, transported by boat with the sheepish governor at its helm.

They didn't trouble us for several years after that.

We lived well, practicing our songs, our magic, and talking of dreams and ambitions. I had always felt a hunger to change the world, to make it a better place. During my youth I had seen such poverty and sickness and I had myself barely escaped their smothering grasp. While rich folk ate greedily, my family clawed about the corners of the city for a loaf of bread. This did not leave me bitter, nor hopeless, as it did to so many who grew up in such circumstance, but with an understanding of the world; there simply wasn't enough to go around.

The girls were fourteen when the latest governor (they changed as often as the wind) sent a new envoy to speak with me.

He offered gifts of silk, gold, and the finest deer meat on the island, as well as words of deference and respect. I took these with a smile and a promise that I could grant their request of fine weather for the following years. My powers were waning by now, but I still held the strength for such simple magic.

The next few years were blissful. We ate well, gorging ourselves on the finest veal and turtle soup. We dressed finely, adorning ourselves in the red and blue silks sent to us by the governor; expensive, ornate garments from both sides of the ocean. The girls' singing voices grew more intricate and adept, and they had a hunger for learning that matched the hunger of any shark. Caitlin bubbled with enthusiasm for each new song, or verse, or true name-of-a-thing, smiling widely at every new lesson. Isla kept pace, but was never so engaged as her sister. Never as interested.

Not during my lessons, anyway, though I knew she practiced when I was not watching. I could see the hesitancy in her heart and doubt in her mind. She needed a spark to ignite the strength I knew she held inside.

And if there was one thing I knew, it was how to start fires.

Icante, now

I have spent too long back on Icante and now must move on again and begin my search. I have been south and east and west. North is next, as unlikely as it may be. Unlikely and hard-going. I study the cold gray sky; the delicate clouds; the blank ocean slate. It is with a sigh that I place my empty glass down. Bottle loosely in hand, I head inside.

I descend the stairs slowly.

Carefully, I step across those wild rocks. Amorphous sea-creatures built of blubber and slime moil around, sucking limpets off of rock faces. I take a final slug from my bottle and clear my throat, close my eyes, think of soothing words. I bend the air around my tongue and shape it in artisanal ways before sending it out alongside my song. One of the creatures shudders, then stalls, before waiting, expectantly. I depart. It follows across the shingle, undulating like a vast slug, as I stagger around the causeway to my rowing boat, *Birdcall*, which sits sullenly on the shingle, pale blue paint chipped and flaking. With a coarse rope I bind the thing—I shall call her Amb—with loops around two appendages and tie her tightly to the front of *Birdcall*.

I sing a few bright notes—dancing, summer notes—and Amb drags us out into the ocean. She carries me over the gentle roll of the tides, and we head north.

Icante, then

The twins were born on a warm evening on Blessday. I have forgotten many things over the years, but remember the exhaustion and elation well. Scars, both physical and mental, that bring me nothing but joy. My fifth spouse—my second husband—beamed at me and held my hand as I lay. We watched them for hours, marveling at each breath, wriggle and yawn; their small miracles bewitched us both. We were never happier than in those fleeting moments.

Sadly, it didn't take long for us to return to quarreling. It had been his lighthouse alone before he met me and he struggled to change with the blossoming of our pairing into a family. His complaints about slovenliness were bitter and spiteful, not to mention unfair. He had lived alone for too long and the girls and I were too much for

162

him, close-minded and insular as he was. Set in his ways, too old of mind. Cleaning dishes in the morning is no different from the night before, once all is said and done. To say otherwise is a lie and I never had time for liars.

He didn't leave until the girls were nearly eight, which was an uncharacteristic feat of endurance for him. The last time I saw him he was leaning over the balcony of the lighthouse, sipping bourbon straight from the bottle, gazing out over the ocean. I heard he was seen near the docks on the day he vanished, but nobody could tell me what ship he had boarded, or if he had embarked at all. For all we knew, he had walked into the ocean with his pockets full of rocks.

It would have been just his style to take my curses so damn literally.

I raised the girls on my own and did a fine job of it too. He may have taught them to tie their shoes and ride their bikes down the hill toward the town, but I taught them to sing to the world and shape it with their words. How we could sing to the elements and to the wild things of the world, but that we must never try to sing to those greater powers. Not to time, the sun and stars, nor to death itself. Not until they were ready. Not until I was certain we had prepared enough and we would sing together and change the world.

And change the world we would. Once the girls had learned enough, once they had turned their voices into fine crafting tools, we would carve out a new world together, our strength combined. A world without darkness or fear or death. Together, once fully prepared, we would sing to the moon and the sun and take their magic. Use it to grant ourselves everlasting life and to end war, famine, and cruelty.

What better gift could they have had than this? What better purpose?

They adored my lessons. Caitlin, so full of joy and energy, visibly shook with anticipation of learning new names and tricks, thirstily drinking in new skills. Isla never showed her emotions. She always watched quietly and rarely wanted to practice with Caitlin and me. Caitlin was all aspiration and vigor for songcraft, yet Isla seemed so lackluster in comparison, so disappointing. I never let my feelings on the matter show, of course.

I would never have done that to her.

Northbound, now

I pull my scarf tighter and wrap my arms around my body. The sky is a ferocious blue. Bergs jut out of the water like teeth, and as I shiver I wonder if the North is going to devour me whole. Vast plates of ice surround me as I sail ever onward, pulled along by the diligent Amb. Foreign birds watch curiously, hop from foot to foot and caw to me. *Birdsong* has done well.

The journey has been long and cold, but I am confident. I sang words of inspiration to a school of dolphins and they told me of a girl who rode in a great wooden fish that cut through the waves and was chased by monstrous winds.

I rub my hands together and slap them against my thighs. My heart sings for the first time in years. It won't be long now until I can apologize and make it all fine once again. I don't blame her anymore. I realize now that I made mistakes too.

My dear Isla is here. I can feel it in the marrow of my bones.

Icante, then

"Mama! Mama!" Caitlin's voice bounced down the stairs of the lighthouse. "Come and see what I've made!"

As I reached the top of the lighthouse and stepped out onto the balcony, she was dancing from foot to foot and pointing to the sky. Isla stood in the shade of the lighthouse spire, watching. The clouds had been shaped into a fleet of galleons. My chest swelled with pride and I rested my hand on her back. "Beautiful, Caitlin."

"Watch," she laughed. She cleared her throat and began to sing. Familiar syllables, sung in a pitch I could never reach, cast out into the sky.

The galleons moved. Slowly at first, they slipped across the sky-sea and glided effortlessly toward the town, their white sails drifting apart in the wind. Caitlin raised her voice and they grew faster. Her voice took on sharp edges, full of hard geometry where it had been soft moments earlier, and the clouds quickly darkened. From their side puffed several dark rings of cloud, and rainfall burst over the houses.

"So boom, sung the cannons!" laughed Caitlin. "And the people did turn wet." She chortled and hopped from foot to foot, beaming at me. Her face was radiant. It was at times like this I saw just how similar to me she was. She looked just like I did as a girl, with long dark hair and wide features; not beautiful, but full of *life*. She also shared my sense of humor and wild imagination.

The ships continued to drop their payload, having moved across the town from the villagers' houses to the open-air market. Such clever magic. So creative. "Beautifully worked, my darling." I gripped her by the shoulders. "Such wonders. I adore the style of your ships. You'll have to teach me the song one day."

"I will, Mother," she grinned. Her eyes flickered to her sister. Isla's lips twitched, just slightly, but she remained silent, a glazed look on her face. She went indoors and disappeared down the stairs.

"Isla thought it was stupid." Caitlin's face crumpled like crushed origami. "Didn't she?"

"No, my dear. I'm sure that's not true. She is probably just feeling sad today." Or envious. Isla had never been an artist, not like Caitlin or me. She could sing to the world and form it to her will, but not with the craft that Caitlin showed. Long ago I had seen resentfulness building in her, but what could I do? Hold back Caitlin? I had made my choice. Caitlin wanted to learn and to grow her songcraft. I could sense the dormant power in her and together we would change the world for the better. If Isla couldn't give me her focus, that must not stop Caitlin from achieving all she was capable of. Isla could still sing in support of us, despite her weakness.

"Are you sure?" Caitlin nuzzled against my shoulder. The cloud-ships had almost dissipated now, though still cast heavy rain upon the town. The people would be most upset. Not that I care any longer.

The gifts from the town had dried up. The former governor's generosity had been an oddity; the new governess—a sharp-eyed woman with a nose like a fish hook and the instincts of a magpie—had returned to the ways of the old island rulers. And with that, we had also returned to our old ways, toying with the townsfolk for our own pleasure. I told the girls that this was just, hence Caitlin's rainfall song. They should have showed more respect.

"Do not worry, Caitlin. Isla just finds it difficult to see magic she cannot yet do herself. That's why she likes to practice on her own so much."

"Like when she goes down to the bay?"

"Exactly." In the distance, I could see Isla walking down the winding path toward the bay. She often went there to sing on her own and to practice magic without my discerning eye pulling her up on errors, or pushing her onward to greater heights. Seeing Caitlin's eyes wet, I pulled her tight to me and hugged her. Yet as I relished her closeness, my nose wrinkled; she smelled of sweat and smoke both.

I frowned and pulled her in front of me, gripping her shoulders firmly. "Why do you smell of smoke?" I had thrown my pipe into the ocean once the girls grew old enough to start imitating me. Their father had insisted. I hadn't started again, even after he left.

Caitlin's face turned pale. "We weren't smoking!"

I raised an eyebrow and shifted my gaze from steely to savage. She shuddered.

"It was Isla's idea ..." she mumbled, her eyes dropping to the floor. "She said we could bottle the smoke and then shape it into birds ..."

"Of course she did."

I glowered for a moment longer, then stormed inside and after foolish, selfish Isla.

The North, now

Isla is here. Whatever remains of her. I am so happy to have the chance to apologize for everything that I did, and for everything that I did not. How many mothers can say the same after making the same mistakes that I had? I make landfall and drag *Birdsong* onto the ice. There is no fear of someone stealing her here, so I do not try to hide my trusted boat. It is with warmth in my heart that I pat thanks across her bow.

I can tell Isla is within reach by the closeness and shapes of the aurora. Vast birds and horses and dolphins of vibrant blues and greens flicker across the black curtain of the night, dancing across the polar skies like carnival beasts. Just like the girls used to make out of the clouds, back on Icante. Isla had never been as powerful as Caitlin, but what she could now shape with her songs was resolutely beautiful. Her songcraft had blossomed in her isolation. Perhaps I should have believed in her more.

Of course I should have. That much is obvious now. But to see how strong she has become lifts my heart. Perhaps all is not lost. Perhaps we can still accomplish our destiny.

With a few quiet words, I shape the ice around me. I form a char-iot, basic and lacking in the pomp I would once have insisted upon in my youth. It is enough to travel and that is all that matters now. No intricacy nor artistry is needed.

I just need to find Isla and say sorry. And ask her to come home.

Amb drags me forward, faster than one would imagine possible. Her many appendages clutch at the permafrost and drag us across the bleak and lonely icescape, toward the dancing circus of light that marks the whereabouts of Isla.

Icante, then

It was summer. The sun had already melted away after a burning hot day where I did little but read and drink. The stars were brighter than ever and decorated the sky like jewels.

The world was content.

I sat on the balcony of the lighthouse and rattled the ice in my glass. The girls would be back from the town soon; they had gone drinking together to celebrate their nineteenth birthday. Privately I had told Isla to make sure her sister did not drink too much. She needed a clear head for practice.

Caitlin's training over the past years had gone well. Her voice reached notes mine never could and she always wanted to please me, so she worked hard and listened to my commands with infinite diligence. Watching her develop had been joyous. Isla had grown too, of course, though never quite showed the strength of her sister. She didn't have the courage, I suppose; it was as if she had leashed herself, kept her greatest strengths bound and tied. Something a true artist would never do.

An unseasonal wind blew across the eyrie. I shivered and took a swig of whiskey.

Fireworks crackled over the docks, showers of color and light bursting over the dull, limpet-strewn hulls of the ships, over the forest of their white masts. The distant merriment of the townsfolk reached me, a whisper on the breeze, and my lip curled with disdain. I finished my glass and poured another. I didn't mind the solitude; it gave me time to work on my wordcraft without distraction. Once the world was ours, and was saved, only then there would be time to be merry.

A streak of light caught my eye. It came from the east, over the secluded bay where the girls and I would go crabbing; where Isla liked to practice her singing alone. I clumsily stepped across the balcony to get a better vantage point, and as I did, the streak appeared again, running through the night sky like a stream of light and down into the bay. The moon glowed brighter than I had ever seen, and the stream of light quickly turned into a river. It fell for several seconds, disappearing into the bay, then faded.

Suddenly, the moon dulled.

There was another burst of light from the bay and I saw them, just for a moment. Two figures stood upon the rocks, holding hands.

Caitlin and Isla.

The river of moonlight ran into the bay once more and, carried by the rising wind, I heard distant song words. I dropped my glass but didn't hear it shatter, my mind already ablaze with worry as I rushed down the stairs, taking them three at a time despite my creaking knees and unsteady gait, out of the lighthouse, and flew down the path. It is a wonder I did not fall myself.

What were they doing? So foolish! They couldn't sing without me. Not to something so powerful as the moon!

My legs felt leaden and it was as if my lungs had been covered in steel webbing that grew tighter and tighter, yet I couldn't stop running toward the bay, couldn't slow even for a moment. Caitlin knew she should be resting for tomorrow, when we would sing together. Isla should have stopped her; why didn't she stop her?

As I half-ran, half-stumbled, I pushed past townsfolk who were also following the light show. They murmured excitedly, thinking it an extension of the Blessday frivolities. My elbows were sharp, my bellowed words still sharper. Any complaints they may have made fell on dead ears.

I rounded the corner and froze. Crowds lined the bay, jaws slack. The twins stood in the water, waves lapping at their ankles, hand in hand and facing the moon. They both sang different songs. I recognized neither the words nor the tune; this was something of their own creation. They were drenched in ferocious moonlight that fell from the sky in torrents.

"Caitlin, no!" I cried as I ran toward them.

It was Isla who spun to face me, her song lost in distraction. "Mother?" Her voice was full of disbelief and irritation.

As she turned, the light intensified, burned bright and scorched my eyes. It rushed into Caitlin, like water sucked into a whirlpool. I squinted and tried to keep my eyes on the girls.

Caitlin screamed as she was enveloped by the light. Isla screamed alongside her.

I realized I was screaming too as the girls both disappeared into an ocean of blinding white. I could no longer tell them apart, their shapes so similar, all individuality—every dimple, scar and pore—masked by the incandescence.

Caitlin—it must have been, I am sure, for she stepped forward with such confidence—took several steps closer to me.

"It was working!" she screamed. My insides shook. She had never spoken to me like this before. "Why did you interrupt? Why did you have to ruin this? It was working!" Her voice turned hoarse as she continued to bellow. "It was going to make everything better! Why couldn't you just stay away?! We were doing it on our own!"

And with that, she screamed a baleful cry that shook the blood in my veins and the sky tore open: moonlight streaming all around; stars burning furiously; gathered crowds fleeing, barging, stampeding. I couldn't make out the girls anymore, but I watched in horror as their silhouettes pulsed in the light. A final scream, so ferocious it made my heart weep, and Caitlin exploded in a firework of blood and brine and both girls disappeared into the waves.

The sky sundered and rain began to lash down like a thousand whips, tearing at my clothes as I rushed forward and dove into the red-and-white foam. I thrashed around the water, but of my daughters, there was no sign. They had both melted away and become one with the waves, or the light, or perhaps even the dark of the bleak night itself.

I searched until the sun rose.

Both of my daughters were gone.

The North, now

Close.

I know she must be nearby now. The aurora continues to dance wildly above. Vast pillars of ice line the valley through which Amb pulls my chariot, like great sentinels created to watch and protect.

Then I see her. A hunched shadow. It can only be her, surely? She is facing away from me, watching a colossal horse made of sapphire light charge across the sky. I whisper the words and Amb immediately halts. She curls into a spiral, ammonite-like, and quietly waits. Stepping from my chariot, I approach, my heart full of joy at finding my daughter. I am almost fighting to keep the smile from my face, but as I draw close the words evaporate.

It is not Isla, but Caitlin.

My brow furrows and I think back to that night. Was I remembering it wrong?

"Caitlin?"

The girl starts, and turns. She looks up at me, her face black and charred, hair recently torn from her scalp, leaving sore red patches. Her cheeks are hollow and she is all rag and spindles. Her mouth opens but words do not come; eyes wide with surprise and writhing emotion. I try to decide what to say. All this time I had only considered the verse and script of what I would say to Isla, the damned daughter, the terrible influence that broke my pride and joy just when she was reaching her greatest triumph. Just as she was about to sing with me and change the world. I have never been one for improvising.

"My love, I've missed you," I start. She is shaking. "Why did you come so far north?"

Her face, as broken and hard to read as it is, sours. "I've been finding myself," she whispers and points at her grotesquely misshapen face with a three-fingered hand. "That night I was spread far and wide."

A question burrows its way through my heart. "Is Isla …"

"She's gone."

I nod. An idea comes to me. "Would you …" I continue, uneasily. "Would you like to sing together? As we had planned? Perhaps we can fix this together? Fix you." Even as the words fall, I know they were the wrong ones.

Impossibly, her eyes grow wider. Her irises are void black, the whites stark even amid the snow. Caitlin stands, staggers backward, and draws breath. She sings a song I do not know.

A snowstorm rises, violently.

That is not all.

Searing pain strikes me across the back and I cry out at the first stroke. Her song cuts—fervently cuts—like a hot knife. Not cleanly or precisely, but with uneven teeth that tear at my skin like a rusty saw. I fall to my knees and try to black out the pain as she flays my arms and legs and back, my cheeks, forehead and nose.

"Mother." Her voice ragged, but calm. "This is you. This is all you." She points at her ruptured face. "Isla is on you. Icante is on you."

Tears drip down my cheeks. "I'm sorry," I say. I am not sure why. I only wanted to help her.

Caitlin's song changes. From fast, guttural tones it shifts to something calmer, more serene. The searing pain that covers my body does not leave, though it is blunted, and I feel my skin tighten. I pull up my thick coat sleeves to see; my wounds are healing, sewn up neatly by lyric and verse, leaving thick, ugly scar tissue. I choke with shock and my tears fall faster.

Scarification: she has cut me open with words and sung them into permanence.

"Isla …" I read the name upon my skin, hot tears rolling down my cheeks. Caitlin has carved her sister's name across me and left it as an ever-cruel reminder of the past.

"Go home, Mother," she screams. "You ruined us all. You never cared about the right things. Not for Isla, or Dad, or anything but your own vision. For your own greed!"

And with that, she disappears into the snowstorm, her silhouette vanishing all too quickly as I stumble after, desperately reaching out for her. To have come so far, I cannot have lost her again!

I wail her name to no avail and when I try to summon up the words to break the storm, I cannot find them. I know a thousand songs and ten times as many verses, yet not one will come to my lips. Slumping into the thick snow, I hang my head and hug my coat close. The storm will subside, I am sure.

It takes longer than expected.

Icante, latterday

I sit inside my lighthouse on Icante, a good book in my lap, a pitcher of water on the table beside me. I can no longer climb the stairs to the eyrie, and I have long stopped singing. Since I returned to the island, I have not offered a word to a soul since Amb delivered me home and

I said goodbye. My molluscan friend has stayed at the island, finding a dwelling amid those wild rocks, even though her brethren are long gone. I am beyond grateful for the company.

Many years ago, stories were told about my daughter and the day she vanished into the ocean. I remember my trips to the mainland where I heard them, tales of the violent storm she called down on our island and the lightning that came, fierce enough to split the ocean in two and burn the sky black for a month and a day. These stories don't mention the details of her disappearance; not the curses she screamed until her throat ran red, nor the torrent of starlight that burst from her pores as she became one with the white foam of the sea.

I know she is still out there, in part, and I only wish I had told her it was okay when I had the time. That it was never her fault and that I should have been kinder, and wiser, and, certainly, less ambitious. I should have trusted in her talent, as her twin obviously had.

I want to speak with Isla one more time, and I want to apologize. It should never have been her. It should never have been either of them.

It wasn't just that I chose one over the other, but the choosing itself that was wrong.

And, girls, I am sorry for that.

Who Smiles Last

All I know is I don't want to be here.

Not again.

The gray waiting room smells like cheap disinfectant. In three years, everything will smell like that because of the global pandemic, but now it's just a scent. It matches with the endless thickly written papers hanging from the walls, like frozen ants on display below the yellowish neon light.

I'm sitting in a corner, beside a door that keeps opening and closing. People I barely know storm in, noisy beyond tolerable. Everybody is older than me, so I guess they have no chance of *growing up*.

"See all these people, Carlo?" Mom says, excited in her elegant blue suit.

I won't smile, even if I could. She crouches down to hug me, chair and everything.

"They are all here for you, don't you see?" She studies my face. "Aren't you happy? Just a bit?"

I stifle a sigh and tilt my head, just to make her happy. "I am."

The grief flashes in her eyes like a falling, wounded crow.

"Believe me, Mom," I insist. "This is an amazing day, even if you can't see it in my face."

She pushes back tears, unconvinced, scanning the room to make sure nobody has seen her. We are celebrities, indeed. The crowd is here to see Carlo Arconte, the young genius, getting a degree ahead of time—that's me, for what it matters.

She stands, straightening her suit.

"I want you to promise me, Carlo, honey," Mom says. "But please look into my eyes, so I can *know* you're listening to me, behind your *mask*."

That's how she calls my impairment. My autism would have always made it awkward for me to express emotions in a socially accepted way, but I also had some form of paralysis in my facial muscles, so I couldn't even fake a smile. Some kind of nerve damage that been attributed to some trauma occurring during my birth.

"I'm listening, Mom," I reply. "Please, go on."

But I don't want to listen. All I want is to be in my room, alone, inventing new toys. The whole business of getting a piece of paper proving that I'm smart, from a board of dumb people, makes little sense.

Everything darkens around me.

All I can think of is whether things might have gone differently, had my mother and I been different.

Then it's all black.

Readings-Check-LowHeartbeat
DataTransfer-Continue-73674563H3H
F/554/HJ3D-Command-JumpingForward

The debriefing office is cozy in its anonymity. The disinfectant is slightly mint-scented, just because I wanted it to be. Privileges of being the lead scientist—and the boss. Keeping the workplace free of distractions is crucial when you work day and night. I'm too energized by the recent developments to need rest.

We brought the patient here after the operation, then my crew left for safety reasons. Seventeen months in the lab, seeing nobody besides the boy who brought me my carefully sanitized meals, have paid off. Mom would say I spent my quarantine time well.

My patient sits on the bench by the light blue wall. His attention is drawn to his new arm, robotic from the joint of the shoulder down to the tip of his new fingers. A cool prototype indeed—my best work until now.

"Can you see it too, Doctor?" the patient asks me, looking into my face for validation.

I nod as his robotic fingers curl into a closed, functional fist. The patient holds his breath while he repeats the operation backward. Then he brings his fingers to his palm one at a time.

My phone beeps in my lab coat pocket. I glance at the screen as I take it out. It's Mom, checking on me.

"Can I ...?"

The patient looks at me in expectation. It takes a few seconds—*so darn slow, again*—to realize he's asking for my phone. A quick scan makes me realize there is nothing else in the room he can try to grasp. I'll complain with my crew as they get back.

"Can I hold it?" the patient repeats, hopeful. The robotic hand assumes the ancient gesture for begging.

I hesitate, all the rules against contagion flooding my mind.

"I'm not sure I should ..."

"Please ..."

I hand him my phone. The robotic hand takes it. The fingers wrap around it in an affectionate fashion.

That, and the light in his eyes, would make anybody think the patient is the father of a newborn, staring at his baby who just came into this world. I suppose the feelings are comparable.

"Doctor, ever since losing my arm in the accident, I had lost any hope for a better life." His voice trembles as he hands back my phone. "You've just made a true miracle."

Circumstances would require a smile from me, now. So I pretend to do it, the lower part of my face conveniently covered by the sanitary mask.

Readings-Check-Pressure
DataVerify-Ongoing-93684536H3H
Y/534/6T3D-Command-FindingEdge

"So, your life is just the lab—and nothing else?"

I observe Sarah closely, from the black bangs covering her green eye—the other is blue—down to her perfect teeth, to make sure she's not mocking me.

175

She smells good.

"I'm not sure I understand your question." I caress her naked back while stretching my legs in the bed. "I'm the one who can't show his emotions here, but you have quite an amazing poker face."

She giggles, then leans closer to brush my lips with hers. "You showed quite a lot of passion tonight …"

"That's not what I meant."

She sits up and covers herself with the blanket. Her eyes frame my relaxed pose. She softens. "You're not angry right now, huh?"

"I'm not." I tilt my head. "See? I'm smiling."

She sighs, then laughs again.

I love her happy face. I wish I could stay here forever.

"My friends say that I always end up with troubled people," she says in an amused tone. "You're the champion of troubled, aren't you?"

"That's a compliment, in a way." Am I deluding myself, or was a shade of irony just conveyed in my voice?

Sarah gets closer again. She caresses my arm with her skinny hand, a tattoo starting from the wrist to cover most of her forearm. It shows a heart and a feather on a scale.

"Really, Carlo, I'm worried for you," she says. "You live only to work. You never step out of your lab."

"I've been seeing remarkable results," I object. "We're waiting for the approval of a new research fund in less than a week. We're going to expand beyond simple, artificial-limb research into new, undiscovered territories."

"Like what?"

"What about a full, artificial neural system?"

She puts a hand in the middle of my chest. Her palm is warm. "This is the marketing guy speaking, I see." She frowns. "But what about you? How do you feel?"

The question still makes me uncomfortable, even after all this time. I welcome the expected beep of my phone. I step out of the bed and pull it from the pocket of my trousers.

"It's her, right?" Sarah's mood darkens.

"Yeah."

"You must do something about that."

I nod. "We have a meeting in an hour."

"You're faking it, right?" she asks. "Pretending not to understand."

I love my mask. "Am I?"

176

Sarah sighs. "Do it for me, please. Talk to your mother. Tell her you need free time."

She squints, hearing another beep from my phone.

"There's no need." I almost shrug as I put my phone back. "She's just very good at managing my time."

What follows is too painful, so I let the world fade around me.

I know this day is as important in my life as the one I met Sarah, when she took the place of her food-delivery colleague. I also know that she's just reopened a wound I was well aware of.

Readings-Check-Heartbeat-Increasing
DataStabilize-Continue-83737583H3H
W/889/HJ3D-Command-FindSpike

I zone out for a few seconds when I realize that the tiny faces of both the fighting robots—created with buttons, screws and a terrible use of a black marker—are more expressive than mine.

I brighten inside as the large, sharp saw I had attached on the right arm of my robot finds the body of its opponent and cuts it in half in a firework of sparkles. Considering I've not been at the labs to hunt for spare parts in months, my robot is still the one with the edge in this battle. I'm doing an impressive job.

Among the smells in the dusty warehouse, the burnt rubber is the strongest. It reaches my nostrils even if I'm wearing—like everybody else—the portable breather filtering out viruses. My company is the leader in the market.

The dirty teenagers who think they are my friends attempt a group hug with me.

"We've won, Carlo! We've won again!" Lucienne cheers, pecking my cheek.

I'm able to wriggle myself free from any further, joyful expressions of happiness from my team. I leave the fighting arena and walk to the desk by the exit to get my money. The thug seems unhappy, but he delivers me our winnings. I split the money into shares as I turn back.

I stumble into Sarah. She looks different from the punk I met twenty-four months ago. Now that she works for my company, she only wears tailor-made suits.

"Oh, hey," I say.

I have already given up on trying to find alternative ways to show emotions to the people around me.

"Carlo, we need you back," Sarah says.

Lucienne, shorter and somehow even skinnier, confronts Sarah. It looks like it is the same person meeting herself at different stages of life.

"Who are you, respectable lady? Can't you see he's busy?"

Sarah sneers. "Oh, yeah, he is. That's why I'm bringing him home."

"I'm not coming. I'm done with that crap," I say.

Sarah grabs my shoulder, ignoring the complaining Lucienne. The other teenagers buzz in the background.

"You know you're not," she says.

I watch her. A glare, now, would be cute—if only I could.

"You know me better than I do, now?"

I attempt a tilt, but she blocks my head with her hand. Her fingers press gently on my cheek.

"Please, save me the bullshit," Sarah begs, torn between sadness and anger. "You know you can't stop building, researching, and studying." She hints at the robot the teenagers are holding. "Even if it's just for … underground gambling."

"I'm having fun."

Sarah scoffs. "You have fun when you make an impact."

I push away all the memories her words bring back. I'm getting vertigo. *All those people who can now walk, work, or simply move again— their smile of joy is my smile. I* said it publicly many times. I had first gotten into robotics to help others replace the parts of their body they couldn't feel or move—knowing what that experience was like with my own face.

Sarah is right.

I must go back.

Hiring Sarah was Mom's idea.

A truly flawless plan.

Readings-Alarm-BloodPressure
DataVerify-Blocked-57383845738G&G
F/465/HJ3D-Command-Reload

The old wood of the ancient German theater doesn't smell as good as I wish. I notice it as I leave the VIP door behind and cross the bare secondary hallways leading to the dressing room. Something in the renovation, in the days after the pandemic was declared over, went wrong—probably for the lack of good trees left.

A team bigger than needed, both from my company and the award ceremony organization, keep swarming around me in the broad relax area. In the soft light, their shadows over the crimson curtains and the rich furniture sway like crazy grasshoppers.

I whisper my request to an assistant and they finally leave me alone.

I let myself appreciate how little time has affected my face. It's more or less like looking at myself in the mirror fifteen years ago. My hair is less thick, with some graying areas, but being unable to express facial emotions surely prevented a lot of wrinkles from ever developing.

"Have you seen the crowd out there, Carlo?" Mom says.

Even if I was expecting her visit, her voice almost makes me jump. Mom shines in her new purple dress, the coiffure and the beauty treatments making her appear much younger. I wonder if a stranger would believe she's my mother.

"The audience is so crammed," she says. "I didn't think I'd ever see such a crowd all together again."

I tilt my head. Mom comes closer and grabs me by my shoulders.

"So, you're happy, huh? I'm so glad for you." Her words are a bit too loud, like she needs to hide something behind the volume.

I pretend I don't notice it.

"Please promise not to cry when I thank you at the end of my acceptance speech," I say.

She surprises me again, pecking my cheek. "You'll be awesome, Carlo, I know."

If I could frown only once this would be the time for it.

"Won't you be out there?" I ask.

Sadness sparks in Mom's eyes. I wish I could read emotions better.

"Oh, no, Carlo. I'm leaving," she says. "We're going to Miami with Andrea."

"Your boyfriend? Couldn't you choose a different time for your vacation?"

She blushes, and this is something I can read. "Well," she hesitates. "It's not my usual trip to the States. I'm here to visit you so I can tell you in person, honey." She holds her breath. "We're getting married."

I swallow, too many thoughts flooding my brain.

But then, out of some remote instinct, I hug my mother hard. Her perfume has a slight scent of mint, resonating deep. So many emotions all at once.

So little ability to cope with them.

"Are you okay, honey?" Mom asks.

"I am," I say. "Have I grown pale, maybe? My body is creating its own way to redirect the emotions, I guess."

She scoffs, in a gentle way. "I mean, are you fine with … this? I'm setting you free, after all these years. That's what you wanted. That's what a man like you, that's gone this far, deserves." She gasps, and the tears glimmer in her eyes. "You're the man you promised me you'd become."

I hug her again. Because I want to.

What follows is a blur. I go on autopilot to speak in public as I climb on stage. The audience is huge. Every word I utter gets a smile. Every joke a laugh. Every full sentence an applause. Would it be the same if they knew I'm not really here?

But then I do what I always did. I have a problem and an idea pops into my mind. I picture a device that translates feelings into shades of color. It could be helpful. The simple enthusiasm for it overcomes my shell, letting me give a stunning, heartfelt conclusion to my speech. I get a long-standing ovation.

I head backstage while I'm already discarding the first options about how such a machine could work. This is probably why I don't notice the man in the trench coat until I almost bump into him.

"Excuse me, I have work to do," I mutter.

"Doctor, I need a minute of your time," the stranger says.

There is something wrong—off—in his expression, in the squinting eyes on an unshaven face framed by long, dirty hair.

"Call me Tom—"

I freeze as a gun appears in the hand of the stranger. A robotic hand. Poorly kept, indeed, but every single component screams the name of my company—even where there's no logo. I gasp as I recognize my first patient. The one whom I gave the first working prosthetic limb I created.

The whirring is almost inaudible as the robotic hand puts the gun to my forehead.

"Hold on, Mister," I say. "There must be something—"

"You're not scared," he says. "I only wanted to scare you, at first. My life went to hell, after I got your arm. I left my wife who was never quite adapt to my superhuman prosthetic, then—thanks to my extraordinary strength—I became a mobster thug—"

I always thought that if someone would kill me, it would come from my time in the underground robot fights. I certainly didn't expect *this*.

"You're not scared because you think you're a god, huh?" He sounds desperate. "You performed a miracle, but you're no god!"

I raise my hands. "I'm scared, believe m—"

He shoots as the security grabs him. When they disarm him, the bullet is already in my brain. I'm fading out, into the abyss.

Readings-Check-Stabilizing
DataTransfer-Ends-463884377Y7
F/013/98HY-Command-Start-NeuroSystem

"Carlo, can you hear me?"

I register an unexpected face, a young man. I can't smell anything. I suppress the instinct of moving my head to look around. Something is wrong.

"Can you hear me?"

It's a young scientist I remember hiring. I had little contact with the newest members of the crew after I had returned to my company, lost in making my own creations. It felt like everything could go on without me. Not being essential made me happy.

"Carlo, please, move your eyes if you can hear me."

His face brightens as I execute. Two more crew members join him, looking at me like a strange animal. Any attempt to vocalize the annoyance goes wrong.

"You can't talk yet, Carlo," the scientist says. "We're bringing the systems online one at a time." A flash of grief. "Every other different procedure before this failed."

181

A suspicion sparkles in my mind. Still, it can't be possible. We aren't there yet.

"Please, Carlo, nod now," the scientist says.

I tilt my head, like if I was smiling, to reassure him. I then complete my move, running a check of the room around me. I know every single piece of hardware in the operation room.

But I've never seen it from the bed.

"It's working!" the scientist bursts out.

The group cheers as they make me run simple movements of arms, legs, and torso. My gaze ends up on my limbs. I recognize the smooth perfection of my synthetic parts. Something snaps as I put the last piece of memory in place.

I'm dead. A bullet pierced my brain. My sight blurs. Darkness falls on me.

"Don't go! Please!" The scientist sounds frantic.

I open my eyes. His sudden relief feels nice.

"Activate his vocal interface!" the scientist orders.

"… solve the neuroconnection?" I hear a voice saying. It's reasonably similar to mine.

The scientist smiles broadly. "It was already there. All in your notes."

"But it didn't work," I insist. "With the others, I mean."

"They were all standard neural-system gifted people," the scientist explains. "Your brain, even damaged … it was special. Different."

My autism made me the perfect subject to make the human conscience transfer into an artificial body work. My mind had always worked on so many more levels than most humans. Was in many ways more advanced, so this is fitting—something worth celebrating. Not the darn degrees or awards. An actual, effective step forward in human science.

They let me change from laying to a sitting position. The reactivity of every part of my new body is impressive.

"One last thing, Mister," a woman with a square jaw intervenes. She's in formal clothes. I hadn't noticed her before, since the nerds are always more interesting to see.

I know, I am one of them. Or maybe, *I was.*

"Please, go on," I reply, enjoying the sound of my new voice.

"Although you may have all the memory of the former, great scientist Carlo Arconte, and somewhat his conscience, I need you to agree that you are *not* him. Not technically."

"I don't understand."

"After Mr. Arconte's death, the property of the company, went to his mother. A board of scientists, Mr. Arconte's best pupils, now run the company. And you—" She can't hide some concern, as she mentions my actual state, "—are an asset of the company. The most valuable, to be honest."

"Seems understandable," I say.

My quick response seems to startle the businesswoman even more. And something connects in my many new artificial pathways. My memories—or, rather, Carlo's—are still reconstituting in this new body. But I recognize that face. That voice.

Sarah.

The various machines connected to my artificial body start beeping in reaction to increasing neural output. If I had a heart, I think it would have skipped a beat. I have to wonder whether a robot can experience emotion. Something for further study.

The scientists mutter to themselves, perplexed over the sudden spike in their readings. They ask me several questions about how I am feeling, processing, before allowing Sarah to continue.

"I mean, do you agree to collaborate with the crew—with me— from now on, anytime of the night and the day, to understand and improve the technology that brought you to your so-called second life, and find a way to implement it and replicate it as far as the company will be able to?" My new visual interface picks up the merest hint of moisture in her eyes.

I'm about to tilt my head in a simple agreement. On a second thought, I search through the neural connections of my artificial body. I narrow the search to the head, then I find the face muscles. Eventually, I focus my intentions on the lower half of my face.

I smile, for the first time in my life.

Tracks on the Moon

They say NASA's about to cancel Project Artemis, the return to the Moon. I think I agree. What's the point, really?

Of course, maybe they'd want to go to get the bodies. And there's some who say that they should because the bodies are littering up the place and making it harder for everyone. There's something to that, too.

No one quite knows how it first started, but these days it's all about footie. Football. Not the daft American sort, the sort the rest of the world plays.

Except these days you don't really go to see the match, not even when it's a girl's game. (Unless you're Neville. He's all about "the integrity of the sport!" But I reckon it's because he can't take the Path.)

You come to a match and about half the people are naked. Starkers. No one minds. It's amazing how boring the human body—male *or* female—becomes when you've seen so many.

Anyway, it's not the nudies that matter—it's the dust on their feet. And the grins on their faces when they come "back" from the corridors.

You see, it's in the corridors of the football stadiums—like our local, Villa Park—that you can really run. And that's why everyone comes to the matches. To run. To follow the Path. Open their minds. Make the leap. And walk on the Moon.

I've done it. Done it three times. The first time I couldn't believe my luck. The second time I wasn't sure I'd be able to do it again. The third time … I tripped. Over a body. She was very young.

I reported it, of course. You see, the Watchers are always there these days. Watching.

At first we called them Voyeurs. Because they just stood there watching the people run—starkers—down the corridor, disappear, then reappear. But after a while people noticed that they weren't looking at the nakedness of the runners, any more than the rest of us. Like us, they were looking at their feet upon their return. And the tracks of dust. Moon dust.

After a while, the Watchers weren't impressed by the Moon dust. Everyone could get that. They were looking for more. And they also reported when people didn't come back.

But it was when Ludmilla Tsenko—you all know her—when she came back with *red* dust on her feet that the Watchers took notice. All the sudden, Luddy was back and gasping for air and crying and jumping up and down excitedly. Mars, you see. She had found a Path to Mars. The Watcher on duty spoke into his cell and—just like that—she was surrounded by these burly types asking all sorts of questions. Not mean or scary; interested and curious. But burly and serious all the same. They worked for the government.

Soon after that, everyone was running the corridors, trying for red dust. I never did. Because of that girl.

So it's pretty simple. You train up if you want to do it right. Go for long runs—in clothes, of course—until you have the stamina. Practice holding your breath until you can hold it for minutes and more. Because the longer you can hold your breath, the longer you'll stay, the further you can go. And then you start to learn how to focus—*really* focus—until you can get onto the Path. Some people like to call it "the Zone" but it sounds too American to me. The Yanks aren't all that good at it—they get all uptight about going nudders and they're always trying to make lists: do this, do that, and so on. You won't get there that way. You've got to let yourself go, to find the pull, to reach out … and step on the Path.

Some like to say that it's a Buddhist thing—The Eightfold Path. Rubbish! It might be similar but it's more like the high runners get when they push themselves. Only, in this case, it's not the finish line that's the goal. It's the moon. Or Mars.

Scientists are trying to figure it out, of course. Clothes don't work. Anything you wear gets left behind. No wrist watches, nor rings, nor necklaces. Birthday suits only. But they're trying. Me, I hope they figure it out. I'd like to go further than I can on one breath of air. I'd like to have my clothes on or, better, a spacesuit—proper, like.

There's this girl who's all shy. She keeps on running down the corridor in her clothes. Of course, when she Jumps her clothes all stay behind. One second a fully clothed girl, the next—a pile of clothes fluttering to the ground. A minute or so after that, a naked girl returns with dust on her feet.

The ones who can't do it, the naysayers, they all whine. They don't want to believe it, so they can't make the leap—literally. "You can't survive in a vacuum! Nude!"

Bollocks! You're not there long enough to get cold, so it doesn't matter. And you're holding your breath.

The scientists say that there are side effects—even from just a short Jump. But no one notices, so we keep on trying.

They've got telescopes that have picked out the tracks on the Moon. For some reason, everyone pretty much goes down the same track. That's why there's the problem with the bodies. Some people—no one knows why for certain—they don't make it back. Bodies on the moon. Maybe they trip or they get afraid. Maybe they panic and try to draw in a breath, and there is none. Not on the moon. They lose their concentration and can't find the Path back.

There's a rumor that the Pope went once. And now they're getting a new Pope. Because the old one's body is on the Moon.

Maybe the Yanks should keep up with that Project Artemis: retrieve all the bodies. Or just bury them.

People are going for red dust mostly these days. Moon dust just doesn't cut it.

Ludmilla Tsenko was the first, but she wasn't the last. Of course, she's famous. Not just for Mars, of course.

I was there when she made her last run. Everyone was, by then. We'd gathered in the corridor when she was getting ready, because we wanted to cheer her on. She'd smile at us and wave, quite the rock star. She'd pre-breathe, deep breaths of air, and she'd bounce up and down, limbering up. And then she turned down the corridor and—just like that—she was off. A proper gazelle. No! A cheetah in motion. She was all out, arms and legs pumping as she gained speed and then—gone.

She wasn't back for a long time.

"Did she go beyond Mars?" We all started wondering. Worried. Awestruck.

The Watcher was looking nervous. He spoke urgently into his mobile. A moment later a bunch of the burly types arrived. And a gurney, just in case.

There was a cry—a muffled shriek, really—from the crowd when she appeared again, stumbled and fell moments later. She was all blue. Dead.

Blue and smushed. Hardly a body at all.

The burly guys took her away but before they could hide her from our view, I got a good look. Her hair was frozen. Clumped in strands, stuck like in ice. Only, I realized, it wasn't ice—there were drops of Jupiter in her hair.

Pleasing the Parallels

by Alvaro Zinos-Amaro

When Mom started reminiscing about Dad's stint as an army chemical engineer, I told myself that I'd misheard, but deep down I suppose I knew better.

"What were you saying about Dad?" I asked.

"Oh, nothing."

She retreated into her bedroom, me in tow, and began brushing her long white hair, a task that seemed to take a little longer each day.

"No, really," I said, "I'd love to hear it."

She stopped the smooth, repetitive downward motion and smiled, brown eyes furtive like those of a child caught with candy. She set down the brush on her oak drawer chest—or *commode,* as she insisted on calling it. "I was thinking about his knack for chemistry, that's all. He was almost as good at it as I was at physics." She grinned mischievously.

"Mom," I said, "Dad served in the army for less than a year before being honorably discharged and becoming a teacher. He never worked as a chemical engineer."

"I know that," she said, looking down. And then: "Do you mind if I take a nap? I just want to lie down for a while."

Hard as it was, I had to do something. So, while she rested, feeling discomfited by my own actions but pushing myself forward anyway, I raised a privacy e-blanket and called Dr. Hartwood.

He asked if I'd noticed any other memory incidents. I reflected. Normally I discern patterns with ease—it's why overseas film studios pay me to analyze their pre-releases, because I can catch subtle things the algorithms miss—but it was only when Dr. Hartwood put me on the spot that I recalled other instances of Mom's memory going awry. Little things, like her not remembering the title of a book she'd read a few months before, or asking if we needed milk after buying some two days earlier. I'd swept each event aside, convincing myself that it was an isolated occurrence. Simply old age encroaching, I told myself. But now the pattern, and my complicit self-deception, were obvious. "Yeah, I suppose I have," I said, trying to hide my embarrassment.

A few days later, the three of us met in person. I told Mom the visit was an ordinary age-related checkup. Dr. Hartwood asked her a lot of questions about major life events—where she'd grown up, when she'd gotten married, my birth, Dad's death, and so on.

When, a minute in, she said I'd been born in Pittsburgh—instead of Ithaca—I felt like someone had dumped ashes inside my mouth. Her accounts over the next dozen questions departed from reality with increasing severity. I'm not sure what depressed me more: how wrong she was, or how calm and confident she sounded.

The doctor subjected her to several bio-scans and consulted with an AI. A week, he said. We made the follow-up appointment.

A recent spike in urban crime was causing my boyfriend, Kyle, to put in a lot of overtime, and things had been rocky between us for a while anyway, so I didn't share the details of these visits with him.

During our second appointment, Dr. Hartwood performed an even more comprehensive salvo of tests. As we were wrapping up, he scanned his tablet and looked at Mom. "Thank you very much. You've done great, Connie. We're almost finished here. One last question: could you tell me about your early research on quantum entanglement?"

I was annoyed because I didn't see how Mom's research, now forty years in the past, could possibly be relevant to her current condition.

But Mom wasn't upset at all. "Sure," she replied. "I was part of the first group that showed that it was possible to transfer information from one place to another instantaneously, and without degradation. My work killed the cryptography industry," she continued placidly. "More importantly, it led to the full-body teleporter that we use today."

I stared at her. Her imagination was really out of control.

189

"So that's how you remember things, then," Dr. Hartwood said, unfazed. He turned to me. "Well, I've got bad news and good news for you both. Those memories *are* accurate. Unfortunately, they don't correspond to *our* reality."

I leaned forward, trying to make sure I'd heard correctly.

"It's true," he said, in response to my discomfort-cum-disbelief. "You see, Pat, in *our* reality your mother performed early pioneer work on quantum teleportation that ultimately didn't pan out, but that's not the whole story. Part of the reason the research died was the government's fear that the scientists involved were being exposed to potentially unsafe side effects. Your mom's present state is the result of one such lingering issue finally catching up to her in her old age. It's extraordinarily rare, which is why I needed all these extra tests, and even then, once I knew the field your mother had worked in and suspected what was going on, I had to verify the results with a specialist. The papers on this have always fascinated me. The condition is called *dementia parallela*—or, less technically, memory fingers." He turned back to my mom. "Our multiverse consists of infinite parallel realities, and your consciousness, Connie, is starting to reach out to these realities. Due to detrimental proximity to your past experiments, your memory is tuning in to events that have happened in these other worlds. As a result, your grasp on your life *here*, in this reality, is weakening. Your consciousness is de-cohering."

So this was why Mom was so sure of what she described. It really *had* happened.

But not in this reality.

I cleared my throat. "What are our options?"

Dr. Hartwood said, "I'm very sorry, but the de-coherence will continue to progress until it leads to a final...collapse."

"There's no treatment?"

"I'm afraid that we don't know any way to stop this," he said. "But we *can* slow things down."

"How?" Mom asked.

"If you want us to," Dr. Hartwood said, "we can undertake a search for someone whose brain wave functions are similar enough to yours to be a compatible sharer of the de-coherence effect. We can then use quantum entanglement to displace your decoherence to the volunteer—up to a point. The volunteer would be paid handsomely. This procedure would help us learn more about this rare effect, while giving you some additional time."

"You want to transmit my sickness to someone else? That doesn't sound very nice," Mom said. "I don't think I—"

"Mom," I interrupted, surprising myself with the forcefulness of my tone. "The person would be a volunteer. They'd be rewarded. And science would benefit. Can we not jump to conclusions, please?"

Mom looked sad. "I don't like the sound of it."

I glanced at the doctor. "How long do you think it would take to locate a compatible sharer?"

"We'll scan our database and I'll let you know."

I replied before Mom could. "Please start the search right away. We can always back out if we change our minds, right?"

"Of course," Dr. Hartwood assured. His tone wasn't silky enough to distract me from Mom's sullen expression.

During the next three weeks my sleep cycle eroded. I'd been a regular consumer of toss-and-turn angst ever since Kyle had moved out, but now I was assaulted by epic nightmares. Thick, stalk-like tendrils would grow out of Mom's nose and ears, followed by writhing vines that burst through her skull to reveal a swollen, palpitating mess of tangled roots where her brain should have been. I'd wake up with cold sweats and skim-read papers I didn't understand on quantum entanglement. During the daytime I was bleary-eyed and cranky, nodding off at the least appropriate times. I developed a "don't-argue-with-me-or-else" rudeness I disliked, but which ironically proved helpful in dealing with Mom's condition. Bit by bit, I wore her resistance down until she finally agreed to the transfer procedure. I recorded her consent and forwarded it to Dr. Hartwood, all the while suppressing the hollow sensation in my chest.

The few times I spoke with Kyle he expressed concern about my obvious irritability. I finally explained to him what was happening.

"I know things are complicated between us right now, but you don't have to go through this alone," he said.

"Yes they are, and of course I do," I said. "She's *my* mom, and I'm her support system."

"I just meant—"

"You were advertising what might be," I said. "But I'm only in the market for what is."

He knew better than to argue.

The following week Dr. Hartwood contacted me. "We've found a match," he said. "We can begin as soon as your mother is ready."

A chill passed over me. It was really happening. "Who is it?"

"I'm afraid I can't disclose that," he said. "To protect both parties involved, you understand."

"I don't need protection," I replied. "What I want is to express my gratitude to the volunteer personally."

Dr. Hartwood swallowed. "Pat, I realize this must be taking a tremendous toll on you. But I can't."

"Help me out here," I pleaded. "Let me say thanks."

"Believe me, I'm helping you by not telling you."

I tried a different approach. "Why would anyone agree to take on the mental confusion that comes with 'memory fingers' anyway? I mean, besides the money?"

"No one's being duped here, if that's what you're implying," Dr. Hartwood said, sitting very straight. "There's a group of New Age types interested in consciousness de-coherence. They say it's an ancient phenomenon, accessible through meditation, and that experiencing manifold realities brings them closer to transcendence."

"Misremembering your life as nirvana? You've got to be kidding."

"Religion might provide a plausible motivation for some."

"Fine, whatever," I said. "Let me check in with Mom. I'm pretty sure we can meet you at nine a.m. tomorrow for the first session."

"Here's the address," he said, and the data transferred into my system.

The following morning we bundled ourselves up in our autumn jackets and sat in the back of my car as it drove us to the lab through a steady downpour. The windshield wipers did all the talking. Once we got upstairs I was surprised by the size of the main device, a kind of super-MRI tunnel. The temperature inside the chamber was almost colder than it had been out in the rain; our jackets stayed on.

During the session I found myself thinking about the identity of the recipient almost as much as about Mom's wellbeing. Whoever it was, he or she was likely in this same building, maybe a few rooms away from us, probably hooked up to a device like the one currently encompassing my mom. What was going through the volunteer's mind, I wondered? Was he or she really being impelled to action because of a belief in some numinous, multi-reality bliss?

The session lasted a little over an hour. "Everything went well," the tech told us.

He confirmed our following appointment and my car drove us back home. En route, Mom looked at me with a curious intensity, as though seeing me clearly for the first time in weeks. "So what ever happened to that friend of yours—I think her name was Lorrie? Didn't you two used to have lunch on Fridays?"

I was speechless for five seconds. "Yes," I said. I couldn't help but smile. "That's exactly right. What else do you remember about her?"

"You know I don't like being quizzed," Mom said, tensing up. Then she relaxed, because showing off her improvement was fun. "She was one of your office friends, before you started telecommuting."

I held back a giggle of delight. How *was* Lorrie, anyway? "Maybe I should check in with her. It's been a while."

By the time we walked up to the apartment door and the identity sensor unlocked it, we were in the middle of a conversation about music and math and old TV shows and relationships and anything and everything. I felt light. Like years had been shed from me. *Maybe,* I thought, *the last few weeks have been a bad dream; a terrible misunderstanding.* That's what I told myself as I drifted off that night, because I was afraid that otherwise my newfound peace would dissolve in the night.

The next morning Mom was up before me, hair in a ponytail. I found her in the kitchen. Assorted breakfast ingredients lay on the counter, over which she leaned, frowning. "Honey, what's the access code to the stove?" she asked. "I thought I knew it, but it's not working."

My stomach lurched. Had the procedure's effects worn off so quickly? *Please, no.* "What are you punching in?" I asked, and reminded myself to breathe normally.

"Clytemnestra-6," she said.

Phew. When Mom's memory issues had flared up I'd changed the code to prevent an accidental fire. "Sorry, Mom, I updated it. The new code is Erigone-8."

Mom got the stove on. "There, much better. You like your eggs runny, don't you?"

"Well done," I said. "I mean, the eggs."

"Oops," she said. "Thanks."

While she prepared the coffee, eggs, and toast, I yawned and stretched. My right shoulder made a popping sound and my neck clacked with pent-up tension. I tried to recall last night's dreams. For once they hadn't been about Mom. *Someone* had been shuffling down a drab street under crimson clouds and a barrage of lightning. I feared the stranger was hurt and needed my help. I was trying to catch up, but no matter how much I ran I always remained twenty steps behind, disoriented by the stroboscopic flashes from the fiery heavens above. "Hey you!" I yelled. When the stranger turned around, I saw he was faceless; emptiness incarnate.

Mom sat down and we ate. It didn't take long for her to notice that I was only pecking away at my food.

"Pat, look at me."

I did.

"I'm still going to make mistakes," she said. "This isn't a cure. We need to remember that. Let's enjoy whatever time we have together."

"Of course," I said. "I had some weird dreams last night, that's all. More coffee will help." I poured myself a second cup and put on a brave face, pretending my sorrow was a physical object I could push out of the way. "When we're done here I need to make a few calls. This is delicious, by the way. Thank you so much." Mom had seasoned the eggs with black pepper and a smattering of tarragon, exactly how I liked them, even if she had undercooked them in the end.

"My pleasure. Calling anyone I know—like Kyle, maybe?"

"So nosy," I said, and laughed. "Maybe I am."

"I'll be in my room," she said.

A short while later, Kyle said, "Nice to see you."

I was going to pay him some kind of compliment, but then I noticed his stubble, along with the rumpled collar of his normally stiff, pristine shirt. So I settled for, "How are things?"

"Busy," he said, which I easily believed. Then I wondered if he was being vague on purpose: one of his talents, keeping people out. *Maybe that's what I'm becoming to him,* I thought. *Just people.* Funny. That aloofness had been part of the appeal—a long time ago. "How's Connie doing?" he asked, voice grave and formal.

"First session has worked wonders." I elided in my own thoughts the little mistake she'd made with my eggs, rewriting my memory so that it never happened. "In fact, that's why I was calling you."

194

"Oh?"

"I wanted to take you up on your offer for help after all," I said. "I'd really like to thank the person who's helping Mom get better."

Kyle's right eyebrow arched. "How does that involve me?"

"The process is officially anonymous. Some medical rule designed to keep everyone out of everyone else's hair."

"Gotcha," he said. "A medical rule—or a law?"

"Not sure."

"It sort of makes a difference," he said, his tone droll. He scratched at his nascent beard. For the thousandth time, I thought about how I missed sharing a bed with him. I was sure he missed it too. Despite my best intentions to keep it bottled up, the longing must have manifested on my features. "I can look into it," he said. "No promises, though."

"Thank you," I said. "Seriously."

"You're welcome. What can you tell me about the volunteer?"

"Not much." I described our most recent appointment: where we'd gone, how long we'd stayed there, and so on. I told him when the next one was and repeated what the doctor had said about New Age mystics being into consciousness de-coherence. A few minutes later the conversation drew to the kind of awkward silence we were training ourselves to accept, and so, like civilized people, we said goodbye.

After the second session, Mom and I went for a long stroll at Druid Hill Park, Baltimore's largest park and my favorite ever since I was a kid. Throughout our walk, light shifted through the ponderous cloud mantle, turning the somber gray sky silver-sheened.

"Wonder what Dad would have made of all this," I said. I probably shouldn't have brought it up, considering the circumstances. On the other hand, why not take advantage of Mom's clarity?

"He never cared much for quantum mechanics," Mom said. "He was a regular Einstein in that respect."

I chuckled. "I'm sure that memory fingers would have rubbed Dad the wrong way." Lame, but the best I could manage under the circumstances. Mom smiled in appreciation.

We passed one of the park's tennis courts, not in use during the rainy season. I remembered how shocked I'd been in school when they'd taught us that these same tennis courts had been for whites only since the park's opening in the 1860s all the way through the 1940s. *A fear of different realities blending*, I thought, and only after caught the irony.

We walked on, silently marveling at the beauty of cherry blossoms and tall striped maples. In a few months they'd be dusted with snow.

When Mom spoke again her demeanor was different. "Do you think there might be a way to find out?" she said.

We reached one of the park's main gates and exited. "Find what out?"

"What *he* would think." She paused. "What he *does* think."

Mom's words stopped me in my tracks. "Are you talking about Dad?"

"Consider it, sweetie." She hugged herself. Her breath was visible in little ghostly exhalations. "My mind is reaching out to all these other worlds where events played out differently. Countless imaginable scenarios. In one of them your father may still be alive. What if I could find that reality?"

My mouth felt dry and my eyes stung. The bracing air seemed to blur my vision and our luck with the clouds finally ran out. Rain pelted down and darkened the pavements, moving us along.

"Dad is gone," I said. Anger crept into my voice. I stared at Mom, wanting her to register the intensity of my response. "*My* dad, *your* husband—he's the only one that matters to me. I'm not interested in some other version of that man. I want us to remember *this* life."

Mom seemed to shrink inside her large brown jacket. "You're right," she said, with a tenderness that killed me.

"The person helping your mom," Kyle said, "is a young man by the name of Derek. Twenty-three-year-old Harvard psych student holding down a part-time job as a counseling assistant to help cover his tuition. Until recently, anyway."

"Oh?"

Kyle hesitated, then continued. "He quit his job and dropped out of school. Two semesters shy of graduation."

I thought about the faceless man in my dream. Not so faceless after all. "Shit."

"Please don't start with the self-blame," Kyle chided. "You didn't make him do this. *He* volunteered. He has his reasons. And I'm sure he was aware of the consequences."

196

"He's twenty-three. How good were your reasons for doing anything at that age?"

Kyle shrugged, then shook his head. "Look, this is it. I'm not doing any more spying for you."

Digesting what Kyle had shared was keeping me from forming cogent thoughts. But before he disconnected the call I raised my hand, as though I could reach through the screen and touch him. "Wait," I said. "One more thing. Did anything come up about his religious affiliations?"

"Pat, religion or no, this is *his* life. I know you don't want my advice, but here it is: focus on *yours.*"

He had a point. But no matter how hard I tried, I couldn't get the name Derek out of my head.

The nightmares returned. I dreamt I pushed an old man through a trapdoor that opened up on an infinite void. He screamed for help as he plummeted through the abyss; his voice was Dad's voice, desperate, the way he'd sounded when he was on the last round of chemo.

To try and alleviate my sense of helplessness and guilt, I researched the group that Dr. Hartwood had alluded to. Their core tenet, as he had suggested, seemed to be that parallel realities offered a gateway to a true transcendence of self. The purpose of life, according to them, was to open up one's mind, through whatever means available, and sample as many alternate realities as possible. *Pleasing the parallels,* they called it. *Is that what you're trying to do, Derek?*

Mom's voice pulled me out of my thoughts. She was speaking out loud, without a privacy e-blanket, and it was clear she wasn't talking to me. I walked into her room and saw her sitting on the bed, holding up a tablet. "Everything okay?" I asked.

She tapped the pause icon. "For the last few days I've been making these recordings." She nodded in a soulful way. "They're for you, Pat. Now that everything is straight in my head I want to set down my thoughts. Preserve the moments. Not sure how many are left."

Trembling a little, I reached forward to hug her.

Still locked in the embrace, I imagined Derek's parents hugging their son, trying to get to him through the increasingly thick fog of other realities.

In that moment I knew what I had to do.

Kyle was angry. I'd been nervous about sharing my decision with him, but after his help finding Derek I felt it fair to be honest.

"One more retreat," he was quick to say. "You've been pulling away from your friends lately, Pat. People who care about you, who are invested in your happiness. Is this what you really want—to become even *less* aware of the world around you?"

"I wasn't asking for your permission," I replied, crossing my arms.

"Noble, self-sacrificing Pat," he went on. "But how are you going to take care of your mom if you need help taking care of yourself? And what makes you even think you're a compatible recipient?"

"I'm her daughter, so the chances are good," I snapped. "I'll do whatever it takes." Truth be told, Kyle was making solid points. But I didn't feel like I had a choice. I couldn't let the young man—Derek, Derek, Derek—continue to take on our woes. And Mom still deserved to have her mind remain clear for as long as possible.

"Look, Pat," Kyle urged, seeing that I wasn't any closer to changing my mind. "Sorry for being on the offensive. All I'm saying is that I think this is a bad idea. I'm sure you haven't told Connie because you know she'll disapprove too. Despite everything that's gone wrong between us ..." In that silence I visualized another world, one where Kyle and I didn't need sentences like that. Perhaps that was one of the realities I'd find myself remembering in a few days. Small consolation it would be.

"I know you'll be here for me," I said, which was maybe presumptuous on my part. But I knew it was true.

The next day I received a call from Dr. Hartwood. Mom had apparently contacted him on her own—and not only had she asked to stop the transfers to the volunteer, but to actively *speed up her de-coherence.*

I was livid.

"How could you go behind my back and do that?" I demanded, barely holding back tears. "And why now? Did you bypass my privacy screen and eavesdrop on my chat with Kyle?"

She was calm. Her serene demeanor only fueled my frustration. "This is what I want," she said. "I feel like I'm supposed to move along this path. And the volunteer's life isn't worth mine. I'm old and he's young. It's a simple equation."

I wanted to sit down next to Mom, but I was still too upset. I settled for lowering my voice and pacing not-quite-frantically. "This isn't one of your physics experiments," I said. "You're not some *variable*."

Mom was quiet. Her eyes journeyed to a place I couldn't follow. When they returned to the here and now, a sliver of her remained in that other realm.

In a soft voice she said, "The doctors can apply these intense fields around my brain to accelerate the consciousness de-coherence."

"I don't understand. Then why couldn't they use the same technique in reverse to decelerate it?"

"Not so simple," Mom said. "My de-coherence is like a hole in the hull of a sinking ship—hard to plug, but easy to widen. In a way, it'll be a beautiful thing."

"What?"

"My mind will disperse through a panoply of parallel worlds." She fell quiet. "Dandelion seeds of consciousness scattered in the winds of the multiverse."

I imagined fairy dust thinning until it was too faint to perceive: my mom's entire life, the fading tail of a comet in its death throes.

"In a way, I won't really be gone," she went on. "Not in the strict scientific sense. Bits of me, infinitesimally small, will endure for a long time. Please understand that my decision doesn't mean I love you any less."

Then I've failed, I thought. I couldn't accept what she was telling me.

"No," I said, quivering. "I won't sign the agreement. And without my endorsement as your primary caregiver, I doubt the doctors can speed up your de-coherence. I'll argue that your decision is the result of mental confusion."

She looked more disappointed than upset. "You wouldn't do that," she said. "That's not the daughter I raised."

"Nevertheless," I shot back, "it's the daughter you have."

For the next few weeks we didn't revisit our conversation. Mom didn't try to cajole me into changing my mind. Nor did she sulk. In fact, she was the best, sunniest version of herself.

I sought refuge in my work, but it was impossible to focus for more than small intervals. It wasn't just the uncertainty of the future that wrecked my concentration: I started experiencing severe headaches. I'd never felt migraines like this before. The pain would appear without warning, a devastating pressure that seemed to arise in both temples simultaneously and then bridged my forehead, encasing my head in an invisible bubble of crippling pain. The world seemed to press in against my cranium from every which side. I had to stop whatever I was doing and lie down in the dark. Often, tears would slide down my face, and during peak intensity the simple effort of raising my hand to wipe them away was too great, so they pooled and dried on my skin. Meds did nothing against the onslaught.

I consulted a doctor, though not Hartwood—I was too ashamed to tell him I was road-blocking Mom's wishes, that we were at an impasse because of me. The physician couldn't find anything wrong with me besides stress. She recommended regular social interactions and more consistent exercise. "Often these things take care of themselves," she said. "But we can help the body's natural mechanisms along."

I scoffed at her platitudes and dismissed her advice. Social interactions were the furthest thing from my mind. Besides, even if I'd wanted to, I reasoned circularly, I couldn't spend time with others to overcome my migraines because my migraines were preventing me from spending time with others. Heck, I was barely even talking to Mom.

One day, acting on impulse, I solicited Kyle's opinion on Mom's request. If he sided with me, I thought, maybe that would bring us closer together. And maybe Mom would reconsider.

I should have known better.

"If that's what she truly wants," Kyle said, ever the irritating paragon of reasonableness, "shouldn't you consider it?"

"You're no help at all," I said.

But Kyle's words lingered, came back as whispers in my head during quiet moments. And eventually, the terrible headaches became less frequent, then faded altogether. Once the pain subsided, a curious thing happened: I was left with an inexplicable feeling of tranquility. At first I thought it was simply relief at the absence of pain, an internal overcompensation. But after the second or third day I knew it was more than that. A warm, reassuring sensation at the core of who I was. For the first time in years, I felt centered. More patient. Things improved with Mom, even as her mis-memories worsened.

One evening, after running errands in the city and visiting the park again, Mom and I were watching a cooking show at home and I started feeling light-headed. A sudden tingling washed over me. It grew in intensity until I felt pins and needles in every part of my body. Reality blacked out for a dizzying instant. I wanted to throw up. Then all of it passed.

I blinked. When I looked around, Mom wasn't there, and the living room had changed. It was larger, warmer, more brightly lit. A voice spoke to me, but I couldn't tell if it was coming from somewhere in this room or my own mind.

We apologize for any discomfort. Those are the side effects of dematerialization. Your recent headaches: that was us too. We were reaching into your reality and preparing your mind for this jump. A kind of brain "immunization," if you will.

I should have been terrified, but I wasn't. In that strange way in which absurdities seem entirely plausible in dreams, I accepted this preposterous explanation without question. These people had a teleporter and had bridged our worlds. Sure, why not?

Who is us? I asked.

We're a research group studying the effects of memory fingers. Your sister, in fact, is the project lead. It was her idea to bring you over to our dimension.

My sister? Even amidst the surreal-ness of this situation, I retained enough sanity to know I didn't have any siblings. But the *idea* of a sister, one who had perhaps followed in Mom's steps, felt no more unlikely to me than the notion of memory fingers themselves.

Why did you bring me here?

The response was at once banal and mysterious. *So that you could see.*

I looked around.

There was no one in the room besides me. On closer inspection, I realized some of its furnishings might be mine—or at least they might have belonged to this reality's me. A few items I could recognize. An antique portico clock with its familiar pendulum swinging between its two black columns; several lush potted *Dieffenbachia* with variegated bright green-and-white leaves; Mom's prized oak *commode*; other assorted knick-knacks. But beyond these familiar mementos, nothing seemed remarkable, except perhaps the room's inviting feeling. I felt strangely at home here.

At peace.

See what? I asked.

Take a good look, the voice said. *There's nothing to be afraid of. The realities your mom is slipping into aren't dangerous or threatening.*

The room's stillness was the opposite of oppressive—it seemed to invite warm memories, peaceful reflection. In the far corner I spotted a picture of me and Mom. I feared it would make me cry, but it didn't. We looked happy. An uncomplicated, spontaneous joy of the sort that's impossible to stage—not dismissive of reality, but rooted in its ultimate acceptance. I hadn't felt that way in real life for …

Too long.

Was this what the absence of loneliness felt like?

This is a silly dream, I said. *Wake up. Wake up, wake up, wake up.*

I opened my eyes and I was in my own living room once more, Mom beside me. "Welcome back," she said.

I frowned.

"You nodded off."

"How long was I out?"

"They finished the kingfish tails with smoked pipi broth and wakame oil, and now they're working on blueberry-pecan galettes."

Exhausted, I yawned, rose, and asked Mom if she needed anything before I went to bed.

"I think I'll call it a night too," she said.

Sometime during the following week Mom sensed the shift in me.

We never even had to talk about it.

After she felt it, she used her lucid periods to say her goodbyes to the people in this life that she cared about, and to put her affairs in order.

On the appointed day it took about an hour for the doctors to configure the enormous parasol-shaped screen several feet above Mom's head. Dr. Hartwood was in attendance, though he wasn't running the show—that required Dr. Singh. Still, it was nice of him to visit, and it made Mom more comfortable.

At one point I was asked to wait outside. Nobody could be in the OR with Mom because it would upset the device's hyper-fine readings. Glumly, I complied.

In a sterile adjoining room I found myself calling Kyle. "I'm here," I said. My voice quavered. "With Mom."

He paused, understanding. "You're doing the right thing, Pat," he said. "Do you want me to come over?"

I hadn't expected the offer. "No—no—it'll be all right—but maybe later we … I dunno, maybe we could talk a bit."

"Sure. Of course. Whatever you want."

He waited, probably thinking the conversation was over. But there was one more thing on my mind I needed to get out. I told Kyle about my experience the week before. "Suppose for a second that it wasn't a dream," I whispered. "For argument's sake, of course."

"Okay."

"Why would this putative research group care about me at all? Why go to all that trouble?"

"Hmmm," he said. "If the problem spills over across realities, affecting not only the sufferer but each of the many versions of the sufferer broached by the memory fingers, maybe they wanted to help all those versions of Connie?"

"They just showed me a room."

"But it influenced your decision, right? What if by ending your Mom's suffering here you're restoring the mental health of a multitude of other Connies?"

I wished he were right—if only to make my immediate future more bearable. "Thank you," I said. "I'll let you know once it's over."

About ten minutes later I was admitted back in. Dr. Singh walked us through what would happen next, emphasizing that Mom wouldn't feel any pain. It was only when she was done talking that it really hit me.

This is it.

Three techs came in and performed one final calibration. After they left, Dr. Singh asked Mom to take a seat under the huge dome-shaped machine.

Mom stood, immobile, and I kissed her on the cheek and squeezed her hand.

"I love you," I said.

"You'll be with me everywhere," she replied.

She shivered, and I held her. Then, finally, she sat down and they wrapped the thin mesh interface over her clothes and attached several cables to her arms and hands. The oversized helmet began to descend, emitting a deep, rumbling sound, until it was inches above Mom's head.

Dr. Singh gave the signal and a high-pitched sound emanated from the machine.

Mom closed her eyes.

As I stared at her, I had the weirdest sensation.

I felt something settle and click into place in the back of my head.

Like a key entering a lock.

Pleasing the parallels, I thought.

The Negotiator

by The Winner Twins

The face is sacred, for the face is the doorway to the soul, and we only show our souls to those closest to us. Thus, it baffled me how despicable Duelum Empire was, with all the death they had brought to my people, that they still believed the same. That they, too, followed the Jupiter Scriptures.

My mentor seemed to know what I was thinking, and placed his wrinkled hands on my shoulders. "These people are barbarians who want the bloodshed to never end," he said. "If you can create peace today, that would be an unlikely miracle. But you must remember, an honorable death is not a failure—it is a holy victory."

He removed his hands. "On the moons of Jupiter, was it not said that truth must never be clouded by fear, or by dogma? Was it not said that the path to truth is always known in the soul, but it's signs often frighten us at first? We both know the truth, Ara. That is, if you do not prevail today, we must do what needs to be done."

Through the window, I saw our ship entering the atmosphere. It was almost time.

"I will do what must be done. You have my word," I said, lowering my veil.

I stared below at the planet of endless red desert. It was neutral territory, with no resources, no life, nothing of value. The perfect place for a negotiation.

I felt uneasy. Who would the Duelum send? Surely an older man. That is what my empire would have sent, if they had not chosen me.

Negotiation was my job, my purpose. I could not let insecurity get the best of me. My age and my gender, though unusual, would not get in my way. It was my strength, just as my mentor had said so many times.

Two soldiers marched in, their faces covered with black and crimson helmets.

"Ma'am, please follow us," one of them said.

I nodded, and my mentor said, "Pretend to drink their tea, but don't actually drink it."

"You think it's poisoned?" I asked, incredulous.

"No, you just tip some on you when you get nervous," he said with a chuckle, trying to break the tension.

I replied with a nod, and a smile he could not see, and I followed the soldiers and exited the ship.

It was in the desert that I saw her for the first time. Luckily my veil hid my surprise at her feminine form. It seems that the Duelum, too, had not sent an old wizened man as a negotiator. This encounter should prove more interesting than I was expecting.

She walked toward me, soldiers on either side of her, just as soldiers from my empire flanked me. Her robes were white, with a matching long white veil down to her waist. Gold embroidery was stitched into the bottom hems in the shape of vines.

Although it matched the white and gold armor of her empire's soldiers, I still thought her clothing gaudy and overdone. My robes and veil were much superior, made with a simple crimson red velvet and chiffon.

The tent was placed between our two vessels, with both ships facing each other, their weapons locked on vital systems and ready to fire at any moment.

"The tent is safe, the tea is *not* poisoned, and the other negotiator is unarmed. All she carries is a small holo-projector, which has not been tampered with," one of my soldiers whispered to me after performing routine security scans. I nodded and saw one of the white-clad soldiers speak to the other woman. I reasoned that he had said the same thing mine had, because a moment later she stepped forward and bowed.

I followed suit, and together, alone in silence, we walked to the tent, closing the fabric door behind us.

It was then we were alone. We took our places on opposite sides of the low circular table. Between us was a copper tea kettle and the two small floral tea cups. She poured the tea and handed one to me and we both lifted them, placed the cups under our long-flowing face veils to our lips. Heeding my mentor's advice, I did not take a sip. It was a type of tea I had never smelled, but it enticed me. Was it cardamom? Whatever it was, it was just my taste. Which is why it could be a trap.

I lowered the tea cup and placed it on the table, then straightened my back. She did the same. It felt eerily like we were matched but opposing pieces on a chess board, each trying to anticipate the other's move before they made it.

"You don't like the tea?" she said.

Her voice bothered me. Her accent was different than mine, which was to be expected, but the intonation of her voice was the problem. It unsettled me for a reason I couldn't put a finger on.

"No, no. It is delightful, just a bit hot. I'll wait to have more when it cools down," I said.

"Well, I am relieved, Ara. I want you to feel at ease," she said.

I shifted in my chair. Who was chosen as negotiator on either side was a closely guarded secret. Her knowing my name meant a security breach, and she knew I would realize that from her words. She was *trying* to discomfort me to get the upper hand. It was times like these I was grateful for my veil, so she could not see my fear.

"The tea, the atmosphere …. Even this harsh desert is serene. How can I not be at ease?" I lied. "Though, you seem to know my name, and I don't know yours."

"Zayden," she said with what sounded suspiciously like veiled amusement.

She was laughing at me, toying with me! Because she could—because we were losing the war.

"I regret to inform you that we cannot accede to any of your terms. But hopefully, considering the position you are in, you will be understanding and amendable to ours," she said.

207

Rage swelled in my chest and I took a deep breath. I had to get centered. I just had to make this work.

"Now, what position would that be, exactly? We still have many of your territories under occupation. This negotiation is meant to be a matter of give *and* take. I know you came in here with something to give," I said.

"Ara, you seem like a reasonable woman. You know the demands of your government are absurd. I mean, they even asked for the original copy of the Jupiter Scriptures, which has nothing to do with our conflict," Zayden said.

"Well Zayden, actually—"

She interrupted. "Actually Ara, their demands are absurd because they *want* you to fail and you know it," she said.

I thought back to my mentor, and what he had told me. If she was going to be aggressive, if she wasn't going to bend, I didn't have a choice: I couldn't negotiate. I could only be a messenger, but maybe that message could persuade her.

"They want no such thing. We follow the Jupiter Scriptures, word by word, unlike you and your government. We believe in peace and purity, and we also believe in honorable cleansing instead of endless violence," I said, my voice raised more than I intended. She'd rattled me and now she knew it. "Since we do follow the scriptures, we know what's required of us. We know we cannot let this bloodshed persist. If it continues, the world must be renewed—it must be cleansed. Continued bloodshed will contaminate all living beings," I added as definitively as I could.

Zayden leaned forward. "What your government threatens is immoral in every regard and not true to the scriptures."

Her voice wavered slightly, and that was all I needed to hear. She was afraid of our resolve. I had to continue.

"We are a people dedicated to a single divine purpose, and we cannot surrender—we will *not* bend. If we must purify humanity, then we will."

These were not my words; they were my mentor's. I spoke them anyway. What choice did I have? This was what I was instructed to do if the impure would not come to an agreement, but even I recognized that my passionate resolve made me sound more like a crazed zealot than a loyal citizen of my nation, when spoken out loud. *I am doing the right thing, aren't I?*

There was a long moment of silence until we eventually shifted positions, one more nervously, and the other more determinedly, both of us crossing our arms in unison.

I could not help but feel that Zayden was mirroring my physical actions. I know it's the role of a negotiator to try and find equal footing with their counterpart, but this was getting ridiculous. Was she toying with me, even after all I had threatened?

"Why are you toying with me?" Zayden snapped. "Mimicking my movements will not help you in any way."

I was taken aback. "I'm not mimicking *you*. *You* are mimicking *me*. I don't know what game you are playing at, but I don't appreciate it. I came here in good faith for us to try to come to an understanding."

Zayden paused, seeming to consider me seriously for the first time through her veil. "So you've seen it? You know *how* your government is going to 'purify' humanity?" she asked quietly. I could hear the import of her words. Did I also hear pain?

"Of course I have!" I lied. I actually had never seen the process, only heard about it. That it was painless, and quick. It was a humane and honorable death, and it prevented those infected with impure thoughts from contaminating others. Destroying others.

"Then let me show you," she said, then brought the small circular holo-projector out of her robes.

I waved my hand, dismissively. "That won't be necessary. I want to talk about our terms, about coming to an agreement," I said.

She leaned forward even further. "Ara, you are lying and I know it. You have not seen it."

"Now is not the time and the place for—"

Zayden placed the holo-projector between us on the table, beside the teapot, then pressed a button in the middle of it. It quickly projected a life-sized image of a child crying in the air between them.

"What is this?" I exclaimed, frowning.

"What will purify humanity," Zayden responded, voice clipped. "Now watch."

The child was barefaced, with her small chubby hands gripping a white child-sized veil. Her cheeks were red and eyes bright blue. Her hair was beautiful, shoulder length and tightly curled.

"This footage was transmitted from a source in one of our territories that your people occupy," Zayden said.

"How do I know whatever this is isn't a forgery?" I said.

She paused the video. "You are welcome to take the device with you when you leave—ask your techs to analyze the truth of the holo-video for yourself," she said, then pressed the play button on the projector once more, and the image began to move and expand.

The child was wailing, tears streaming down her face. I heard other people screaming in the background. As her distress intensified, I noticed a crimson stain in her eye that then spread to her skin, moving through her veins until it was eating her flesh away, exposing nerves, muscle, bone, until it left nothing behind.

Tears came to my eyes and I looked away, but the wails continued.

"Make it stop," I said, my hands growing clammy.

"Isn't this what you want? To purify humanity?" she asked, fists now clenched. "That child was in *pain*! This isn't honorable! This isn't 'cleansing'—this is murder!"

"That holo-video is a forgery!" I exclaimed, needing it to be true.

The wails stopped, and I made myself look back at the holo-video. All that was left was a small robe and veil. The child was gone.

I sat back in my chair, stunned. Zayden poured more tea into my cup, and then into hers. "On the moons of Jupiter, it is said truth must never be clouded by fear or dogma."

Did my mentor know it wasn't painless? Did he know and never told me? Or maybe this was a forgery to manipulate me. Their choice of negotiator—her voice, her mannerisms. Everything about her seemed off. Too familiar.

Zayden lifted her cup, and I noticed her hand was shaking. I looked down and noticed mine were as well.

A suspicion began to form in my mind. "How were you picked for this mission?"

"Well," she said, raising her veil slightly, then lifting her cup underneath it to take a sip of tea, before continuing. I heard her choke, then slam the cup back on the table, where it shattered. Then I heard her strained intake of breath as she tried to cough up the tea she had inhaled and saw the white veil being sucked into her mouth. She was choking on it!

She started to rock violently side to side, and I rushed to her. I ripped the veil from her face and pounded her back. Her choking stopped and I rubbed her back for a minute while her breathing settled. Then she peered up at me.

I grimaced, my shock hidden behind my own veil. Now I knew why she had known my name. Her people *had* done intel on me. They *had* been prepared for this negotiation.

She was that preparation.

My clone.

Who better to battle wits with me than someone who would know me as intimately as she knew herself?

"What is wrong with you?" she asked, and I realized I was touching her face (my face, in a way) in wonder.

I looked into her eyes. Eyes that perfectly mirrored my own. She didn't know. She really didn't know. It looked like it wasn't just my own mentor who was keeping secrets.

"Were you designed for this negotiation?" I wondered out loud.

Her veil was back in her hand now and she was shaking it out. "Well, in the sense that our people are all trained in our professions from birth—yes. Why?" she asked.

We had been trying to cleanse humanity because our clones—created servants of our empire—had risen up and claimed independence centuries ago. At first, a faction of our ancestors—pure humans—had believed the clones had earned the right to claim independence.

Until they had become a problem. Until they had started encouraging others to question our divine rule.

I studied Zayden carefully. We had long suspected the majority of her nation didn't know of their origins in laboratory test tubes, except for the ruling class, which was why we wanted to retrieve the scriptures stolen from us during the revolution. To prove that *we* were the humans. That *they* were the aberrations—impure. A vermin in the galaxy.

The cleanse was just our way of undoing a failed science experiment.

Or is it murder? The image of the little girl flashed in my head, her screams echoing through my mind. I straightened, reached up and removed the veil from my eyes.

Zayden stood up and screamed, "Why do you have my face?"

I pushed my teacup over to her side of the table. She was going to need it more than me. "Lets talk."

Grave 657

by Mica Scotti Kole

The little robot scurried up to the grave site: a long, concrete tomb with no headstone. He had navigated around this place for the past twenty-one days in order to avoid a [SIGNAL: CROSS RISK]. *He* couldn't manage his tasks around too many other robots, and this grave site had been busy with them.

This same thing happened every now and then, in his memory. Sometimes it was only a week, sometimes a month, where the [SIGNAL: CROSS RISK] persisted above one site or another. Today, though, the little robot only had to contend with one other signal: that of a FlowerBot 2.5E, which was placing a garland of delivery flowers atop the concrete slab.

[QUERY: TASK]?[QUERY: STATUS]? the little robot asked the FlowerBot, as he asked every robot that ever came within collision distance.

[TASK: MOURNING RITUAL, CATHOLIC][STATUS: ONGOING] said the FlowerBot. It crossed itself at the same time it asked the little robot the same question. [QUERY: TASK]?[QUERY: STATUS]?

The little robot answered, [TASK: SANITATION][STATUS: STALLED]. Then silence again as both robots waited sixty seconds. In the meantime, the FlowerBot bowed its head, and though it had no mouth, it relayed a recording:

"I'm going to miss you, Jimmy," said a man's voice, breaking up from emotion and static. "You were a good kid. My little boy. I'll never forget you. May the souls of all the faithful departed, through the mercy of God, rest in peace ..." A sob. "Amen."

The little robot, whose processor was more advanced, counted to sixty slightly faster than the FlowerBot.

[QUERY: TASK]?[QUERY:STATUS]? it asked.

[TASK: MOURNING RITUAL, CATHOLIC][STATUS: COM-PLETE] ... [QUERY: TASK]?[QUERY: STATUS]?

The little robot replied that his task remained sanitation and stalled. Then he stayed in place, idling, for another sixty seconds. By the time he could have asked again, the FlowerBot had gone.

With nothing further within his collision radius, the little robot extracted its legs and began to scrape the refuse off the concrete. Candle wax, handwritten notes of endearment and mourning, photo frames and their contents—even the fresh flowers left by the FlowerBot (flowers were tagged with [REMOVE: ALWAYS]). All of this he disintegrated within his acid reservoir, releasing the byproducts as harmless gas.

He was etching dirt out of the stone's laser-inscription—a name, two years, a dash—when another signal came into his collision radius. He recognized it as a HomeBot 7-R.

[QUERY: TASK]?[QUERY: STATUS]? the little robot inquired.

[TASK1: DELIVERY][TASK2: MOURNING RITUAL, RECORD-ING PLAYBACK][TASK1: ONGOING][TASK2: ONGOING]... [QUE-RY: TASK]?[QUERY: STATUS]? the HomeBot replied.

The little robot dutifully replied in the same way he always had, and he waited patiently while the HomeBot deposited a stuffed pur-ple hippopotamus on the paving. When the HomeBot had gone, the little robot scanned the hippopotamus to check for freshness, as cloth toys were tagged [REMOVE: IF STAINED]. A dark handprint clung to the stomach of the purple hippopotamus, so the little robot retract-ed its claw-like arms and began to pry apart the sewing, disintegrating the stuffing and the fabric in small chunks until nothing was left.

He was just touching up the slots in the edges of the paving—holes which were used by PallBots to lower caskets, grave markers, and other stones into the ground—when yet another robot entered his collision radius. This time the little robot kept working, however, because the signal came from an immobile source—an iWatch 11.

[QUERY: TASK]?[QUERY:STATUS]? he asked the iWatch, out of habit. The iWatch reported a list of ongoing tasks: clock, GPS, call forwarding, and so on. It appeared to be on ultra-power-saver mode, so it did not ask the little robot for its own [QUERY: TASK]?[QUERY: STATUS]?

Thus unthreatened, the little robot continued to clean the Pall-Bot slots in the paving stone as a human woman approached and stood over the grave, the iWatch 11 content on her wrist. She didn't cry or cross herself, nor did she produce any of the typical objects the little robot was used to disintegrating. He finished what he was doing while the human still stood there, and he began to move toward the next grave.

"Wait," the woman said. The little robot analyzed the direction of her voice, and it was aimed at him. He then analyzed whether the words were imperative. They were. So he stopped.

"Sit there for a moment," she told him, kneeling over the grave.

The little robot considered this. [TASK: ORDER OVERRIDE] [ORDER: WAIT][TRANSLATE<MOMENT>][TASK: <WAIT>FIVE MINUTES].

He began counting down as the woman bent over the paving. He processed and analyzed a small buzzing sound, identifying it as a laser, non-commercial grade. It was neither directed at the human, nor himself, and so he processed it and analyzed it endlessly without performing any action in response.

The laser sound stopped twice, and each time the woman bowed her head and her shoulders shook, but he was not trained to analyze human movement which was not directed at him. He tried twice to leave again, but both times she made him stop and wait another [<MOMENT>] until she stood up.

"There," she said. "Clean this grave again. Then go on and do whatever you do."

With that, she pulled her scarf up over her mouth and turned away to walk out of the cemetery. The little robot did as instructed, realigning his daily subtask list to re-include grave number 657. He scanned for any significant sanitation issues, and found a great deal of stone dust at the base of the paving. As he ran over it using his vacuum function, he noted that the paving had been defaced. A small camera poked out of his top-plate and snapped a picture.

[SUBTASK INITIATED: VANDALISM REPORT][STATUS: ANALYSIS]

Carefully, the little robot scanned the words carved into the paving and translated them into a text-based report.

[REPORT: VANDALISM][LOCATION: RICHARDI CEMETERY <GRAVE NUMBER: 657>][VANDALISM TYPE: GRAFFITI, STONE ETCHING][VANDALISM TEXT: I HOPE THE HIPPOS ARE PURPLE IN HEAVEN. MISS YOU ALWAYS.—AUNTIE.].

Then the little robot finished with all the stone dust, and he moved on to grave 658.

Against the Current

by Robert Silverberg

About half past four in the afternoon Rackman felt a sudden red blaze of pain in both his temples at once, the sort of stabbing jab that you would expect to feel if a narrow metal spike had been driven through your head. It was gone as quickly as it had come, but it left him feeling queasy and puzzled and a little frightened, and, since things were slow at the dealership just then anyway, he decided it might be best to call it a day and head for home.

He stepped out into perfect summer weather, a sunny, cloudless day, and headed across the lot to look for Gene, his manager, who had been over by the SUVs making a tally of the leftovers. But Gene was nowhere in sight. The only person Rackman saw out there was a pudgy salesman named Freitas, who so far as he recalled had given notice a couple of weeks ago. Evidently he wasn't gone yet, though.

"I'm not feeling so good and I'm going home early," Rackman announced. "If Gene's around here somewhere, will you tell him that?"

"Sure thing, Mr. Rackman."

Rackman circled around the edge of the lot toward the staff parking area. He still felt queasy, and somewhat muddled too, with a slight headache lingering after that sudden weird stab of pain. Everything seemed just a bit askew. The SUVs, for instance—there were more of the things than there should be, considering that he had just run a big clearance on them. They were lined up like a whopping great phalanx of tanks. How come so many? He filed away a mental note to ask Gene about that tomorrow.

He turned the ignition key and the sleek silver Prius glided smoothly, silently, out of the lot, off to the nearby freeway entrance. By the time he reached the Caldecott Tunnel twenty minutes later the last traces of the pain in his temple were gone, and he moved on easily through Oakland toward the bridge and San Francisco across the bay.

At the Bay Bridge toll plaza they had taken down all the overhead signs that denoted the FasTrak lanes. That was odd, he thought. Probably one of their mysterious maintenance routines.

Rackman headed into his usual lane anyway, but there was a toll-taker in the booth—why?—and as he started to roll past the man toward the FasTrak scanner just beyond he got such an incandescent glare from him that he braked to a halt.

The FasTrak toll scanner wasn't where it should be, right back of the tollbooth on the left. It wasn't there at all.

Feeling a little bewildered now, Rackman pulled a five-dollar bill from his wallet, handed it to the man, got what seemed to be too many singles in change, and drove out onto the bridge. There was very little traffic. As he approached the Treasure Island tunnel, though, it struck him that he couldn't remember having seen any of the towering construction cranes that ran alongside the torso of the not-quite-finished new bridge just north of the old one. Nor was there any sign of them—or any trace of the new bridge itself, for that matter, when he glanced into his rearview mirror.

This is peculiar, Rackman thought. Really, really peculiar.

On the far side of the tunnel the sky was darker, as though dusk were already descending—at 5:10 on a summer day?—and by the time he was approaching the San Francisco end of the bridge the light was all but gone. Even stranger, a little rain was starting to come down. Rain falls in the Bay Area in August about once every twenty years. The morning forecast hadn't said anything about rain. Rackman's hand trembled a little as he turned his wipers on. I am having what could be called a waking dream, Rackman thought, some very vivid hallucination, and when I'm off the bridge I better pull over and take a few deep breaths.

The skyline of the city just ahead of him looked somehow diminished, as though a number of the bigger buildings were missing. And the exit ramps presented more puzzles. A lot of stuff that had been torn down for the retro-fitting of the old bridge seemed to have been put back in place. He couldn't find his Folsom Street off-ramp, but the long-gone Main Street one, which they had closed after the 1989 earthquake, lay right in front of him. He took it and pulled the Prius to curbside as soon as he was down at street level. The rain had stopped—the streets were dry, as if the rain had never been—but the air seemed clinging and clammy, not like dry summer air at all. It enfolded him, contained him in a strange tight grip. His cheeks were flushed and he was perspiring heavily.

Deep breaths, yes. Calm. Calm. You're only five blocks from your condo.

Only he wasn't. Most of the high-rise office buildings were missing, all right, and none of the residential towers south of the off-ramp complex were there, just block after block of parking lots and some ramshackle warehouses. It was night now, and the empty neighborhood was almost completely dark. Everything was the way it had looked around here fifteen, twenty years before. His bewilderment was beginning to turn into terror. The street signs said that he was at his own corner. So where was the thirty-story building where he lived?

Better call Jenny, he thought.

He would tell her—delicately—that he was going through something very baffling, a feeling of, well, disorientation, that in fact he was pretty seriously mixed up, that she had better come get him and take him home.

But his cell phone didn't seem to be working. All he got was a dull buzzing sound. He looked at it, stunned. He felt as though some part of him had been amputated.

Rackman was angry now as well as frightened. Things like this weren't supposed to happen to him. He was fifty-seven years old, healthy, solvent, a solid citizen, owner of a thriving Toyota dealership across the bay, married to a lovely and loving woman. Everyone said he looked ten years younger than he really was. He worked out three times a week and ran in the Bay-to-Breakers race every year and once in a while he even did a marathon. But the drive across the bridge had been all wrong and he didn't know where his condo building had gone and his cell phone was on the fritz, and here he was lost in this dark forlorn neighborhood of empty lots and abandoned warehouses with a wintry wind blowing—hey, hadn't it been sticky and humid a few minutes ago?—on what had started out as a summer day. And he had the feeling that things were going to get worse before they got better. If indeed they got better at all.

He swung around and drove toward Union Square. Traffic was surprisingly light for downtown San Francisco. He spotted a phone booth, parked nearby, fumbled a coin into the slot, and dialed his number. The phone made ugly noises and a robot voice told him that the number he had dialed was not a working number. Cursing, Rackman tried again, tapping the numbers in with utmost care. "We're sorry," the voice said again, "the number you have reached is not—"

A telephone book dangled before him. He riffled through it—Jenny had her own listing, under Burke—but though half a dozen J Burkes were in the book, five of them lived in the wrong part of town, and when he dialed the sixth number, which had no address listed, an answering machine responded in a birdlike chirping voice that certainly wasn't Jenny's. Something led him then to look for his own listing. No, that wasn't there either. A curious calmness came over him at that discovery. There were no FasTrak lanes at the toll plaza, and the dismantled freeway ramps were still here, and the neighborhood where he lived hadn't been developed yet, and neither he nor Jenny was listed in the San Francisco phone book, and therefore either he had gone seriously crazy or else somehow this had to be fifteen or even twenty years ago, which was pretty much just another way of saying the same thing. If this really is fifteen or twenty years ago, Rackman thought, then Jenny would be living in Sacramento and I'd be across the bay in El Cerrito and still married to Helene. But what the hell kind of thing was that to be thinking, *If this really is fifteen or twenty years ago?*

He considered taking himself to the nearest emergency room and telling them he was having a breakdown, but he knew that once he put himself in the hands of the medics, there'd be no extricating himself: they'd subject him to a million tests, reports would be filed with this agency and that, his driver's license might be yanked, bad things would happen to his credit rating. It would be much smarter, he thought, to check himself into a hotel room, take a shower, rest, try to figure all this out, wait for things to get back to normal.

Rackman headed for the Hilton, a couple of blocks away. Though night had fallen just a little while ago, the sun was high overhead now, and the weather had changed again, too: it was sharp and cool, autumn just shading into winter. He was getting a different season and a different time of day every fifteen minutes or so, it seemed. The Hilton desk clerk, tall and balding and starchy-looking, had such a self-important manner that as Rackman requested a room he felt a little abashed at not having any luggage with him, but the clerk didn't appear to give a damn about that, simply handed him the registration form and asked him for his credit card. Rackman put his Visa down on the counter and began to fill out the form.

"Sir?" the desk clerk said, after a moment.

Rackman looked up. The clerk was staring at his credit card. It was the translucent kind, and he tipped it this way and that, puzzledly holding it against the light. "Problem?" Rackman asked, and the clerk muttered something about how unusual the card looked.

Then his expression darkened. "Wait just a second," he said, very coldly now, and tapped the imprinted expiration date on the card. "What is *this* supposed to be? Expires July 2010? *2010*, sir? *2010*? Are we having a little joke, sir?" He flipped the card across the counter at Rackman the way he might have done if it had been covered with some noxious substance.

Another surge of terror hit him. He backed away, moving quickly through the lobby and into the street. Of course he might have tried to pay cash, he supposed, but the room would surely be something like $225 a night, and he had only about $350 on him. If his credit card was useless, he'd need to hang on to his cash at least until he understood what was happening to him. Instead of the Hilton, he would go to some cheaper place, perhaps one of the motels up on Lombard Street.

On his way back to his car Rackman glanced at a newspaper in a sidewalk rack. President Reagan was on the front page, under a headline about the invasion of Grenada. The date on the paper was Wednesday, October 26, 1983. Sure, he thought. 1983. This hallucination isn't missing a trick. I am in 1983 and Reagan is president again, with 1979 just up the road, 1965, 1957, 1950—

In 1950 Rackman hadn't even been born yet. He wondered what was going to happen to him when he got back to a time earlier than his own birth.

He stopped at the first motel on Lombard that had a VACAN-CY sign and registered for a room. The price was only $75, but when he put two fifties down on the counter, the clerk, a pleasant, smiling Latino woman, gave him a pleasant smile and tapped her finger against the swirls of pink coloration next to President Grant's portrait. "Somebody has stuck you with some very funny bills, sir. But you know that I can't take them. If you can pay by credit card, though, Visa, American Express—"

Of course she couldn't take them. Rackman remembered, now, that all the paper money had changed five or ten years back, new designs, bigger portraits, distinctive patches of pink or blue ink on their front sides that had once been boringly monochromatic. And these bills of his had the tiny date "2004" in the corner.

So far as the world of 1983 was concerned, the money he was carrying was nothing but play money.

1983.

Jenny, who is up in Sacramento in 1983 and has no idea yet that he even exists, had been twenty-five that year. Already he was more than twice her age. And she would get younger and younger as he went ever onward, if that was what was going to continue to happen.

Maybe it wouldn't. Soon, perhaps, the pendulum would begin to swing the other way, carrying him back to his own time, to his own life. What if it didn't, though? What if it just kept on going?

In that case, Rackman thought, Jenny was lost to him, with everything that had bound them together now unhappened. Rackman reached out suddenly, grasping the air as though reaching for Jenny, but all he grasped was air. There was no Jenny for him any longer. He had lost her, yes. And he would lose everything else of what he had thought of as his life as well, his whole past peeling away strip by strip. He had no reason to think that the pendulum *would* swing back. Already the exact details of Jenny's features were blurring in his mind. He struggled to recall them: the quizzical blue eyes, the slender nose, the wide, generous mouth, the slim, supple body. She seemed to be drifting past him in the fog, caught in an inexorable current carrying her ever farther away.

✧ ✧ ✧

He slept in his car that night, up by the Marina, where he hoped no one would bother him. No one did. Morning light awakened him after a few hours—his wristwatch said it was 9:45 p.m. on the same August day when all this had started, but he knew better now than to regard what his watch told him as having any meaning— and when he stepped outside the day was dry and clear, with a blue summer sky overhead and the sort of harsh wind blowing that only San Francisco can manage on a summer day. He was getting used to the ever-changing weather by now, though, the swift parade of seasons tumbling upon him one after another. Each new one would hold him for a little while in that odd *enclosed* way, but then it would release its grasp and nudge him onward into the next one.

He checked the newspaper box on the corner. *San Francisco Chronicle*, Tuesday, May 1, 1973. Big front-page story: Nixon dismisses White House counsel John Dean and accepts the resignations of aides John Ehrlichman and H.R. Haldeman. Right, he thought. Dean, Ehrlichman, Haldeman: Watergate. So a whole decade had vanished while he slept. He had slipped all the way back to 1973. He wasn't even surprised. He had entered some realm beyond all possibility of surprise.

Taking out his wallet, Rackman checked his driver's license. Still the same, expires 03-11-11, photo of his familiar fifty-something face. His car was still a silver 2009 Prius. Certain things hadn't changed. But the Prius stood out like a shriek among the other parked cars, every last one of them some clunky-looking old model of the kind that he dimly remembered from his youth. What we have here is 1973, he thought. Probably not for long, though.

He hadn't had anything to eat since lunchtime, ten hours and thirty-five years ago. He drove over to Chestnut Street, marveling at the quiet old-fashioned look of all the shop fronts, and parked right outside Joe's, which he knew had been out of business since maybe the Clinton years. There were no parking meters on the street. Rackman ordered a salad, a Joe's Special, and a glass of red wine, and paid for it with a ten-dollar bill of the old black-and-white kind that he happened to have. Meal plus wine, $8.50, he thought. That sounded about right for this long ago. It was a very consistent kind of hallucination. He left a dollar tip.

Rackman remembered pretty well what he had been doing in the spring of 1973. He was twenty-two that year, out of college almost a year, working in Cody's Books on Telegraph Avenue in Berkeley while waiting to get into law school, for which he had been turned down the first time around but which he had high hopes of entering that autumn. He and Al Mortenson, another young Cody's clerk—nice steady guy, easy to get along with—were rooming together in a little upstairs apartment on Dana, two or three blocks from the bookshop.

What ever had happened to old Al? Rackman had lost touch with him many years back. A powerful urge seized him now to drive across to Berkeley and look for him. He hadn't spoken with anyone except those two hotel clerks since he had left the car lot, what felt like a million years ago, and a terrible icy loneliness was beginning to settle over him as he went spinning onward through his constantly unraveling world. He needed to reach out to someone, anyone, for whatever help he could find. Al might be a good man to consult. Al was level-headed; Al was unflusterable; Al was *steady*. What about driving over to Berkeley now and looking for Al at the Dana Street place? —"I know you don't recognize me, Al, but I'm actually Phil Rackman, only I'm from 2008, and I'm having some sort of bad trip and I need to sit down in a quiet place with a good friend like you and figure out what's going on." Rackman wondered what that would accomplish. Probably nothing, but at least it might provide him with half an hour of companionship, sympathy, even understanding. At worst Al would think he was a lunatic and he would wind up under sedation at Alta Bates Hospital while they tried to find his next of kin. If he really was sliding constantly backward in time he would slip away from Alta Bates too, Rackman thought, and if not, if he was simply unhinged, maybe a hospital was where he belonged.

He went to Berkeley. The season drifted back from spring to late winter while he was crossing the bridge: in Berkeley the acacias were in bloom, great clusters of golden yellow flowers, and that was a January thing. The sight of Berkeley in early 1973, a year that had in fact been the last gasp of the Sixties, gave him a shiver: the Day-Glo rock-concert posters on all the walls, the flower-child costumes, the huge, bizarre helmets of shaggy hair that everyone was wearing. The streets were strangely clean, hardly any litter, no graffiti. It all was like a movie set, a careful, loving reconstruction of the era. He had no business being here. He was entirely out of place. And yet he had lived here once. This street belonged to his own past. He had lost Jenny, he had lost his nice condominium, he had lost his car dealership, but other things that he had thought were lost, like this Day-Glo tie-dyed world of his youth, were coming back to him. Only they weren't coming back for long, he knew. One by one they would present themselves, tantalizing flashes of a returning past, and then they'd go streaming onward, lost to him like everything else, lost for a second and terribly final time.

He guessed from the position of the pale winter sun, just coming up over the hills to the east, that the time was eight or nine in the morning. If so, Al would probably still be at home. The Dana Street place looked just as Rackman remembered it, a tidy little frame building, the landlady's tiny but immaculate garden of pretty succulents out front, the redwood deck, the staircase on the side that led to the upstairs apartment. As he started upward an unsettling burst of panic swept through him at the possibility that he might be going to come face to face with his own younger self. But in a moment his trepidation passed. It wouldn't happen, he told himself. It was just *too* impossible. There had to be a limit to this thing somewhere.

A kid answered his knock, sleepy-looking and impossibly young, a tall lanky guy in jeans and a t-shirt, with a long oval face almost completely engulfed in an immense spherical mass of jet-black hair that covered his forehead and his cheeks and his chin, a wild woolly tangle that left only eyes and nose and lips visible. A golden peace-symbol amulet dangled on a silver chain around his neck. My God, Rackman thought, this really is the Al I knew in 1973. Like a ghost out of time. But *I* am the ghost. *I* am the ghost.

"Yes?" the kid at the door said vaguely.

"Al Mortenson, right?"

"Yes." He said it in an uneasy way, chilly, distant, grudging.

What the hell, some unknown elderly guy at the door, an utter stranger wanting God only knew what, eight or nine in the morning: even the unflappable Al might be a little suspicious. Rackman saw no option but to launch straight into his story. "I realize this is going to sound very strange to you. But I ask you to bear with me. Do I look in any way familiar to you, Al?"

He wouldn't, naturally. He was much stockier than the Phil Rackman of 1973, his full-face beard was ancient history and his once-luxurious russet hair was close-cropped and gray, and he was wearing a checked suit of the kind that nobody, not even a middle-aged man, would have worn in 1973. But he began to speak, quietly, earnestly, intensely, persuasively, his best one-foot-in-the-door salesman approach, the approach he might have used if he had been trying to sell his biggest model SUV to a frail old lady from the Rossmoor retirement home. Starting off by casually mentioning Al's roommate Phil Rackman—"he isn't here, by any chance, is he?"—no, he wasn't, thank God—and then asking Al once again to prepare himself for a very peculiar tale indeed, giving him no chance to reply, and swiftly and smoothly working around to the notion that he himself was Phil Rackman, not Phil's father but the actual Phil Rackman who been his roommate back in 1973, only in fact he was the Phil Rackman of the year 2008 who had without warning become caught up in what could only be described as an inexplicable toboggan-slide backward across time.

Even through that forest of facial hair Al's reactions were readily discernible: puzzlement at first, then annoyance verging on anger, then a show of curiosity, a flicker of interest at the possibility of such a wild thing—hey, man, far out! Cool!—and then, gradually, gradually, gradually bringing himself to the tipping point, completing the transition from skepticism verging on hostility to mild curiosity to fascination to stunned acceptance, as Rackman began to conjure up remembered episodes of their shared life that only he could have known. That time in the summer of '72 when he and Al and their current girlfriends had gone camping in the Sierra and had been happily screwing away on a flat, smooth granite outcropping next to a mountain stream in what they thought was total seclusion, 8,000 feet above sea level, when a wide-eyed party of Boy Scouts came marching past them down the trail; and that long-legged girl from Oregon Rackman had picked up one weekend who turned out to be double-jointed, or whatever, and showed them both the most amazing sexual tricks; and the great moment when they and some friends had scored half a pound of hash and gave a party that lasted three days running without time out for sleep; and the time when he and Al had hitchhiked down to Big Sur, he with big, cuddly Ginny Beardsley and Al with hot little Nikki Rosenzweig, during Easter break, and the four of them had dropped a little acid and gone absolutely gonzo berserk together in a secluded redwood grove—

"No," Al said. "That hasn't happened yet. Easter is still three months away. And I don't know any Nikki Rosenzweig."

Rackman rolled his eyes lasciviously. "You will, kiddo. Believe me, you will! Ginny will introduce you, and—and—"

"So you even know my own future."

"For me it isn't the future," Rackman said. "It's the long-ago past. When you and I were rooming together right here on Dana Street and having the time of our lives."

"But how is this possible?"

"You think I know, old pal? All I know is that it's happening. I'm me, really me, sliding backward in time. It's the truth. Look at my face, Al. Run a computer simulation in your mind, if you can—hell, people don't have their own computers yet, do they?—well, just try to age me up, in your imagination, gray hair, more weight, but the same nose, Al, the same mouth—" He shook his head. "Wait a second. Look at this." He drew out his driver's license and thrust it at the other man. "You see the name? The photo? You see the birthdate? *You see the expiration date?* March 2011? Here, look at these fifty-dollar bills! The dates on them. This credit card, this Visa. Do you even know what a Visa is? Did we have them back in 1973?"

"Christ," Al said, in a husky, barely audible whisper. "Jesus Christ, Phil. —It's okay if I call you Phil, right?"

"Phil, yes."

"Look, Phil—" That same thin ghostly whisper, the voice of a man in shock. Rackman had never, in the old days, seen Al this badly shaken up. "The bookstore's about to open. I've got to get to work. You come in, wait here, make yourself at home." Then a little manic laugh: "You *are* at home, aren't you? In a manner of speaking. So wait here. Rest. Relax. Smoke some of my dope, if you want. You probably know where I keep it. Meet me at Cody's at one, and we can go out to lunch and talk about all this, okay? I want to know all about it. What year did you say you came from? 2011?"

"2008."

"2008. Christ, this is so wild!—You'll stay here, then?"

"And if my younger self walks in on me?"

"Don't worry. You're safe. He's in Los Angeles this week."

"Groovy," Rackman said, wondering if anyone still said things like that. "Go on, then. Go to work. I'll see you later."

The two rooms, Al's and his own just across the hall, were like museum exhibits: the posters for Fillmore West concerts, the antique stereo set and the stack of LP records, the tie-dyed shirts and bell-bottom pants scattered in the corner, the bong on the dresser, the macramé wall hangings, the musty aroma of last night's incense. Rackman poked around, lost in dreamy nostalgia and at times close to tears as he looked at this artifact of that ancient era and that one, *The Teachings of Don Juan, The White Album, The Whole Earth Catalog.* His own copies. He still had the Castaneda book somewhere; he remembered the beer stain on the cover. He peered into the dresser drawer where Al kept his stash, scooped up a pinch of it in his fingers and sniffed it, smiled, put it back. It was years since he had smoked. Decades.

He ran his hand over his cheek. His stubble was starting to bother him. He hadn't shaved since yesterday morning on Rackman body time. He knew there'd be a shaver in the bathroom, though—he was pretty sure he had left it there even after he began growing his Seventies beard—and, yes, there was his old Norelco three-headed job. He felt better with clean cheeks. Rackman stuffed the shaver into his inside jacket pocket, knowing he'd want it in the days ahead.

Then he found himself wondering whether he had parked in a tow-away zone. They had always been very tough about illegally parked cars in Berkeley. You could try to assassinate the president and get off with a six-month sentence, but God help you if you parked in a tow-away zone. And if they took his car away, he'd be in an even worse pickle than he already was. The car was his one link to the world he had left behind, his time capsule, his home, now, actually.

The car was still where he had left it. But he was afraid to leave it for long. It might slip away from him in the next time-shift. He got in, thinking to wait in it until it was time to meet Al for lunch. But although it was still just mid-morning he felt drowsiness overcoming him, and almost instantly he dozed off. When he awakened he saw that it was dark outside. He must have slept the day away. The dashboard clock told him it was 1:15 p.m., but that was useless, meaningless. Probably it was early evening, too late for lunch with Al. Maybe they could have dinner instead.

On the way over to the bookstore, marveling every step of the way at the utter weirdness of everybody he passed in the streets, the strange beards, the flamboyant globes of hair, the gaudy clothing, Rackman began to see that it would be very embarrassing to tell Al that he had grown up to own a suburban automobile dealership. He had planned to become a legal advocate for important social causes, or perhaps a public defender, or an investigator of corporate malfeasance. Everybody had noble plans like that, back then. Going into the car business hadn't been on anyone's screen.

Then he saw that he didn't have to tell Al anything about what he had come to do for a living. It was a long story and not one that Al was likely to find interesting. Al wouldn't care that he had become a car dealer. Al was sufficiently blown away by the mere fact that his former roommate Phil Rackman had dropped in on him out of the future that morning.

He entered the bookstore and spotted Al over near the cash register. But when he waved he got only a blank stare in return.

"I'm sorry I missed our lunch date, Al. I guess I just nodded off. It's been a pretty tiring day for me, you know."

There was no trace of recognition on Al's face.

"Sir? There must be some mistake."

"Al Mortenson? Who lives on Dana Street?"

"I'm Al Mortenson, yes. I live in Bowles Hall, though."

Bowles Hall was a campus dormitory. Undergraduates lived there. This Al hadn't graduated yet.

This Al's hair was different too, Rackman saw now. A tighter cut, more disciplined, more forehead showing. And his beard was much longer, cascading down over his chest, hiding the peace symbol. He might have had a haircut during the day but he couldn't have grown four inches more of beard.

There was a stack of newspapers on the counter next to the register, the *New York Times*. Rackman flicked a glance at the top one. *November 10, 1971.*

I haven't just slept away the afternoon, Rackman thought. I've slept away all of 1972. He and Al hadn't rented the Dana Street place until after graduation, in June of '72.

Fumbling, trying to recover, always the nice helpful guy, Al said, "You aren't Mr. Chesley, are you? Bud Chesley's father?"

Bud Chesley had been a classmate of theirs, a jock, big, broad-shouldered. The main thing that Rackman remembered about him was that he had been one of about six men on campus who were in favor of the war in Vietnam. Rackman seemed to recall that in his senior year Al had roomed with Chesley in Bowles, before he and Al had known each other.

"No," Rackman said leadenly. "I'm not Mr. Chesley. I'm really sorry to have bothered you."

So it was hopeless, then. He had suspected it all along, but now, feeling the past tugging at him as he hurried back to his car, it was certain. The slippage made any sort of human interaction lasting more than half an hour or so impossible to sustain. He struggled with it, trying to tug back, to hold fast against the sliding, hoping that perhaps he could root himself somehow in the present and then begin the climb forward again until he reached the place where he belonged. But he could feel the slippage continuing, not at any consistent rate but in sudden unpredictable bursts, and there was nothing he could do about it. There were times when he was completely unaware of it until it had happened and other times when he could see the seasons rocketing right by in front of his eyes.

Without any particular destination in mind Rackman returned to his car, wandered around Berkeley until he found himself heading down Ashby Avenue to the freeway, and drove back into San Francisco. The toll was only a quarter. Astonishing. The cars around him on the bridge all seemed like collector's items, with yellow-and-black license plates, three digits, three letters. He wondered what a highway patrolman would say about his own plates, if he recognized them as California plates at all.

Halfway across the bridge Rackman turned the radio on, hoping the car might be able to pick up a news broadcast out of 2008, but no, no, when he got KCBS he heard the announcer talking about President Johnson, Secretary of State Rusk, Vietnam, Israel refusing to give back Jerusalem after the recent war with the Arab countries, Dr. Martin Luther King calling for calm following a night of racial strife in Hartford, Connecticut. It was hard to remember some of the history exactly, but Rackman knew that Dr. King had been assassinated in 1968, so he figured that just in the course of crossing the bridge he probably had slid back into 1967 or even 1966. He had been in high school then. All the sweaty anguish of that whole lunatic era came swimming back into his mind, the Robert Kennedy assassination too, the body counts on the nightly news, Malcolm X, peace marches, the strident 1968 political convention in Chicago, the race riots, Nixon, Hubert Humphrey, Mao Tse-tung, spacemen in orbit around the moon, Lady Bird Johnson, Cassius Clay. *Hey hey hey, LBJ, how many kids did you kill today?* The noise, the hard-edged excitement, the daily anxiety. It felt like the Pleistocene to him now. But he had driven right into the thick of it.

The slippage continued. The long hair went away, the granny glasses, the Day-Glo posters, the tie-dyed clothes. John F. Kennedy came and went in reverse. Night and day seemed to follow one another in random sequence. Rackman ate his meals randomly too, no idea whether it was breakfast or lunch or dinner that he needed. He had lost all track of personal time. He caught naps in his car, kept a low profile, said very little to anyone. A careless restaurant cashier took one of his gussied-up fifties without demur and gave him a stack of spendable bills in change. He doled those bills out parsimoniously, watching what he spent even though meals, like the bridge toll, like the cost of a newspaper, like everything else back here, were astoundingly cheap, a nickel or a dime for this, fifty cents for that.

San Francisco was smaller, dingier, a little old 1950s-style town, no trace of the high-rise buildings now. Everything was muted, old-fashioned, the simpler, more innocent textures of his childhood. He half expected it all to be in black and white, as an old newsreel would be, and perhaps to flicker a little. But he took in smells, breezes, sounds, that no newsreel could have captured. This wasn't any newsreel and it wasn't any hallucination, either. This was the world itself, dense, deep, real. All too real, unthinkably real. And there was no place for him in it.

Men wore hats, women's coats had padded shoulders. Shop windows sparkled. There was a Christmas bustle in the streets. A little while later, though, the sky brightened and the dry, cold winds of San

Francisco summer came whistling eastward at him again out of the Pacific, and then, presto jingo, the previous winter's rainy season was upon him. He wondered which year's winter it was.

It was 1953, the newspaper told him. The corner newspaper rack was his only friend. It provided him with guidance, information about his present position in time. That was Eisenhower on the front page. The Korean war was still going on, here in 1953. And Stalin: Stalin had just died. Rackman remembered Eisenhower, the president of his childhood, kindly old Ike. Truman's bespectacled face would be next. Rackman had been born during Truman's second term. He had no recollection of the Truman presidency but he could recall the salty old Harry of later years, who went walking every day, gabbing with reporters about anything that came into his head.

What is going to happen to me, Rackman wondered, when I get back past my own birthdate?

Maybe he would come to some glittering gateway, a giant sizzling special effect throwing off fireworks across the whole horizon, with a blue-white sheen of nothingness stretching into infinity beyond it. And when he passed through it he would disappear into oblivion and that would be that. He'd find out soon enough. He couldn't be much more than a year or two away from the day of his birth.

Without knowing or caring where he was going Rackman began to drive south out of San Francisco, the poky little San Francisco of this far-off day, heading out of town on what once had been Highway 101, the freeway that led to the airport and San Jose and, eventually, Los Angeles. It wasn't a freeway now, just an oddly charming little four-lane road. The billboards that lined it on both sides looked like ads from old National Geographics. The curving rows of small ticky-tacky houses on the hillsides hadn't been built yet. There was almost nothing except open fields everywhere, down here south of the city. The ballpark wasn't there—the Giants still played in New York in this era, he recalled—and when he went past the airport, he almost failed to notice it, it was such a piffling little small-town place. Only when a DC-3 passed overhead like a huge droning mosquito did he realize that that collection of tin sheds over to the left was what would one day be SFO.

Rackman knew that he was still slipping and slipping as he went, that the pace of slippage seemed to be picking up, that if that glittering gateway existed he had already gone beyond it. He was somewhere near 1945 now or maybe even earlier—they were honking at his car on the road in amazement, as though it was a spaceship that had dropped down from Mars—and now a clear, cold understanding of what was in store for him was growing in his mind.

He wouldn't disappear through any gateway. It didn't matter that he hadn't been born yet in the year he was currently traveling through, because he wasn't growing any younger as he drifted backward. And the deep past waited for him. He saw that he would just go endlessly onward, cut loose from the restraints that time imposed, drifting on and on back into antiquity. While he was driving southward, heading for San Jose or Los Angeles or wherever it was that he might be going next, the years would roll along backward, the twentieth century would be gobbled up in the nineteenth, California's great cities would melt away—he had already seen that happening in San Francisco—and the whole state would revert to the days of Mexican rule, a bunch of little villages clustered around the Catholic missions, and then the villages and the missions would disappear too. A day or two later for him, California would be an emptiness, nobody here but simple Indian tribes. Farther to the east, in the center of the continent, great herds of bison would roam. Still farther east would be the territory of the Thirteen Colonies, gradually shriveling back into tiny pioneering settlements and then vanishing also.

Well, he thought, if he could get himself across the country quickly enough, he might be able to reach New York City—Nieuw Amsterdam, it would probably be by then—while it still existed. There he might be able to arrange a voyage across to Europe before the continent reverted entirely to its pre-Columbian status. But what then? All that he could envisage was a perpetual journey backward, backward, ever backward: the Renaissance, the Dark Ages, Rome, Greece, Babylon, Egypt, the Ice Age. A couple of summers ago he and Jenny had taken a holiday in France, down in the Dordogne, where they had looked at the painted caves of the Cro-Magnon men, the colorful images of bulls and bison and spotted horses and mammoths. No one knew what those pictures meant, why they had been painted. Now he would go back and find out at first hand the answer to the enigmas of the prehistoric caves. How very cool that sounded, how interesting, a nice fantasy, except that if you gave it half a second's thought it was appalling. To whom would he impart that knowledge? What good would it do him, or anyone?

The deep past was waiting for him, yes. But would he get there? Even a Prius wasn't going to make it all the way across North America on a single tank of gas, and soon there weren't going to be any gas stations, and even if there were he would have no valid money to pay for gas, or food, or anything else. Pretty soon there would be no roads, either. He couldn't *walk* to New York. In that wilderness he wouldn't last three days.

He had kept himself in motion up until this moment, staying just ahead of the vast gray grimness that was threatening to invade his soul, but it was catching up with him now. Rackman went through ten or fifteen minutes that might have been the darkest, bleakest moments of his life. Then—was it something about the sweet simplicity of this little road, no longer the roaring Highway 101 but now just a dusty, narrow two-laner with hardly any traffic?—there came an unexpected change in his mood. He grew indifferent to his fate. In an odd way he found himself actually welcoming whatever might come. The prospect before him looked pretty terrifying, yes. But it might just be exciting, too. He had liked his life, he had liked it very much, but it had been torn away from him, he knew not how or why. This was his life now. He had no choice about that. The best thing to do, Rackman thought, was to take it one century at a time and try to enjoy the ride.

What he needed right now was a little breather: come to a halt if only for a short while, pause and regroup. Stop and pass the time, so to speak, as he got himself ready for the next phase of his new existence. He pulled over by the side of the road and turned off the ignition and sat there quietly, thinking about nothing at all.

After a while a youngish man on a motorcycle pulled up alongside him. The motorcycle was hardly more than a souped-up bike. The man was wearing a khaki blouse and khaki trousers, all pleats and flounces, a very old-fashioned outfit, something like a scoutmaster's uniform. He himself had an old-fashioned look, too, dark hair parted in the middle like an actor in a silent movie.

Then Rackman noticed the California Highway Patrol badge on the man's shoulder. He opened the car window. The patrolman leaned toward him and gave him an earnest smile, a Boy Scout smile. Even the smile was old-fashioned. You couldn't help believing the sincerity of it. "Is there any difficulty, sir? May I be of any assistance?"

So polite, so formal. *Sir.* Everyone had been calling him *sir* since this trip had started, the desk clerks, the people in restaurants, Al Mortenson, and now this CHP man. So respectful, everybody was, back here in prehistory.

"No," Rackman said. "No problem. Everything's fine."

The patrolman didn't seem to hear him. He had turned his complete attention to Rackman's car itself, the glossy silver Prius, the car out of the future. The look of it was apparently sinking in for the first time. He was staring at the car in disbelief, in befuddlement, in unconcealed jaw-sagging awe, gawking at its fluid streamlined shape, at its gleaming futuristic dashboard. Then he turned back to Rackman himself, taking in the look of his clothing, his haircut, his checked jacket, his patterned shirt. The man's eyes seemed to glaze. Rackman knew that there had to be something about his whole appearance that seemed as wrong to the patrolman as the patrolman's did to him. He could see the man working to get himself under control. The car must have him completely flummoxed, Rackman thought. The patrolman began to say something but it was a moment before he could put his voice in gear. Then he said, hoarsely, like a rusty automaton determined to go through its routine no matter what, "I want you to know, sir, that if you are having any problem with your—ah—your car, we are here to assist you in whatever way we can."

To assist you. That was a good one.

Rackman managed a faint smile. "Thanks, but the car's okay," he said. "And I'm okay too. I just stopped off here to rest a bit, that's all. I've got a long trip ahead of me." He reached for the ignition key. Silently, smoothly, the Prius floated forward into the morning light and the night that would quickly follow it and into the random succession of springs and winters and autumns and summers beyond, forward into the mysteries, dark and dreadful and splendid, that lay before him.

Echoes of Gliese

The two ships inside the Maternity Bay looked nothing alike. Gideon Roe's starship, *Nergüi*, looked like a giant caterpillar. Her hull arched slightly in her center, and her neat rows of gravity claws wriggled as gracefully as a swimmer treading water. But there was nothing caterpillar-like about her newborn starship, *Pai*. During gestation, *Pai*'s exoskeleton had shattered. The cartilage overlapped and then refused. By the time she was born two hours ago, *Pai* looked more like a crushed beetle than a caterpillar. Yes, she was ugly. But Gideon would be damned if he'd see her killed.

Gideon stepped away from the observation window in the director's office and shook his head. "I've heard enough. She'll be fine."

Raj Patel, director of the station's Organic Starship Health Facility, glared at Gideon through horn-rimmed glasses and a plume of salt-and-pepper eyebrows. "Mr. Roe, be reasonable. No amount of care can help *Pai*. For her own good, she must be euthanized."

Gideon bristled. The word *euthanasia* was coined by PhDs like Patel so they didn't have to think of themselves as murderers. But Gideon knew better. "No. End of discussion." He nodded curtly and made for the door.

Director Patel spoke into the comm. "Starship *Nergüi*, what do you have to say?"

"*Nergüi* is with me," Gideon said. He'd been *Nergüi*'s captain for ten years; he spoke for both of them.

The intercom crackled, translating *Nergüi*'s neuro-pulses into a digital voice. "Please help my baby. If she cannot be healed, then please end her suffering."

Nergüi's words sucked the air out of Gideon's lungs. This felt like Gliese all over again. Following the eruptions on the planet Gliese-832c, the doctors had recklessly euthanized hundreds of thousands of people. Many of these were mistakes, the same as euthanizing *Pai* would be.

Director Patel cleared his throat bringing Gideon back to the matter at hand.

"Mr. Roe, I invited you to this meeting as a courtesy. While I appreciate that you are *Nergüi*'s captain, this decision sits solely with her, as the mother. I apologize for not making this clear earlier." Director Patel laced his fingers together and flared his thumbs. "I am sorry. But *Pai* will be euthanized within the hour."

Gideon turned back to the observation window. *Pai* was a fragile dot next to her mother's bulk. "Don't do this," he said to *Nergüi*. "Please. She deserves life."

"Don't make this harder on me, Gideon. I've made up my mind," *Nergüi* said then cut the comms.

Gideon stormed from the office and down the station's corridors. There was no way he would let them euthanize *Pai*. There was no way he'd let this turn into another Gliese.

To save *Pai*, Gideon had to get her out of the station. That meant opening the Maternity Bay's main gate. The problem was he didn't have access to the controls. To get around this, he needed to hack the controls from the auxiliary exchange.

Gideon marched through the public cafeteria two levels down. He slipped past the queue and waited beside a bulkhead door labeled Restricted Area: Warehousing. When it opened, he caught the door with his boot and slipped inside.

The warehousing area swept in a slow arc with the curvature of the station. It was like walking through a giant doughnut two miles long. A wide hall ran longways down its center with towering shelves of used equipment on either side. At the end of the aisles, hugging the innermost portion of the doughnut, was a wall of transparent polycarbonate. Through it, Gideon could see *Nergüi* and *Pai*.

Gideon found the auxiliary exchange behind a stack of used solar converters. It was old Earth tech: color-coded resistor crystals that were set in a grid. Seeing the crystals, Gideon grimaced wryly. If he rearranged the crystals then he could overload the system. The emergency protocol would kick in, and the doors would open. Hope sparked inside him. He could do this.

A high-pitched voice startled him. "Yoo-hoo. You awake?"

Gideon swung around. A voluptuous woman with frizzy auburn hair smiled down at him. Her cheeks pulled into tight rosy knots.

"Wow, you were totally zoned." She chuckled. "I'm Molly. You new here?"

"Hi. Yes. Just … concentrating." Gideon didn't want to be rude, but idle conversation would have to wait. He turned his attention back to the crystals and silently recited the mnemonic phrase he learned in trade school: *R.E.D.S* (*resistor, entangle, displace, superposition*). The sequence dictated the order the crystals had to be replaced.

Molly hovered over Gideon's left shoulder. "Did you see the birthing?"

"No."

"That's too bad. This one had complications. Poor thing's going to have to be put down. But, you know, sometimes it's for the best."

Gideon gnashed his teeth. He pulled the last crystal in the sequence and counted them. There were thirteen; one was missing. He sighed, replaced the crystals, and started over.

"I hope they do it soon," Molly said. "I've got a friend in the lab, and she said this little ship nearly exploded when it hit hard vacuum. Poor thing must be in agony. Anyway, there's no coming back from something like that."

Gideon pulled the crystals again and laid them on the floor in a new sequence. "Your friend is an idiot. You don't just kill something because it's in pain."

Molly scoffed. "You can't be serious. I mean, what if it was your mom or sister? You wouldn't honestly leave them to suffer?"

Gideon's fingers brushed an unlabeled crystal, and an electrical shock jolted through his arm. It felt like someone grabbing and shaking him a hundred times in a fraction of a second before he could let go.

He sucked his finger and turned to scowl back at Molly. "What I would do is find someone competent enough to help them."

Gideon slid the last crystal back into place then levered himself up. Outside the observation window, he could see the maternity bay's twenty-story-high doors. The lights on either side of them flickered and pulled apart. They opened like a slow eclipse, revealing Proxima Centauri against a backdrop of darkness. Gideon's body tingled from head to toe.

But *Pai* moved away from the bay doors. Drones had latched onto her with towing cables and corralled her into a room thirteen levels down. Gideon pressed his face to the glass and read the words stenciled above the door: Annex 319-F.

Gideon cursed and kicked the stack of solar converters. He raked back his hair. He'd been so close: seconds from saving *Pai*.

He glared at Molly. She wasn't smiling anymore. Her gaze shifted from the crystals, to the opening bay doors, to the solar converters Gideon had kicked.

Molly backed away. "You're not supposed to be here, are you?" She turned and broke into a jog.

Gideon cursed his stupidity.

Gideon sprinted through the warehouse. He rounded a bin of used bolts then skidded to a stop, nearly running into a man in a hoverchair.

"S-sorry." Gideon stumbled backward. He bumped into a CO_2 tank but caught it before it fell. "Hey, that annex down there. Do you know how to get to it?"

The lanky man in the hoverchair wore a pair of welding goggles on his forehead and a greasy blue jumpsuit. The name Murdoch was embroidered across the jumpsuit's chest pocket. The man, Murdoch, rubbed his finger under his nose leaving a stain across his upper lip. "Sure, which one?"

"319-F."

Murdoch hesitated a second too long then swallowed. "The euthanasia job."

The way Murdoch said it made Gideon's stomach squirm. And yet, this posed an unexpected opportunity.

"Yeah," Gideon said. "That's me."

Murdoch lowered his gaze and fingered the beveled edge of his hoverchair. "I don't envy you, man." He shook his head. "Come on."

He led the way to a maintenance elevator with extra-wide doors. He thumbed the down button and somewhere deep within the shaft, the elevator jostled to life.

At the end of the hall, a security guard rounded the corner. He wore a stunner against his hip and a comms unit clipped to his collar. His attention shifted with his gaze swinging like a pendulum down each aisle.

The elevator pinged and the doors skidded open. Gideon ducked inside, gasping for breath, but Murdoch didn't move.

"Craaap." Murdock crooked his head to one side and nodded toward the back of his chair. "Hey, there's a battery cable that keeps slipping off. Would you mind popping it back on?"

The last thing Gideon wanted was to step where the guard could see him. Instead, he keyed level 319 into the elevator. A prompt appeared on the display, asking for his access. He swiped away the message and tried to close the elevator doors. But the prompt returned.

"Everything all right?" the guard said.

Murdoch nodded in acknowledgement. "Sergio. Battery cable again."

"Need some help?"

Gideon ducked behind the hoverchair and waved. "No problem. I got it."

The battery cable was as thick as his pinkie finger, sticky, and wrapped in yellow electrical tape. He slipped it back over the battery post and waited for the chair to reboot.

"So, why are you lurking in my domain?" Murdoch chortled at Sergio.

"Ah, Molly called in about some rambling psychopath." Sergio stopped a few feet away and exhaled a long breath.

"I'm offended." Murdoch pulled his hoverchair into the elevator; Gideon followed using the chair as a barrier between him and Sergio. "I've never rambled in my life."

Sergio hooted a laugh, and Murdoch swiped his access card. The elevator doors jostled closed.

Relief flooded through Gideon like a cool drink of a hot day. But he relaxed a moment too soon. Sergio peered back through the gap in the closing doors, and for a moment they locked gazes.

The elevator jostled and descended down the shaft. Gideon rubbed his temples. He'd be arrested when this was over. But that was okay. *Pai* was worth it.

Murdoch said, "This has got to be the slowest elevator in the system. But at least it fits my chair."

Gideon eyed the chair. "Ain't seen one of those since I was a kid."

"It's a classic. The ladies dig it."

A moment passed before Gideon realized it was a joke. By then it was too late to laugh. "What happened?"

"Gliese." Murdoch said. "I was on the far side of the planet when it blew. But man, I swear I could feel it from there." He shook his head and his gaze seemed to lose focus. "You remember those old twenty-man Arlo Darts? They crammed eighty of us onto one of those, piled us from floor to ceiling. Tight enough to break my back on a pipe joint on our way out."

Gideon had never set foot on Gliese-832c. But in the last ten years he'd thought of little else.

"It took a couple days to get to Hawkings Station field hospital. But by then there were only a few of us left. Most choked to death on the ash in their lungs. And even after we got there, most of those left didn't leave."

Gideon stared fixedly on the elevator's digital readout. The numbers on the display dropped slowly. 326. 325. 324. "Euthanasia?"

"Some," Murdoc said. "Sergio was on the Dart with me. We helped each other through. Been together ever since."

Gideon stared at his reflection in the digital display. There were lines beneath his eyes, and he looked thin.

"You lost someone?" Murdoch asked.

Gideon closed his eyes. "Daughter." *Her name was Acadia.*

The elevator chimed, and the doors pulled open. Gideon held it open for Murdoch then followed him down a narrow corridor.

Unlike the warehousing area upstairs, level 319 was strictly maintenance. The ceiling was low, the walls painted a gray-green. The pipes lining the halls intersected and branched with welded cup links, pressure gauges, and regulator valves.

"There she is." Murdoch nodded down a narrow passage. At its end was an airlock door with a small window in its center. Beside the door was a wall-mounted control panel and four EVA suits.

Gideon splayed his fingers against the window, breathing patches of fog against its surface. Inside, *Pai* stalked the annex like a caged animal, from the bulkhead to the emergency exit on the opposite wall.

Emergency exit. He didn't have to bring *Pai* back through the annex and out the Maternity Bay's main gate. All he had to do was open the exit. Behind it was empty space.

At the control panel, he tapped the option for emergency protocol. A warning message blinked: *Initiating emergency protocol will result in a yellow alert. Do you wish to proceed?*

"Hey-hey-hey. Hold on," Murdoch said over Gideon's shoulder. "What are you doing?"

Gideon pressed *yes*. But the emergency exit didn't open, and the yellow alert didn't sound. The control panel flashed a new message: *Error. Please close all airlocks before proceeding.*

The back of Gideon's neck flashed hot, and at the same time, the station intercom crackled to life. "This is a station-wide announcement. Be on the lookout for unauthorized personnel: Tau Ceti male in his early to mid-forties wearing gray fatigues and a long-sleeve black shirt. Last seen accessing the maintenance elevator in level 332 warehousing area. May be in the company of Murdoch McCarthy, identifiable by his hoverchair. If seen, please notify security immediately."

Defeat chafed against the lining of Gideon's stomach as a whirl of gyros sounded behind him. He turned to find Murdoch speeding away.

Gideon darted after him. He caught up with Murdock a few feet from the extra-large elevator and ripped the battery cable from the back of Murdoch's hoverchair. The chair drifted to a stop.

Murdoch cursed and called for help, but Gideon darted back for the annex.

Gideon climbed into the largest EVA suit and opened the annex door. "I'm sorry," he called back. "I ain't got time to explain."

The annex was a giant cube-shaped room. Its walls were the color of eggshells and dotted with air vents.

Pai hovered an arm's length away, unmoving. Up close, Gideon could see the tiny sacs of infection hanging where her gravity receptors should have been. Without those, she'd never be able to burrow into the fabric of space.

Beneath *Pai* was a manhole with its hatch cracked ajar. That's what was preventing the emergency protocol from running.

"Air pressure 0.7%," Gideon's EVA suit informed him. He'd not checked the pressure before putting the suit on, but he wasn't worried. He only needed to step back out the door and then take it off.

Gideon laid flat on the floor and shuffled beneath *Pai*. He muscled the hatch closed, and the indicator lights on its top changed from green to red. Unless there were any other pressure doors opened in here, all he had to do was leave and close the annex door behind him. From there, the emergency protocol should resume automatically.

Gideon shuffled out from under *Pai*. He levered himself up with his hands on his knees. When he lifted his gaze toward the door, he saw the security guard, Sergio, round the corner.

Panic lurched from the pit of Gideon's stomach and lodged in his throat. He slammed the door closed between them, initiating the door's auto-lock. Through the dinner-plate-sized window, Sergio's face stared back at him, brow furrowed in a rage. He appeared to be yelling, but Gideon couldn't hear him.

The lights in the annex flickered and dimmed. Unsure what had changed, Gideon looked around until his gaze rested on the wall-mounted vents and the puffs of rust-colored mist snaking through them.

Euthanasia.

"Air pressure 0.6%," the EVA said.

The gravity of the situation hit Gideon like an asteroid. He yanked furiously on the door release, but it didn't budge. He entered the *open* command on the control panel, but it didn't move. "Open the door!" he screamed, locking gazes with Sergio through the small window.

Sergio appeared ill. He blinked twice as if pulled from a dream then yanked on the door. It didn't help. Then he grabbed one of the EVA helmets from the shelf behind him and pulled it down over his head. The words "Can you hear me?" blasted in Gideon's ear.

Gideon nodded. "Get me out of here."

Before Sergio could answer, the rust-colored mist licked at *Pai*'s hull. *Pai* sprang forward, ramming the emergency exit. The impact sounded like a hammer against an anvil, and Gideon stumbled back, breathless.

The impact left a gap three inches wide between the emergency exit and its frame. Air whistled through the gap, venting into space and carrying most of the mist with it.

Pai tottered back, and the mist continued to pour into the room.

"Air pressure 0.5%," the EVA said.

"You still with me?" Sergio jerked his thumb behind him. "I've got Murdoch here. He said that's nerve gas, supposed to euthanize that ship. Is that right?"

"Patel's doing this. Tell him to turn it off!" Gideon said.

Sergio nodded, removed his helmet, and spoke into the comms device clipped to his shirt collar. His expression morphed from urgent to relieved to concerned before he pulled the helmet back over his head to speak to Gideon. "That's a no-go. The system's design prevents it. But it'll turn off once the ship is … dead."

Anxiety crawled up Gideon's spine. "Well, then we got a major problem here. Because *Pai* just busted a three-inch gap between the emergency exit and its frame. We're venting atmosphere in here and it's taking most of the gas with it."

"Okay," Sergio said. "Then it will take a little longer? It's not ideal, but—"

"And this EVA suit is out of oxygen. I'm down to half a percent."

Sergio relayed the message to Director Patel then lifted his gaze. Gideon could see the bad news carved into the security guard's face. "They're developing a plan," he said sheepishly.

"Developing a plan? Did you tell them—"

Sergio raised his hand. "You need to stop talking. Breathe slowly. Conserve air. And he recommends that you get out of that nerve gas as quickly as possible …. That suit is pretty old."

"Air pressure 0.4%."

Gideon's face flushed hot, and fog condensed inside his helmet. "Where am I supposed to go?"

Sergio's brow furrowed. He lifted his gaze to a point over Gideon's left shoulder. "Inside that baby ship."

Gideon switched on the light mounted to his helmet and surveyed *Pai*'s inner cavity. Gobs of mucus wept from the blisters lining her hull. He'd never seen the inside of a starship before it was outfitted for human occupants, but he guessed this wasn't what a healthy ship should look like.

Hunkered on the floor, he leaned against the soft tissue lining *Pai*'s inner hull. His eyes burned. He wanted to take off his helmet and rub them but knew that would kill him. Better to let the oxygen run out and fall asleep.

The air tank dropped to 0.3%, and Gideon felt a gentle pressure against his chest. He was slipping away now. His eyes jittered and their lids sagged.

Darkness came, and Gideon drifted into a memory.

His fifteen-year-old daughter, Acadia, was preparing for her first day of high school. She wore a crop top that showed too much skin. "No. No. No!" Gideon didn't want to yell but Acadia just wasn't getting the message. "I'm not letting you out of this house wearing that. Go change now."

"Quit treating me like a child," Acadia said. "I'm not a little girl anymore. You don't even know me!"

Eventually, she changed, but she didn't speak to Gideon for the rest of the day. The distance between them widened. Every time Gideon tried to be a responsible parent, he made things worse.

That memory faded, and in the next one Gideon was in the Tau Ceti Interplanetary Spaceport. Acadia and her classmates huddled with travel bags draped over their shoulders. "I'm not comfortable with this," Gideon said to her. It didn't matter that teachers would chaperone the kids; Gideon didn't like the thought of Acadia being on another planet without him. What if she got into trouble?

"Dad, you're embarrassing me," Acadia said. "Can you please go?"

Acadia's friends snickered into their hands. The *Now Boarding* sign flickered.

Gideon swallowed hard. This was his last chance. He had to put his foot down, demand that Acadia stay here on Tau Ceti with him. Yes, she'd be angry. Furious. But he'd make it up to her. He didn't know how, but he would. He just had to keep her from boarding that damned starship.

"I …" *don't want you to go. I want you to stay. I want you here where I can watch over you, not gallivanting around another star system.* "I … want you to be safe."

Acadia hugged her dad, somewhat awkwardly, rejoined her friends, and they migrated into the boarding terminal. The display above them flashed their destination: *Gliese-832c, Final Boarding.*

The memory faded. In the next, Gideon, covering his mouth and nose, squeezed through the field hospital. The acrid scent of charred flesh and chemical cleaners clawed at the back of his nose and throat. He searched the common room on the lowest deck. It was crammed with makeshift cots and looked like a volcanic sea of burnt and writhing bodies. Those bodies spilled into the corridors and every room on the station's lower level. Gideon checked each one—some alive, some dead—but Acadia wasn't here. Nor was she on the next level up, or the three hundred and nineteen after that.

Gideon found her laying on a towel on the floor. Acadia's right arm was fused to her chest as if she'd died shielding her face or batting something away. Her eyes were open, and her mouth gaped slightly ajar. There was a needle sticking out of her neck.

Gideon pressed his hand against Acadia's cold cheek then brushed her hair from her face. This was his fault. She died because he wasn't there to protect her from the doctors' medical mercy.

Here the memories ended, and darkness came: an immeasurable expanse of emptiness more vast than space. The waypoint between the living and the dead.

"Dad. Dad," a whisper said.

Something electric sparked inside of Gideon. His emotions twitched and his voice trembled. "I'm sorry."

"It wasn't your fault."

"I wasn't there when you needed me."

"Dad," Acadia said, her voice sweet in its whisper, "I'm gone now. You have to accept that. You have to let go."

"I can't."

"You have to. And you have to let go of *Pai* too."

"But I can't. *Pai* deserves life—*you* deserved life."

"I did. *Pai* does." The voice started to fade, still washing over him in the gentlest of caresses. "But the life she deserves is one without endless agony—one without a body that can't even function in the environment for which she was born. Would you have wanted me in endless agony, Dad? Wouldn't you have done anything to take my pain away—to give me peace?"

There was a pause where time and space moved, displaced from this reality. Gideon grappled to hold on to it—to hold onto Acadia. But she was gone.

Her words echoed in his mind.

A distant glow appeared to the side of Gideon's vision. It grew until it overtook his field of view, and he was back inside *Pai*.

"Air pressure, 0.1%," the EVA suit said.

Pai trembled and jerked to one side, rousing Gideon's senses.

Gideon gathered his resolve and shouldered *Pai*'s hatch open. Outside, the air carried a hue of orange rust. He stumbled out of *Pai*, falling to one knee on the annex floor. Then he rose. Burning images of light cluttered Gideon's vision, but he pressed forward. He stopped before the emergency exit. From here the air and gas whistled through the gap so loud that he could hear nothing else.

Gideon turned and pressed his back against the gap in the emergency exit. The pull of the atmosphere sucked him tightly against the gap, pinning him and clogging the hole. The noise subsided and the mist stopped venting out the gap.

The vents in the walls continued to pour the toxic mist into the room. Gideon could no longer see the other end of the annex, though he saw *Pai* floating gently toward him. She stopped within an arm's length of him, and Gideon placed his hand on her misshapen exoskeleton.

"If you see Acadia on the other side," he said wistfully, "tell her I love her."

Pai hovered there a moment longer. She shuddered. Her anti-gravity system stopped, and she clanked against the annex floor. She did not move again.

Then Gideon closed his eyes and let go.

Gideon spent the next week in the station's infirmary. The room smelled of disinfectant, and the machine beside his bed beeped every hour to break the silence. A nurse came in to check his blood pressure, another brought his meals. Then Gideon slept again. But unlike the last ten years, his sleep was not riddled with nightmares or images of the past. He slept deeply, dreamlessly.

A knock at the door drew his attention. Director Patel stood in the hospital's corridor, an eyebrow raised. "I can come back later ..."

Gideon shook his head then gestured toward a faux-leather chair beside him. Their meeting was inevitable. What he didn't expect was the director to come alone.

"Thought you'd bring Sergio?"

Director Patel leaned back in the chair and crossed his legs at the knee. "I interviewed Sergio and Molly and Murdoch." He focused his attention on a picture hanging at the end of Gideon's bed.

"How'd that go?"

"Mr. Roe, you should not expect a Christmas card from any of them." Director Patel turned back to Gideon wearing a half-smile.

"Fair assumption."

Out in the corridor, two nurses giggled amidst private banter.

"Am I going to be arrested?" Gideon said.

"No. You are banned from the station for a period of ten years. But you are otherwise free to go once you are healed."

This didn't make sense. Surely Director Patel had enough evidence to put him behind bars for years. Gideon's shook his head. "Why?"

"Because, Mr. Roe, last week someone reminded me how precious life is. I wish to follow this example."

Later that day, Gideon collected his belongings from the duty nurse and made his way to the hangar bay.

He placed an open palm on *Nergüi*'s warm hull. "I'm sorry about *Pai*. Sorry that I didn't listen to you or consider your feelings. If you could forgive me, then maybe we can help each other through this."

"I would like that very much." *Nergüi*'s rear hatch opened, and Gideon climbed aboard.

When it was their turn to launch, *Nergüi* arched her back then sprang forward. Her claws shuffled like tiny swinging pistons. They raked the fabric of space, propelling them through the bay doors and out of the station. Proxima Centauri b shone before them, a bright gleaming beacon of hope in an endless expanse of possibility.

They accelerated. The sensors on the control panel chimed as they exited the no-gravity wake zone.

"On your command," *Nergüi* said.

Gideon took a deep, cleansing breath. "I'm ready now. Thank you."

"It's good to have you back, Captain."

The tips of *Nergüi*'s caterpillar-like legs sparked then glowed. They sank deeper into the fabric of space and tore open a small hole. The hole widened and she burrowed inside.

Timely Visitor

She looked as if she'd just stepped out of one of those television series set at the beginning of the twentieth century. She was probably in her forties, wearing a rose-colored blouse and a dark skirt that
stretched to her ankles. She carried a large purse, and her hair was
bundled in a fashion you just didn't see any more. But the feature
that stood out was a smile that suggested she was amused. "Professor
Glazer?" she said.

"Yes? How can I help you?"

"May I have a moment?"

It was shortly after one o'clock on a Thursday afternoon. I was
due in the auditorium in twenty minutes to speak to members of the
Advanced Physics Foundation. My topic would be quantum optics. I
was putting my thoughts together and, while there was no immediate
rush, I had no interest in becoming distracted. "I really don't have
much time," I said. "What can I do for you?"

"My name is Mileva Maric." She sounded as if she thought I
should recognize it. "I only need a minute. I just want to leave something with you." She opened the purse, removed an index card, and
laid it on my desk. "I suspect you'll want to get in touch with me
tomorrow." Her index finger tapped the bottom of the card. "This is
my cell number. And my hotel." Her smile widened. "I'll be waiting
for your call."

I thought about telling her to just go away, that she looked good but I was happily married. My attention though focused on the card. She'd placed it just out of my reach. Above the cell number were a couple of what looked like basketball scores. "Ms. Maric," I said, "I'm sorry, but I just haven't time for nonsense." I got out of my seat.

"I understand, Professor. I'll look forward to hearing from you tomorrow. Good luck with your address this afternoon."

I shook my head to let her know that any connection she expected with me wasn't going to happen.

She nodded, wished me a good afternoon, and walked out of the office, closing the door gently behind her.

They *were* basketball scores.

I put my jacket on, glanced at the windows and saw that a light rain had begun to fall. I started for the door, trying to ignore the card. I was at the height of my career at the Swiss Federal Institute of Technology. And I just had too much to think about at the moment. But I picked it up anyhow.

Two games were listed. Lausanne Foxes 88 against Goldcoast Wallabies 86. The other was our local team: the Zurich Wildcats 97 against the Morges-Saint-Prex Red Devils 96, in overtime. I don't follow the Foxes, so I didn't know anything about them, but the Wildcats had lost their last game, and it had been not to the Red Devils but to Sion. So she had them wrong. And why on earth did she think I'd care anyway?

She was staying at the Adler.

The presentation went fine. I got some laughs and Jerry Lawson, a longtime friend and math professor at the University of Zurich, told me it was outstanding. I've known Jerry a long time and he's not accustomed to exaggerating his feelings.

Janet and I took the girls out for a pizza dinner. I told her about Mileva and she rolled her eyes. "Don't go near her, Mack," she said.

When we got home she settled in with a Lord Peter novel and I worked with the kids on a jigsaw puzzle. At ten we turned on the news. They covered the usual political stuff. Also, Russia was denying charges they were interfering in Kazakhstan's elections. The weather report warned us of approaching thunderstorms. They ran a couple of commercials and then told us the Wildcats were tied at 79 with the Red Devils and the game was going into overtime.

All right, there was no way I could miss that. It sounded as if the game was heading to the score Maric had given me. We switched over to the channel that was carrying the game. They were down to the last couple of minutes with the Red Devils leading 87-84. And they reported on the Foxes. They'd beaten the Wallabies 88-86.

"That can't be right," said Janet. She'd retrieved the woman's index card and was frowning at it. "That was the score."

"Something's wrong here."

"It must have been yesterday."

We checked the sports channel. The game had just ended. "What the hell is going on?"

"I have no idea."

While we kicked it back and forth, the Wildcats overtook the Red Devils in the dying seconds and won by a point at 97-96. So she had that one right, too. Maybe they were fixed. Even if someone was throwing the games, though, I doubted there'd be any way to fix the scores. "In any case, Jan, why does she think I would care?"

But I did. I wasn't going to sleep until I settled what was happening. I tried calling. Her cell rang twice and got picked up by voicemail. "The person you are trying to reach is not accepting calls at this time. Please try again later."

"Maybe you're right," I told Janet. "Something *is* going on." I called the Adler.

"Sorry," they said. "We have nobody by that name staying here.

Janet was in the kitchen when I came downstairs in the morning. "That name ring a bell with you?" she asked. "Mileva Maric?"

"No. Should it?"

"The woman's a liar. Stay clear of her."

"Why should it ring a bell?"

"It just hit me this morning: Mileva Maric was Einstein's first wife. She died in 1948."

"Maybe she's a niece or something. Look, Janet, I'm going to try again to call her."

"Don't do it."

"You want to be *still* wondering ten years from now how she managed last night's basketball scores?"

"I don't care about it, Mack. The whole thing just feels … off. I just want us to stay away from her." She opened the refrigerator. "You want some eggs?"

"Sure."

"So, will you just back off?"

"I'm going to call her today. I have to. No way I can walk away from this. But don't worry—everything'll be fine. I'll get some answers, hopefully. And then it's over."

At a few minutes past eleven, I called. I listened to it ring while I told myself to calm down. She picked up. "Professor Glazer?"

"Yes, Ms. Maric. Good morning."

"To you as well, Professor."

"That was very interesting yesterday. How did you know about the scores?"

"I saw the papers."

"The games hadn't been played yet. Would you like to explain what this is about?"

"Why don't we meet for lunch?"

"What is going on, Ms. Maric?"

"My friends call me Mileva."

"So where do you want to eat, Mileva?"

"The hotel has an excellent restaurant."

"You're back at the Adler?"

She hesitated. "I will be shortly."

"You weren't there yesterday."

"I decided to go home."

I sighed. "What time?"

"Does one o'clock work for you?"

Janet was furious with me. She wanted me to call the woman back and cancel. Then she tried to insist on coming. But I couldn't let her do that. Whatever was happening, her presence wasn't going to help.

The woman was seated at a corner table when I walked in. She seemed to be wearing exactly the same clothes she'd had the day before. "It's good to see you again, Mileva," I said. I sat down. A waiter came over and took our orders. When he was gone, she asked if I understood what had happened. There was no one seated close to us, but she nevertheless kept her voice down.

"I've no idea," I said. "Before we start, can I ask you what your name is? Your *real* name?"

She smiled. "I have not lied to you."

"So it *is* Mileva Maric. Are you related to Einstein's first wife? You part of the family?"

"No, Professor. I'm not a relative. I *am* Mileva. I *was* Albert's first wife."

"Would you please get serious?"

"I understand your skepticism. But I *am* her."

"She died seventy years ago."

"Let me ask *you* a question: how did I know in advance the outcome of the two basketball games?"

I shook my head. "I have no idea."

She took another index card from her purse and handed it to me. A number was written on it: 11,118.46. "Do you follow the Swiss Market Index?" she asked.

"No. We don't own any stock."

"When the market closes today, check the numbers."

I looked again at the card. "It's going to be this one?"

"I'll leave that to you to determine."

"What's going on, Mileva?"

"My husband, in 1905, released his particle theory of light. In fact, he virtually rewrote physics in that year. Or, rather, *we* did. I did a lot of the groundwork but never got any credit for it. It's not that he claimed the credit; he simply didn't correct what was believed. It was an era when no one could or would take seriously research done by a woman. We could not do anything other than housework. So the physics community laid all the credit at his door. I don't think Albert himself understood the depth of my assistance. In any case, my name never got mentioned."

The waiter was back with napkins and two cups of coffee. He put them in front of us, smiled, and left. A couple of men arrived and sat down at the table behind me. The woman inched closer and leaned forward, lowering her voice even more. "I did other work for him until finally our marriage collapsed."

"Hold on," I said. "Tell me again who you really are. What's your part in all this?"

"I'll admit that I was frustrated that no one knew who I was. That Albert started collecting awards, and occasionally mentioned my name. It sounded as if I took notes for him."

I took a deep breath. "Mileva died in 1948."

"That is correct."

"Are you claiming you're a spirit?"

"Of course not. I'm simply a physicist who invented a time travel device."

"You have a *time machine*?"

"How else could I have gotten the scores last night? Or picked up today's closing Swiss Market Index?"

I sat staring at her. I could think of no alternative explanation. Other than a couple of incredibly lucky guesses. "Why?" I asked. "Why am I involved in all this?"

"Professor, I live in a five-story house at Huttenstrasse 62. Or I guess I should say I used to live there. It still exists in your era as a tourist site." She went into her purse again and came out with a folder. "This contains a document tracking everything I did during the 1905 research. It's in my handwriting and it's dated. It should provide sufficient evidence that I played a major role in Albert's breakthrough work. If I give this to you, could you arrange to visit Huttenstrasse 62? Be sure you log in. There's a closet on the second floor. Please claim you found this on the top shelf." She handed me the folder. "I know I'm asking you to lie but I don't want to take the chance of leaving it over there until you could get to it."

"Why? Why are you doing this?"

"I want credit for my share of the work. And I want it handled by someone who knows who I was. The truth is, I did *more* than Albert. For all of us, I would like it to be acknowledged."

"But you've invented a *time machine*. That makes everything else minor league."

"I know."

"You have the time travel device in your purse, too?"

She grinned at me. "Let's not get into details."

"Mileva, time travel is a huge step forward. I'd think that taking credit for that would be more than enough."

"Please lower your voice, Professor. We're drawing attention."

"Why screw around with relativity when you have time travel? Assuming you actually do?"

"I do. The problem is that it is dangerous."

"In what way? Have you gone back to visit some historical figures? Aristotle? Rousseau? Descartes?"

"No. The device doesn't work that way. I built it in 1922. It can only operate from that date forward. I can travel to the future, and I can return to any time after 1922."

"So why is it dangerous?"

"It will radically change the world in which we live. What do our lives become when we know what tomorrow will bring? What research will be done if we think we need do nothing other than travel forward to get data? If I make this device available, the future will become simply vast flat turf. An area where nothing happens other than decay. For that reason I'll ask you not to mention the time travel aspect. I plan to bury its existence."

"What good would that do? If you could devise it, someone else will eventually do the same thing."

"You're right. Eventually, I'm sure it will happen again. But the person who does it will understand its effect. Just as I do. Hopefully she will take the same course."

"Did your husband know about it? The time device?"

"No. You are the only person I've told."

"If it's so dangerous, why did you construct the machine at all?"

"Why? Because I wanted to travel through time. Because I wanted people to know that women matter. I wanted someone to know about my part in the development of relativity. To know I was there. That would be you." She finally picked up her cup and sipped the coffee. "So will you help me?"

I told Janet. She doesn't believe the device exists, but she had a hard time discounting the validity of Mileva's claims when she saw the

Swiss Market's closing numbers. In any case, she agreed to say nothing and, as far as I know, has kept her word.

I don't know why I've recorded all this. I always make notes after a significant experience. But I've no intention of releasing them. Maybe one day I'll put it all together and ship it off to a publisher and claim it's a piece of fiction.

How Does My Garden Grow?

by David Cleden

"Are you ill, Elke?" the ship's physician asks.

"No," I lie. Whatever I am, it's no one else's concern.

"I think you should have these." He slides a blister pack full of blue-white pills across the dispensing table. They nestle in their cocoons like tiny, fragile eggs.

I want to say that Dr. Vajrani has a kindly face. I think he used to, back in those heady early years soon after embarkation. Now though, he just looks tired and emaciated; skin drawn tight over cheekbones as though at some point on this great journey of ours he's forgotten how to smile.

My eyes drift to the shelf behind his head. There's a cluster of little toy Flexi-fun figures peeping down that I remember from my own childhood. Are they distractions for his younger patients or merely sentimental keepsakes? It seems each of us needs to cling to a bit of our past.

I suppose eventually they'll figure out I'm not taking my other medication. They'll be able to measure some imbalance in the chemical and mineral constituents entering the recycling loop. One more piece of Closure lost.

Because everyone frets over the C number.

The entire sum of everything we are and everything we will be is contained within this ship. We're the ultimate closed environment.

Maintaining resource equilibrium; well … how often have we been told it's not so much a goal as a pre-requisite for survival? No stopping off for supplies at some gas station along the way for us.

A C number of 1.0—perfect closure—is unattainable. Something about violating the laws of thermodynamics, I think? Don't ask me. But as long as we stay close to 1.0, stay *in the zone*, we're good for a couple of centuries.

So the higher-ups watch the C number as though our fate is determined by those numerals. Which it is, I suppose.

There's even a kind of clock. It's mounted on a plinth in the central municipal space where all the stunted trees grow and birdsong chirps on a loop from hidden speakers. It's there as a reminder that Closure hangs over us like some dark thundercloud. Not for us directly—it will be our children, or our children's children who'll pay the price of today's recklessness—even though no one knows for sure what awaits us around the dim, cold star that is our destination.

Why is the C-clock there at all? It's not as if any of us can forget.

Dr. Vajrani is studying me. I know this game. He's waiting so that sooner or later I'll spill some of my thoughts to fill the silence.

So I say nothing. I'm good at this game too.

"Very well. I think we're done, Elke. But if there's anything—"

I don't hear the end of his sentence because I'm already out the door, on the way back to my soul garden.

Soul gardens.

Who came up with that name, I'd like to know? Someone like Dr. Vajrani, I bet.

They're just about the only things on the ship that aren't there for a practical reason. Everything else, the engines, life-support machines, fabrication units, agri-bays, schools and creches for the children—even the tiny parks for people to relax in—they all have a clear function.

Soul gardens have no purpose. They're just whatever you want them to be. It's good for the soul to have something to nurture.

Mine has three growing shelves, subdivided and planted according to a plan of my own devising. Soon I'm going to add a fourth. Right here, there's a patch of lime grass (symbolizing ambition and drive), growing tall and straight. Over there, the fading purple of chive flowers are hung with melancholy, drooping as though under some invisible burden. A section of the bottom tray is given over to *Fulmina partaxis,* one of my favorites. I often imagine my pent-up anger flowing into its tight little blood-red flowers. Right in the corner is a tiny patch where I scattered love-in-the-mist seed but it hasn't taken, still just bare soil. No wonder I feel so alone.

I draw off a little water from my allowance and moisten the bedding material. I trim here, neaten there. I add a few drops of liquid fertilizer made from rotting organics I've kept back. (That's going to land me in trouble if anyone finds out. All waste is supposed to be returned to central recycling.)

I can't begin to describe how much comfort I draw from my soul garden, often tending it three or four times a day when my work rota allows. Sometimes I take from it, and sometimes I give. It serves me well.

I think about the lie I told Dr. Vajrani as I caress the blue-black stem of an *Alchema dorix.* I let the lie drain out of me, flowing from my fingertips, imagining those dark flowers darkening a little more, unseen roots spreading outwards like ink stains beneath the soil—until I am calm again.

Home for me is in the deepest level of the ship. I like to imagine all those roots forcing their way down through hull material, thrusting at last into the blackness of space. I picture them turning blindly towards the dimming light of the old sun, or the faint pinprick of the new.

But Dr. Vajrani has told me it's not healthy to think about what's outside.

A softly chiming alarm reminds me that my work shift is about to start. Four days a week I serve on the Infrastructure Maintenance Crew. Mostly it involves scraping mold from inaccessible cabling conduits. We have robot moles to do this work but sometimes they get stuck and it's our job to figure out how to get them out. Usually we do, but sometimes it means lifting floor gratings or dismantling wall panels and that tends to get the higher-ups very agitated. Occasionally even that doesn't work and we have to abandon the mole where it is. Everybody hates it when that happens. It means valuable resources put beyond use; another ding in the C number.

Closure.

It's the only topic of conversation these days.

I often think about those poor little robotic creatures burrowed deep into the skin of our ship, dead and slowly fossilizing, never to see the light of day again.

To me, those are the best days of all.

We're standing inside Municipal Space #3, the largest on the ship, keeping vigil.

Not everyone's here because we wouldn't all fit in the space, so several hundred more are watching on screens elsewhere. But I'm near the front of the crowd, an invited special guest.

The Mayor is standing next to the C-clock making his speech. The Captain stands next to him, her face gray and impassive as though her mind is far away dealing with more important matters. I'm sure only half the crowd are listening anyway. Everyone's staring at the glowing numerals of the C-clock:

0.99726

It's not a good number, but a lot better than a year ago. That was when Closure dipped below 96 percent for the first time ever, and we knew we were in trouble if people didn't act.

So people did. Thirty of them, my parents included.

The Mayor drones on and we watch and wait, transfixed.

When it finally happens—that last digit morphing from a 6 to a 7—a ripple runs through the crowd. People smile and nudge their neighbors. The Mayor falters, glancing back over his shoulder at the clock. Then he turns back to the crowd beaming and raising his arms as though accepting their praise.

Malia Ng, my neighbor from across the corridor, leans close. "See?" she says, an unwanted arm snaking round my shoulders. "Such a brave sacrifice, but it's working. It really is! You should feel so proud."

My vision goes a little blurry and I wonder if I'm about to faint. I dip my hand into a pocket, finding the little bouquet of river mint freshly picked not half an hour ago from my soul garden. I crush a leaf and inhale the rich scent from my fingertips: a little pepperminty, a little sharp; hints of lime and sulfur. It centers me again and my vision clears.

I get such joy from my soul garden. But I also get contentment and melancholy, bliss and despair, hope and fear—and much more besides. It's all there: all the fragrances and flavors. I pour my soul into it, and then I take from it whatever I need.

This last year has undoubtedly been tough. So much anger and resentment. *Fulmina partaxis* has colonized the bottom tray more than I'd like, a red stain under the artificial lights.

The Mayor is still talking about sacrifice, but I don't bother listening.

Oscar Brandt is the leader of the Five-Nines Crew that comes calling. I know him a little (I know everyone a little—it can't be helped when you live in a community of five hundred, I suppose) but we're not exactly friends.

"You can't keep these flower trays in your room," he tells me.

"But I *need* my soul garden."

He's a big man, broad-shouldered and a little intimidating up close. But it's the others in the Five-Nines Crew who make me nervous. They shuffle around the apartment, fingering the few precious things I brought from Earth—photographs, a competition trophy, a faded cloth doll. They peer into cupboards, checking to make sure I'm not hoarding recyclables.

"I understand. But we all have to do our bit and get the C number back up to where it should be." His dark-eyed stare is unwavering and I don't like that. It makes me feel as though he can see right inside my head. "It's the least we can do to honor the Thirty."

OK. Well *that's* a low blow.

I can't make any counter-argument, not against the Thirty. They did, after all, sacrifice themselves, in a desperate bid to fix the Closure problem once and for all. Six percent of the citizens. Six percent of daily resource consumption removed from the loop. More of everything to go round for the rest of us.

And we still don't know if that was enough.

Slowly, slowly, we saw the C-number creep back up—just not nearly as much as everyone hoped.

"You hear about the disease outbreak in a couple of the agri-bays?" Brandt asks me. "And no one can figure out why seed germination rates are declining. Could be very bad news for harvest yields if we can't turn it around. So they've upped the bio-security protocols." He shrugs. "Soul gardens have to go. An order from the Captain herself. We can't take any risks."

Something flutters inside my chest like a wild, untamed creature trying to batter its way out.

"You can't! My soul garden—it … it means the world to me."

The world? Now *that's* a quaint expression. I don't have a world anymore. We are all of us between worlds.

"Sure, it's a big ask, Elke, but we have to get the C number back to five-nines. Or better, if we can. Remember the Thirty." His smile is thin, and I know what he's thinking. One more would have helped things along nicely.

The Five-Nines Crew are back the next day, come to destroy my soul garden. Two of them hold me tight by the arms while I scream and sob and struggle uselessly in a grip that is never going to relent.

I watch the precious contents of those trays transferred into recycling sacks: uprooted plants for the micro-shredder and compost processor, growing medium for sterilization; all of it destined to become part of an agri-bay once more. Everything weighed and accounted for.

I feel sick in the pit of my stomach. I can taste a little of the kava on my tongue, but also miller's-tail and white sage and cilantro—a little of everything that I've sampled from my soul garden, roiling in my stomach just as the matching emotions churn in my head.

The crew seals the last sack tight and leave.

My soul garden is both gone and not gone.

There's a hateful part of my job which is attending to the air-filtration machines that keep our atmosphere fresh and viable. Sometimes it means wriggling deep inside their conduits, checking filters, replacing worn bearings, and scraping away any thriving colonies of mold. (Which must be carefully collected and recycled for composting, of course. Everything is part of the cycle. Feed the C number! Help close the loop!)

Altering the maintenance roster to gain access to conduit 43-B isn't hard. It's not as if anyone's going to fight me for the privilege of grabbing a respirator and mold-scraper and crawling into those tight spaces.

43-B is one of the larger ducts. There's an access panel right next to a big air filtration unit and about thirty meters of conduit just wide enough to wriggle along before the next booster fan. There'll be all kinds of holy hell if my secret growing space is discovered, but honestly, I don't see how it can be hurting anyone.

It's hardly anything. My torch-beam picks out one little growing tray duct-taped to the floor. There's no lighting because I couldn't figure out how to rig something that wouldn't be detected.

Only ... now I see it's all been for nothing. My dancing beam picks out a shriveled tuft of mint, ghost pale, its leaf tips curling in on themselves. Myrtle, chicory, lemon verbena—all are dead or dying. Only the blood-red heads of *Fulmina partaxis* seem to cling impossibly to life.

What had I expected—with near darkness and a constant airflow wicking away moisture? Only mold survives those conditions.

Something in my chest tightens with an angry, vice-like grip.

My fingers gently caress the dying stems as I let my frustration and rage bubble and froth like a pan of milk on the boil. I grow aware of this cramped space pinning me down; a tiny, sightless mite burrowed into the ship's flesh, and an odd thought comes to me. Why are there no windows on the ship? No relayed images of the shrinking Sun?

Because we're not supposed to remember the past, that's why.

My rage boils over, turning to hissing steam as my breaths come louder and faster, amplified within the confines of my respirator. I let it flow out of me. In the torchlight, the *partaxis* flowers look darker than before; blood-red become black. I crush their fragile heads in my fingers, watching their powdery dust drawn away on the gentle air currents.

Hours pass as I sit in the semi-darkness, alone with my churning thoughts, waiting for calmness to return. I am mourning the very last part of my soul garden, now broken up and scattered to the four artificial winds.

When at last I haul myself out of the conduit, I'm grateful there's no one around to see. I make my way back to my apartment and drop into a deep and welcoming sleep, already missing my little garden which has left a fathomless hole in my soul that can never be filled.

Only silence and solitude can comfort me.

✧ ✧ ✧

I ask Dr. Vajrani if I can start a new soul garden.

"I think that would be a wonderful idea, Elke."

"You do? Because I don't think I can carry all of it around in my head for much longer. Everything's jammed up inside. All those different scents and fragrances tangled like a big ball of string. They're pressing to get out and making my head hurt."

"Then you should start at once, Elke. In fact, I know what. I think you should use one of the agri-bays. I'm sure there's room to spare now."

"Really? That's wonderful!"

I waggle my little cloth doll happily so that it smooches with one of the Flexi-fun figures I've swiped from Vajrani's shelf. The figure has a frown and a tiny stethoscope around its neck; a perfect avatar for Dr. Vajrani. "Let me give you a big sloppy kiss to thank you!" my doll says.

Bored now, I wander out of Vajrani's consulting room, not meeting anyone as I wander the curving corridors, stroll in the green spaces, help myself to snacks from the food dispensary.

That's good. People make the ship seem crowded, the spaces a little smaller than they really are. Sometimes the ship reminds me of a resort complex we holidayed in once when I was tiny. It's comforting to imagine I could just step outside whenever I want. Maybe there'd be an ocean nearby with waves breaking on an endless golden beach, and seagulls turning lazy circles in the air. Maybe it really is there, just waiting for me. All I have to do is find the door.

My head still hurts. Three days and the pain and nausea are only now beginning to ebb. There are fat, unseen fingers drumming on my skull, sending little stabby waves of pain through my brain. That's my soul garden anxious to be free again.

I turn and begin walking toward the closed-off sections of the ship where the agri-bays are. Naturally, access is tightly controlled; only the palm prints of the hydroponic techs open those doors. I've only ever seen pictures of what's inside.

I thrust my hand into the deep pockets of my coveralls. There is already a hand in there. It isn't mine. The door to the agri-bay opens to its palm print.

Plans for my new soul garden bubble and fizz in my mind. I'll only need a little space. At first.

More *partaxis*, that'll be important. I have a lot of pent-up anger to offload. And lemon balm too, just because it smells so wonderful.

I halt outside Municipal Space #3. The numerals on the Closure clock are a fierce bright red, the color of a dying sun. In all the time I can remember, I've never seen it set like this.

But why not? There are many fewer mouths to feed now. All the nutrients and rare elements from those who are no longer living are being recycled via the composting machines. Consumables stores have been replenished. Nothing has gone to waste. And the daily resource demands of nearly five hundred people have been slashed; a big strain on the system removed.

Come on, Elke, I tell myself, *there's work to be done.* Heart-wrenching, back-breaking work. So many bodies! It takes all I've got just to drag each one to the composter. I try my hardest not to look at their faces, but the marks of toxin-induced asphyxia—those blued lips and tortured expressions—are soon etched deep into my brain.

Traces are still in the recycled air. Even now, I can feel a ghost-hand tightening around my own throat. I think it will take a few more days before the air-scrubbers have removed the last traces of *partaxis* toxin.

I stare at the numbers on the C-clock, marveling at the straight row of nines that stretch as far as there are digits to display. Of course a 1.0 would be even better, but that's not possible. No system is perfect. Closure is a goal you chase but don't ever reach. It has bought time and solitude and serenity, though.

I doubt I'll live long enough to feel real soil beneath my feet again, breathe the wonderful scents of an unfiltered atmosphere, wander where I please without boundaries. But if I grow tired of waiting, maybe I'll go looking for that door. One day I'll step outside onto the golden beach that awaits.

And that's a thought that brings its own kind of closure.

Barnaby in Exile

by Mike Resnick

Barnaby sits in his cage, waiting for Sally to come into the lab. She will give him the puzzle, the same one he worked on yesterday. But today he will not disappoint her. He has been thinking about the puzzle all night. Thinking is fun. Today he will do it right, and she will laugh and tell him how smart he is. He will lay on his back and she will tickle his stomach, and say, "Oh, what a bright young fellow you are, Barnaby!" Then Barnaby will make a funny face and turn a somersault.

Barnaby is me.

It gets lonely after Sally leaves. Bud comes when it is black and cleans my cage, but he never talks. Sometimes he forgets and leaves the light on. Then I try to talk to Roger and his family, but they are just rabbits and cannot make the signs. I don't think they are very smart, anyway.

Every night when Bud comes in I sit up and smile at him. I always make the sign for "Hello," but he doesn't answer. Sometimes I think Bud isn't any smarter than Roger. He just pats me on the head. Sometimes he leaves the pictures on after he leaves.

My favorite pictures are Fred and Barney. Everything is so bright and fast. Many times I ask Sally to bring Dino to the lab so that I

265

can play with him, but she never does. I like Barney, because he is not as big or loud as Fred, and I am not big or loud either. Also, my name is Barnaby and that is like Barney. Sometimes, when it is black and I am all alone, I imagine that I am Barney, and that I don't sleep in a cage at all.

This day it was white out, and Sally even had white on her when she came to the lab, but it all turned to water.

Today we had a new toy. It looks like the thing on Doctor's desk, with lots of little things that look like flat grapes. Sally told me that she would show me something and then I should touch the grape that had the same picture on it. She showed me a shoe, and a ball, and an egg, and a star, and a square.

I did the egg and the ball wrong, but tomorrow I will do them right. I think more every day. Like Sally says I am a very bright young fellow.

We have spent many days with the new toy, and now I can speak to Sally with it, just by touching the right grapes.

She will come into the lab and say, "How are you this morning, Barnaby?" and I will touch the grapes that say, "Barnaby is fine" or "Barnaby is hungry."

What I really want to say is "Barnaby is lonely" but there is no grape for "lonely."

Today I touch the grapes that say, "Barnaby wants out."

"Out of your cage?" she asks.

"Out there," I sign. "Out in the white."

"You would not like it."

"I do not like the black when I am alone," I sign. "I will like the white."

"It is very cold," she says, "and you are not used to it."

"The white is very pretty," I say. "Barnaby wants out."

"The last time I let you out you hurt Roger," she reminds me.

"I just wanted to touch him," I say.

"You do not know your own strength," she says. "Roger is just a rabbit, and you hurt him."

"I will be gentle this time," I say.

"I thought you didn't like Roger," she says.

"I don't like Roger," I say. "I like touching."

She reaches into the cage and tickles my belly and scratches my back and I feel better, but then she stops.

"It is time for your lesson," she says.

"If I do it right, can you bring me something to touch?" I ask.

"What kind of thing?" she says.

I think for a moment. "Another Barnaby," I say.

She looks sad, and doesn't answer.

One day Sally brings me a book filled with pictures. I smell it and taste it. Finally I figure out that she wants me to look at it.

There are all kinds of animals in it. I see one that looks like Roger, but it is brown and Roger is white. And there is a kitten, like I see through the window. And a dog, like Doctor sometimes brings to the lab. But there is no Dino.

Then I see a picture of a boy. His hair is shorter than Sally's, and not as gray as Doctor's, or as yellow as Bud's. But he is smiling, and I know he must have many things to touch.

When Sally comes back the next morning, I have lots of questions about the pictures. But before I can ask her, she asks me.

"What is this?" she says, holding up a picture.

"Roger," I say.

"No," she says. "Roger is a name. What is this animal called?"

I try to remember. "Rabbit," I say at last.

"Very good, Barnaby," she says. "And what is this?"

"Kitten," I say.

We got through the whole book.

"Where is Barnaby?" I ask.

"Barnaby is an ape," she says. "There is no picture of an ape in the book."

I wonder if there are any other Barnabys in the world, and if they are lonely too.

Later I ask, "Do I have a father and a mother?"

"Of course you do," says Sally. "Everything has a father and a mother."

"Where are they?" I ask.

"Your father is dead," says Sally. "Your mother is in a zoo far away from here."

"Barnaby wants to see his mother," I say.

"I'm afraid not, Barnaby."

"Why?"

"She wouldn't know you. She has forgotten you, just as you have forgotten her."

"If I could see her, I would say, 'I'm Barnaby,' and then she would know me."

Sally shakes her head. "She wouldn't understand. You are very special; she is not. She can't sign, and she can't use a computer."

"Does she have any other Barnabys?" I ask.

"I don't know," says Sally. "I suppose so."

"How does she speak to them?"

"She doesn't."

I think about this for a long time.

Finally I say, "But she touches them."

"Yes, she touches them," says Sally.

"They must be very happy," I say.

Today I will find out more about being Barnaby.

"Good morning," says Sally when she comes into the lab. "How are you today, Barnaby?"

"What is a zoo?" I ask.

"A zoo is a place where animals live," says Sally.

"Can I see a zoo through the window?"

"No. It is very far away."

I think about my next question for a long time. "Are Barnabys animals?"

"Yes."

"Are Sallys animals?"

"In a way, yes."

"Does Sally's mother live in a zoo?"

Sally laughs. "No," she says.

"Does she live in a cage?"

"No," says Sally.

I think for a while.

"Sally's mother is dead," I say.

"No, she is alive."

I get very upset, because I do not know how to ask why Sally's mother is different from Barnaby's mother, and the harder I try the worse I do it, and Sally cannot understand me. Finally I start hitting the floor with my fist. Roger and his family all jump, and Doctor opens the door. Sally gives me a little toy that squeaks when I hit it, and very soon I forget to be mad and start playing with the toy. Sally says something to Doctor, and he smiles and leaves.

"Do you want to ask anything else before we begin our lesson?" asks Sally.

"Why?" I ask.

"Why what?"

"Why is Barnaby an ape and Sally a man?"

"Because that is the way God made us," she says.

I start getting very excited, because I think I am very close to learning more about Barnabys.

"Who is God?" I ask.

She tries to answer, but I do not understand again.

When it gets black and I am all alone except for Roger and his family, and Bud has already cleaned my cage, I sit and think about God. Thinking can be very interesting.

If he made Sally and he made me, why didn't he make me as smart as Sally? Why can she talk, and do things with her hands that I can't do?

It is very confusing. I decide that I must meet God and ask him why he does these things, and why he forgot that even Barnabys like to be touched.

As soon as Sally comes into the lab, I ask her, "Where does God live?"

"In heaven."

"Is heaven far away?"

"Yes."

"Farther than a zoo?" I ask.

"Much farther."

"Does God ever come to the lab?"

She laughs. "No. Why?"

"I have many questions to ask him."

"Perhaps I can answer some of them," she says.

"Why am I alone?"

"Because you are very special," says Sally.

"If I was not special, would I be with other Barnabys?"

"Yes."

"I have never hurt God," I say. "Why has God made me special?"

The next morning I ask her to tell me about the other Barnabys.

"Barnaby is just a name," explains Sally. "There are other apes, but I don't know if any of them are named Barnaby."

"What is a name?"

"A name is what makes you different from everything else."

"If my name was Fred or Dino, could I be like everyone else?" I ask.

"No," she says. "You are special. You are Barnaby the Bonobo. You are very famous."

"What is famous?"

"Many people know who you are."

"What are People?" I ask.

"Men and women."

"Are there more than you and Doctor and Bud?"

"Yes."

Then it is time for my lessons, but I do them very badly, because I am still thinking about a world that has more People in it than Sally and Doctor and Bud. I am so busy wondering who lets them out of their cages when the dark goes away, that I forget all about God and don't think about him any more for many days.

I hear Sally talking to Doctor, but I do not understand what they are saying.

Doctor keeps repeating that we don't have any more fun, and Sally keeps saying that Barnaby is special, and then they both say a lot of things I can't understand.

When they are through, and Doctor leaves, I ask Sally why we can't have fun any more.

"Fun?" she repeats. "What do you mean?"

"Doctor says there will be no more fun."

She stares at me for a long time. "You understood what he said?"

"Why can't we have any fun?" I repeat.

"Fund," she says. "The word was *fund*. It means something different."

"Then Barnaby and Sally can still have fun?" I ask.

"Of course we can."

I lay on my back and sign to her. "Tickle me."

She reaches into the cage and tickles me, but I see water in her eyes. Human People make water in their eyes when they are unhappy. I pretend to bite her hand and then race around my cage like I did when I was a baby, but this time it doesn't make her laugh.

I hear voices coming from behind the door. It is Sally and Doctor again.

"Well, we can't put him in a zoo," says Doctor. "If he starts signing to the spectators, they'd have a million people demanding his freedom by the end of the month, and then what would happen? What would become of him? Can you picture the poor bastard in a circus?"

"We can't destroy him just because he's too bright," says Sally.

"Who will take him? *You?*" says Doctor. "He's only eight now. What happens when he becomes sexually mature, when he is a surly adult male? It's not that far away. He could rip you apart in seconds."

"He won't—not Barnaby."

"Will your landlord let you keep him? Are you willing to sacrifice the next twenty years of your life caring for him?"

"We might get renewed funding as early as this fall," says Sally.

"Be realistic," says Doctor. "It'll be years, if ever. This program is being duplicated at half a dozen labs around the country, and some of them are much farther along. Barnaby's not the only ape that has learned to use articles and adjectives, you know. There's a twenty-five-year-old gorilla, and three other Bonobo chimps that are well into their teens. There's no reason to believe that anyone will restore our funding."

"But he's *different*," says Sally. "He asks abstract questions."

"I know, I know … once he asked you who God was. But I studied the tape, and you mentioned God first. If you mention Michael

Jordan and he asks who that is, it doesn't mean that he's developed an abiding interest in basketball."

"Can I at least talk to the committee? Show them videotapes of him?"

"They know what a chimpanzee looks like," says Doctor.

"But they don't know what one *thinks* like," says Sally. "Perhaps this will help to convince them …"

"It's not a matter of convincing them," says Doctor. "The funds have dried up. Every program is hurting these days."

"Please …"

"All right," says Doctor. "I'll set up a meeting. But it won't do any good."

I hear it all, but I do not understand any of it. Before it got white today, I dreamed of a place filled with Barnabys, and I am sitting in a corner, my eyes shut, trying to remember it before it all drifts away.

We keep doing the lessons each day, but I can tell that Sally is unhappy, and I wonder what I have done to upset her.

This morning Sally opens my cage door and just hugs me for a long time.

"I have to talk to you, Barnaby," she says, and I see her eyes are making water again.

I touch the grapes that say, "Barnaby likes to talk."

"This is important," she says. "Tomorrow you will leave the lab."

"Will I go outside?" I ask.

"You will go very far away."

"To a zoo?"

"Farther."

Suddenly I remember God.

"Will I go to heaven?" I ask.

She smiles even as her eyes make more water. "Not quite that far," she says. "You are going to a place where there are no labs and no cages. You will be free, Barnaby."

"Are there other Barnabys there?"

"Yes," she says. "There are other Barnabys there."

"Doctor was wrong," I say. "There will be more fun for Sally and Barnaby."

"I cannot go with you," she says.

"Why?"

"I have to stay here. This is my home."

"If you are good, maybe God will let you out of your cage," I say.

She makes a funny sound and hugs me again.

They put me in a smaller cage, one with no light in it. For two days I smell bad things. Most of my water spills, and there are loud noises that hurt my ears. Sometimes People talk, and once a man who is not Bud or Doctor gives me food and more water. He does it through a little hole in the top of the cage.

I touch his hand to show him that I am not angry. He screams and pulls his hand away.

I keep signing, "Barnaby is lonely," but it is dark and there is no one to see.

I do not like my new world.

On the third morning they move my crate, and then they move it again. Finally they lift it up and carry it, and when they set it down I can smell many things I have never smelled before.

They open the door, and I step out onto the grass. The sun is very bright, and I squint and look at People who are not Sally or Doctor or Bud.

"You're home, boy," says one of them.

I look around. The world is a much bigger place than the lab, and I am frightened.

"Go on, fella," says another. "Sniff around. Get used to the place."

I sniff around. I do not get used to the place.

I spend many days in the world. I get to know all the trees and bushes, and the big fence around it. They feed me fruits and leaves and bark. I am not used to them, and for a while I am sick, but then I get better.

I hear many noises from beyond the world—screams and growls and shrieks. I smell many strange animals. But I do not hear or smell any Barnabys.

Then one day the People put me back in my crate, and I am alone for a long time, and then they open the crate, and I am no longer in the world, but in a place with so many trees that I almost cannot see the sky.

"Okay, fella," says a Person. "Off into the forest with you now."

He makes a motion with his hands, but it is a sign I do not recognize. I sign back: "Barnaby is afraid."

The Person pets me on the head. It is the first time anyone has touched me since I left the lab.

"Have a good life," he says, "and make lots of little Barnabys."

Then he climbs into his cage, and it rolls away from me. I try to follow it, but it is much too fast, and soon I can no longer see it.

I look back at the forest and hear strange sounds, and a breeze brings me the sweet smell of fruit.

There is no one around to see me, but I sign "Barnaby is free" anyway.

Barnaby is free.

Barnaby is lonely.

Barnaby is frightened.

I learn to find water, and to climb trees. I see little Barnabys with tails that chatter at me, but they cannot sign, and I see big kittens with spots, and they make terrible noises and I hide from them.

I wish I could hide in my cage, where I was always safe.

Today when the black goes away I wake up and go to the water, and I find another Barnaby.

"Hello," I sign. "I am a Barnaby too."

The other Barnaby growls at me.

"Do you live in a lab?" I ask. "Where is your cage?"

The other Barnaby runs at me and starts biting me. I shriek and roll on the ground.

"What have I done?" I ask.

The other Barnaby runs at me again, and I screech and climb to the top of a tree. He sits at the bottom and stares at me all day until the black returns. It gets very cold, and then wet, and I shiver all night and wish Sally was here.

In the morning the Barnaby is gone, and I climb down to the ground. I smell where he has been, and I follow his scent, because I do not know what else to do. Finally I come to a place with more Barnabys than I ever imagined there could be. Then I remember that Sally taught me counting, and I count. There are twenty-three of them.

One of them sees me and screams, and before I can make any signs all of them charge at me and I run away. They chase me for a long time, but finally they stop, and I am alone again.

I am alone for many days. I do not go back to the Barnabys, because they would hurt me if they could. I do not know what I have done to make them mad, so I do not know how to stop doing it.

I have learned to smell the big kittens when they are still far away, and to climb the trees so they cannot catch me, and I have learned to hide from the dogs that laugh like Sally does when I make somersaults, but I am so lonely, and I miss talking, and I am already forgetting some of the signs Sally taught me.

Last night I dreamed about Fred and Wilma and Barney and Dino, and when I woke up my own eyes were making water.

I hear sounds in the morning. Not sounds like the big kittens or the dogs make, but strange, clumsy sounds. I go to see what is making them.

In a little clearing I see four People—two men and two women—and they have brought little brown cages. The cages are not as nice as my old cage, because you cannot see in or out of them.

One of the men has made a fire, and they are sitting on chairs around it. I want to approach them, but I have learned my lesson with the Barnabys, and so I wait until one of the men sees me.

When he doesn't yell or chase me, I sign to him.

"I am Barnaby."

"What has it got in its hands?" asks one of the women.

"Nothing," says a man.

"Barnaby wants to be friends," I sign.

A woman puts something up in front of her face, and suddenly there is a big *pop!* It is so bright that I can't see. I rub my eyes and walk forward.

"Don't let him get too close," says the other man. "No telling what kind of diseases he's carrying."

"Will you play with Barnaby?" I ask.

The first man picks up a rock and throws it at me.

"Shoo!" he yells. "Go away!"

He throws another rock, and I run back into the forest.

When it is black out, and they sit around the fire, I sneak as close as I can get, and lay down and listen to the sounds of their voices, and pretend I am back in the lab.

In the morning they throw rocks at me until I go away.

And then one day, after they throw the rocks at me and I go for water, I come back and find that they are gone. They were not very good friends, but they were the only ones I had.

What will I do now?

Finally, after many days, I find a single Barnaby, and it is a female. She has terrible scars on her from other Barnabys, and when she sees me she bares her teeth and growls. I sit still and hope that she will not go away.

After a long time she comes closer to me. I am afraid to move, because I do not want to frighten her or make her mad. I ignore her and stare off into the trees.

Finally she reaches out and picks an insect off my shoulder and puts it into her mouth, and soon she is sitting beside me, eating the flowers and leaves that have fallen to the ground.

Finally, when I am sure she will not run away, I sign to her, "I am Barnaby."

She grabs at my hands as if I was playing with a fruit or an insect, then shows her teeth when she sees that I am not holding anything.

She is really not any smarter than Roger, but at least she does not run away from me.

I will call her Sally.

Sally is afraid of the other Barnabys, so we live at the edge of the forest where they hardly ever come. She touches me, and that is very nice, but I find that I miss talking and thinking even more.

Every day I try to teach her to sign, but she cannot learn. We have three baby Barnabys, one after each rainy season, but they are no smarter than Sally, and besides I have forgotten most of the signs.

More and more People come to the forest in their brown cages. My family is afraid of them, but I love talking and listening and thinking more than anything. I always visit their camps at night, and listen to their voices in the darkness, and try to understand the words. I pretend I am back in the lab, though it is harder and harder to remember what the lab is like.

Each time there are new People I show myself and say, "I am Barnaby," but none of them ever answers. When one finally does, I will know that he is God.

There were many things I wanted to ask him once, but I cannot remember most of them. I will tell him to be nice to Sally and the other two People at the lab—I forget their names—because what has happened to me is not their fault.

I will not ask him why he hated me so much that he made me special, or why People and Barnabys always chase me away. I will just say, "Please talk to Barnaby," and then I will ask if we can do a lesson.

Once, when I was a very bright fellow, there were many things I wanted to discuss with him. But now that I have left the world, that will be enough.

Giant Mechs in the Distance, Forever Fighting

by ZZ Claybourne

Birdsong, of the few birds that hung around, barely carried in the omnipresent haze. Behemoth mechs—some shaped like spiders, some like angry giants, others like pieces of war held together by magnets—fought along every horizon. They always fought and always in the outlying areas, as there was no point fighting inside a city meant to be taken over. Even the lowliest taggers didn't spar for turf if the turf was unusable rubble.

Birdsong came short and swift; each tiny, fragile winged body had a point to make and made it without waiting to be felled by a drone or eaten by whatever feral animal was nearest; they twittered for a moment hoping for a mate. They took off before a rival answered the call instead.

Life in general was primarily chaotic as mechs fought. The mechs were glorious. War had never been so aspirational until the first two rolled off the line two continents away from each other. Seeing that much science, ingenuity, and high expenditure brought to bear for killing genuinely stirred folks. Up close, the neighborhoods fought about water, they fought about air, they fought about footsteps and living space. They fought at all hours of the day and night. Even the people with jobs fought, but not as often.

Marshall had a job. Marshall usually stayed indoors. Fighters heard him playing now and then when they were quiet, which wasn't often. He played each day in his rundown home with the shiniest guitar in the world. It was played for however long a tune needed, polished after each use, and replaced carefully as a babe on fur when done.

Marshall peered outward, but not at the giant mechs along the horizon of the flat barren land stretching forever away from his border home. He observed a group of fighters in the middle of the street. The group got bigger and bigger the longer he peered between the slats of his blinds. Half of them wore masks to protect themselves from the ash of nearby warfare, half did not. All were angry, nearly feral, except for the fact that they worked in organized groups with rules and roles, but Marshall had long since supposed feral cats acknowledged hierarchy and structure. The fight was going to be ugly since it was about absolutely nothing. Those fights usually ended with lots of blood for loud, crazed gulls to land atop, leaving strange, red art on the broken roads. The municipality took care of the bodies; ash rain eventually washed the gulls' prints away.

Scavengers, all. One day the gulls would learn that there was never food following these deaths.

He couldn't tolerate a fight today. He was too old for it. He was too frightened for it. That morning he'd said the customary prayer to remake the world, but had done so in front of the glow of a monitor showing three pre-determined pictures over and over. The house computer forever asked him if he'd like it to import additional images. He never responded to it. Marshall Monday-nee-Wellis always hated the day the world's spy machines had been made cheap enough for poor people to be able to buy their conveniences. The lovely Anna Monday said she'd marry him if he took her name—after kissing his ear while they cuddled against a gray, rotted tree—to which he'd mellifluously sang yes. Anna had loved the idea of things being done for her for a change.

The first 3-dimensional image showed Anna holding tongs; smiling and grilling before the ash had become an everyday thing.

The second photo was one she'd taken at his birthday twenty-three years ago. Pre-ash again. They were all pre-ash. Photography had died after that first intercontinental bomb. A part of her hand was in the photo, owing to her laughing at the expression on his face at the misshapen cake guitar she'd attempted.

In their locked home it had tasted wonderful.

279

Lemon and butter, not at all like the bitter taste of being old and alone.

The last picture was Anna's face up close, each freckle and blemish a sun on honeyed skin, with the real sun—that now-permanent smudge behind haze—haloing her gray twists brilliantly.

Life now was nothing but peering between blinds and working. He never left the house on this day—this anniversary—not even for the nightly cleaning of the air vents at the various municipal offices he toiled. Today had been *his* day for ten years, no matter what clanked on the horizon. He'd fought for it tooth and nail, wearing the bosses down year after year.

"I just need this one day off, sir—"

"I never ask for anything at all—"

"I don't make trouble, sir, I just—"

The municipality no longer even docked his pay.

He narrowed his eye at the fighters. Hven gave a disinterested glance toward the mechs. One—at this distance just a confluence of lines and angles—toppled in a huge cloud of cartoon dust. The other fired another rocket at it.

In the middle of his street, several people shoved each other. Marshall was inured to the shouting. That was background noise—that and the random bursts of gunfire. This, though, was the type of gathering that gained strength, like the old hurricanes used to do. Its threat potential leaving people wondering if it would become a one, a three, or a five—

"Just go away," he muttered. He was grumpy and old enough to have muttered "Get off my lawn," had there been any lawns left under the constant haze of warfare.

It was merely a matter of time before the flash of an ancient blade or the glint off a silver-painted printed gun made its way through the quarter-inch view of the world he allowed. Every light in the home was turned on, except for this closed-off room. The living room. It was the smallest room in the house, but it faced the street, and Anna had claimed the space as their place of daily respite.

He didn't want them to see or notice him.

He just wanted to sit on his stoop and play his guitar without wondering who was coming to fight him for it.

Marshall's tight breath displaced motes on the blinds. The fighters jostled far enough away that they wouldn't see the slat vibrating from his nervous heartbeat shaking his wrinkled fingers.

Still, the hurricane category worsened. The sounds of escalation were invading his personal space. *Their* personal space.

"Not today!"

He dropped the blind and rushed to his polished guitar.

He pulled his mask off the nail by the door.

He yanked the door open so angrily it frightened him at the same time.

The fighters didn't notice at first. They shouted, pushed, and were probably about to kick or punch. Kicks and punches led to weapons being drawn.

He played as he walked.

It stopped everything.

The notes, even though they didn't fly far, took to the air.

He kept his eyes closed and played to calm them. It was an impromptu arrangement, a melody of awakening and creation, a G chord which wandered the crowd like a small bystander. He stopped inside a wide, shallow pothole while the fighters stared at him. He played as if there was no one but him, his guitar, and music for Anna Monday at the curb of that city street, keeping his eyes closed because otherwise the reality of the world would have knocked his music from the sky and eaten it.

The fighters stared at him. He didn't want to feel their stares. They murmured. He didn't want to hear their noise. This strange concert kept everyone's hands away from knives and guns, and when they realized he wasn't going anywhere—that he was going to stand there with eyes closed and continue playing music—several fighters went away.

He'd done this before. He hated it each time.

Neighbors told Marshall Monday he was going to get killed doing that. He agreed it was likely.

But today was Anna's day. He had fought this ragged city to hold this day away from the hungry world. If he had to fight a mech along the border too, he would. Getting smooshed wouldn't matter. What was life but blood under a thumb anyway.

He played in the pothole that would never be repaired. After a short time, everybody left, disappearing into the gloom of ash to put on spyglasses to see which mech toppled another. There was always fighting, whether it was man or machine.

Marshall Monday kept playing until all he heard was his music. He opened his eyes. Even all the neighbors had gone inside. He played a little more, then he stopped strumming only long enough to carry his guitar to his cracked stoop. He sat on the top step where the rusted awning placed him in deeper shadow, and played the tune out to the end. Then he too disappeared inside. He locked his front door and glanced out one last time. He thought of Anna, her face in what used to be the sun.

In the distance, soundlessly and surely, a toppled mech righted itself to begin again. Marshall didn't care. He carefully placed his guitar on the table and went to get polish to wipe dust and ash from it yet again.

No more fighting today.

Worrywart

by Effie Seiberg

Fairy gifts are great if they come from a smart fairy. A *smart* fairy knows not to deal in too many abstracts without defining them. But my fairy godfather, Morningflower, gifted me with "being able to confront my biggest problems head-on," which meant that instead of having a baseline level of anxiety neatly tucked into my head, I had Bub.

Bub was my anxiety. He looked like a navy-blue goblin, and was the size of a big watermelon. Not that he was visible to anyone else, but I'd been able to see him since the age of eight. He hadn't left my side once.

And today he was cranky.

"No respect!" he grumped. "None! The nerve of that guy!"

"Calm down," I said. My horse half-tripped on a rock in the path and jolted us, but kept going through the autumn breeze. "He couldn't see you and he was trying to be helpful."

I couldn't see Bub behind me in his stiff leather basket attached to the side of my saddle, but I knew he had his arms crossed in his huff. "He loaded five dead chickens onto my head! This is on you, really. You coulda told him I was there."

"Not if I want any more monster-killing business. Besides, they're in the other bag now so you're fine." We'd had this fight so many times before. Who's gonna hire a freelance adventurer if they're known to have anxiety?

283

"*I* think you're scared of me. You're scared of being scared. You big wuss. Just you wait, it'll be a self-reinforcing cycle of fear and you'll be stuck cowering under a tree somewhere, too scared to keep going."

"Sure, whatever." I looked back and saw he was sticking his tongue out, so I made a point of rolling my eyes. But what if he was right? What if I was a big wuss?

I went through my mental checklist, which always kept Bub a little quieter. Today's assignment was a hydra. I *hated* hydras. But I was ready, hopefully? I had my sword at my side, my big axe strapped to my back, a short dagger on my left leg and a knife in my right boot. Making sure to keep my horse steady, I felt around behind me for the saddlebag that didn't have Bub, and fished beneath the dead chickens until I could touch the box for my poison-tipped crossbow bolts. The crossbow case was just within reach behind the bag.

The plan was simple. Lure out the hydra with the chickens. Shoot it a bunch with the poison-tipped bolts. Easy-peasy—unless I didn't get a good shot and had to defend myself close-up. I should've dipped my sword in the poison when I had it too. Damn. You can't kill a hydra with a sword, just piss it off enough so maybe it thinks you're not worth the trouble. And hydras are so mean they think everything's worth the trouble.

"You can't do it," said Bub.

"Of course I can do it," I said, not believing a word that came out of my mouth. I hated how persuasive Bub was. But I'd spent lots of time working on my crossbow marksmanship before I even took the gig.

I'd also spent lots of time working on not listening to Bub, but that skill was … not as far along as my marksmanship.

"You're gonna fail."

What if I failed? A terribly painful protracted death. Hydras liked to play with their food, the sadistic things, like a bored cat with a slow mouse.

And if I survived? Deep humiliation when I came back empty-handed to the town that hired me. And my reputation would be ruined. And I'd never get work again. And I'd starve to death which honestly sounded a lot worse than being a hydra chew toy.

"You're gonna fa-ail. You ca-an't do it. You aren't rea-dy. You'll never work aga-ain." Bub's taunting singsong was as familiar as the back of my hand. "Now, look at this."

Thanks to Bub I now pictured myself in front of the hydra, all of its heads staring at me. A cluster of red mouths glistened with spit and venom, green scales splitting into evil grins. The heads surrounded me and started biting, one small bloody chunk of me gone each time. I flailed with my sword and axe but they bounced right off the monster's skin. The ground was littered with useless crossbow bolts, blue-stained with the poison that failed to get into the hydra every time I'd missed a shot. Of course I'd missed. And I couldn't run because in this scenario I was backed up to the edge of a cliff—death whether I went forward or back. I was helpless and too scared to do anything, too paralyzed by fear to even pick up a dropped bolt and stab in the poison directly.

I could feel myself starting to sweat, my heart racing and trying to smash its way out my ribcage. What if this was it? Why did I think I was capable of killing a *hydra* of all things? They were awful! I barely escaped the last one!

My hands were sweaty on the horse's reins. The dripping mouths full of awful needle teeth filled my inner eye again, and I started to hyperventilate.

I wiped my hands on my brown woolen tunic and shook my head, trying to clear out the mental image. It didn't work.

"Utter failure, that's what you are," said Bub.

I turned around in the saddle as far as I could and swiped at him. It felt like slapping fog—ineffective and not even good at getting out frustration. And definitely not good at shutting him up.

"Why did you ever think you could do this?" Smug bastard.

I imagined ditching him, flinging him out a trebuchet, boiling him in oil … but none of that made my current panic any easier, or the mental image of venomous hydra-mouth any fainter. Besides, I knew none of these ideas would work.

I counted my breath in for one, two, three … and then counted my breath out for one, two, three, four, five. Gripped the pommel of my saddle and focused on the sensation in my hands. Then repeated the whole exercise nine more times until I felt a bit calmer.

"You ca-an't doooo it," Bub whispered, and something itched at the back of my mind. I was forgetting something.

Wait. Wait a minute.

Wait just a gods-cursed snake-spitting minute.

I eased the horse to a stop and hopped off. Rummaged through the saddlebag to pull out the wooden box of bolts. The iron latch was already open, and inside, nothing but the burlap lining. No bolts at all.

And suddenly I could picture the bolts on the shopkeeper's table, right where I put them after she'd dipped them all in poison for me, and right where I left them when I ran out to deal with the commotion of Bub yelling at the assistant for pouring dead chickens on his head, and the assistant not understanding why the chickens weren't going into the saddle compartment at all even though it was clearly empty, and then the assistant dumping them on Bub's head all over again. And then I'd put the chickens on top of the bolt case in the other bag and forgot about everything.

Dammit.

I *hated* when Bub was right. It didn't happen often, but whenever it did he'd use it as ammo from there on in to make me doubt myself more. I put the case back in the saddlebag, this time on top of the chickens, got on the horse and turned us back on the path.

Two hours later, now properly armed with poison-tipped bolts (I used my checklist twice as we were leaving the shop to make sure I hadn't forgotten anything else), Bub and I approached the hydra's lair.

I armed myself with all my weapons, double-checked and triple-checked my leather armor and steel helmet were bucked on right, and hid myself behind a tree. The mouth of the hydra's cave was right where the town leaders had said it would be, on the other side of the grassy clearing. The rocks nearby were tinged with blood spatters, and I could see what had to be a couple of cow femurs strewn about.

The wait for a deadly creature to come out was always the worst part. It's where Bub went *wild* with terrible scenarios. But before I could preemptively tell him to shut up, a noise sounding like footsteps on gravel came out of the cave. And out stepped … the tiniest hydra I'd ever seen.

It couldn't've been much taller than Bub, and was even the same deep blue color. Nine stubby necks erupted from its shoulders, and nine cranky heads sat atop them. This was gonna be easy for once.

Bub smirked. "Look at you. Even a tiny hydra like this one, and you're gonna fail."

Something itched at the back of my mind again, but I ignored it and loaded up my crossbow.

"You forgot your poisoned bolts before. What else are you forgetting? Look at all this bare vulnerable flesh you've got showing. Bet you forgot some armor."

I patted myself all around, checked the armor, checked the buckles. Looked good. "Shut up, Bub."

"You're gonna fail anyway. Before you know it, you'll be shaking like a leaf and your shot will go wide. And you'll end up dead, and not even from something big and scary. From this piddly little thing."

"Shut up *shut up!*" I said under my breath. I imagined a stone wall going up all around Bub, sealing him away, then brought up my crossbow again. I aimed at the creature, breathed out to steady myself, and fired.

The shot hit right in the middle of the squat creature's chest … and went right through as though the beast were made of smoke.

What the hell?

Bub was right. I couldn't fight back and this thing was going to get me and I was going to die a horrible death from this tiny thing *right now.*

"Hey, whoever you are, that was RUDE and UNNECESSARY!" bellowed the creature.

"*Calm down,*" said a deeper voice from within the cave, and out came *another* hydra.

Easily twelve feet tall, nine elegant long necks shining in scales of teal and green and turquoise, and now that I thought about it, looking a whole lot more likely to be the right size for multiple cow femurs to make sense. Damn damn damn damn.

"*Remember people can't see you?*" said head 3.

"*Or animals,*" said head 7.

"Someone shot me! So rude. This is why you don't have any friends. You don't take care of the people around you," said the mini-hydra.

"Hey, this guy's awesome!" shouted Bub from behind me.

"Who said that!" The mini-hydra started to stomp over in our direction across the clearing.

"Wait, you can hear me?" said Bub.

"*Wait, you can hear him?*" said big-hydra heads 1, 4, and 8 in unison.

Bub stomped out from behind the tree toward the mini-hydra before I could do anything about it. So much for my element of surprise.

The two met midway across and other than the number of heads, they looked weirdly similar. In fact, the mini-hydra walked on the tips of the grass, just like Bub. Like they were both equally weightless and the stalks felt no need to bend underneath them.

I reloaded my crossbow, my hands shaking. Bub got me into enough problems as it was, but if he was gonna sic two different hydras on me, there's no way I could get out of this alive, even with my poison bolts. But I should still try, right? Even worse to go out not fighting.

The two talked quietly together for a moment while both the big hydra and I waited on opposite sides of the clearing. It probably hadn't seen me yet and thought Bub was the only one around. But why could it see Bub?

I aimed again, but the giant monster paced back and forth, and my shaking hands made it hard for me to get a good shot.

Bub turned back to where I was and yelled, "I like this guy!" while the mini-hydra turned to its bigger counterpart and called out, "This one's okay! He's also got a scaredy-cat loser."

I kept my crossbow up. Great, now the big hydra knew where I was.

"Yeah," Bub waved me over. "Turns out we're brothers!"

The big hydra caught my eye with all nine of its heads at once, just like I'd imagined. SHIT SHIT SHIT.

"So … does that mean you have Morningflower as your fairy godfather too?" asked head 3.

My jaw dropped, and things came together really really fast. This hydra also had anxiety!

I had an idea, and inched out from behind the tree. I dropped my crossbow just enough to show I wasn't aiming directly at the monster. "Yeah! He really sucks, right?"

Heads 1, 4, and 8 broke out in laughter. *"He totally does! Did you get that nonsense about facing things head-on too?"*

"Yes! It's the worst!" I yelled back. "How do you manage it?"

"Um … poorly?" said head 3. *"I dunno, some days I don't manage it at all. It's really hard. He's always harping on all of my worst fears."*

"It's even worse when he's right!" I said. I let my crossbow arm drop and started to walk toward the middle of the clearing. "He never lets me forget it!"

"I knoooooooow!" said head 7 with a smile. The hydra moved toward the center too. *"Like Gug's always saying, I'm gonna get killed by some tiny skinny wuss of an adventurer ... wait."*

All eighteen eyes locked on my crossbow. *"Were you gonna ...?"* heads 1, 4, and 8 trailed off.

"Um," I felt sheepish. "I mean yeah, until I met you. You seem cool though. I'd rather we didn't kill each other."

"You're gonna wuss out? Already?" my Bub smirked. "See, I told you you'll fail. Time to starve and die a failure."

"It's a lie." Hydra-Gug turned to the big hydra. "And you're stupid enough to fall for it because you're too desperate to make a friend. You'll get killed and it'll be all your fault and you'll die lonely and friendless AND gullible."

I tensed a bit. It's hard not to believe what anxiety tells you. But I took a deep breath and placed my crossbow in the grass, then stood up and held out my empty hands. "Actually, I'd love to get to know you better. I never met anyone else with anxiety before, and it'd be nice to have the company."

All nine heads grinned and said, "Shut up, Gug," to the nine-headed anxiety goblin, then turned back to me. *"I'm Slee,"* said head 7. *"Come on in. I've got a sheep I was about to roast on the fire, and a cask of wine I swiped."*

Several hours later, I was back on my way to the village. The sun was starting to set and a cool breeze whipped dead leaves around my horse's feet. Bub was in his usual saddle compartment, and the other compartment now held a sheep heart. Strapped to the back of the saddle was a hydra head and neck, which I hadn't known were shed and replaced regularly. (Turns out you can tell a hydra's age by how many heads they have! Slee was ninety.)

"You're gonna fail," said Bub. "People are going to see right through this con. They'll kill you for trying to trick them out of their money."

"No they won't," I said. "They have no idea what a hydra heart looks like. And Slee's gonna be more careful with livestock from this village. Besides, it's the next village that'll have a hydra problem."

"You're not gonna get away with this multiple times. You can't just go village by village causing and 'solving' a hydra problem. You're too stupid to get it right. You'll get caught, and you're gonna fail."

"Maybe, maybe not," I said. "Seems like a pretty good partnership to me."

I tried to focus on the present, which Slee told me they'd found helpful. *Right now* things were good. *Right now* I had a new friend and we could share stories and meals and coping mechanisms together without judgment. *Right now* it looked like Bub was a teeeeeny bit fuzzy around the edges, and talked a teeeeeny bit softer.

It was almost like having someone to share with made managing Bub a little easier. I didn't expect Bub to ever go away completely. But it sure was nice finding a friend to share the burden.

I hummed a little tune.

"You're off-key."

"Shut up, Bub," I said, and smiled.

The Color of Thunder

by Alicia Cay

The sound of alarm bells woke Ella even before Papa's heavy booted feet came pounding down the hall.

"El, we've caught something!" Papa yelled.

Ella wrestled herself out of her blankets. The townsfolk told tales of the winged people seen in the skies over the village on dark days—harbingers of ill fate, they said.

But Ella had never seen a Seraph herself, and excitement filled her from her fingers to her toes. Had they caught one at last?

The grass, damp with early morning dew, was slick beneath Ella's bare feet as she ran to catch up with Papa. Over the past year, the narrow backyard, tucked behind their moss-roofed cottage and the line of aspens that bordered their farm, had been transformed with her father's trap. Laced across the night sky, tied from tree to tree, lay an intricate net of black ropes entwined with bells that danced in alarm. Beneath the net hung glass jars stuffed with lightning-flies that sparkled like stars, designed to lure down their prey.

Papa stood under the ropes, staring up at the creature tangled in the lines. Ella's breath snagged in her chest. The Seraphs were known to be beings of malice, but to her the creature appeared rather harmless. It looked like a man, short and slender, with folded wings as long as its body and skin that shone like a midnight-caught

291

oyster pearl—brilliant and blinding in the waning moonlight. Did all Seraphs shine like stars?

"We've caught the murderous beast," Papa whispered.

Ella bit at her bottom lip. How did they know this was *the* Seraph who had murdered her brother? She slipped her fingers into Papa's big warm hand, needing his comfort, his certainty.

Papa pulled his hand away. He ran to fetch his tools from the shed, calling out as he went, "The gods have smiled on us tonight, El." His voice streamed along behind him, leaving trails of manic-violet color in his wake that only Ella could see.

She craned her head to catch a glimpse of the Seraph's face. The ropes were pulled tight across its shimmering skin—ropes that Ella's hands had woven. For this was her family's lone pastime: to sit long into the gathering dark in front of the fire, weaving strong strands of rope for Papa's revenge. She rubbed calloused hands against the fabric of her nightgown, wiping the damp of fear and anticipation from them. *Had* this thing murdered Cord?

Suddenly, from behind a wing covered in sunlight-tinted feathers, the Seraph's face emerged. Ella gasped. Fear prickled across her skin as she met its stare—there was nothing human in that dark gaze. Flickers of light, like dancing galaxies, moved across its pitch-black eyes.

A memory stirred in Ella. Last summer, the day after her fifteenth birthday, Cord had woken her in the night to say goodbye. He was running off with the watchman's daughter. "Her father won't let us be together," Cord had whispered in her ear. "Says we're too young, but Daisy and I are in love. We're going to the Capital to be married." Her big brother had wiped the tears from her eyes, then tucked the blanket around her feet the way he'd done when she was little. He promised to write to her as soon as he and Daisy arrived.

That letter had never come.

Papa returned with a hand-axe and began to cut the ropes. The bells tied to them rang in rhythm with the swing of his blade. Lost in her thoughts and the Seraph's gaze, Ella barely registered Papa's shouts. She came to her senses just in time to dodge the ropes as they fell. The Seraph dropped to the ground with a heavy thud.

Papa bore down on the winged man. He pressed a boot against the Seraph's back and pinned it to the ground. The color of her father, these days a frosty-blue of lonely pain, erupted from him in streams of molten lava, banged up in deep reds—the color of rage. Then her Papa—the man who had taught her to ride her first pony and kissed her skinned knees when she fell from climbing trees—reached down, unfurled one wing with both hands, and wrenched it sideways.

The thick bone snapped, the sound as deafening as a crack of lightning heard up close. Papa grabbed the other wing and twisted, snapping it like a broken branch. Auburn-tinted waves of torture rolled across the Seraph's body. Papa, who could not see these colors as Ella did, bent over the prone creature, his foot firmly between its shoulder blades. Using the axe, he hacked through the bone and sinew that still held.

Flecks of blood splashed onto Papa's arms and face. As they landed on his skin, ripples of a color Ella had never seen on her father before streamed around his chest in circles of rancid-green, and moved outward in waves of scarlet-black, dark as death's cloak.

Ella reeled. She wanted to scream, wanted to crash into her father's arms—once a harbor from bullies and bad dreams—and remind him she was still here, that he was doing this in front of her. She wanted Cord back, but more than that, she wanted Papa back. The person who was meant to protect her from all harm.

Tears lined Ella's cheeks as she stumbled into the cottage. The smell of heated pine rushed to meet her and pulled her into the front room. Sometime during the commotion out back, Mama had woken. She swayed in her rocking chair before a fresh fire.

A rush of relief and affection flooded through Ella. "Mama, you're up?"

"There was such a racket, I could hardly rest." Mama looked at Ella, but her gaze was adrift.

Mama's hair, as gray as the pewter pall of mourning that surrounded her, hung in wisps around her frown-lined face. She had been a gifted healer once, sought after for her tinctures and poultices. Now she spent her days rocking in her chair, mending clothing, and recounting half-forgotten stories.

Ella settled on the woven rug at her mother's feet. Unable to face the ugly color consuming her father, she had left him to drag the Seraph to the barn on his own. Ella took a deep breath, trying to loosen the tightly wound spring of turmoil twisted in her chest. She held her trembling hands before the fire. Its orange warmth drifted into the room, shot through with pops of heated sap that licked out in bursts of bright white, like reaching arms.

"I knew a girl once," Mama said, "with clouds in her eyes."

Ella knew this story, a blend of real and imagined things melded together in her mother's chipped memory, but she leaned her head against Mama's leg and listened anyway, grateful to have her close. Grateful for something to take her thoughts away from what Papa was doing in the barn.

"This girl lived in the village, oh"—Mama waved a hand—"many years ago. She was about your age, I'd say, just coming into her womanhood, when she began to speak of things no one else could see. Her words frightened us, but there were some who also feared her. They said her sorcery would bring the wicked Seraphs down upon our heads. So, she was sent away—"

"Never to return," Ella said, finishing the line she'd heard so many times.

"Listen now, child." Mama stroked Ella's long dark hair. "There is a road, hidden in the Far Woods on the other side of the village. It leads west into the mountains. That girl lives there now, in a cabin by the Salt-Crusted Cliffs." Mama sighed. "Should you ever leave here, dear, go and find her, and give her a kiss for me, would you?"

Ella smiled up at her mother, her heart heavy. "I will, Mama."

The back door banged open. Papa's boots clumped on the smooth stone floor as he made his way into the front room.

Ella watched her father in the firelight. Like Mama, he had aged before his time; his black hair gone to silver, his beard more salt than pepper. Ella was relieved to see the rancid-green color was gone and the madness from moments ago no longer lingered in his eyes, replaced by the great blue sadness that lived there these days.

He bent and planted a kiss on his wife's forehead. "Did we wake you, my love?"

"So much noise," Mama said.

"I know, my dear, I'm sorry. But, we bring good news. Ella and I have caught the damnable creature."

Mama scowled. "Out fishing, at this hour?"

Papa swallowed hard and squeezed Mama's hand. A shot of long-ing tore through Ella's chest. He was so tender with Mama; proof that he *was* still in there, somewhere. Ella jumped up and wrapped her arms around his neck. Papa, caught off guard, let out a small chuckle and hugged her back. Ella saw the blue pain on his skin waver, but it held fast. No matter how Papa hugged her or how tender he was with Mama, the golden greens of his prior happiness did not return. She knew he hadn't stopped caring for them. His love was simply lost, buried beneath his grief.

Papa let Ella go and moved to warm his hands in the golden glow of the fire.

"What do we do now, Papa?" Ella asked.

"I must go to the village and seek counsel. I will need the Elders' advice on how to properly kill the wretched thing so that it stays dead."

"Take 'em out of the water," Mama chimed in. "Kill a fish quick."

Papa tried a smile on for Mama's sake, but it wouldn't take, and he let it slip away. Mama smiled back at him in that slack-jawed way of hers. He traced a thumb along her cheek.

When Papa spoke again, his words drifted from him in bruised purples that tangled in the light-blue frost of his pain. "Once that *thing* is dead, you'll come back to me then. We will have justice for his murder and grace will be restored." He cleared his throat and looked at Ella. "I leave first thing in the morning. See to it she doesn't stay up all night."

"Yes, Papa."

He kissed Mama again, then headed down the hall to their bedroom.

The loss of his only son had broken him in different ways than Mama, and Ella could not fault him for wanting to destroy the Seraph. Cord had been the light of Papa's eye; for the little boy who liked to stick his fingers in the jam jar, and the young man he'd become, laugh-ing while he worked beside Papa in the fields. His absence had left a hole in their home none of them had figured out how to fill.

Papa needed to do this to the Seraph to find peace, but … uncer-tainty knotted in her belly. What if the stories were true? The Ser-aphs were said to come in the night and steal away people possessed by magic, whisking them from their families to far-away corners in nightmare lands.

Ella worked at her bottom lip with her teeth. She was like the girl in Mama's stories, able to see things no one else could. *Had* they caught the creature that murdered her brother, or had it come here for her?

Papa left early the next day, the sun just beginning to rise. Long rays of light glinted off the Plum-Shaded Mountains perched on the western horizon.

Her father shouldered the bag she'd packed for him and strode down the foot-worn path through the heather that led off their farm. He would stay on that path until it met the road that took him into the village; where smoke curled from the chimneys of straw-roofed homes and the Elders waited to give counsel on how to kill a winged man.

Questions about the Seraph burned in Ella, a heat she could feel in her chest. She threw herself into her farm chores to try and keep the treacherous thoughts at bay, and to stay away from the barn as Papa had ordered.

As evening approached, Ella settled on the log fence to watch the goats and pigs in their paddock. Fed and content with life, the farm animals lounged in the shade of her favorite oak tree. How she envied them.

She sighed. Duty called. It was time to go in and start supper for Mama.

Ella swung her legs over the railing and froze, struck by a thought. Did Seraphs need to eat? She should find out. Papa wanted it dead, but she'd been raised to cause no harm. Even prisoners to be executed were given a last meal.

She told herself that was why she was going against Papa's orders. That it wasn't her curiosity, or her need to fix things, that drew her to the creature.

She ran inside to gather a few things, then made her way up the field toward the barn. Wild lavender and long heather swung their purple heads in the breeze and bent to tickle her knees.

The smell of alfalfa hay, sweet and green, hit Ella as she slid back the barn door. She paused, hesitating on the threshold, then continued inside. Her boots kicked up plumes of dust as she shuffled toward the stall where her father had confined the creature. When she reached the gate, the sight of Papa's brutality hit her like a blow to the stomach.

The Seraph lay on its side on a wooden cot, facing the wall. Spikes of bone protruded from its back at the shoulder blades, and smears of dried blood stained its pearled skin. Ella had gone through Mama's cabinets and mixed a quick poultice of pungent herbs. They rang with the colors of renewal and cleanliness—green and hot white—a peace offering to show the Seraph she meant no harm.

Ella opened her mouth to speak, but she could not make the words come out.

"Hello, Ella," the Seraph said. Its voice drifted like dust caught on shafts of sunlight, in motes of pastel pink and aquamarine.

Ella let out a garbled caw. How did it know her name? She cleared her throat. "I came to tend to your wounds."

"I smell the herbs. Will they help with the hurt?"

Mama did have some laudanum tucked away in the back of the cabinet, but Ella hadn't thought to bring any. "No, but I could get you something."

"That would be a kindness."

Ella hesitated. Seraphs were dangerous creatures with blackened hearts, but without its wings did it still have the means to cause her harm?

"You are in no danger from me, child. I have been restrained." The Seraph held up a length of rope. Papa had fastened it around the winged man's neck and secured it to one of the barn's timbers.

Ella bit her lip, unnerved by its response to her unspoken thoughts, but the Seraph's colors never wavered toward anger or deception, so she approached. With trembling hands, she applied the poultice around the broken shards of bone, wishing she could do more.

Lyrical light sang off its skin—except around the wounds, where gaping holes of yellow and black marred it. Touching this oth-er-worldly creature was difficult. The clash of clean and dirty colors riled up the fear inside of her, but what Papa had done to its wings made her chest ache. She wrapped the area in strips of clean cloth. "It's done now."

"May I face you?" the Seraph asked.

Ella nodded, too nervous for words. Again, the creature somehow knew of her affirmation. She moved back as the Seraph turned over. Its movements were fluid and unflinching, like water poured from a fountain. Up close its face was human enough, smooth forehead, delicate nose—all except for those galaxy-eyes.

Ella found herself caught in them again and unexpected fond memories swelled in her: riding her brown and blond Shetland pony through Papa's fields; Cord working next to Papa, making silly faces at her to get her to laugh; tall stalks of wheat dancing around her like waves of a golden ocean; Mama singing in notes of sea green as she rolled biscuits for supper.

The Seraph's voice pulled her back. "You have clouds in your eyes."

Heat licked along Ella's skin beneath the collar of her cotton tunic. *No she didn't.* She turned her face away.

The Seraph sat up, movements graceful, but clearly pained. "Do you see me? My essence?"

Ella stayed quiet. She did not speak to anyone about her Sight— the way the colorful world waltzed around her.

"I see yours," the Seraph said.

Ella's heartbeat fluttered against her ribs like a battering of butterfly wings. Though she could not see herself the way she saw others, she must have her own colors. Mama's had been pale green dappled with brilliant blushes of pink that had turned gray from the thunderstorm clouds of sadness shrouding her after Cord's death. And Papa, whose colors once shone in the emerald greens and glowing golds of a man who worked the land, had faded into the frosty pale blue of abysmal pain. Every once in a while, when he held Mama's hand, Ella would catch a flash of that old color on him—sparkles of sunshine yellow would mist around his chest, though never enough to thaw the cold completely.

"I can see you," Ella blurted, then covered her mouth.

The Seraph tilted its head. "How, I wonder?"

Ella smiled shyly behind her hand. "You cast rainbow shadows."

The Seraph nodded, a smile flickering on its lips.

"Do you eat?" Ella asked. "I can make you something."

"Water and food would be a kindness."

Ella turned to leave.

"Nothing with flesh in it," the Seraph added, pale distaste coloring its words.

Ella nodded and left the barn. She returned a while later with a bowl of turnip and thyme stew cradled in the crook of her arm, a few drops of laudanum added to help with the Seraph's pain, and a small jug of water. The creature took the food and began to eat.

She made to leave the Seraph with its meal, but at the stall opening, spun on her heel. Ella had gathered all her courage to come out here, not only to bind its wounds or feed it, but to find out ... "I want to know."

"The answer to which question?" the Seraph asked.

Ella dug a tooth into her lip. She had so many that needed answers. "Why did you kill my brother?"

"I did not," the Seraph said through mouthfuls of stew.

Frustration and pain erupted in Ella. "My Papa believes that you did. Why would he, if there was no truth to it?" She banged balled-up hands on her thighs. "I *need* to know. My family is broken because of this!"

The Seraph stopped, as if suddenly aware of its seeming indifference, the spoon halfway to its mouth. It returned the spoon to the bowl and set them on the ground. "Your brother was not killed by one of us."

"You were there, over the woods where Cord's body was found. The village folk saw you. My people often see yours at the moment of our deaths."

"We are only guides. One of my kind arrived to assist your brother across the threshold, but we did not harm him. We mourn the loss of any Magicis."

Hot tears leaked from Ella's eyes. "What do you mean, Magicis?"

"A human that possesses a spark of the divine. They have the ability to see beyond this earthly plane, into a world where much more is possible. It is what attracts us to your kind. Your brother had—"

"You lie!" Ella was in front of the Seraph before it could blink twice. She kicked the bowl of stew over, splashing turnip chunks onto its legs. "Papa said a winged man killed him. *You* killed Cord!" Ella couldn't stomach the thought that Papa might have tortured an innocent being. That couldn't be what had happened. She raised a fist, intending with every fiber of her being to smash it into the thing's lying mouth.

The Seraph leaned back, eyes closed, its cheek turned to meet her wrath.

Ella's fist wavered. She lowered her hand. In expectation of being hit, the Seraph's color had changed. Not to one of anger—bashed in reds—but into silver threads that streamed from its chest up around its head. They curled and knotted in on themselves like a twisted crown. Ella had seen this color before, on the village folk after Cord's funeral; it was the color of compassion.

Ella shivered as though she'd been plunged into a mountain stream so cold it crushed the breath from her. She staggered back. Her legs gave way and she fell in the straw.

"His love for the girl was not the only reason he ran away that night," the Seraph said.

"Shut up," Ella croaked.

"You asked—"

"For answers, not lies!"

"Did you not see it on him yourself?" the Seraph asked.

Waves of anger and sorrow flooded through her, so big she felt her body might crack apart. "The colors, they were so new then, I didn't ..." Ella hid her face in her hands as memories she'd pushed down returned.

In the last year of her brother's life, his colors had begun to change from forest-greens and playful peeks of apricot, into a soft shifting curtain of hues she did not comprehend. Ella thought it was his love for Daisy showing through. She hadn't understood then that something in him was emerging.

"If it wasn't you, then who killed my brother?"

The Seraph blinked, and lights like falling stars fell across the blacks of its eyes. "The girl's father."

Ella gasped. "Mr. Thomas?"

"He caught your brother with his daughter."

"It's not true. It can't be. He was at Cord's funeral."

"You see my words. You know I do not lie."

Ella did know. The color of lies was a sickly brown, like faded dirt baked in the sun until dull and lifeless.

"And, Daisy—she knows?"

The Seraph lifted a shoulder. "I could not say." Its eyelids drooped and its head bobbed, no doubt from the laudanum making its way through its system.

Ella nodded as this truth seeped in. Then she pulled her knees to her chest and wept. The Seraph rested a gentle hand on her shoulder, offering a comfort she'd gone so long without.

When Ella had let out enough sorrow to breathe again, she wiped her face. "Papa, if I tell him—he won't believe me. I have no proof but the colors I see on you."

"I understand." The Seraph struggled to keep its eyes open, and its voice grew quiet. "He is as the people in the village. In building a sanctuary to hide from their fears, they have created a prison instead. They cannot see beyond their walls."

"That must be why Cord left. Papa would never accept us if he knew."

The Seraph considered this, nodded, then laid down gingerly on the cot. Its eyes drifted shut.

Ella sighed. There would be no more answers tonight. She locked the stall and quietly pulled the barn door closed behind her.

Uneasiness settled like a stone in her belly as she trudged across the field to the cottage. She brushed her palms along the lavender and heather, lifting their scent into the air—a perfume of purple—to calm her.

She was so close to having Papa back. He needed only justice to seal the wound in his heart. Somehow, she must convince him the Seraph hadn't killed Cord. But how, without giving herself away as—what had the Seraph called her?—a Magicis? And what if she couldn't? Would she stand by and let him kill an innocent creature? A creature drawn here, like a moth to a flame, because of her.

After a night of tossing and fretting, Ella rose weary. Outside her bedroom window, the morning looked the same as she felt, shrouded in mist and full of rain. She dressed warmly in a wool tunic and pants and went to prepare breakfast.

Mama stood in the kitchen, her hands covered in flour, kneading the morning bread and singing a song in *Hen Gymraeg,* the old tongue, meant to chase away the rainy day. Her gray was gone. She was covered in moss-green trimmed at the edges by pale pink.

"Mama!" Ella called.

Mama turned, a smile on her face. "Good morning, Ella dear. Breakfast will be on soon. Go and fetch me some eggs, would you?"

Her mother's eyes were clear and bright as the hues humming around her, and she had used Ella's name, recognized her.

Ella choked on the sob welling in her throat. "Mama." She hurried into the kitchen, wrapped her arms around her mother's waist, and buried her face in Mama's blouse. Her mother smelled of flour and rose water.

"My darling, what's gotten into you?" Mama wiped her hands on the sides of her apron, then stroked Ella's hair. "Oh, honey, come now. Sit down." She ushered Ella into a chair at the dining table and grabbed her hand. Mama's touch was warm and gentle.

Ella dabbed her eyes on a sleeve. "I've missed you, is all."

"Missed me?" The colors on Mama's skin deepened into a worried peach. "I've been here all morning."

"Has Papa returned?"

"He must be in the back field with Cord. They'll be in soon, I'm sure. Our boys wouldn't miss breakfast." Mama winked.

Ella had to push hard to get her words over the lump in her throat. *Cord.* Mama had spoken his name as if he were still alive. "No, Mama. Papa's gone into the village."

Mama's eyebrows shot up. "Has he, for what?"

"To seek counsel from the Elders, on how to …" Ella hesitated.

"To what, dear?"

"To kill the Seraph."

Mama frowned. "Why in creation's name would he want to do that?"

Ella couldn't bring herself to say Cord's name, afraid it would send her mother away again.

"One got caught on some ropes in the backyard. He aims to get rid of it."

"Oh, dear." Mama sighed. "That is a shame." She returned to the kitchen counter, a troubled look creasing her face. Her hands moved in rhythmic motions on the bread dough.

"What's a shame, Mama?"

"Have I ever told you about the girl from the village, Ella? The one with clouds in her eyes."

Of course Mama had, but never when she'd been aware like this. "I don't think so."

"I grew up with a girl called Agnes. As she got older, she began to change. Pale clouds appeared in her eyes, and she spoke of things …" Mama pressed into the dough—*push, pull.* When she spoke again, her voice was hoarse and fragile as gossamer strings of moonglow on snow. "She came into my room one evening, weeping. The girls from school had cornered her on the way home. There were bruises on her skin and blood on her dress." Mama rolled the dough up, slapped it onto the floured counter, then leaned into it—*push, pull, roll, slap.* "My mother was teaching me about healing, so I mixed up what I knew and tended to her as best I could." *Push, pull, dig, push, pull.*

"That night, I begged her to leave the village. When the Elders found out the girls had attacked her, they would find out why as well. Their fear that Agnes would bring the Seraphs down on our heads would have been too great to ignore, and they might have …" Mama stopped kneading and stared out the window at the mountains.

Ella came and leaned on the counter next to her mother. "What happened to her?"

"My family kept a small cabin out by the Salt-Cliffs that overlook the Mad Sea, and I … well, there was no other choice." Tears clung to her mother's cheeks. "I sent my sister away."

Ella's eyes went wide. "Agnes was your sister?"

Mama nodded. "I have missed her every day since. You remind me so much of her, El. It does my heart good." She smiled at Ella as tears trickled across her lips. "I can tell you, if there was a Seraph in the yard, it did not get tangled in loose ropes. It came for a reason."

Mama's words lingered, bright swatches of lemon-silver in the air. Ella had no clouds in her eyes to give her away, but she wondered how much her mother knew—about her, maybe even about Cord.

"Papa wants it dead," Ella said. How could she explain why the Seraph needed to die, for Papa's sanity, without treading into the risky territory of terrible memories?

"I love your father dearly. He is a good man with a kind heart, but when it comes to things he does not understand, he feels the same to me as those schoolgirls did. People like her are mysteries to plain folk, and where there is a mystery there will be a story told to explain it, true or not. Sometimes those stories take root and become superstitions." Mama clucked her tongue. "Deadly things."

She turned away to stoke the coals in the woodstove. "Go and do your chores, El, before your father and Cord come in, and bring me those eggs when you're done."

Gratitude and affection spilled through Ella. She wrapped her arms around her mother and squeezed. "I will, Mama."

Mama laughed, a beautiful sound wrapped in cinnamon notes. Ella kissed her on the cheek and ran from the cottage, her uncertainty gone. She knew what to do.

Papa would be upset at first, but when he found his wife with life in her eyes again, all would be forgiven. Mama was back. She'd come back to them. And wasn't that the healing Papa had needed all along?

Would she disappear into her grief again after she found out about Cord? Ella shook her head. She couldn't think about that. Surely there was a reason Mama came back to them this day.

Ella ran through the field. Rain slipped from the sky, pattering onto her face and shoulders. Her heart hammered with love for her family, and with hope—perhaps broken things could be mended after all. She laughed with her mouth wide open, catching raindrops as they fell. One day, with Mama's help, Ella would tell her father everything. Then he would understand and accept her not just as his daughter, but as a girl possessed of magic.

Ella dashed into the barn. She would set the Seraph free before Papa returned and spare them all more bloodshed.

The Seraph sat on the edge of the cot as though waiting for her. He watched her haul two large burlap sacks from an adjoining stall and take the wings from them.

Ella used an old pair of shears to cut through the rope around the Seraph's neck, then removed the bandages from his back. She was shocked to see how fast his injuries had healed. The skin around the wounds no longer echoed of sickly green but had already faded back to its natural iridescence. Ella dragged the wings over to the Seraph— they were heavier than she expected, for something that could lift someone into flight toward the heavens—and with no small feat of sweat and tears, she fit the broken ends of bone back together, like mending jagged shards of shattered pottery. She wound long lengths of cloth smeared with resin around the new joins, then tied them off and stood back, wiping sticky hands on her pants. "Will they heal?"

"In time, yes. There is magic in your hands—just like your Mama's." The Seraph rubbed his feet in the dirt, a small smile on his lips. "I will have to walk until then."

"Ella Marie!" Papa's voice crashed into the back of her head. She jumped and spun to face him.

Pops of angry red flared off him. "What in the hell are you doing?"

"I was … I think we …." She straightened her back, unconsciously blocking the Seraph from her Papa's view. "We've made a mistake."

"Blessed be, I left you alone with it and …" His voice dropped to a growl. "What has that thing done to you?"

Ella's stomach churned with fear for the Seraph—fear for her Papa. "He's not what you think."

Her father marched across the barn, fumbled between bales of hay and pulled out his hatchet. "Move out of the way." His words dripped from his mouth in amber hues laced with ebony-ink bitterness. He stared at the Seraph. "I don't care the Elders say your kind can't be killed. I'll take you apart piece by piece!" He raised the hatchet and tried to move around his daughter.

Ella hands raised her hands to halt him as she stepped between the Seraph and her father. Fear wrapped icy hands around her back-bone, and her voice shook when she spoke. "Papa, *stop.*"

Her father's color twisted in spirals of orange surprise. He froze, the gray-lipped blade hanging in the air.

"He didn't kill Cord."

Papa blinked at the use of Cord's name. He had not spoken his son's name since he'd thrown the first handful of dirt onto Cord's plain pine coffin. Hints of green and gold flared from Papa's chest. He lowered the hatchet.

"The village watchman. It was him—" Ella broke off, unable to bring herself to say the words.

Papa wasn't stupid. "How could you know that?" he asked, eyes intent.

Ella swallowed hard. Her pulse beat in her temples, blurring her vision. "Because, he told me. The Seraph."

Her father's jaw clenched. The bright colors on his chest simmered back to a hoar blue.

"A Seraph *was* with Cord that night," Ella said, "but only to guide him to his final resting place *after* he was mortally injured."

Papa's hand tightened on the handle of his hatchet, the blade wavering.

"Mr. Thomas caught Cord trying to leave with Daisy and then—"

"Thomas?!" Papa yelled.

"I … I … don't think …" the words jumbled in Ella's mouth. "Maybe … he didn't mean to …. Maybe he only meant to scare—"

"It would have you think one of my oldest friends did this?"

"Please, listen. Cord woke me that night. He told me he was going to the Capital with Daisy." Ella glanced back at the Seraph, hesitating. He stood watching, his wings unfolded, feathers draped across the straw. She firmed her resolve. "I can see the Seraph speaks the truth."

"You can *see*?" Papa blinked. "You mean ... the Sight? You're one of *them*? Possessed."

"No, Papa, I'm not. I'm your daughter." Ella, reached forward, laid a hand on her father's arm. Her fingers tingled.

Colors rippled on her father's skin—circles of rancid green that moved outward from her fingertips in waves of scarlet black—the same colors she'd seen on him when he'd severed the Seraph's wings.

Ella snatched her hand back as though she'd grazed hot iron. His knuckles were white around the hatchet's handle.

"Papa, please. Don't do anything you'll regret."

"Regret? You've allowed yourself to be tainted by wickedness while my son .... He was perfect." Papa swallowed hard. "The only thing I regret"—rancid green leaked from the corners of his mouth like froth from a rabid dog—"is that the wrong child died last summer."

Papa may as well have buried the blade of his hatchet deep into her chest. Ella's mouth fell open.

Movement behind her father pulled her attention over his shoulder, to the barn door.

Papa turned to look. The hatchet dropped from his hand. "Margaret, what are you doing out here?"

Mama stood in the doorway. Rain had matted her hair flat, drops glittered on her cheeks—and, to Ella's eyes, those familiar charcoal whispers streamed around Mama's head like a shroud.

Relief crashed into Ella. "Oh, Mama, thank heaven. Papa knows. You must tell him what we talked about this morning. Tell him about Agnes."

Mama's brow creased, confusion and the ravages of grief marring her features. "Something in the stove is burning, and I haven't had my breakfast yet. Will you be long, child?"

Ella's chest tightened. Pinpricks of heat stung the back of her eyes. Her Mama was lost again. Words fell from Ella's mouth in a crushed whisper. Just one. "No," was all her heart could manage.

Mama's gaze moved from Ella to Papa, then flickered over to the Seraph. Her jaw dropped. "Wha— wha—?" she pointed a finger. Her bottom lip trembled, and she began to scream.

Papa rushed to her, turned her away from the sight of the winged man. "Come, my darling. You shouldn't be out here."

"That's not a fish," Mama said. "You haven't been fishing. Where's Cord?" She beat weak fists against Papa's chest, trying to get out of his grasp. "Put it back. Back in the water!"

"I will, Margaret. *Shhh, shhh*," Papa soothed, curls of concerned carnelian on his lips. He looked back at Ella. "Take your mother into the house, now."

Ella's knees wobbled, but she could not make her legs move.

"*Now*, Ella Marie. I will deal with you when my business out here is finished." His eyes lingered on the hatchet laying in the straw, then moved to the Seraph.

A wing brushed Ella's arm. Heat trickled along her skin and sank into her bones. She took a deep breath. Her knees steadied, and she stepped forward. "No."

Papa stared at her; his teeth gritted.

"Throw it back!" Mama cried.

Papa turned his attention to his wife and held her close.

As Ella watched her mother weep against Papa's chest, a blush of pink glimmered along the streams of gray draped around Mama's chest. Ella wanted to join them, to hug her mother the way she had that morning. She wanted to beg her father to turn the Seraph loose and come back to their family whole again.

Ella worked at her bottom lip with her teeth. Had Mama been watching at the kitchen window when Papa returned? She must have known the truth Ella refused to acknowledge—that Papa's mind would not be changed. Maybe Mama had come out here to send Ella away, the way she'd sent Agnes, and those thunderstorm clouds of gray sadness had come rumbling back into her broken heart—too many things lost.

Ella knew what to do. She cleared her throat. "We must set the Seraph free. It's the only thing that will calm Mama down."

Her father sneered, all the care gone from his face.

Mama yelled again. "Something is burning! Throw the fish back! The stove is on fire!" She yanked on his arms.

Papa looked toward the cottage. His eyes widened at the sight of black smoke trickling from the kitchen window. He clenched his jaw. The rancid-scarlet-black on his skin grew, sliding down his arms and legs, devouring him. When he spoke again, he would not meet Ella's gaze. "If that thing walks off my land, you go with it."

Never to return, Ella finished the line she'd heard so many times before.

Papa led Mama into the rain and hurried toward the smoke-filled cottage.

Ella stood there a moment, breathing in the smell of alfalfa hay, sweet and green. She clutched the sides of her pants, fists twisting in the fabric. Cord was gone. Mama was gone. And Papa—wasn't coming back. None of them ever would. Sometimes things did just break and could not be mended.

Ella reached out and slipped her fingers into the Seraph's waiting hand.

Ella and the Seraph walked down the foot-worn path through the heather that led off the farm. The sun hid behind silver clouds that wept rain on them. She looked back only once.

Papa stood on the porch, watching them go, his color as blue gray as the misty morning. Next to the house, a cluster of goats huddled beneath her favorite oak tree, its branches a shelter from the storm. How she envied them.

Ella's clothes were soaked through. She shivered and leaned against the Seraph's body. The Seraph winced as he stretched a wing over her head.

"Where will we go, Seraph?"

"I have a friend, who I think will be glad to know you."

Ella peered past the sunlight-tinted feathers, into the Seraph's face. "Your friend will welcome me?"

"Yes," the Seraph said.

"Who is this person?"

"Her name is Agnes—"

"My aunt!" Ella's feet tangled together, and she stumbled. The Seraph caught her in the cup of his wing.

"What? How? I—"

"She asked me to come," the Seraph said.

"But we trapped you." Ella's voice went quiet. "We hurt you."

The Seraph smiled, a slight thing that hardly turned the corners of his mouth, yet made his eyes shine with starlight. "You cannot catch one of us that does not want to be caught, and I am unharmed. I came to you in the only way you would accept me—as something broken and in need of mending."

Ella shook her head. With every answer she received from the Seraph, a new question appeared.

A flash of lightning, made of watercolor-fire wrapped in satin strips of gold, sizzled through the gloomy sky. The clap of thunder that followed rolled out in peals of ocean-tormented teal, trailing ribbons of tangerine stars.

Ella's heart fluttered. She knew those colors. They were the same ones she'd seen on Cord as he came into his magic. Perhaps in time she would be strong enough to return and seek justice for her brother's death. At least Papa knew the truth now and, like Ella, it was his decision what to do with it.

Silken feathers brushed against her cheek in the breeze. She turned her attention to the road ahead. Beyond the edges of the storm, the light was clear and bright over the Plum-Shaded Mountains. Ella was headed there, to a cabin by the Salt-Crusted Cliffs—a kiss for her aunt from Mama on her lips, and the color of thunder shimmering on her skin.

Men of Greywater Station

by George R.R. Martin & Howard Waldrop

The men of Greywater Station watched the shooting star descend and they knew it for an omen.

They watched it in silence from the laser turret atop the central tower. The streak grew bright in the northeast sky, divided the night though the thin haze of the spore dust. It went through the zenith, sank, fell below the western horizon.

Sheridan, the bullet-headed zoologist was the first to speak. "There they went," he said, unnecessarily.

Delvecchio shook his head. "There they are," he said, turning towards the others. There were only five there, of the seven who were left. Sanderpay and Miterz were still outside collecting samples.

"They'll make it," Delvecchio said firmly. "Took too long crossing the sky to burn up like a meteor. I hope we got a triangulation on them with the radar. They came in slow enough to maybe make it through the crash."

Reyn, the youngest of the men at Greywater, looked up from the radar console and nodded "I got them, all right. Though it's a wonder they slowed enough before hitting the atmosphere. From the little that got through jamming, they must have hit pretty hard out there."

"If they live, it puts us in a difficult position," said Delvecchio. "I'm not quite sure what comes next."

310

"I am," said Sheridan. "We get ready to fight. If anybody lives through the landing, we've got to get ready to take them on. They'll be crawling with fungus before they get here. And you know they'll come. We'll have to kill them."

Delvecchio eyed Sheridan with new distaste. The zoologist was always very vocal with his ideas. That didn't make it any easier for Delvecchio, who then had to end the arguments that Sheridan's ideas usually started "Any other suggestions?" he asked, looking to the others.

Reyn looked hopeful. "We might try rescuing them before the fungus takes over." He gestured toward the window, and the swampy, fungus-clotted landscape beyond. "We could maybe take one of the flyers to them, shuttle them back to the station, put them in the sterilization ward ..." Then his words trailed off, and he ran a hand nervously through his thick black hair. "No. There'd be too many of them. We'd have to make so many trips. And the swampbats ... I don't know."

"The vaccine," suggested Granowicz, the wiry extee psychologist. "Bring them some vaccine in a flyer. Then they might be able to walk it."

"The vaccine doesn't work right," Sheridan said. "People build up an immunity, the protection wears off. Besides, who's going to take it to them? You? Remember the last time we took a flyer out? The damn swampbats knocked it to bits. We lost Blatt and Ryerson. The Fungus has kept us out of the air for nearly eight months now. So what makes you think it's all of a sudden going to give us a free pass to fly away into the sunset?"

"We've got to try," Reyn said hotly. From his tone, Delvecchio could see there was going to be a hell of an argument. Put Sheridan on one side of a fight and immediately Reyn was on the other.

"Those are men out there, you know," Reyn continued. "I think Ike's right. We can get them some vaccine. At least there's a chance. We can fight the swampbats. But those poor bastards out there don't have a chance against the fungus."

"They don't have a chance whatever we do," Sheridan said "It's us we should worry about. They're finished. By now the fungus knows they're there. It's probably already attacking them. If any survived."

"That seems to be the problem," said Delvecchio quickly, before Reyn could jump in again. "We have to assume some will survive. We also have to assume the fungus won't miss a chance to take them over. And that it will send them against us."

311

"Right!" said Sheridan, shaking his head vigorously. "And don't forget, these aren't ordinary people we're dealing with. That was a troop transport up there. The survivors will be armed to the teeth. What do we have besides the turret laser? Hunting rifles and specimen guns. And knives. Against screechers and seventy-five mikemikes and God knows what else. We're finished if we're not ready. Finished."

"Well, Jim?" Granowicz asked. "Is he right? What do you think our chances are?"

Delvecchio sighed. Being the leader wasn't always a very comfortable position. "I know how you feel, Bill," he said with a nod to Reyn. "But I'm afraid I have to agree with Sheridan. Your scheme doesn't have much of a chance. And there are bigger stakes. If the survivors have screechers and heavy armament, they'll be able to breach the station walls. You all know what that would mean. Our supply ship is due in a month. If the fungus gets into Greywater, then Earth won't have to worry about the Fyndii anymore. The fungus would put a permanent stop to the war—it doesn't like its hosts to fight each other."

Sheridan was nodding again. "Yes. So we have to destroy the survivors. It's the only way."

Andrews, the quiet little mycologist, spoke up for the first time. "We might try to capture them," he suggested. "I've been experimenting with methods of killing the fungus without damaging the hosts. We could keep them under sedation until I got somewhere."

"How many years would that take?" Sheridan snapped.

Delvecchio cut in. "No. We've got no reason to think we'll even be able to fight them, successfully. All the odds are with them. Capture would be clearly impossible."

"But rescue isn't." Reyn was still insistent. "We should gamble," he said, pounding the radar console with his fist. "It's worth it."

"We settled that, Bill," Delvecchio said. "No rescue. We've got only seven men to fight off maybe hundreds—I can't afford to throw any away on a useless dramatic gesture."

"Seven men trying to fight off hundreds sounds like a useless dramatic gesture to me," Reyn said. "Especially since there may be only a few survivors who could be rescued."

"But what if all of them are left?" said Sheridan. "And all of them have already been taken over by the fungus? Be serious, Reyn. The spore dust is everywhere. As soon as they breathe unfiltered air, they'll take it in. And seventy-two hours they'll be like the rest of the animal life on this planet. Then the fungus will send them against us."

Goddamnit, Sheridan!" yelled Reyn. "They could still be in their pods. Maybe they don't even know what happened. Maybe they're still asleep. How the hell do I know? If we get there before they come out, we can save them. Or something. We've got to try!"

"No. Look. The crash is sure to have shut the ship down. They'll be awake. First thing they'll do is check their charts. Only the fungus is classified, so they won't know what a hell of a place they've landed on. All they *will* know is that Greywater is the only human settlement here. They'll head toward us. And they'll get infected and possessed."

"That's why we should work fast," Reyn said. "We should arm three or four flyers and leave at once. Now."

Delvecchio decided to put an end to the argument. The last one like this had gone all night. "This is getting us nowhere," he said sharply, fixing both Sheridan and Reyn with hard stares. "It's useless to discuss any longer. All we're doing is getting mad at each other. Besides, it's late." He looked at his watch. "Let's break for six hours or so and resume at dawn when we're cooler and less tired. We'll be able to think more clearly. And Sanderpay and Miterz will be back then, too. They deserve a voice in this."

There were three rumbles of agreement. And one sharp note of dissent.

"No," said Reyn. Loudly. He stood up, towering over the others in their seats.

"That's too late. There's no time to lose."

"Bill, you—" Delvecchio started.

"Those men might be grabbed while we sleep," Reyn went on, plowing right over his superior. "We've got to *do* something."

"No," said Delvecchio. "And that's an order. We'll talk about it in the morning. Get some sleep, Bill."

Reyn looked around for support. He got none. He glared at Delvecchio briefly. Then he turned and left the tower.

Delvecchio had trouble sleeping. He woke up at least twice, between the sheets that were cold and sticky with sweat. In his nightmare, he was out beyond Greywater, knee-deep in the grey-green slime, collecting samples for analysis. While he worked, he watched a big amphibious mud-tractor in the distance, wallowing toward him.

313

On top was another human, his features invisible behind a filter mask and skinthins. In the dream Delvecchio waved to the tractor as it neared, and the driver waved back. Then he pulled up nearby, climbing down from the cab, and grasped Delvecchio in a firm handshake.

Only by that time, Delvecchio could see through the transparent filter mark. It was Ryerson, the dead geologist, his friend Ryerson. But his head was swollen grossly and there were trails of fungus hanging from each ear.

After the second nightmare he gave it up as a bad show. They never found Ryerson or Blatt after the crash. Though they knew from the impact that there wouldn't be much to find. But Delvecchio dreamed of them often, and he suspected that some of the others did, too.

He dressed in darkness, and made his way to the central tower. Sanderpay, the telecom man, was on watch. He was asleep in the small ready bunk near the laser turret, where the station monitors could awaken him quickly if anything big approached the walls. Reinforced duralloy was tough stuff, but the fungus had some pretty wicked creatures at its call. And there were the airlocks to consider.

Delvecchio decided to let Sanderpay sleep, and went to the window. The big spotlights mounted on the wall flooded the perimeter around Greywater with night white lights that made the mud glisten sickly. He could see drifting spores reflected briefly in the beams. They seemed unusually thick, especially toward the west, but that was probably his imagination.

Then again, it might be a sign that the fungus was uneasy. The spores had always been ten times as thick around Greywater as elsewhere on the planet's surface. That had been one of the first pieces of evidence that the damned fungus was intelligent. And hostile.

They still weren't sure just how intelligent. But of the hostility there was no more doubt. The parasitic fungus infected every animal on the planet. And had used most of them to attack the station at one point or another. It wanted them. So the blizzard of spores had rained on Greywater for more than a year now. The overhead force screens kept them out, though, and the sterilization chambers killed any that clung to the mud-tractor or skinthins or drifted into the airlocks. The fungus kept trying.

Across the room, Sanderpay yawned and sat up in his bunk. Delvecchio turned toward him. "Morning, Otis."

Sanderpay yawned again, and stifled it with a big red hand. "Morning," he replied, untangling himself from the bunk in a tangle of long arms and legs. "What's going on? You taking Bill's shift?"

Delvecchio stiffened. "What? Was Reyn supposed to relieve you?"

"Uh-huh," said Sanderpay, looking at the clock. "Hour ago. The bastard. I get cramps sleeping in this thing. Why can't we make it a little more comfortable, I ask you?"

Delvecchio was hardly listening. He ignored Sanderpay and moved swiftly to the intercom panel against one wall. Granowicz was closest to the motor pool. He rang him.

A sleepy voice answered. "Ike," Delvecchio said. "This is Jim. Check the motor pool, quick. Count the flyers."

Granowicz acknowledged the order. He was back in less than two minutes, but it seemed longer. "Flyer five is missing," he said. He sounded awake all of a sudden.

"Shit," said Delvecchio. He slammed down the intercom, and whirled toward Sanderpay. "Get on the radio, fast. There's a flyer missing. Raise it."

Sanderpay looked baffled, but complied. Delvecchio stood over him, muttering obscenities and thinking worse ones, while he searched through the static.

Finally an answer. "I read you, Otis." Reyn's voice, of course.

Delvecchio leaned toward the transmitter. "I told you no rescue."

The reply was equal parts laughter and static. "Did you? Hell! I guess I wasn't paying attention, Jim. You know how long conferences always bored me."

"I don't want a dead hero on my hands. Turn back."

"I intend to. After I deliver the vaccine. I'll bring as many of the soldiers with me as I can. The rest can walk. The immunity wears off, but it should last long enough if they landed where we predict."

Delvecchio swore. "Dammit, Bill. Turn back. Remember Ryerson."

"Sure I do. He was a geologist. Little guy with a pot belly, wasn't he?"

"Reyn!" There was an edge to Delvecchio's voice.

Laughter. "Oh, take it easy, Jim. I'll make it. Ryerson was careless, and it killed him. And Blatt too. I won't be. I've rigged some lasers up. Already got two big swampbats that came at me. Huge fuckers, easy to burn down."

"Two! The fungus can send hundreds if it gets an itch. Damnit, listen to me. Come back."

"Will do," said Reyn. "With my guests." Then he signed off with a laugh.

Delvecchio straightened, and frowned. Sanderpay seemed to think a comment was called for, and managed a limp, "Well …" Delvecchio never heard him.

"Keep on the frequency, Otis," he said. "There's a chance the damn fool might make it. I want to know the minute he comes back on." He started across the room.

"Look. Try to raise him every five minutes or so. He probably won't answer. He's in for a world of shit if that jury-rigged laser fails him."

Delvecchio was at the intercom. He punched Granowicz' station. "Jim again, Ike. What kind of laser's missing from the shop? I'll hold on."

"No need to," came the reply. "Saw it just after I found the flyer gone. I think one of the standard tabletop cutters, low power job. He's done some spot-welding, left the stat on the power box. Ned found that, and places where he'd done some bracketing. Also, one of the vacutainers is gone."

"Okay, Thanks, Ike. I want everybody up here in ten minutes. War council."

"Oh, Sheridan will be so glad."

"No. Yes. Maybe he will." He clicked off, punched for Andrews.

The mycologist took a while to answer. "Arnold?" Delvecchio snapped when the acknowledgment finally came.

"Can you tell me what's gone from stores?"

There were a few minutes of silence. Then Andrews was back. "Yeah, Jim. A lot of medical supplies. Syringes, bandages, vaccine, plastic splints, even some body bags. What's going on?"

"Reyn. And from what you say, it sounds like he's on a real mercy mission there. How much did he take?"

"Enough, I guess. Nothing we can't replace, however."

"Okay. Meeting up here in ten … five minutes."

"Well, all right." Andrews clicked off.

Delvecchio hit the master control, opening all the bitch boxes. For the first time in four months, since the slinkers had massed near the station walls. That had been a false alarm. This, he knew, wasn't.

"Meeting in five minutes in the turret," he said.

The words rang through the station, echoing off the cool humming walls.

"... that if we don't make plans now, it'll be way too late." Delvecchio paused and looked at four men lounging on the chairs. Sanderpay was still at the radio, his long legs spilling into the center of the room. But the other four were clustered around the table, clutching coffee cups.

None of them seemed to be paying close attention. Granowicz was staring absently out the window, as usual, his eyes and forebrain mulling the fungus that grew on the trees around Greywater. Andrews was scribbling in a notepad, very slowly. Doodling. Ned Miterz, big and blond and blocky, was a bundle of nervous tension; Bill Reyn was his closest friend. He alternated between drumming his fingers on the tabletop, swilling his coffee, and tugging nervously at his drooping blond mustache. Sheridan's bullet-shaped head stared at the floor.

But they were all listening, in their way. Even Sanderpay, at the radio. When Delvecchio paused, he pulled his long legs back under him, and began to speak. "I'm sorry it's come to this, Jim," he said, rubbing his ear to restore circulation. "It's bad enough those soldiers are out there. Now Bill has gone after them, and he's in the same spot. I think, well, we have to forget him. And worry about attacks."

Delvecchio sighed. "It's hard to take, I know. If he makes it, he makes it. If he finds them, he finds them. If they've been exposed, in three days they'll be part of the fungus. Whether they take the vaccine or not. If he brings them back, we watch them three days to see if symptoms develop. If they do, we have to kill them. If not, then nobody's hurt, and when the rest walk in we watch for symptoms in them. But those are iffy things. If he doesn't make it, he's dead. Chances are, the troopers are dead. Or exposed. Either way, we prepare for the worst and forget Reyn until we see him. So what I'm asking for now are practical suggestions as to how we defend ourselves against well-armed soldiers. Controlled by some intelligence we do not understand."

He looked at the men again.

Sanderpay whooped. He grabbed the console mike as they jumped and looked at him.

"Go ahead, Bill," he said, twisting the volume knob over to the wall speaker. The others winced as the roar of frequency noise swept the room.

"... right. The damn thing's sending insects into the ship. Smear ... ing ... smear windscreen ... on instruments." Reyn's voice. There was a sound in the background like heavy rain.

"… swampbats just before they came … probably coming at me now. Goddamn laser mount loosened …" There was a dull thud in the background. "No lateral control … got that bastard … ohmigodd …" Two more dull thuds. A sound like metal eating itself.

"… in the trees. Altitude … going down … swampbats … something just got sucked in the engine …. Damn, no power … nothing … if …"

Followed by frequency noise.

Sanderpay, his thin face blank and white, waited a few seconds to see if more transmission came through, then tried to raise Reyn on the frequency. He turned the volume down again after a while.

"I think that's about what we can expect will happen to us in a couple of days," said Delvecchio. "That fungus will stop at nothing to get intelligent life. Once it has the soldiers who survive, they'll come after the station. With their weapons."

"Well," snapped Sheridan. "He knew not to go out there in that flyer."

Miterz slammed down his coffee cup, and rose. "Goddamn you, Sheridan. Can't you hold it even a minute? Bill's probably dead out there. And all you want to do is say I-told-you-so."

Sheridan jumped to his feet too. "You think I like listening to someone get killed on the radio? Just because I didn't like him? You think it's fun? Huh? You think I want to fight somebody who's been trained to do it? Huh?" He looked at them, all of them, and wiped sweat from his brow with the back of his hand. "I don't. I'm scared. I don't like making plans for war when men could be out there wounded and dying with no help coming."

He paused. His voice, stretched thin, began to waver. "Reyn was a fool to go out there. But maybe he was the only one who let his humanity come through. I made myself ignore them. I tried to get you all to plan for war in case any of the soldiers made it. Damn you. I'm afraid to go out there. I'm afraid to go near the stuff, even inside the station. I'm a zoologist, but I can't even work. Every animal on this planet has that—that stuff on it. I can't bear to touch it. I don't want to fight either. But we're going to have to. Sooner or later."

He wiped his head again, looked at Delvecchio. "I—I'm sorry, Jim. Ned, too. The rest of you. I'm—I have—I just don't like it any more than you. But we have to."

He sat down, very tiredly.

Delvecchio rubbed his nose, and reflected again that being the nominal leader was more trouble than it was worth Sheridan had never opened up like this before. He wasn't quite sure how to deal with it.

"Look," he finally said. "It's okay, Eldon" It was the first time he could remember that he—or any of them—had used Sheridan's first name. "This isn't going to be easy on any of us. You may be right about our humanity.Sometimes you have to put humanity aside to think about … well, I don't know.

"The fungus has finally found a way to get to us. It will attack us with the soldiers, like it has with the slinkers and the swampbats and the rest. Like it's trying to do now, while we're talking, with the burrowing worms and the insects and the arthropodia. The station's defenses will take care of those. All we have to worry about are the soldiers."

"All?" said Granowicz, sharply.

"That, and what we'll do if they breach the wall of the field. The field wasn't built to take screechers or laser explosives. Just to keep out insects and flying animals. I think one of the first things we've got to do is find a way to beef up the field. Like running in the mains from the other power sources. But that still leaves the wall. And the entry chambers. Our weakest links. Ten or twenty good rounds of high explosives will bring it right down. How do we fight back?"

"Maybe we don't," said Miterz. His face was still hard and angry. But now the anger was turned against the fungus, instead of Sheridan. "Maybe we take the fight to them."

The suggestions flew thick and fast from there on. Half of them were impossible, a quarter improbable, the most of what were left were crazy. At the end of an hour, they had gotten past the points of mining, pitfalls, electrocution.

To Delvecchio's ears, it was the strangest conversation he had ever heard. It was full of the madnesses of men who plan against each other, made more strange by the nature of the men themselves. They were all scientists and technicians, not soldiers, not killers. They talked and planned without enthusiasm, with the quiet talk of men who must talk before being pallbearers at a friend's funeral, or the pace of men who must take their turns as members of a firing squad the next morning.

In a way, they were.

✧ ✧ ✧

An hour later, Delvecchio was standing up to his ankles in grey-green mud, wrestling with a power saw and sweating freely under his skin-thins. The saw was hooked up to the power supply on his mud-tractor. And Miterz was sitting atop the tractor, with a hunting laser resting across his knee, occasionally lifting it to burn down one of the slinkers slithering through the underbrush.

Delvecchio had already cut through the bases of four of the biggest trees around the Greywater perimeter—about three-quarters of the way through, anyway. Just enough to weaken them, so the turret laser could finish the job quickly when the need arose. It was a desperate idea. But they were desperate men.

The fifth tree was giving him trouble. It was a different species from the others, gnarled and overhung with creepers and rock-hard. He was only halfway through, and already he'd had to change the blade twice. That made him edgy. One slip with the blade, one slash in the skinthins, and the spores could get at him.

"Damn thing," he said, when the teeth began to snap off for the third time. "It cuts like it's half petrified. Damn."

"Look at the bright side," suggested Miterz. "It'll make a mighty big splat when it falls. And even duralloy armor should crumple pretty good."

Delvecchio missed the humor. He changed the blade without comment, and resumed cutting.

"That should do it," he said after a while. "Looks deep enough. But maybe we should use the lasers on this kind, if we hit any more of them."

"That's a lot of power," said Miterz. "Can we afford it?" He raised his laser suddenly, and fired at something behind Delvecchio. The slinker, a four-foot-long mass of scales and claws, reared briefly from its stomach and then fell again, splattering mud in their direction. Its dying scream was a brief punctuation mark. "Those things are thick today," Miterz commented.

Delvecchio climbed up into the tractor. "You're imagining things," he said.

"No, I'm not." Miterz sounded serious. "I'm the ecologist, remember? I know we don't have a natural ecology around here. The fungus sends us its nasties, and keeps the harmless life forms away. But now there's even more than usual." He gestured with the laser. Off through the underbrush, two big slinkers could be seen chewing at the creepers around a tree, the fungus hanging like a shroud over the back of their skulls. "Look there. What do you think they're doing?"

"Eating," said Delvecchio. "That's normal enough." He started the tractor, and moved it forward jerkily. Mud, turned into a watery slime, spouted out behind the vehicle in great gushes.

"Slinkers are omnivores," Miterz said. "But they prefer meat. Only eat creepers when there's no prey. But there's plenty around here." He stopped, stared at the scene, banged the butt of the laser rifle on the cab floor in a fit of sudden nervous tension.

Then he resumed in a burst of words. "Damn it, damn it. They're clearing a path!" His voice was an accusation. "A path for the soldiers to march on. Starting at our end and working toward them. They'll get here faster if they don't have to cut through the undergrowth."

Delvecchio, at the wheel, snorted. "Don't be absurd."

"What makes you think it's absurd? Who know what the fungus is up to? A living ecology. It can turn every living thing on this planet against us if it wants to. Eating a path through a swamp is nothing to something like that." Miterz' voice was distant and brooding.

Delvecchio didn't like the way the conversation was going. He kept silent. They went on to the next tree, and then the next. But Miterz, his mind racing, was getting more and more edgy. He kept fidgeting in the tractor, and playing with the rifle, and more than once he absently tried to yank at his mustache, only to be stopped by the filtermask. Finally, Delvecchio decided it was time to head in.

Decontamination took the usual two hours. They waited patiently in the entry chamber and sterilization rooms while the pumps sprays, heat lamps, and ultraviolet systems did their work on them and the tractor.

They shed their sterilized skinthins as they came through the final airlock.

"Goddamn," said Delvecchio. "I hope we don't have to go out again. Decon takes more time than getting the work done."

Sanderpay met them, smiling. "I think I found something we could use. Nearly forgot about them."

"Yeah? What?" Miterz asked, as he unloaded the laser charge and placed it back in the recharge rack. He punched several buttons absently.

"The sounding rockets."

321

Delvecchio slapped his head, "Of course. Damn. Didn't even consider them." His mind went back. Blatt, the dead meteorologist, had fired off the six-foot sounding rockets regularly for the first few weeks, gaining data on the fungus. They had discovered that spores were frequently found up to 50,000 feet, and a few even reached as high as 80,000. After Blatt covered that he still made a twice-daily ritual of firing the sounding rockets, to collect information on the planet's shifting wind patterns. They had weather balloons, but those were next to useless; the swampbats usually vectored in on them soon after they were released. After Blatt's death, however, the readings hadn't meant as much, so the firings were discontinued. But the launching tubes were still functional, as far as he knew.

"You think you can rig them up as small guided missiles?" Delvecchio asked.

"Yep," Sanderpay said with a grin. "I already started. But they won't be very accurate. For one thing, they'll reach about a mile in altitude before we can begin to control them. Then, we'll be forcing the trajectory. They'll want to continue in a long arc. We'll want them back down almost to the launching point. It'll be like wrestling a two-headed alligator. I'm thinking of filing half of them with that explosive Andrews is trying to make, and the rest with white phosphorus. But that might be tricky."

"Well, do whatever you can, Otis," said Delvecchio. "This is good news. We needed this kind of punch. Maybe it isn't as hopeless as I thought."

Miterz had been listening carefully, but he still looked glum. "Anything over the commo?" he put in. "From Bill?"

Sanderpay shook his head. "Just the usual solar shit, and some mighty nice whistlers. Must be a helluva thunderstorm somewhere within a thousand miles of here. I'll let you know if anything comes in, though."

Miterz didn't answer. He was looking at the armory and shaking his head.

Delvecchio followed his eyes. Eight lasers were on the racks. Eight lasers and sixteen charges, standard station allotment. Each charge good for maybe fifty fifth-second bursts. Five tranquilizer rifles, an assortment of syringes, darts, and projectiles. All of which would be useless against armored infantry. Maybe if they could adapt some of the heavier projectiles to H.E. ... but such a small amount wouldn't dent duralloy. Hell.

"You know," said Miterz. "If they get inside, we might as well hang it up."

"If," said Delvecchio.

Night at Greywater Station. They had started watch-and-watch. Andrews was topside at the laser turret and sensor board. Delvecchio, Granowicz, and Sanderpay lingered over dinner in the cafeteria below. Miterz and Sheridan had already turned in.

Sanderpay was talking of the day's accomplishments. He figured he had gotten somewhere with the rockets. And Andrews had managed to put together some explosive from the ingredients in Reyn's lab.

"Arnold doesn't like it much, though," Sanderpay was saying. "He wants to get back to his fungus samples. Says he's out of his field, and not too sure he knows what he's doing. He's right, too. Bill was your chemist."

"Bill isn't here," Delvecchio snapped. He was in no mood for criticism. "Someone has to do it. At least Arnold has some background in organic chemistry, no matter how long ago it was. That's more than the rest of us have." He shook his head. "Am I supposed to do it? I'm an entomologist. What good is that? I feel useless."

"Yep, I know," said Sanderpay. "Still. It's not easy for me with the rockets, either. I had to take half the propellant from each one. Worked nine hours, finished three. We're gonna be fighting all the known laws of aerodynamics trying to force those things down near their starting point. And everybody else is having problems, too. We tinker and curse and it's all a blind alley. If we do this, we gotta do that. But if we do that, it won't work. This is a research station. So maybe it looks like a fort. That doesn't make it one. And we're still scientists, not demolition experts."

Granowicz gave a thin chuckle. "I'm reminded of that time, back on Earth, in the twentieth century, when that German scientist ... von Brau? Von ... von Braun and his men were advised that the enemy forces would soon be there. The military began giving them close-order drill and marksmanship courses. They wanted them to meet the enemy on the very edge of their missile complex and fight them hand to hand."

"What happened?" said Sanderpay.

"Oh, they ran 300 miles, and surrendered," Granowicz replied dryly.

Delvecchio downed his two hundredth cup of coffee, and put his feet up on the table. "Great," he said. "Only we've got no place to run to. So we're going to *have* to meet them on the edge of *our* little missile complex, or whatever. And soon."

Granowicz nodded. "Three days from now. I figure."

"That's if the fungus doesn't help them," said Delvecchio.

The other two looked at him. "What do you mean?" asked Granowicz.

"When Ned and I were out this morning, we saw slinkers. Lots of them. Eating away at the creepers to the west of the station."

Granowicz had a light in his eyes. But Sanderpay, still baffled, said "So?"

"Miterz thinks they're clearing a path."

Uh oh," said Granowicz. He stroked his chin with a thin hand. "That's very interesting, and very bad news. Clearing away at both ends, and all along, as I'd think it would do. Hmmmmm."

Sanderpay looked from Delvecchio to Granowicz and back, grimaced, uncoiled his legs and then coiled them around his chair again in a different position. He said nothing.

"Ah, yes, yes," Granowicz was saying. "It all fits, all ties in. We should have anticipated this. A total assault, with the life of a planet working for our destruction. It's the fungus ... a total ecology, as Ned likes to call it. A classic case of the parasitic collective mind. But we can't understand it. We don't know what its basic precepts are, its formative experiences. We don't know. No research has been carried out on anything like it. Except maybe the water jellies of Noborn. But that was a collective organism formed of separate colonies for mutual benefit. A benign form, as it were. As far as I can tell, Greywater, the fungus, is a single all-encompassing mass, which took over this planet starting from some single central point."

He rubbed his hands together and nodded. "Yes. Based on that, we can make guesses as to what it thinks. And how it will act. And this fits, this total hostility."

"How so?" asked Sanderpay.

"Well, it's never run up against any other intelligence, you see. Only lower forms. That's important. So it judges us by itself, the only mind it has known. It is driven to dominate, to take over all life with which it comes in contact. So it thinks we are the same, fears that we are trying to take over this planet as it once did.

Only, like I've been saying all along, it doesn't see us as the intelligence. We're animals, small, mobile. It's known life like that before and all a lower form. But the station itself is something new, something outside its experience. It sees the station as the intelligence, I'll bet. An intelligence like itself. Land, establishing itself, sending out extensions, poking at it and its hosts. And us, us poor animals, the fungus sees as unimportant tools."

Delvecchio signed. "Yeah, Ike. We've heard this before. I agree that it's a persuasive theory. But how do you prove it?"

"Proof is all around us," said Granowicz. "The station is under a constant around-the-clock attack. But we can go outside for samples, and the odds are fifty-fifty whether we'll be attacked or not. Why? We don't kill every slinker we see, do we? Of course not. And the fungus doesn't try to kill us, except if we get annoying. Because we're not important, it thinks. But something like the flyers—mobile but not animal, strange—it tries to eradicate. Because it perceives them as major extensions of Greywater."

"Then why the spores?" Delvecchio said.

Granowicz dismissed that with an airy wave. "Oh, the fungus would like to take us over, sure. To deprive the station of hosts. But it's the station it wants to eradicate. It can't conceive of cooperating with another intelligence—maybe, who knows, it had to destroy rival fungus colonies of its own species before it came to dominate this planet. Once it perceives intelligence, it is threatened. And it perceives intelligence in the station."

He was going to go on. But Delvecchio suddenly took his feet from the table, sat up, and said, "Uh oh."

Granowicz frowned. "What?"

Delvecchio stabbed at him with a finger. "Ike, think about this theory of yours. What if you're right? Then how is the fungus going to perceive the spaceship?"

Granowicz thought a moment, nodded to himself, and gave a slow, low whistle.

"So? How?' said Sanderpay. "Whattaya talking about?

Granowicz turned on him. "The spaceship was mobile, but not animal. Like the station. It came out of the sky, landed, destroyed a large area of the fungus and host forms. And hasn't moved since. Like the station. The fungus probably sees it as another station, another threat. Or an extension of our station."

"Yes," said Delvecchio. "But it gets worse. If you're right, then maybe the fungus is launching an all-out attack right at this moment on the spaceship hull. While it lets the men march away unharmed."

There was a moment of dead silence. Sanderpay finally broke it, looking at each of the others in turn, and saying in a low voice, "Oh. Wow. I see."

Granowicz had a thoughtful expression on his face, and he was rubbing his chin again. "No," he said at last. "You'd think that, but I don't think that's what is happening."

"Why not?" asked Delvecchio.

"Well, the fungus may not see the soldiers as the major threat. But it would at least try to take them over, as it does with us. And once it had them, and their weapons, it would have the tools to obliterate the station and the spaceship. That's almost sure to happen, too. Those soldiers will be easy prey for the spores. They'll fall to the fungus like ripe fruit."

Delvecchio clearly looked troubled. "Yeah, probably. But this bothers me. If there's even a slight chance that the soldiers might get here without being taken over, we'll have to change our plans."

"But there's no chance of that," Granowicz said, shaking his head. "The fungus already has those men. Why else would it be clearing a path?"

Sanderpay nodded in agreement. But Delvecchio wasn't that sure.

"We don't know that it's clearing a path," he insisted. "That's just what Miterz thinks is happening. Based on very scant evidence. We shouldn't accept it as an accomplished fact."

"It makes sense, though," Granowicz came back. "It would speed up the soldiers getting here, speed up the ..."

The alarm from the turret began to hoot and clang.

"Slinkers," said Andrews. "I think out by those trees you were working on."

He drew on a pair of infrared goggles and depressed a stud on the console. There was a hum.

Delvecchio peered through the binoculars. "Think maybe it's sending them to see what we were up to?"

"Definitely," said Granowicz, standing just behind him and looking out the window over his shoulder.

"I don't think it'll do anything," said Delvecchio, hopefully. "Mines or anything foreign it would destroy, of course. We've proved that. But all we did is slash a few trees. I doubt that it will be able to figure out why."

"Do you think I should fire a few times?" Andrews asked from the laser console.

"I don't know," said Delvecchio. "Wait a bit. See what they do."

The long, thick lizards were moving around the tree trunks. Some slithered through the fungus and the mud, others scratched and clawed at the notched trees.

"Switch on some of the directional sensors," said Delvecchio. Sanderpay, at the sensor bank, nodded and began flicking on the directional mikes. First to come in was the constant tick of the continual spore bombardment on the receiver head. Then as the mike rotated, came the hissing screams of the slinkers.

And then the rending sound of a falling tree.

Delvecchio, watching through the binoculars, suddenly felt very cold. The tree came down into the mud with a crashing thud. Slime flew from all sides, and several slinkers hissed out their lives beneath the trunk.

"Shit," said Delvecchio. And then, "Fire, Arnold."

Andrews pushed buttons, sighted in the nightscope, lined the crossnotches up on a slinker near the fallen tree, and fired.

To those not watching through goggles or binoculars, a tiny red-white light appeared in the air between the turret laser and the group of lizards. A gargling sound mixed with the slinker hissing. One of the animals thrashed suddenly, and then lay still. The others began slithering away into the undergrowth. There was stillness for a second.

And on another part of the perimeter, a second tree began to fall.

Andrews hit more buttons, and the big turret laser moved and fired again. Another slinker died. Then, without waiting for another crash, the laser began to swivel to hit the slinkers around the other trees.

Delvecchio lowered the binoculars very slowly. "I think we just wasted a day's work out there," he said. "Somehow the fungus guessed what we were up to. It's smarter than we gave it credit for."

"Reyn," said Granowicz.

"Reyn?" said Delvecchio. With a questioning look.

327

"He knew we'd try to defend the station. Given that knowledge, it's logical for the fungus to destroy anything we do out there. Maybe Reyn survived the crash of his flyer. Maybe the fungus finally got a human."

"Oh, *shit*," said Delvecchio with expression. "Yes, sure, you might be right. Or maybe it's all a big coincidence. A bunch of accidents. How do we know? How do we know anything about what the damned thing is thinking or doing or planning?" He shook his head. "Damn. We're fighting blind. Every time something happens, there are a dozen reasons that might have been behind it. And every plan we make has to have a dozen alternatives."

"It's not that bad," said Granowicz. "We're not entirely in the dark. We've proved that the fungus can take over Earth forms. We've proved that it gets at least some knowledge from them; that it absorbs at least part of what they knew. We don't know how big a part, true, however—"

"However, if, but, maybe," Delvecchio swore, looking very disgusted. "Dammit, Ike, how big a part is the crucial question. *If* it has Reyn, and *if* it knows everything he knew, then it knows everything there is to know about Greywater and its defenses. In that case, what kind of chance will we have?"

"Well," said Granowicz. He paused, frowned, stroked his chin. "I—hmmmmm. Wait, there are other aspects to this that should be thought out. Let me work on this a while."

"Fine," said Delvecchio. "You do that." He turned to Andrews. "Arnold, keep them off the trees as best you can. I'll be back up to relieve you in four hours."

Andrews nodded. "Okay, I think," he said, his eyes locked firmly on the nightscope.

Delvecchio gave brief instructions to Sanderpay, then turned and left the turret. He went straight to his bunk. It took him the better part of an hour to drift to sleep.

Delvecchio's dream:

He was old, and cool. He saw the station from all sides in a shifting montage of images; some near the ground, some from above, wheeling on silent wings. In one image, he saw, or felt as a worm must feel, the presence of the heavy weight of sunlight.

He saw the station twisted, old, wrecked. He saw the station in a series of images from inside. He saw a skeleton in the corner of an indefinite lab, and saw through the eyes of the skull out into the broken station. Outside, he saw heaped duralloy bodies with grey-green growths sprouting from the cracked faceplates. And he saw out of the faceplates, out into the swamp. Everywhere was grey-green, and damp and old and cold. Everywhere.

Delvecchio awoke sweating.

His watch was uneventful. The slinkers had vanished as suddenly as they had assembled, and he only fired the laser once, at a careless swampbat that flew near the perimeter. Miterz relieved him. Delvecchio caught several more hours of sleep. Or at least of bunk time. He spent a large chunk of time lying awake, thinking.

When he walked into the cafeteria the next morning, an argument was raging.

Granowicz turned to him immediately. "Jim, listen," he began, gesturing with his hands. "I've thought about this all night. We've been missing something obvious. If this thing has Reyn, or the soldiers, or *any* human, this is the chance we've been waiting for. The chance to communicate, to begin a mutual understanding. With their knowledge, it will have a common tongue with us. We shouldn't fight it at all. We should try to talk to it, try to make it understand how different we are."

"You're crazy, Granowicz," Sheridan said loudly. "Stark, raving mad. *You* go talk to that stuff. Not me. It's after us. It's been after us all along, and now it's sending those soldiers to kill us all. We have to kill them first."

"But this is our *chance*," Granowicz said. "To begin to understand, to reach that mind, to—"

"That was your job all along," Sheridan snapped. "You're the extee psych. Just because you didn't do your job is no reason to ask us to risk our lives to do it for you."

Granowicz glowered. Sanderpay, sitting next to him, was more vocal. "Sheridan," he said, "sometimes I wish we could throw you out to the fungus. You'd look good with grey-green growths coming out of your ears. Yep."

Delvecchio gave hard glances to all of them. "Shut up, all of you," he said simply. "I've had enough of this nonsense. I've been doing some thinking too."

He pulled up a chair and sat down. Andrews was at another table, quietly finishing his breakfast. Delvecchio motioned him over, and he joined them.

"I've got some things I want to announce," Delvecchio said. "Number one, no more arguments. We waste an incredible amount of time hashing out every detail and yelling at each other. And we don't have time to waste. So, no more. I make the decisions, and I don't want any screaming and kicking. If you don't like it, you're free to elect another leader. Understand?" He looked at each of them in turn. Sheridan squirmed a little under the gaze, but none of them objected.

"Okay," Delvecchio said finally. "If that's settled, then we'll move on." He looked at Granowicz. "First thing is this idea of yours, Ike. Now you want us to talk. Sorry, I don't buy it. Just last night you were telling us how the fungus, because of its childhood traumas, was bound to be hostile."

"Yes," began Granowicz, "but with the additional knowledge it will get from—"

"No arguments," Delvecchio said sharply. Granowicz subsided. Delvecchio continued. "What do you think it will be doing while we're talking? Hitting us with everything it's got, if your theory was correct. And it sounded good to me. We're dead men if we're not ready, so we'll be ready. To fight, not talk."

Sheridan was smirking. Delvecchio turned on him next. "But we're not going to hit them with everything we've got as soon as we see them, like you want, Sheridan," he said. "Ike brought up a point last night that's been bothering me ever since. Nagging at me. There's an outside chance the fungus might not even try to take over the soldiers. It might not be smart enough to realize they're important. It might concentrate on the spaceship."

Sheridan sat up straight. "We *have* to hit them," he said. "They'll kill us, Delvecchio. You don't—"

Sanderpay, surprisingly, joined in. "It's eating a path," he said. "And the trees. And this morning, Jim, look out there. Slinkers and swampbats all around. It's got them, I know it. It wouldn't be building up this way otherwise."

Delvecchio waved them both silent. "I know, Otis, I know. You're right. All signs say that it has them. But we have to be sure. We wait until we see them, until we *know*. Then, if they're taken, hit them with everything, at once. It has to be hard. If it becomes a struggle, we've lost. They outnumber and outgun us, and in a fight, they'd breach the station easy. Only the fungus might just march 'em up. Maybe we can kill them all before they know what hit them."

Granowicz looked doubtful. Sheridan looked more than doubtful. "Delvecchio, that's ridiculous. Every moment we hesitate increases our risk And for such a ridiculous chance. Of *course* it will take them."

"Sheridan, I've had about enough out of you," Delvecchio said quietly. "Listen for a change. There're two chances. One that the fungus might be too dumb to take them over. And one that it might be too smart."

Granowicz raised his eyebrows. Andrews cleared his throat. Sheridan just looked insulted.

"If it has Reyn," Delvecchio said. "Maybe it knows all about us. Maybe it won't take the soldiers over on purpose. It knows from Reyn that we plan to destroy them. Maybe it will just wait."

"But why would it have slinkers clearing a ..." Sanderpay began, then shut up. "Oh. Oh, no. Jim, it couldn't ..."

"You're not merely assuming the fungus is very intelligent, Jim" Granowicz said.

"You're assuming it's very devious as well."

"No," said Delvecchio. "I'm not assuming *anything*. I'm merely pointing out a possibility. A terrible possibility, but one we should be ready for. For over a year now, we've been constantly underestimating the fungus. At every test, it has proven just a bit more intelligent than we figured. We can't make another mistake like that. No margin for error this time."

Granowicz gave a reluctant nod.

"There's more," said Delvecchio. "I want those missiles finished *today*, Otis. In case they get here sooner than we've anticipated. And the explosive too, Arnold. And I don't want any more griping. You two are relived of your watches until you finish those projects. The rest of us will double up."

"Also, from now on we all wear skinthins inside the station. In case the attack comes suddenly and the screens are breached."

Everyone was nodding.

"Finally, we throw out all the experiments. I want every bit of fungus and every Greywater life form within this station eradicated." Delvecchio thought of his dream again, and shuddered mentally.

Sheridan slapped the table and smiled. "Now that's the kind of thing I like to hear! I've wanted to get rid of those things for weeks."

Granowicz looked unhappy, though. And Andrews looked very unhappy. Delvecchio looked at each in turn.

"All I have is a few small animals, Jim" Granowicz said. "Root-snuffs and such. They're harmless enough, and safely enclosed. I've been trying to reach the fungus, establish some sort of communications—"

"No," said Delvecchio. "Sorry, Ike, but we can't take the chances. If the walls are breached or the station damaged, we might lose power. Then, we'd have contamination inside and out. It's too risky. You can get new animals."

Andrews cleared his throat. "But, well, my cultures," he said. "I'm just getting them broken down, isolating properties of the fungus strains. Six months of research, Jim, and, well, I think—" He shook his head.

"You're got you research. You can duplicate it. If we live through this."

"Yes, well—" Andrews was hesitant. "But the cultures will have to be started over. So much time. And Jim—" He hesitated again and looked at the others.

Delvecchio smiled grimly. "Go ahead, Arnold. They might die soon. Maybe they should know."

Andrews nodded. "I'm getting somewhere, Jim. With *my* work, the real work, the whole reason for Greywater. I've bred a mutation of the fungus, a non-intelligence variety, very virulent, very destructive of its hosts.

I'm in the final stages now. It's only a matter of getting the mutant to breed in the Fyndii atmosphere. And I'm near. I'm so near." He looked at each of them in turn, eyes imploring. "If you let me continue, I'll have it soon. And they could dump in on the Fyndii homeworlds, and well, it would end the war. All those lives saved. Think about all the men who will die if I'm delayed."

He stopped suddenly, awkwardly. There was a long silence around the table.

Granowicz broke it. He stroked his chin and gave a funny little chuckle. "And I thought this was such a bold, clean venture," he said, his voice bitter. "To grope toward new intelligence, unlike any we had known, to try to find and talk to a mind perhaps unique in this universe. And now you tell me all my work was a decoy for biological warfare. Even here I can't get away from that damned war." He shook his head. "Greywater Station. What a lie."

"It had to be this way, Ike." Delvecchio said. "The potential for military application was too great to pass up, but the Fyndii would have easily found out about a big, full-scale biowar research project, But teams like Greywater's—routine planetary investigation teams—are common. The Fyndii can't bother to check on every one. And they don't."

Granowicz was staring at the table. "I don't suppose it matters," he said glumly. "We all may die in a few days anyway. This doesn't change that. But—but—" He stopped.

Delvecchio shrugged. "I'm sorry, Ike." He looked at Andrews. "And I'm sorry about the experiments, too, Arnold. But your cultures have to go. They're a danger to us inside the station."

"But, well, the war—all those people." Andrews looked anguished.

"If we don't make it through this, we lose it all anyway, Arnold," Delvecchio said.

Sanderpay put a hand on Andrews' shoulder. "He's right. It's not worth it."

Andrews nodded.

Delvecchio rose. "Alright," he said. "We've got that settled. Now we get to work. Arnold—the explosives. Otis—the rockets. Ike and I will take care of dumping the experiments. But first, I'm going to go brief Miterz. Okay?"

The answer was a weak chorus of agreement.

It took them only a few hours to destroy the work of a year. The rockets, the explosives and the other defenses took longer, but in time, they too were ready. And then they waited, sweaty and nervous and uncomfortable in their skinthins.

Sanderpay monitored the commo system constantly. One day. Two. Three, a day of incredible tension. Four, and the strain began to tell. Five, and they relaxed a bit.

The enemy was late.

"You think they'll try and contact us first?" Andrews asked at one point.

"I don't know," said Sanderpay. "Have you thought about it?"

"I have," Granowicz put in. "But it doesn't matter. They'll try either way. If it's them, they'll want to reach us, of course. If it's the fungus, it'll want to throw us off our guard. Assuming it has absorbed enough knowledge from its hosts to handle a transmission, which isn't established. Still, it will probably try, so we can't trust a transmission."

"Yeah," said Delvecchio. "But, that's the problem. We can't trust anything. We have to suppose everything we're working on. We don't have any concrete information to speak of."

"I know, Jim, I know."

On the sixth day, the storms screamed over the horizon. Spore clouds flowed by in the wind, whipped into random gaps. Overhead the sky darkened. Lightning sheeted in the west.

The radio screeched its agony and crackled. Whistlers moved up and down the scale. Thunder rolled. In the tower, the men of Greywater Station waited out the last few hours.

The voice that had come in early that morning, had faded. Nothing intelligible had come through. Static had crackled most of the day. The soldiers were moving on the edge of the storm, Delvecchio calculated.

Accident? Or planning? He wondered. And deployed his men. Andrews to the turret laser. Sanderpay at the rocket station. Sheridan and himself inside the station, with laser rifles. Granowicz to the flyer port, where the remaining flyers had been stocked with crude bombs. Miterz on the walls.

They waited in their skinthins, filtermasks looked on but not in place. The sky, darkened by the coming storm, was blackening toward twilight anyway. Soon night and the storm would reach Greywater Station hand in hand.

Delvecchio stalked through the halls impatiently. Finally, he returned to the tower to see what was happening. Andrews, at the laser console, was watching the window. A can of beer sat next to him on the nightscope. Delvecchio had never seen the quiet little mycologist drink before.

"They're out there," Andrews said. "Somewhere." He sipped at his beer, put it down again. "I wish that, well, they'd hurry up or something." He looked at Delvecchio. "We're all probably going to die, you know. The odds are so against us."

Delvecchio didn't have the stomach to tell him he was wrong. He just nodded, and watched the window. All the lights in the station were out. Everything was down but the generators, the turret controls, and the forcefield. The field, fed with the extra power, was stronger than ever. But strong enough? Delvecchio didn't know.

Near the field perimeter, seven or eight ghosting shapes wheeled against the storm. They were all wings and claws, and a long, razor-barbed tail. Swampbats. Big ones, with six-foot wingspans.

They weren't alone. The underbrush was alive with slinkers. And the big leeches could be seen in the water near the south wall. All sorts of life were being pick up by the sensors.

Driven before the storm? Or massing for the attack? Delvecchio didn't know that, either.

The tower door opened, and Sheridan entered. He threw his laser rifle on the table near the door. "These things are useless," he said. "We can't use them unless they get inside. Or unless we go out to meet them, and I'm not going to do *that*. Besides, what good will they do against all the stuff they've got?"

Delvecchio started to answer, but Andrews spoke first. "Look out there," he said softly. "More swampbats. And that other thing. What is it?"

Delvecchio looked. Something else was moving through the sky on slowly moving leathery wings. It was black and *big*. Twice the size of a swampbat.

"The first expedition named them hellions," Delvecchio said after a long pause.

"They're native to the mountains, a thousand miles from here." Another pause.

"That clinches it."

There was general movement on the ground and in the water to the west of Greywater Station. Echoes of thunder rolled and then piercing the thunder came a shrill whooping shriek.

"What was *that*?" Sheridan asked.

Andrews was white. "That one I know," he said. "It's called a screecher. A sonic rifle breaks down cell walls with concentrated sound. I saw them used once. I-it almost makes flesh liquefy."

"God," said Sheridan.

Delvecchio moved to the intercom. Every box in the station was on full volume. "Battle stations, gentlemen." He said, flipping down his filter mask. "And good luck."

Delvecchio moved out into the hall and down the stairs. Sheridan picked up his laser and followed. At the base of the stairs, Delvecchio motioned for him to stop.

"You stay here, Eldon. I'll take the main entry port."

Rain had begun to spatter the swamps around Greywater, although the field kept it off the station. A great sheet of wind roared from the west and suddenly the storm was no longer approaching. It was here. A blurred outline of the force bubble could be seen against the churning sky.

Delvecchio strode across the yards through the halls and cycled through decon quickly to the main entry port. The large viewplate gave the illusion of a window. Delvecchio watched it sitting on the hood of a mud-tractor. The intercom box was on the wall next to him.

"Burrowing animals are moving against the under-field, Jim," Andrews reported from the turret. "We're getting, oh, five or six shock inputs a minute. Nothing we can't handle however."

He fell silent again and the only noise was the thunder. Sanderpay began to talk, gabbing about the rockets. Delvecchio was hardly listening. The perimeter beyond the walls was a morass of rain-whipped mud. Delvecchio could see little. He switched from the monitor he was tuned to and picked up the turret cameras. He and Andrews watched with the same eyes.

"Under-field contacts are up," Andrews said suddenly. "A couple of dozen a minute now."

The swampbats were wheeling closer to the perimeter. First one, then another, skirting the very edge of the field, riding terribly and silently on the wet winds. The turret laser rotated to follow each, but they were gone before it could fire.

Then, there was motion on the ground. A wave of slinkers began to cross the perimeter. The laser wheeled, depressed. A spurt of light appeared, leaving a quick vanishing roil of steam. One slinker died, then another.

On the south, a leech rose from the grey waters near the base wall of the station. The turret turned. Two quick spurts of red burned. Steam rose once. The leech twisted at the second burst.

Delvecchio nodded silently, clutched his rifle tighter.

And Andrews voice came over the intercom. "There's a man out there," he said. "Near you, Jim."

Delvecchio slipped on his infrared goggles and flicked back to the camera just outside the entry port. There was a dim shape in the undergrowth.

"Just one?" asked Delvecchio.

"All I read," Andrews said.

Delvecchio nodded and thought. Then, "I'm going out." Many voices at once on the intercom. "That's not wise. I don't think," said one, Granowicz? Another said, "Watch it, Jim. Be careful," Sanderpay, maybe. And Sheridan, unmistakable, "*Don't,* you'll let *them* in!"

Delvecchio ignored them all. He hit the switch to open the outer port doors and slid down into the driver's seat in the mud-tractor. The doors parted. Rain washed into the chamber.

The tractor moved forward, rattling over the entry ramp and sliding smoothly into the slime. Now he was out in the storm and the rain tingled through his skinthins. He drove with one hand and held the laser with the other.

He stopped the tractor just outside the port and stood up. "Come out!" he screamed as loud as he could, out-shouting the thunder. "Let us see you! If you can understand me— If the fungus doesn't have you— Come out now."

He paused and hoped and waited a long minute. He was about to shout again when a man came running from the undergrowth.

Delvecchio had a fleeting glimpse of tattered torn clothes. Bare feet stumbling in the mud. Rain drenched dark hair. But he wasn't looking at those. He was looking at the fungus that all but covered the man's face and trailed across his chest and back.

The man—the thing—raised a fist and released a rock. It missed. He kept running and screaming. Delvecchio, numb, raised his rifle and fired. The fungus thing fell a few feet beyond the trees.

Delvecchio left the tractor where it was and walked back to the entry port on foot. The doors were still open. He went to the intercom. "It has them," he said. Then, again, "It has them. And it's hostile. So now we kill them."

There were no answers. Just a long silence, and a stifled sob, and then Andrews's slow, detached voice. "A new reading. A body of men—thirty, forty, maybe—moving from the west. In formation. A lot of metal—duralloy, I think."

"The main force," Delvecchio said. "They won't be so easy to kill. Get ready. Remember, everything at once."

He turned back into the rain, cradled his rifle, walked to the ramp. Through his goggles, Delvecchio saw the shapes of men. Only a few at first. Fanned out.

He went outside the station to the tractor, knelt behind it. As he watched, the turret turned. A red line reached out, touched the first dim shape. It staggered.

New sheets of rain washed in, obliterating the landscape. The laser licked out again. Delvecchio very slowly, lifted his rifle to his shoulder and joined it, firing at the dim outlines seen through the goggles.

Behind him, he felt the first sounding rocket leave up the launch tube, and he briefly saw the fire of its propellant as it cleared the dome. It disappeared into the rain. Another followed it, then another, then the firings became regular.

The dim shapes were all running together; there was a large mass of men just a few yards deep in the undergrowth. Delvecchio fired into the mass, and noted where they were, and hoped Arnold remembered.

Arnold remembered. The turret laser depressed, sliced at the trunk of a nearby tree. There was the sound of wood tearing. Then the tree began to lean. Then it fell.

From what Delvecchio could see, it missed. Another idea that didn't quite work, he reflected bitterly. But he continued to fire into the forest.

Suddenly, near the edge of the perimeter, water gouted up out of the swamp in a terrific explosion. Dwarfing all else. A slinker flew through the air, surprised at itself. It rained leech parts.

The first rocket.

A second later, another explosion, among the trees this time. Then more, one after another. Several very close to the enemy. Two among the enemy. Trees began to fall. And Delvecchio thought he could hear screaming.

He began to hope. He continued to fire.

There was a whine in the sky above. Granowicz in the flier. Delvecchio took time to glance up briefly and watch it flit overhead towards the trees. Other shapes were moving up there too however, diving on the flier, but they were slower. Granowicz made a quick pass over the perimeter dumping bombs. The swamp shook and the mud and water from the explosions mixed with the rain.

Now, definitely, he *could* hear screaming.

And then the answer began to come.

Red tongues and pencil of light flicked out of the dark, played against the walls causing steam whirlpools which washed away in the rain. Then projectiles. Explosions. A dull thud rocked the station. A second. And somewhere in the storm, someone opened up with a screecher.

The wall behind him rang with a humming glow. And there was another explosion much bigger overhead against the forcefield dome. The rain vanished for an instant in a vortex of exploding gases. Wind whipped the smoke away and the station rocked. Then the rains touched the dome again in sheets.

More explosions. Lasers spat and hissed in the rain. Back and forth the grizzly light show. Miterz was firing from the walls. Granowicz was making another pass. The rockets had stopped falling. Gone already?

The turret fired, moved, fired, moved, fired. Several explosions rocked the tower. The world was a madness of rain. Of noise. Of lightning. Of night.

Then, the rockets began again. The swamp and nearer forest shook from the hits. The eastern corner of the station *moved* as a sounding missile landed uncomfortably close.

The turret began to fire again. Short bursts lost in rain. Answering fire was thick. At least one screecher was shrieking regularly.

Delvecchio saw the swampbats appear suddenly around the flier. They converged from all sides, howling, bent on death. One climbed right up into the engine, folding its wings neatly. There was a terrible explosion that lit the night to ghosts of trailing rain.

More explosions around the force dome. Lasers screened off the dome and turret. The turret glowed red, steamed. On the south, a section of wall vanished in a tremendous explosion.

Delvecchio was still firing regularly, automatically. But, suddenly, the laser went dead, uncharged. He hesitated, rose. He turned just in time to see the hellion dive on the turret. Nothing stopped it. With a sudden chill, Delvecchio realized that the forcefield was out.

Laser riffles reached out and touched the hellion, but not the turret laser. The turret was still silent. The hellion hit the windows with a crash, smashing through, shattering glass and plastic and duralloy struts.

Delvecchio began to move back toward the ramp and the entry port. A slinker rose as he darted by, snapped at his leg. There was a red blur of pain, fading quickly. He stumbled, rose again, moved. The leg was numb and bleeding. He used the useless laser as a crutch.

Inside, he hit the switch to shut the outer doors. Nothing happened. He laughed suddenly. It didn't matter. Nothing mattered. The station was breeched. The fields were down.

The inner doors still work. He moved through, limped through the halls out to the yard. Around him he could hear the generators dying.

The turret was hit again and again. It exploded and lifted moaning. Three separate impacts hit the tower at once. The top half rained metal.

Delvecchio stopped in the yard, looked at the tower suddenly unsure of where he was going. The word "Arnold" formed on his lips, but stayed there.

The generators quit completely. Lasers and missiles and swampbats steamed overhead. All was night lit by lightning. By explosions. By lasers.

Delvecchio retreated to a wall and propped himself against it. The barrage continued. The ground inside the station was torn, turned, shook. Once there was a scream somewhere as though someone was calling him in their moment of death.

He lowered himself to the ground and lay still clutching the rifle while more shells pounded the station. Then all was silent.

Propped up against a rubble pile, he watched helplessly as a big slinker moved toward him across the yard. It loomed large in the rain, but before it reached him, it fell screaming.

There was movement behind him. He turned. A figure in skin-thins waved, took up a position near one of the ruined laboratories.

Delvecchio saw shapes moving on what was left of the walls, scrambling over. He wished he had a charge for his laser. A red pencil of light flashed by him in the rain. One of the shapes crumbled. The man behind him had fired too soon, though, and too obviously. The other figured leveled on him. Stabs of laser fire went searing over Delvecchio's head. Answering fire came briefly, then stopped.

Slowly, slowly, Delvecchio dragged himself through the med, toward the labs. They didn't seem to see him. After an exhausting effort, he reached the fallen figure in skinthins. Sanderpay, dead.

Delvecchio took the laser. There were five men ahead of him, more in the darkness beyond. Lying on his stomach, Delvecchio fired at one man, then another and another. Steam geysers rose around him as the shapes in duralloy fired back. He fired and fired and fired until all those around him were down. Then he plucked himself up, and tried to run.

The heel was shot off his boot, and warmth flooded his foot. He turned and fired, moved on, past the wrecked tower and the labs.

Laser stabs peeled overhead. Four, five, maybe six of them. Delvecchio dropped what had been a lab wall. He fired around the wall, saw one shape fall. He fired again. Then the rifle died on him.

Lasers tore into the wall, burning in, almost through. The men fanned. There was no hope.

Then the night exploded into fire and noise. A body, twisted flat, spun by. A stab of laser fire came on the teeth of the explosion, from behind Delvecchio.

Sheridan stood over him, firing into the men caught in the open, burning them down one by one. He quit firing for an instant, lobbed a vial of explosive, then went back to the laser. He was hit by a chunk of flying rubble, went down.

Delvecchio came back up as he did. They stood unsteadily. Sheridan wheeling and looking for the targets. But there were no more targets. Sheridan was coughing from exertion inside his skinthins.

The rain lessened. The pain increased.

They picked their way through the rubble. They passed many twisted bodies in duralloy, a few skinthins. Sheridan paused at one of the armored bodies, turned it over. The faceplate had been burned away with part of the face. He kicked it back over.

Delvecchio tried another. He lifted the helmet off, searched the nostrils, the forehead, the eyes, the ears. Nothing.

Sheridan had moved away, and was standing over a body in skinthins half covered by rubble. He stood there for a long time. "Delvecchio!" he called finally. "*Delvecchio!*"

Delvecchio walked to him, bent, pulled off the filtermask. The man was still alive. He opened his eyes. "Oh, God, Jim," he said "Why? Oh, *why?*"

Delvecchio didn't say anything. He stood stock still and stared down.

Bill Reyn stared back up.

"I got through, Jim," said Reyn, coughing blood. "Once the flier was down … no trouble. Close … I walked it. They … they were still inside mostly with the heat. Only a few … had gone out."

Delvecchio coughed once, quietly.

"I got through … the vaccine … most, anyway. A few had gone out, infected … no hope. But … but, we took away their armor and their weapons. No harm that way … we … had to fight our way through. Me it … left alone, but, God, those guys in duralloy lost some men … leeches … slinkers."

Sheridan turned and dropped his rifle. He began to run towards the labs.

"We tried the suit radios, Jim … but the storm … should have waited, but the vaccine … short term … wearing off … we tried not … to hurt you … started killing us …"

He began to choke on his own blood. Delvecchio, helpless, looked down. "Again," he said in a voice that was dead and broken. "We underestimated it again. We—no, I—I—"

Reyn did not die for another three or four hours. Delvecchio never found Sheridan again. He tried to restart the generators alone, but to no avail.

Just before dawn the skies cleared. The stars came through bright and white against the night sky. The fungus had not yet released new spores. It was almost like a moonless night on Earth.

Delvecchio sat atop a mound of rubble. A dead soldier's laser rifle in his hands. Ten or eleven charges on his belt. He did not look off to where Reyn lay. He was trying to figure out how to get the radio working. There was a supply ship coming.

The sky to the east began to lighten. A swamp bat, then another, began to circle the ruins of Greywater Station.

And the spores began to fall.

O₂ Arena

by Oghenechovwe Donald Ekpeki

"Where there is no inner freedom, there is no life."

—Radhanath Swami

My sweat ran in rivulets, caught between my skin and the Lycra bodysuit. It slid down my spine and chest, as I regarded my enemy with detached exhaustion. Though my vision was hazy, my focus was sharp. My intention: to do murder, even a murder sanctioned and abetted by the same system that was slowly killing us all.

The man in front of me paced, fatigue showing plainly in his bearing. My body was depleted of the energy needed to carry it, and my breathing came in short, gulping gasps as I inhaled the bittersweet air. Bitter because it reeked of my own possible—no, likely—death, and sweet because of its purpose: winning a life for another, one far more deserving of it than I was. I breathed in that sweetness as if it was a promise, a sustenance of a selfish love, which, to me, was everything.

I knew my opponent was not my enemy, although he might be the instrument of my death, or I the instrument of his. The one I truly needed to defeat, our collective enemy, was unflagging: the society that broke us and engineered our existence as an inexorable journey

343

toward death. Quick or slow, the system forced us into a profound lifelessness just so we could breathe one more day, then yet another.

I was at the arena for the second time, of my own accord, but in a trap by the society to which I had been born.

My opponent shuffled forward, all the humor bleached out of the desperate grin he wore plastered on his frozen features. A snarl spread across my own face, and I rushed at him to take life if I could, that I may cherish and gift it to another.

A small part of me whimpered and briefly wondered at the monster I had become.

A few months earlier

The chattering in the hall faded as the speaker mounted the podium. Four thousand of us fell silent as he removed his O_2 mask and began our induction into the Academy of Laws. The Head of the Department (HoD) of Property Law proceeded to tell us why we were here.

I shook my head ruefully. In the Nigeria of 2030, people still insisted on telling others their purpose, as though we did not know or could not decide for ourselves. Cursed was the one with their own will and individuality, and woe unto them if they aspired to more than the O_2 credits needed to keep them breathing.

What was our daily reality? You had to pay to breathe. Since the global warming crisis had affected phytoplankton and hampered the production of breathable air, our lives were our own to maintain at the requisite cost.

Plodding along, the HoD explained to us that we were amongst the chosen few privileged to earn the Bachelor of Laws (LL.B) degree. Having studied for five years to obtain an LL.B degree, and having passed a very difficult entrance exam to be admitted to the Academy of Laws, one wondered where the "privilege" came from. Here we had to survive a rigorous, nearly militaristic regimen of study and indoctrination and only then would we be allowed to take the almighty Bar exam.

I couldn't help thinking that if I had wanted to show off superhuman stamina, I would have joined the army. Then I reminded myself that I wasn't here by choice. It was the Bar that would usher me into my position in the corrupt system where I could earn the kind of O_2 allowances that would quash my CO_2s. It would be a herculean journey, not helped by these pompous men making it seem like a grand privilege.

The HoD's talk prompted several students, naïve in my opinion, to ask about our rights. He informed them, almost scathingly, that they had no rights.

I inwardly shrugged. I would sort it out the way I sorted everything. Succeeding was all that was required. It didn't matter how.

The HoD introduced a second lecturer, a professor of the Commercial Law Department. Without removing his mask—which he didn't need here, where O_2 generators regulated the air—he outlined the curriculum. A program that should ordinarily take three years was crammed into eight intensive months, giving room for periodic admission of new students. The more students admitted, the greater the fortune of O_2 units the school made. He concluded with a reiteration of our privilege as law students. I shook my head and, slipping on my O_2 mask, left the hall.

Outside, I saw that Ovoke had taken a break from the rhetoric too. She smirked when she saw me and came over to give me a hug. She felt the way she looked: delicate, as if she would crumble if I squeezed her too tightly. What was it about her fragile look that all the boys found irresistible? I held her at arm's length to inspect her as if trying to find her appeal.

She smiled at the confused look on my face, raising an eyebrow.

I never missed an opportunity to tease her, and I couldn't resist it now. "I would say I missed you, but I don't want to lie."

She laughed. "And yet you hold me like you care."

I struggled with a response, and she filled in for me. "Is it because I'm dying?"

"Of course," I agreed, hoping my off-handedness would hide the double bluff. "Why else would I care?"

She smiled again, and I soaked in her presence as we leaned against the parapet in companionable silence.

"Do you want to feel it?" she asked blandly after a moment.

"Feel what?"

"My tumor. The death inside me. I can feel it, you know."

I looked away, over the railing. When we had first met during registration for the program, she'd told me she suffered from ovarian cancer. She'd told no one else, not one of her close friends from our university days when I had been just a course mate she hardly noticed. She hadn't told her new friends here, either. Just me, who didn't fawn over her like everyone else. Me, who teased her like a brother, and never let her take anything too seriously.

The way I was around her was also her preference. Not like everyone else, who were always in puppy-mode around her, even when she wasn't ill. They didn't see what I saw: a strong, intelligent, frighteningly competent woman with teeth and claws and a mind all her own. When I saw her fight, I called her fearsome, horrifying, a raging animal in a world too delicate to cage her. When others saw her fight, they called her "brave."

It was easy then to see why she told just me.

"I told only you," she had said, "for the same reason I left home for this rigorous, unhealthy program. I don't want to be treated like I'm a sick, broken thing. I want to live before I die." And then she'd added, "If not caring is your normal, then that's what I want."

But I had always cared, even when it felt hopeless to do so, even when I didn't want to.

I realized I'd not answered her about touching her tumor. I didn't want to respond. Teasing her about death made it seem less real, but really talking about it was too hard. I had to keep pretending that I didn't care.

"Hey, mumu," I teased her, rather than humor her macabre mood on this, a day to acknowledge the new challenges ahead of us at the Academy of Laws. "We had better go in before the patrollers come looking for us."

She chuckled. "Okay, big head."

We slipped off our oxygen-filtering masks as we returned to the hall. We only needed them in the harsh, oppressive, and barely breathable air of the outside.

The lecturer, while deep in a section on campus rules, had found his good humor. I preferred him without it.

"You are not allowed to eat when classes are on. Not even to chew gum. Unless you are pregnant and carrying a kid, then you can chew like a goat. Hahahaha."

He continued on, outlining all the lack of privileges we had at our privileged school, with the interspersing of jokes, often classist. I grimaced, but some students chuckled. You knew the ones who would succeed early by ass-kissing.

Next up was Dr. Umez of property law. A man in his early forties, he rasped on about his religious, conservative principles and rules that I am sure weren't sanctioned by the institution, as strict as it already was. His last edict was that phones wouldn't be allowed when his lectures were on, and any found would be confiscated, permanently.

"Well, that's not extreme," I quipped sarcastically. "He's trying to go into phone retailing?"

Ovoke leaned closer and whispered conspiratorially, "He trades them back for favors."

I looked at her blankly, not getting her point, so she continued, "He's famous with the ladies."

My eyebrows climbed in realization, then furrowed in confusion again. "But why? For a phone?"

"He promises an easier time for them here, and better chances of passing."

I scoffed. "I have actually looked into bribing people to pass and to game the system. 'Phone Seizer' here can't guarantee anyone will pass. The scripts are marked by external examiners and people in HQ, Abuja. That's where it all happens."

"Well, the average student doesn't know that. Between deceiving the gullible and promising to make their lives hell, Umez has quite a tutoring program."

"How do you even know all this?" I asked.

"I'm a woman. It's our business, our survival, to know about people like this."

I was quiet for a bit. Ovoke touched my angry face.

"If he ever bothers you," I told her softly, "I'll kill him."

"Awww," she said. "You're every girl's dream: a psycho best friend who would kill for her. However, start with my cancer."

"I'm afraid that's beyond the reach of my goons," I said apologetically.

"Are you useful for anything?" she asked with a playful push. We both laughed under our breath.

Mrs. Oduwole was at the podium now. The Head of Hostels began by stating that the generators would be on until midnight for reading and for the making of breathable air. After midnight, we would revert to our O₂ cylinders, which we must keep by our bedsides throughout the night.

The tuition was expensive but was only meant to cover the central hall's oxygen generation when lectures were on. O_2 masks filtered the bad air temporarily, for the brief periods when moving between places. O_2 cylinders were for longer periods when there were no O_2 generators.

We weren't allowed to be in the hostels during the day when lectures were on, for any reason. She didn't care if you were a girl on your flow, no matter how heavy. And this was apparently the only example she felt obligated to give.

Another lecturer talked about modest and decent dressing, and one unfortunate girl was singled out as an example of what not to do.

The female lecturer, gesturing at the girl's long and painted nails, said, "Such is not allowed here. They are an unnecessary distraction to both ladies and gentlemen. The ladies might feel pressured to compete and focus on their looks, and the men might want to … well, we all know what men want from women."

There was a low chuckle from the students, and not for the first time I wondered at the unhealthy focus of this school to use sexist mores to try to keep everyone in their place.

"Well, we know some women also want the same from women," she continued, and the chuckle rang louder. She leaned forward now and whispered, even though she knew the microphone would carry the whisper. "So, with your nails, how do you wash your …"

The laughter rang long and unrestrained now. The girl being queried wilted in shame, and the woman moved on, having achieved her objective.

"Well, that's professional," I whispered sarcastically to Ovoke.

But she wasn't fazed by any of this. Of course, she had more immediate worries on her mind.

I had to wonder why our society still looks down on women so much. Was gasping your lungs out in between toiling to purchase filters and breathable air in an atmosphere ruined by global warming not enough? Or was the audacity of being here, daring to compete with men in the most lucrative and influential profession in the Republic, simply too bold?

At the end of the induction, students remained seated while the lecturers left. There were electronic fingerprint scanners embedded at our desks and, in order to be counted as having attended, we would have to use the scanners to sign in and out. If there wasn't 85 percent attendance over the entire program, you couldn't take the Bar exams. That also ensured that students were holding each other accountable.

Once the teachers were gone, the students rushed out through their exits.

Exit A was left for the Bar 1 students, the elite gang in their expensive-as-hell O_2 regulator masks. They had all schooled in China and America for their LL.B. Foreign schools were attended by only the extremely wealthy and took less time—three years instead of the five in domestic schools. These elite students were generally regarded as "better" and were treated accordingly. They didn't mingle with the students from Nigerian universities. It didn't help that the Chinese government, in partnership with the CAT—Chinese American Tobacco—had donated a stash of high-quality masks for them and took care of O_2 regulation in most of our institutions, in exchange for certain economic and political concessions.

The British American Tobacco (BAT) was consumed by the CAT after the Chinese had bought all the interests, infrastructure, and institutions that had been left over in Nigeria after the Weather Crises. They effectively split the country down the middle to share with American investors in an uneasy alliance. Both former tobacco companies quickly caught on and began to produce air-filtration systems, air regulators, masks, and other paraphernalia needed by all for survival.

Before the Crises, they had sold death in the form of cigarettes when life was in abundance to those who didn't care about life. But after the thinning of the air and the severe climate changes that had made the Earth near uninhabitable, the industrial conglomerate had switched. Now the merchants of death sold life and oxygen because death was in abundance, and life was the commodity in demand. You had to pay to breathe. O_2 credit was life. And your deficits, your debits, were in CO_2. They sold to the highest bidders: the government who purchased and subsidized it for their workers, and for the rich. So there was short supply for the rest.

I made a move to follow as the peacocks trooped through their exit, but Ovoke's hand tugged my arm.

"Not that way, trouble-lover."

I smiled, and we went out through one of the other doors, heading for the hostels. I looked at Ovoke. She had taken the induction far less seriously than me, rolling her eyes through all the nonsense. She was well attuned to my moods and temperament.

"Want to take a walk?" she asked.

"Yes," I replied. "I need a break since there are no more induction classes today."

She clasped my hand as we strolled out.

A security guard was patrolling outside, and I passed him an $O_2$20 card, to forestall his inquiries. He pocketed it smartly and moved on. I bribed the security men at the gate too, and we left campus to walk illegally into the sunset of a quiet afternoon, away from the toxic Law Academy.

Weeks in, we had adjusted to the toxic institution; to the assignments and group work that ran on into late nights and had to be presented in class the next day; to the frantic, extra reading after classes to avoid being embarrassed in the randomly administered, rapid-fire quizzes; to the shaming and disgrace that followed failure to get an answer right; to hoarding our oxygen cylinders in the hostels for when the power generators switched off in the night.

We had a plethora of assignments and projects that kept us buried to our eyebrows, even on weekends. But assignments were rarely my concern on weekdays, much less weekends. And on this weekend, Ovoke was gone.

She had taken a trip home to Ikeja, where her family lived, for chemo sessions scheduled into the middle of next week.

I missed her. Taking care of her at school—buying her food, drawing her water, and keeping her company with jokes and sallies, both of which made her happy—was the one thing that kept me anchored and from snapping at the horrid attitude of everyone here.

Without her here, there was no life to be experienced. I felt acutely every pull of the thin and corrupted air. The mechanically purified and generated atmosphere wasn't much better. We hadn't had good air in a decade.

It's no surprise that Ovoke was my breath of fresh air, my reason for being able to withstand this place—for not exploding at all the verbal abuse and stupidity from lecturers, students, and other staff. I needed to stay here to stay with her.

And it was this realization that sent me on my own little detour. I needed to visit the mainland. Not that the air there was any better there. It was much worse, in fact. The people there were poor. The island that held the school campus was the part of Lagos kept for the elite, with regulated air, as seen to by Governor MC Oluwole.

You see, only the rich deserved to breathe.

Still, the mainland was home. Usually, I would take my Temperature Regulating Suit. I needed the TRS when going to the mainland so as not to suffer heat stress from the ever-rising temperatures, another effect of the warming crises of a decade ago.

But I had given Ovoke my suit, so I stood sweating, waiting for transport until one of the government-regulated Bus Rapid Transit (BRT) vehicles arrived. It would take me to the outskirts of the mainland and was fitted with its own temperature-regulation systems. Inside, I leaned back and let the cold-yet-polluted air fan my anxieties away.

I was fine until I got into the Danfo bus, the first of many on this transfer line that would convey me the last distance to my home. They were usually faulty and broke down a lot, exposing the occupants to serious dangers of heat stress.

I paid the Danfo driver O$_2$17. His bus, at least, had a marginally working air-filtration system, so we could have breathable air. I baked in the heat, but I could tell that the other passengers were not as affected. They were hardy, sturdy folks who looked like they were used to this. People who lived on the mainland but worked on the island made the trip to the high-rise and office complexes they toiled in daily, so they were used to the extremes. The island housed most of the companies and corporations that thrived in this troubled world, along with CAT, the company that owned the breath in our lungs.

I stopped at Oyingbo and took a bus going toward the University of Lagos, my alma mater. I wasn't going to my old school, though. I stopped at the university gate and took another bus to Bariga, the student community that housed most of the 100,000-student population, teachers, and other mostly junior staff that ran the institution. You only got accommodation inside the school if you were senior staff.

The hostels were for foreign students who paid top O$_2$ credits. I was heading downtown, to the most dangerous parts of Bariga, the parts I knew were occupied by the Eiye and Buccaneer cultists.

I paid the keke driver O$_2$4. My mask was already on. I took the Ikoro, the side streets that led to the house of the friends and fellow cultists I came to see, members of the vanilla Buccaneer cult I had belonged to during my years as a University of Lagos student.

It was not as dangerous as it sounded. The Buccaneer was a cult made up of better-off kids who wanted to be dissidents. We paid the Eiye guys to handle the few infractions we got into. The Eiye was a more impoverished fraternity with their members nicknamed "bird," or "winch," for the rough and dirty crowd it attracted. They were always eager to do any jobs for the right pay, which was any pay.

I passed a few people carrying old, crude oxygen cylinders. People on the mainland here, aside those in high-profile jobs, could rarely afford filtration masks sold by CAT, so they made do with old oxygen cylinders they had to refill. The agencies that should have handled filtration and regulation systems here were moribund from having their initially insufficient funding further looted by officials who went on to buy high-rise apartments on the island.

The passing folks glared at me, taking in my fine and obviously expensive air-filtration mask. To them I was a "butty," a rich kid who had lost his way—and I knew some would try to rob me, then severely wound me if I tried to resist. I looked back to see them already preparing to come at me. I flashed one of them the Buccaneer hand sign. He hesitated. I flashed the Eiye hand sign too, thus identifying myself as "brother to pikin of last two years, egede number one." The guy at the head of the company nodded in respect and waved me on as "master."

My destination was the house of one of my old Buccaneer friends yet to graduate. It was crowded with a number of students and indigenes of the Bariga community who hung out with them. Loud music blared from speakers somewhere in the two-bedroom apartment. It was old and decrepit, like most of the houses here.

The generator, running outside for electricity, powered an old air regulator which coughed out good air, marginally improving what we had. Ironically, it was ruining the good air outside, to provide for us inside. Talk about robbing Peter to pay Paul. Not to even mention the noise.

But, anything to breathe better. I could smell igbo, which had become dirt cheap when everyone moved on to drugs and synthetic substances for highs to compensate for an otherwise shitty life. Well, almost everyone. It didn't make sense to me to smoke and damage your lungs and the most precious commodity you had: air that was in such short supply. But then, no one ever accused cultists of wisdom.

I went to my friend's room, where the smell of weed was coming from. Jaiyesimi and some friends were smoking and playing cards while another group was gambling with dice. Some had passed out on a rickety-rackety bed in the corner.

Jaiyesimi nodded at me. He had to finish his game before we could speak.

I greeted the occupants of the room in confralangua, to show I belonged. I had taken off my air-filtration mask when I got into the house, seeing as they had a regulator. But the smell of weed soon overpowered me and it was either choke or put on my mask, neither of which was a good option here; both would make me look weak. So, I signaled to my friend that I would be outside when he was done. I choked down a small cough as I stepped out. I could see them chuckle and one of them say slyly, Ju man.

Outside, I slipped my mask back on and inhaled deeply. Air was life. For this, I was content to be a "Ju man," a slur for people who didn't belong to cults in the university. Or for those who, like me, belonged merely as honorary members for protection, social and other nonviolent reasons, paying dues and not engaging in any of the requisite violent activities that gained one respect and prestige as a cultist. I had joined to be left alone. There was no middle ground in a community like this: you were either the oppressed or the oppressor.

I opted to join the latter, even as an honorary member.

Jaiyesimi soon joined me. Chuckling at something someone inside had said, he took a pull of his blunt. Looking at my disapproving glance, he put it out and deposited it in a pocket.

We both stood in silence for a while, then he asked, "How the academy be na?"

"It's fine. By that I mean everyone there isn't."

"As it should be," he chuckled. "You know, we hear gist from folks there. It sounds like the university all over again."

"Basically," I agreed. "Just more studying, more nonsense. Less time though."

"Mmm," he nodded knowingly. "More of the bad things, less of the good."

"Yea," I agreed. "The academics are really the worst. But I will sort myself out. You know I know how."

He nodded.

We were quiet again, and then he said, "I heard about this guy in your academy, Dr. Umez. Has he been bothering you?"

"How do you mean?"

"You know how I mean," he said, leaning closer. "I heard he pressures folks for sex. Has he …"

"Wait," I stopped him, confused. "Why would you think this would be a problem for me? He pressures g— Oh! You think I'm gay, and Dr. Umez is into boys?"

Silence.

"Dr. Umez does boys?" I asked. "But he's so married, with kids, and religious, and being queer is a …"

"… crime with a fourteen-year jail term here and a death sentence in the North?" He rolled his eyes. "That's for the little people. Not an academy lecturer."

"But he's married, to a woman!"

"That never stopped anybody either. He's either bi or he does girls as a feint. In any case, he does both, so I've heard."

I thought back to what I had learnt about the lecturer. "Isn't he religious and a deacon at church?"

"Definitely a smoke screen."

"First of all, it's a wonder how you know so much about what's going on in the academy from here. Yes, I know gist filters down. But you know so much about the sexual lives of people there. Me, him. I am curious."

"Well, I like to check up on mine and know what's going on in the community."

"Since when was the academy part of the community?" I asked. At his raised eyebrow, I paused. "Wait, are you gay?"

I think he knew I didn't care about a person's sexual orientation. Straight or gay, bi or otherwise—as long as the relationship was healthy, who was I to judge?

He sidled closer. "Well, I could show you," he said softly, winking. "Show, not tell. Right?"

I laughed, knowing he was being playful, but also wondering if he was partly serious. It was so hard to tell in a society that didn't talk about such things openly, for fear of condemnation. "Don't ask, don't tell," I rejoinder. "This is flattering, but I prefer a partner who is cerebral."

"Are you mad?" He laughed too. "Last I checked, your grades weren't all that, so how will you be wanting a cerebral partner? And didn't you graduate with a third class?"

"I said cerebral, not academic. Also, you managed to not graduate at all."

"True," he conceded.

"Also, I'm not ..."

"Right," he said.

We were both quiet after this, till I punctured the silence.

"So, Dr. Umez harasses and rapes both boys and girls, huh."

"Yup," he said without looking at me.

"Dude sounds like he needs killing."

Jaiyesimi now looked at me. "Can you kill someone?"

"I'm not sure. We're going to find out, I guess."

He looked at me askance. Silent.

I hesitated. "You get my text na, didn't you? O₂ Arena."

His eyebrows raised in genuine surprise. "You were serious?"

"Yes na," I confirmed, irritated by the notion I would joke about something like that.

"Wetin you need money for so bad?" But he barely paused to breathe before answering his own question. "Ah ... Law Academy."

It wasn't hard for him to figure out. I was a decent student when I tried. But I rarely did. School was a necessary evil for me. Something I did but had no choice.

I preferred art and writing, which I couldn't get parental approval to pursue. The only thing they endorsed or cared to entertain was a career that allowed one to get a job in the government administration as a civil servant and be entitled to O₂ credits and an allocation of oxygen.

What use was a life where all you did was merely exist? So, I cheated when I could, and bribed my way through when I couldn't cheat or wing it. My dad had died in my third year at the university, and his monetary support had dried up.

Now I required five times the amount of money I had needed in the past to pay my way through the university. And I would need it all at once. So O_2 Arena it was.

Jaiyesimi met my eyes sternly, and I realized he also, on some level, only thought of me as a Ju Man—faking it until I make it. Never completely all in. "You sure?"

I nodded.

"Well, na, your life, sha." He shrugged. "Make I call Papilo to carry us go."

We made our way to the underground square, led by one of the Eiye boys and my friend Jaiyesimi, to the place they called O_2 Arena. It was a fighting pit, a solid Plexiglass cage, its transparent walls harder than steel. Two combatants in skintight black bodysuits were inside, cameras focused from every angle.

This was what had replaced selling your kidneys and internet fraud: the only get-rich-quick scheme, regulated secretly by government and top CAT officials, illegally and discreetly. The cage fights were streamed and sponsored by equally rich and highly placed folks who had an appetite for this kind of entertainment.

Thugs and all sorts of desperate people who were ready to risk it all for a huge payoff came here. Cult members came to settle squabbles. Instead of wasting a death, they came here to fight it out and at least know that one of them stood the chance to make what equalled near three decades of standard wages. Fifty thousand O_2 credits, a lifetime supply of air. You fought and died to keep breathing. And this was how I planned to make money enough to sort my exams.

Jaiyesimi looked at me strangely, trying to figure out my sudden need to make such a huge gamble with my life. I ignored him.

They announced the fighters who got into the arena, glass doors sealed behind them. Pure, breathable air was provided inside so combatants could breathe well, could draw lungs full of the air they fought, and maybe died, for. The irony was not lost on the online spectators.

The fighters in the arena squared and faced off. The mic man and moderator atop the cage commentated, move-by-move, on the entire match, which turned out to be dirty, long, and ugly. I watched as the two men pummelled each other till they were almost too exhausted to stand. I didn't know them, or why they had come here to murder or be murdered, but I understood them. They were both me. I was both of them. Cultist, thug, desperate son, brother, or father—this was as fair a fight for oxygen as any of us would ever have.

One of them slipped, perhaps on the sweat on the floor. The other set to stomping the fallen, on and on. When his target stopped moving, he took him into a choke hold. The other struggled, but not for long. When he finally lay still, the victor stood up, screaming to the rafters.

Then he fell to his knees in exhaustion.

Canned cheering and applause answered him; there were no spectators live here—just the technical staff working the equipment, and thugs and cultists screening fighters or helping victors to process their payment.

The Eiye boy with Jaiyesimi looked at us both. "You don see am abi?"

I nodded. They brought trusted, wannabe participants here for a viewing, to see the action before they committed to their fate.

Jaiyesimi looked at me with disbelief. "Why you wan do this kind thing? For school? You fit read na. You fit pass on your own. And if you fail, e no matter."

I shook my head. He didn't understand. I couldn't risk it. It was not that I could not do it on my own, but if I failed, my mom and family at home, who needed the status of having a graduate from the academy of letters, would miss the income I could contribute to keeping them breathing. Not to mention the stigma of my failing. I would rather die.

The thug who brought us to the arena rapped Jaiyesimi on the shoulder. "He no get the mind." Meaning that I didn't have the guts to do this.

They were right, as I realized on the bus the next day. It's all well and good to think you can do it until you actually have to.

I had only been in school for barely a week when Ovoke called me. A week after my first trip back from the mainland. I had left after she left, because in her absence there was not enough presences to keep me occupied. The campus was filled with students, but while she was gone it was empty of companionship.

I had been lazing through the school activities with disinterest when she called me one evening, her voice such a tiny scratchy whisper, I had to strain to hear her. "Ode, I'm back."

"Oh, really?" I said, feigning disinterest. "Why is your voice so tiny? I could come see you in your room. Or should I wait for you to come downstairs?" I was eager not to seem too eager. She chuckled, no doubt aware of my ruse.

"I'm not in school yet," she said. "I'm outside. Chemo was rough and those hostels are not the best place to recover. That's why my voice is tiny, by the way."

I swallowed a lecture about how she should have stayed at home instead to rest, something she sensed. Instead I said, "Well, you were no Beyonce to begin with, so it's not like your voice is a great loss."

She chuckled and answered my unspoken question. "My parents agreed I could lodge in one of the more affordable hotels around, for a day or two to get over chemo before moving back to the hostel. So, will you come and see me there?"

My phone chimed immediately after and I received the address in my WhatsApp. Golden Tulip Hotels. I knew the place. No wonder it was affordable. It was a not-too-terrible place but in the more run-down part of the island.

"Okay, girl. I'll see you in a bit. Though I have important things to do, so it won't be for a while."

"Of course, busy man," she said mockingly.

"Bye." I hung up, a little annoyed that I was worried and she would know I was. I would have to deliberately delay now. Wait for a whole day before going to see her, so I could be fashionably late, not show how much I care.

It was 8 p.m. when I knocked on the door of her room. She opened the door, looked me up and down, then let me hug her. I held on a bit, then she pushed me away. I sat on the bed and she sat at the table, and in her scratchy voice she told me how her trip went. After a while of listening, punctuating her recollections with sarcastic quips that had her chuckling all throughout, she got up and pulled something from a drawer.

"What's that?"

"Neulasta."

"What's that? Are you doing drugs in addition to your cancer?" I asked, almost impressed.

She sighed.

"It's a follow-up for my chemo, to wake me up."

"Wake you up?"

She sighed and beckoned to me. I pulled closer saying, "Oooh, the sex talk."

She shook her head. "Do you know how chemo works?"

"I know what goes in where and how to use a condom."

She punched me. "Be serious." I affected seriousness and she continued. "What chemo is supposed to do is kill you."

I raised an eyebrow.

"Along with your cancer cells," she added. "It kills you and the cancer, almost. It stops before you are dead. But the cancer is weak, the chemo has made you even weaker, so then you take this after." She held up what she had called Neulasta. "It's for my vitality. Wakes me back up, brings me back from the edge. Rinse and repeat. I slip out of Death's grasp with this, leaving the cancer to die a little more each chemo session, till it's eventually dead. A little game of cat and mouse."

She stopped talking. There was a lingering silence in the room. I didn't say anything but the unspoken question hung between us: what if you lose in this little game of cat and mouse?

I asked, "Does it kill your brain cells then? Cuz that would explain ..."

She punched me and we both laugh.

"I'm supposed to take this by 9.30 p.m.," she continued. "And I must take it before two hours elapse after the last chemo."

I nodded solemnly. "What happens if you don't take it within that time?"

"It's supposed to keep me alive, so ..." she shrugged. "Your guess is as good as mine."

I swallowed.

"Come here, scaredy-cat," she said, pulling more stuff from her drawer. "I had a cannula in my hand from chemo, which I would have simply taken it with. All you would have needed to do was inject it into my cannula. But it fell off you see ..."

"Of course it did," I muttered.

"So I'll need you to ..."

I looked at what she was holding closely now. It was a syringe.

"I'll need you to fix this new one for me."

I felt blank and empty.

"I can't break my skin myself," she continued. "I'm scared of the needles."

I looked at her face now, my disbelief plainly etched in it. She smiled a little, what she must have imagined was an encouraging smile.

"You know I'm not a doctor, or even a nurse," I said. "But I'm supposed to get this straight, pierce your skin, fix a cannula—which I've never done before—and correctly administer this drug—which if I don't, you might die?"

She didn't nod; she just made the encouraging face. I groan and she proceeded to convince me that it wouldn't be that difficult.

It was difficult as hell. Her veins had collapsed from many needles and her general condition. She had what she called "vein trauma," which made it more difficult. And I just couldn't believe how difficult it was slipping a needle into a human vein, especially for someone with no professional training. Her skin was soft under my touch, and she tried to hide the tremble then the tears as I missed the vein over and over and over again. Then before I knew it, I flung the needle away.

"This is supposed to be a normal visit. You just called me to come hang as a friend. Why didn't you warn me? Why didn't you tell me? How am I supposed to do this—which I haven't done before and it means so much, maybe even your life? How can you put this on me?"

I realized I was yelling.

She was quiet. I already knew the answers to my questions. She wanted to make her own choices, not stay home with her stifling family to get proper care and miss out on life and all that. Especially if she was already on borrowed time.

I swallowed the rest of what I was going to say, about this being irresponsible and unsafe. She handed me another needle nonchalantly.

I realize she must be used to these kinds of outbursts. I was one of those worrying people that didn't understand the situation.

So I took a fresh syringe and tried again, and again, and again. This time, I didn't snap; I just tried. But if she took my yelling stoically, she didn't take my failure the same way. She had already been too weak—and time was running out. She was crying. And then I was crying, too. She hugged me and rubbed the back of my head, saying she was sorry.

I snapped out of it. She shouldn't be the strong one, comforting me. I was not the one at risk of dying.

I pulled back and looked at her.

It was an hour before the maximum time limit for when she should take the drug, and she was starting to show signs of damage. Her eyes were dripping an odd, slimy liquid, and she was drooling too. She looked a little distant, not quite herself. Then the realization came to me and I said aloud, "I can't do this. I'm going to get help."

She nodded weakly, as if absentminded and not present. I looked at the time. One hour more, going by the time she said she was supposed to take it. While the chemo might not take her this time, the Neulasta would give her the chance to fight another day.

I was conflicted when I left. Should she lock the door? What if she was in no condition to open it when I got back? Should she leave it open? What if someone came in to do something to her while I was away? Should I lock it and take the key? What if she needed help while I was gone and couldn't get out?

The area where we were in was just rife with criminal opportunists.

I slipped on my O₂ mask and left. One hour to go. I stumbled through the streets, asking directions to a chemist, any chemist. It was dark, past 10 p.m., and I got suspicious looks as I strolled along. I stumbled from closed chemist to another closed chemist, frantic, semi-insane with the urgency of the help I needed. Then someone told me about a lady—not a chemist but a nurse. She sold drugs at home.

I rushed to the location I was given and found the nurse. She was in her backyard smoking weed. She said she'd had a long day and just wanted to chill, maybe noting the desperation in my bearing. She offered me a blunt. I looked at her incredulously and almost started to cry. But there was no time for that …

I walked over to her and said as emphatically as I could: "PLEASE HELP ME."

She simply grunted, wearily dragging herself out of her fold-up chair. She followed me to the hotel. On the way, I explained in more details: we only needed her to administer the injection. She was high and sang all the way. But her hand was rock steady.

She asked no questions; apparently, she was used to strange, odd-hour jobs. I was glad of that. I was in a random hotel with a very sick, near comatose girl and a strange, high nurse injecting something I didn't understand into her at my behest. I briefly wondered what would happen if Ovoke were to die. What kind of narrative would come out of this, and what kind of explanation would I give?

Then I violently shoved the thought from my mind. Ovoke ISN'T DYING.

The nurse finished her job. I gave her a bunch of O$_2$ credits—all the cards I could lay my hands on. She thanked me, lingering to look back at me and Ovoke. She opened her mouth as if to say something, then decided against it and left.

I watched Ovoke for the next thirty minutes, all but paranoid the injection wouldn't work. The color came back to her. Her eyes had stopped dripping and she was not drooling anymore. I crawled into the bed and fell into a dead, dreamless sleep.

When I awoke in the morning, someone was holding me gently, cradling my head to their chest. I extricated myself and she woke.

I got up, frowning at her, trying to brush off the intimacy—to not show her how much I care. Platonically, anyway.

She smiled.

I pointed at the bed. "We're not like that. Also, did you get my consent before cuddling me?"

"Morning, grumpy."

I shook my head.

"Oh, and your breathing is really bad," she said sympathetically. "You slept so badly, I was worried all night."

"Worry about yourself, punk." I said in mock annoyance.

She smiled and got up, pulling a toothbrush from her bag. "You should call a cab now while we get ready for class. You know they usually take forever to get here."

"Why are we going to class again? After last night?" I asked. And then I answered the question myself. "Live before you die, right?"

She beamed at me. Grumbling, I pulled out my phone to call a cab.

The moment I dreaded happening occurred a week after her second trip home for chemo sessions. I had been restive, expecting her call, thinking it was about the time she should return. I knew something was wrong. I could sense it. And I was right, I realized in dread when the call came. My breath was loud in my ears. The filter did what it was meant to, and the air that reached me was clean, but it couldn't stop my labored breathing. My heart was thumping so hard.

My friend, Ovoke, was dying.

Ovoke's brother, Efeturi, had been the one to call; she was asking to see me.

I greeted him at the University of Lagos Teaching Hospital (LUTH) then rushed to where she lay on a stretcher outside the building. She'd always been so full of life but now she looked smaller, diminished.

How she had shrunk in such a short while, I couldn't understand. I held her bony hand in mine, rubbing it on my cheek, desperate to feel something of her as I'd known her before. Her fingers were warm, and I felt a faint throbbing as she breathed laboriously from a cylinder by the side of the bed. Over the edges of the mask, her panicked eyelids fluttered, and I couldn't tell if she knew I was there.

Her dad sat fanning her, and, while I held her and told her it would be all right, I met his stricken eyes.

She was outside, he said, because a year of cancer treatment, of chemo, had exhausted their money. They couldn't afford a ward. A bed would come at the daily cost of O₂200. Getting her into the ICU and hooked up on proper machines would be even more.

So here we were. The chemotherapy treatment had been meant to kill her cancer but it was killing her instead. Now those precious, delicate lungs had stopped coping.

"So what now?" I asked.

He couldn't meet my eyes. "If we could raise the money for the ICU and a proper bed, she would be allowed time to heal her lungs. Then the cancer treatment could proceed. If not …"

I stepped out to talk to Efeturi, leaving her parents and other brother with her.

When we came back, Ovoke was near hysterical from breathlessness and desperately thirsty. With the breathing mask briefly removed, we dribbled water into her mouth, letting her lay back. Everyone could see that it was taking all her energy just to suck what little air was given her by the mask, which we replaced after every paltry drink.

Too tired to talk, she communicated only with her eyes, and I gave her my best reassuring smile as I squeezed that fragile, tiny, bony hand.

"You'll be all right. Your dad says that you're considering surgery now."

She nodded.

I sighed, trying not to let my surprise and heartache at that news show in my eyes.

Back in school, before her chemo, we'd had a discussion about her treatment method. Chemo had burnt her out and she had lost her voice, her hair, her weight, energy, and vitality. And now she had also lost her air, the most precious commodity she, and any of us, had.

But back then, there had been an alternative: surgery. I had suggested she have the ovaries removed, removing the cancer with them. But she had refused because that would also mean losing her chance at future children.

"And what kind of life would that be?" she had asked. She was convinced that she'd be left a broken woman—a woman who wasn't a woman.

I had tried to tell her that her ability to give birth was not what made her a woman or gave her value. But even as I said it, I knew how false it would ring in her ears, as it might in mine, if I had been subjected to the other side of our patriarchal society.

She thought she would be nothing in a patriarchal society that valued men for their ability to provide and women for reproduction. I had never told her that even in such a society, she was everything to me. How could I, when she needed me to tease her, to treat her the same as I always had? When she demanded nothing could change, and I had to pretend I still cared for nothing.

"A freak," she'd insisted, "wanted by no one."

And so she had given up her air for future, unborn children. She'd risked it all. And only now could she see that her ovaries were not her, not worth her life. She was ready to let them go, if it wasn't too late.

Her labored breathing kept me fully focused on our painful reality. I held her hands as air flowed raggedly through her damaged lungs, while she cried in between gasps, calling for her mom, and then pushing the distraught woman away when she came.

Ovoke's dad, gone for a good while during the afternoon, eventually came back. He had gotten the funds, probably by selling something, if they still had anything to sell. Whatever it had been, I could tell from his hushed conversation with his wife, and the stricken and defeated look on her face, that it wasn't good.

But it must have been enough. They would move Ovoke to the ICU. Her lungs would get the chance to stabilize while we looked for the funds to remove the offending cancer.

The surgery was a fortune, one beyond any resource the family could tap. Without it, she would die. At that moment I knew what I had to do.

I told her she would be all right. I held her hand, stroking it again lightly over my cheek. I told her I had to go get something and would be back. She gestured weakly that I should come closer. I leaned over her until I could feel each labored, precious breath against my skin.

"I love you," she whispered in my ear.

I screwed my eyes tightly closed until the flood of tears no longer threatened. Then I smiled as bravely as I could and kissed her on the forehead. I left without telling her I loved her. There would be time later when the fire was back in her eyes and light gleamed from her smile. I would tell her I loved her then because she would know then that my love was not pity, or hopelessness, or humor.

I would tell her. But now, I had to focus on what I had to do.

Life for Life. #SaveVoke

The hashtag had spread throughout the interwebs, leading up to the fight, prompting an increased online viewership for the arena, their corrupt owners resharing the tweet, watching their bank account balance rise with glee.

Jaiyesimi was incredulous, disbelieving; his Eiye friend, our guide in this terrible place, was surprised but impressed.

And my opponent looked eager. His eyes glittered; all he saw in my place was a bag of O_2 units. What I saw was life. A chance at life for the friend I loved, and I was willing to pay the ultimate price: to kill or to die.

My love and desire didn't automatically hand me the fight. I had done a little karate, up to green belt, so I took the stance and threw a flurry of punches. He took the blows, grabbing my hands and then delivering a headbutt that broke my nose and drew first blood, sending me sprawling to the floor.

There was no skill to it, no sparring strategy or technique, only experience and power.

He let me get up, perhaps disappointed by how little excitement such a victory would bring our audience. A mistake, as our next encounter had me rubbing the blood in his eyes and knocking him almost senseless.

Now we had both done damage.

I tried to take advantage of his confusion at his newfound blindness, but then it was me in a choke hold that would have ended things then and there, if I hadn't discovered a last-minute taste for human flesh. I sank my teeth into his arm, and he let me go with a brutal scream. A reverb-heavy roar from the remote spectators filled the air around us, and the announcer's words bounced off the plexiglass walls, feverish with renewed excitement.

This would not be an orderly fight; it was a meaningless grapple for survival, for air—and drowning men didn't struggle prettily.

But I wasn't a fighter like these street thugs were, like he was. They had the crucial advantage of killing before and were ready to kill again. I had paid for protection. I had always taken the easy way out. Cheated, lied, stole. I'd never cared about anything except survival. And here I was, willing to die for something.

Someone.

I had no experience with the instinct to kill, and yet clearly this man had lived that way his entire life.

He pummelled me thoroughly, always darting back after each blow, wary of the bite of my teeth and determined to finish me without getting into close-quarters combat.

It was my reason for being here that kept me from giving up, from dying. I saw then his confusion at not having an easy kill, confusion that turned this thug's eyes into desperate rage. He caught me again in a clumsy choke hold. He was tired, but he was also eager to finish the job, to earn his fortune, to earn air—my air, my life, and Ovoke's right to life as well.

Outside the cage, I could see the Eiye cultist nod at me. I was brave, but I was done. My friend Jaiyesimi turned away. He wasn't ready to see me go.

Covered as I was in blood and sweat and tears, it was easy to slip out of my opponent's grasp. Clearly, he expected me to run then, to retreat in a futile attempt to escape with my life. Instead, I went for him. His stunned response at my small rebellion was only a small advantage. With me a spent and beaten animal, there was little I could do once I had him in my grasp.

But even a wounded wolf is a dangerous thing. I still had my teeth, and his neck was bare inches away, so I went for his throat, biting through his skin into salty, coppery flesh.

He choked and slammed his fists into me repeatedly, but I held on tight, for life, for air. His blood filled my mouth and though I wanted to retch, I tightened my jaw with grim determination and felt skin and tendon cords between my teeth and lifeblood pump against my tongue.

With one final thump, he lifted me off the ground. Ovoke, I thought. I tried …

He slammed me back down.

The lights went out.

I woke days later, surprised to be alive.

Jaiyesimi had stayed by my side and recounted to me what had happened. My opponent had bled to death after he knocked me out

… and I had won. The fortune in O_2 units was already sitting in my account.

I was in some kind of recovery unit for the victors, but there was no time to celebrate my survival. I stumbled out of the bed, found my clothes, and rushed back to the student hospital.

I was met with numb looks and reddened eyes. Ovoke's brothers' faces were filled with restrained pain. Her mother sat weeping, and her dad's defeat was evident in his hunched posture. He straightened when he saw me, letting go of his wife's hand and coming to hold me, to gently break the news.

In my absence, Ovoke had passed. Her oxygen-starved organs had finally given in. The substandard breathing apparatus that was all her family could afford couldn't sustain her through the three cardiac arrests she'd suffered in the night.

She was gone, her delicate, wild spirit, flown, borne away by the wayward winds we dealt so recklessly with. Winds which had paid us in disgruntled O_2 coin, exacted in fulfilment of poetic justice, its pound of flesh.

I had fought and killed so she could breathe. Had taken a life so savagely, so pointlessly—all for her. I had the fortune in O_2 units and now had access to the purest of air. But there were no longer lungs for me to put it in.

I crumbled to the floor and wept.

I walked into one of the admin offices at the Academy of Laws. The man I handed my form to was old, graying, and a bit stooped—old enough to have retired. Probably one of those who falsified their age so they could work longer.

Why anyone wanted more time in this place, I couldn't fathom. His shrewd eyes regarded my narrowed ones. His kindly smile answered the question I hadn't voiced: survival. That was why he stayed. Of course, he worked to keep breathing, for air, for a continued meagre flow of O_2 units for him and for his loved ones.

Survival was overrated. I knew that now. You would live long enough to see your loved ones die.

"Son." His voice stopped me as I went to leave. "Why fill this? Why defer?" He asked, waving the paper at me.

Of course, I thought. The nosy old man wants to make sure I am utilizing my life well, not wasting my "potential."

I could try to explain the futility of it all, the fact that they were trapped here living a life that wasn't worth the O_2 units it took to buy the oxygen to sustain it, but he wouldn't understand. It would shock him, my directness and honesty, my lack of respect, and brazenness.

"This isn't the place for me anymore," I told him.

His brows furrowed. "Why?"

It wouldn't be worth the O_2 units it would take to explain. I had a fortune in oxygen, true, but still, every breath was precious. Instead, I raised my hand toward him, my voice raspy, Darth Vader–like, as if I had smoked a lifetime's worth of cigarettes.

"This world needs a wake-up call that might only be found in an arena of our own making."

I stepped out. The commotion was just starting.

I could hear the siren of the Reddington ambulance driving in as I stepped outside the school and into the world. After Dr. Umez didn't show up for his lecture, and they found his door locked, his calls not being answered, they would have broken in to find him slumped and unmoving, his oxygen air-filtration system in the office mysteriously disabled.

I drew in a loud, raspy breath through my own portable air system. Air that I had earned—air that was now a means to an end.

Most of us had been hiding behind these masks, telling ourselves it was because they let us breathe. It was time for the world to see the true face of things. I placed the call to Efeturi, my second in command, and, in the same raspy quality, breathed out my orders to my men.

"This world, our O_2 arena, is now open."

for the Great and Immortal

by Daniel Burnbridge

Saduk says he was here before the beginning. Before time. He says he saw the beginning when it began. And it's not the first time, either. He'd done it before. He'd lived through many great breaths.

I laugh at him. I say he's the greatest ever freeloader, just along for the ride. He humors me by laughing too.

Saduk says when an inhalation ends, when matter and energy become naught, when time and space cease to exist, when everything is nothing and is everywhere and nowhere, it sort of ignites, begins anew, starts off another great exhalation.

But I don't believe this. It doesn't fit the rules. I know the rules. I'm a product of the rules. I've created my own things by following them.

So I ask Saduk to show me how something can come from nothing. But he says it's beyond his power. He says he knows because he'd seen it.

So I let it be. If it's true, I'll see for myself, one day.

Saduk says he's only here to witness. That he's some sort of residue left after everything had found its purpose. He says he's not part of the cosmos. It must be the same, I suppose, for my brother and I, since we come from Saduk.

"Maybe it's your purpose to witness?" I suggest.

But Saduk says no. He says that's just the only thing left to do. It doesn't mean it's what he's *meant* to do.

"Are there other great breaths, Saduk?" I ask. "Other creators? Other witnesses? Or are we alone?"

"There are others," he says. "There are many," he says. "But there's no way to cross from the one to the other."

"And that's why you made Lim and I," I say. "You made us because you were lonely."

"Yes," says Saduk. "And to have something to rule," he says.

"Look!" says Saduk. "It's light. Now you can see yourself," he says.

I'm just a baby. I've never seen light. The cosmos was too young for that. It seems to change everything. It intrigues me. It sets other rules in motion. New rules. I see them span everything. When I look at it closely, the universe seems smaller, more constrained. Somehow more magnificent.

Lim doesn't like it.

He sees me in the light, and squirms and runs away.

I want Lim to join me in the light. I want to play. I'm used to us being together.

He says no. He doesn't want to play in the light. It's like he's angry at me. I see him kick a baby star, shatter it. I tell him he's just scared because it's new, and once he gets used to it, he'll like it. I tell him it makes things even better, shows them in a different way. "Like your beautiful darkness," I say. "It seems to me even more beautiful next to the light," I say.

He tells me I'm preachy. Says I'm not that much older than him. Says I shouldn't speak to him like he's a baby. Then he turns and goes to where the light has not yet reached, and I give up and join him there, in the dark, so we can play.

For a while, we get along fine.

Saduk doesn't approve of us playing so far out. He says the darkness holds danger. But of course we don't listen. We can't die. We know that. Only Saduk can destroy us. And we know he won't. We know he loves us.

We may get lost. But that's an adventure. Not something to fear.

I know Saduk can stop us. That we cannot resist his will. That we're not free to do as we please.

But he lets us be. And I'm happy for that.

One day, in the darkness, Lim turns to me and says we're not alike. "I think we're made of opposing parts of Saduk," Lim says. He's so serious when he says it, weighed down by a strange melancholy, and there's something rancorous and surreptitious in his gaze.

But that's just nonsense, and I say so. "We can be different without being opposing," I say. "I cannot imagine existence without you, and I know Saduk feels the same," I say. "We give each other meaning. We're both parts of the same picture," I say.

But he doesn't listen. The dark weight stays with him.

"I don't like you," says beautiful Lim. "I think Saduk loves you more. I think you're the better part of it. That's why it made you first. I'm what was left over," says Lim.

"You've changed since the light," I say, worried. "Saduk made you because it was incomplete without you. You know that. We're paired. One day the light will disappear. It won't last forever. Everything is fleeting. And then I'll be vexed by its absence, and you'll be happy again."

But beautiful Lim leaves, his anger trailing darkly, his great presence ramming furiously against time and space, making everything shudder.

I feel in that instant like I don't know him at all. That he's no more than a silly boy throwing a tantrum.

I suppose he'll outgrow that.

Lim and I haven't played in a long time. Saduk is distant, aloof.

I keep myself busy with my worlds, my secret experiments. It's not going well. I'm distracted, impatient. I botch it each time, have to start over again.

Saduk worries. He blames himself. He thinks he did something wrong when he made us. "The light came early this time," he says. The rules are always a bit different, between breaths. Saduk thinks the darkness in beautiful Lim may not have had enough time to settle before it was disturbed. He thinks he should have anticipated that.

So I'm happy when Lim asks me to play with him again. I figure he might be getting better. Maybe he likes me again.

We go out to a cosmic void. Where it's dark, of course. He's not over that yet. When he calls out to me over the distance, he seems warm and kind. Like he used to. Like the brother I know.

We run and play between vortices. Lim seems happy. It's been a long time since he's seemed happy. It's as though something has resolved for him. Like he's found some sort of clarity. And that makes me happy, too.

He shows me a wormhole. He's always liked wormholes. Saduk would not have approved. One can never tell where or when they go, Saduk had told us many times. And sometimes it's a one-way trip, especially if you're big and your gravitational wake collapses it as you fall through.

But it's glorious. And we love playing in its gravity well, spinning round and round, pitting our strength against it, laughing, flailing among the gasses, kicking up quite a mess.

"Where do you think it goes?" I ask, because we always do this fantasy game, where we think of places where the rules are inverted, or different, or where there are no rules at all.

Lim looks at me darkly. For a second I'm lost, because, for all his familiarity, I do not recognize him.

I'm stronger than him, but he catches me off guard. I try to fight back, but it's too late. The wormhole joins forces with his thrust, and I'm drawn in and in and away.

And then I'm sort of drowning in blackness and distorted reality. I flail like a fool. Like I can pull myself out like that.

But it's too late.

I look at Lim through the narrowing window.

He smiles. He seems at peace.

I turn to go back, but the bridge is bust. Just like Saduk had said.

A one-way ticket.

And I know, because of all the light here, that I am a great deal of time ahead of them.

Which is a much bigger problem than the vast spaces between us.

I find myself in a cloud of interstellar gas and dust.

It's inert. There's nothing to it. It's a shapeless, dull jumble.

But it's pleasant. Sort of ductile and homey and unchallenging. There's nothing here threatening to explode or to swallow me whole. And I like what the cloud does to light. How it broadens and softens the colors. It reminds me of the early days. When there wasn't much around. Nothing big, nothing solid. When the cosmos was made of soft gaseous things.

I linger here. Right where I've been spat out. At a loss. No idea what to do. I tarry for a long time, thinking. I put out tendrils into the fabric of the universe, probing, searching.

For my world. For my loved ones.

I detect nothing. Just dead black dark and quiet. Not even a shadow or a breath of the ones I seek.

Wherever they are, they're far, far away.

And I'm lost. Good and proper.

It's not that I cannot leap time. Of course I can. But where to in an infinity of options? That kind of energy does not come cheaply. I can bleed the universe leaping time from point to point, suffocating worlds in my selfish wake.

But I won't do that. Not unless I know what's on the other side. Not unless I know it'll be worth it.

For a while, I let myself drift into thoughtlessness. Loosen my consciousness. It's easy enough. Let time take its time. Maybe they'll find me. In the meantime, my liminal mind watches a distant nebula coalesce, watches it birth a star, watches till it blows grandly in a white-hot supernova.

Always a good show. Helps to pass the time.

But then the interminable starts to bore me, and I pull myself back into my whole and back into the present, and look at the cloud that's my new home, and wonder what I could make of it, since I have the time, and it's so palpably uninteresting.

I like making things. Making things changes me—makes and unmakes little pieces of myself.

I quicken the cloud. Gently. A suggestion, not a command. Not so as to tell it what I think it should be, but just enough to see where it wants to go, what it wants to make of itself, given a little stir to get it going.

It vortices toward its center. Nothing surprising about that. A bit typical, in fact. I've seen this before. I consider stopping the whole thing, return it to the state I've found it in, try something different.

But I don't. It would be like killing something. Something un-formed, unfulfilled.

I don't like that thought.

And so I wait, and watch it twirl and swirl and lighten.

Making the invariable, predictable star.

And a rather average one, at that.

It sparkles awake, bright white, pushes at the protoplanetary mass around it. I hold my face to it to feel its heat. Then I get out of the way to let the planets form, while I try to guess how each will turn out, thinking I should choose one, to make a home, for while I wait.

I don't like the big gassy ones, I decide. I want to see the stars from the surface at night, without having to leap. In fact, I want to stop leaping for a while. I want to rest. And wait. Sleep, maybe, if I find nothing better to do. I want to be a terrestrial thing. Sunk into stone. Solid and slow-moving.

And so I consider the small ones near the sun, even though they all seem red-black and rocky, molten warm, not very pleasant at all.

But wait.

Three of them blink blue. And that's unusual. First just a sparkle, a glint. But, surely, blue.

And blue says water, and water is good. I've made some rudi-mentary things with water before. Self-creating, regenerating little things, unpredictable and full of surprises.

And that was very interesting. Interesting enough, maybe, to pass the time.

I could do that again. Maybe I could do it better this time.

I choose the middle blue one, thinking the first may be too hot, the third too cold. I hope I'm right.

These little subtleties can make all the difference.

I set foot on the world. I know I won't leave any time soon, and so shape myself so I may inhabit, so I'm something that belongs, so my form and nature needn't contest with it.

I take my time, have a nice slow look around. I walk the world's surface, all of it, solid and soft, even as it changes. I breathe the acrid air, feel the hot-hot crust, look at the dead ashen sky.

It's a dead place. Like the rest of the cosmos.

The way Saduk likes it.

It's fine this way, I suppose. But I think it can be better. I think it can be more.

I think there's something missing.

I allow myself to sink all the way in, past the mantle, all the way to the molten core. And then I stretch out my tendrils, so I can feel the whole planet in its entirety, so I can be, for a while, one with it.

And it's good and beautiful, and has its own kind of soul. I like it. It's a bit rough around the edges, for sure, but the important bits are all here. Not too much or too little of anything. No deal-breakers.

I take my time to drink it in. To try and make sure I get it right this time.

It's easy to make mistakes. I've learned this from my other worlds. Worlds now defunct. All for being eager and young and hungry to have something unique of my own.

Neither Saduk nor beautiful Lim knows of these places. They would have considered my work inelegant, menial in relation to what we're capable of.

It's my very own thing. And so I've had to figure it out all on my own. But that was part of the pleasure, too. To be able to do something they couldn't, to understand something they didn't.

But the extinctions had saddened me. I'd given it all up. It's pretty dismal when everything dies and you have to watch.

I'm ready.

It's fear that holds me back, that makes me hesitate.

I take the constituent parts. I put it together. Carefully. Just so.

I put it in the water where its warm and alive and churning, and tell it to *become*.

And then I wait.

Don't meddle, I tell myself. *Remember what happened the other times. When you tried to force it. When you tried to hurry it along. And spoiled it.*

Leave it. Let it be. You can start it, but you cannot finish it. That's the whole point. To let it become. To let it be free. To let it choose.

Leave it. It doesn't need you as badly as you think.

It starts out slowly. But that's expected. Much of it I'd seen before on my other worlds. It follows a familiar pattern, until, ultimately, it becomes too complicated to predict. Even for me.

But there's still some way to go before it gets anywhere near that kind of intricacy.

Once bacteria start converting light into chemical energy, I know I'm on the right track, that I've built a good foundation for what's to follow.

Give it a billion years or so, I figure. I need oxygen. Lots of it. To drive the bodies of bigger, more elaborate things.

Carbon and water I have aplenty.

So I slumber a while, to pass the time, and as oxygen proliferates, it wakes me to a deep blue frozen cold, and a very great quiet dying: a planetary stench of things that had evolved to live without oxygen, now victims of the new.

This is good. These dyings, I know, make space for better things. It's necessary.

This, too, is like breathing, I know. The old feeding the new. Small things progressing into big ones. And sometimes from the ashes arise others with eyes that are brighter, maybe even minds that perceive.

If you're lucky.

It'd happened to me once, but was short-lived. I nearly missed it. The interval between their self-awareness and self-destruction was a fraction of a blink of an eye.

377

This, too, is like breathing, I know. Tectonic plates split, drift apart, meet up again, crush things up, flatten them out. And in between the cracks, from the planet's hot belly, fire bursts forth, scorches, consumes, leaves behind rich black soils.

That feed new things. Things that flourish.

Then die.

All of it a ceaseless rhythm beating between old and new, darkness and light, ignorance and consciousness.

Like the great-great breath that begets and destroys the cosmos, over and over again.

Then, finally, it's ready.

It's good, and I'm pleased. Maybe this time it'll work. Maybe I can make a thing that feels and thinks, stays alive longer than a blink. Something in my very own image, fundamentally indeterminate. Something that can surprise me, that can make me wonder. That can move past and beyond my power.

Something to love.

I shape them from the soil because I love the soil. The feel of it in my fingers. The smell.

I wake them from my own breath, so they'll always be part of me.

And then I watch them smile at day's blue sky and night's star-jeweled black, at yellow savannas, brimming seas, great gray mountains, forests and fjords, desert sands, the whole shebang.

They spread, remake themselves over and over, as though to poke a finger at me, show me where I'd done a bad job. They manipulate the world in a million ways no other creature here would conceive of.

And they always *want*. More and more. They keep on wanting until the world and a lifetime on it is no longer enough.

They yearn to transcend. They create a great many things to worship.

I can wipe them out in an instant, with half a thought, but they carry themselves proudly, like they can defy all the great forces of the universe.

I like that about them.

I am pleased with them. Proud of what I've achieved. Consciousness. The rarest of things. Meant only for the great and immortal. My gift to them. And that out of a few bits and pieces of organic matter.

It's beyond anything I'd imagined. Beyond what I'd hoped for.

Sometimes I think they sense me. I think they're looking for me. I think they know I'm watching. And maybe, it seems to me, that explains why they always yearn.

It's my fault. For not showing myself. But I've set them in motion to become their own, apart from me. I've never wanted to make them beyond the form and the essences I'd given them. That was just to kick them off, to get them going.

I do not want their prayers. I will not answer them.

I will not bind them to my will, like Saduk had bound me to his.

If they could ascend to my plane, I think they would. One day, I think, they will. I'm not sure what they'll tell me. I think they'll be angry. I think they'll ask me why I didn't make things better, after I've seen where I've gone wrong, once I saw the bad things.

But, no, I only want to watch. It's always been the plan.

And they don't need me to fix the bad things. It's in their own power.

Beautiful Lim finds me first. He's never been a subtle one. He strikes the planet with such force it kills quite a lot of things.

He says he's sorry, but I think he did it on purpose.

I want to be angry, to chide him, but he's my brother. Who I haven't seen in such a long time. Who I love. I'm so happy to see him, I let go of my anger, and embrace him.

The planet heals quickly, I know. Scabs over in no time. And the living is extraordinarily resilient.

He's tight-lipped, cagey. I don't like that. It makes me nervous. I can see he's changed. He skirts the light, as though it burns. He's not gotten used to it at all. His aversion has grown.

His dark heart has deepened. Now he can hide the larger part of him there, just eyes peeking out. He refuses to tell me where Saduk is, how to find him. He won't say how he's found me, even though I cannot understand it. To find me in space would have been formidable indeed. To find me in time as well boggles the mind.

Saduk must have helped.

But Lim just laughs. He laughs all the time. I don't know what he's laughing at.

He laughs at the ones I love. My creation. "Dismal little things," he says, "beginning and ending in blinks of time, living their lives on specks of reality, little clods made of mud and water. They understand nothing," he says. "You've doomed them to ignorance," he says. "You shouldn't hide yourself. You should master them. You should show them who you are, then watch them shudder with fear."

He's always teased me. But it's different now.

Because deep-deep down there's something hurt and broken and monstrous inside. Something that hisses and sneers. The rest is for show. A façade.

And it frightens me. Because I cannot see Saduk allowing something so powerful and unhinged free passage of the cosmos.

Lim threatens to crush them, sees something in my face, snickers nervously.

He knows I'm gentle. It's my nature. He knows my power too. He's seen it before.

He backs away into a shadowy sneer. A hateful submission. Not a good look.

"You really care." He smirks. "You've been on your own too long. Your little games, your experiments, have addled your mind," he says.

And still he doesn't tell me how to find Saduk. Even though my longing is deep and real. I plead with him. Stop short of begging. I consider hurting him. But decide against it.

He's my brother.

I think he takes pleasure from my pain. The thought makes my skin crawl.

He hates me. I don't know why.

He does the unforgivable.

He takes them.

Even though he hasn't made them. Even though he doesn't care for them. Even though he doesn't know what's good for them, hasn't watched them grow from random little nothings.

He shows himself to them, in all his blinding beautiful irresistible glory. He seduces them with vanity and greed, knowing they would embrace him, knowing they'd been looking for something greater than themselves.

And he did it for no other reason but to hurt me.

And it does. Hurt.

Because I've made them. And I love them. My children.

I wonder whether he knows that I thought of hurting him. The pain I could inflict would have blown a most wonderful chasm in the fabric of space and time.

How I savored the thought! To flex my muscle. All of it.

But, most of all, it hurts that they embraced him. That they did not know the difference between the mother who had made them, who had left them to become what they are, and the intruder from afar, the manipulator, the broken one.

They did not know that they were free. They took up their chains, and were happy for the chance to do so.

And then beautiful Lim lost interest, of course. Once he'd broken it.

My perfect thing.

When Saduk comes, he's not pleased with my work.

Life, I call it, and watch Saduk mull the word over with distaste. "It's something I've made, and that I've come to love," I explain. "And those are *humans*"—I point—"and I know you don't like it, but they've earned their consciousness. It did not come easy for them. It took a long time and a lot of death and suffering. But they do it justice," I say. "You'll see if you take the time. They'll surprise you. They, too, can create beautiful things."

"Get rid of it," says Saduk. "It's unbecoming. It's unnatural. It's not what matter was meant for. It's wrong to allow something as rare as consciousness to subsist in such minusculae," he says. "Such great things are meant for us. For the ones who witness the great breaths."

Lim snickers. Loves that I'm in trouble. Loves to see something he knows I treasure being taken from me.

And I know Saduk won't budge.

I ask for time to say goodbye, and, even though he doesn't like it, doesn't approve of the sentiment, he still loves me, I suppose, because he agrees.

If he'd forced his will against me, I would not have been able to resist.

I love him for not doing it. I resent that he could.

And then Saduk and Lim wink away, leave me.

I've never disobeyed Saduk. It's never crossed my mind.

I know he wants me to obliterate the whole thing. To throw it into a sun or something.

But I don't.

While I extricate myself from the world, it turns dark, and everything hushes. Some of them know what I'm doing. They sense it. They know I'm abandoning them. I tear a hole in space and time, and tuck them away, out of sight, where no one can see.

And then I leave them there. All alone. But alive. With a future ahead.

If Saduk took the time to poke around, he would find them, for sure. But I don't think he will. I don't think he really cares. A star system lasts a short time only. Whatever I do, they'll die soon enough.

What Saduk wants is for me to rejoin him and beautiful Lim. And I have no choice. I'm not free. I belong to Saduk.

I hope they make it. I don't think I'll see them again. I hope for them to become whatever they choose for themselves.

I hope for them to be free.

It's why I made them.

The Space-Time Painter

by Hai Ya

translated by Roy Gilman

Introduction

A flash of pale-blue lightning tore suddenly through the inky darkness of the night sky. The magnificent palace slept like a great beast in the pouring rain, lying quietly between the heavens and the earth.

Lao Li rubbed at his aching arm. The rainy days brought on the old pains of his rheumatism. The plan for the palace exhibition had been finalized since the beginning of the year, and among the exhibits would be several national treasures that had rarely been seen since the founding of the People's Republic of China. But just as work was due to begin, the unexpected heavy rains had brought humidity to the air, adding another variable to the inherently difficult work of cultural relic protection. Suppose the exhibition was postponed or even canceled due to the weather. How could they explain to those who had anxiously awaited and, now arriving with high expectations, had to be turned away disappointed?

Despite his concerns, Lao Li remained dutiful in his work. He patrolled the empty exhibition hall, fastidiously examining every installation and power source. He had faith that the expert staff at the institution would carefully deliberate on the arrangements in order to protect the national treasures. And if his own work contributed in some small way to the cause of cultural preservation, he could not tolerate the slightest carelessness. He took pride in his work as one of the old hands at the Palace Museum.

And so, when the outline of the shadow gradually emerged, Lao Li did not panic. Initially, it was no more than a dark spot on one of the pillars in the exhibition hall, and Lao Li assumed there was something wrong with the spotlight at the base of the column. But the spotlight was functioning normally, even as the dark spots wriggled and squirmed like living creatures, then formed a pattern! The dark figure slowly raised itself up, its joints clicking and clacking, and the shadow took the form of a living human skeleton.

"Who are you?" Lao Li cried out instinctively, wanting to drive away the mysterious figure. Yet there was no one in the exhibition hall, no sound but for his own heavy breathing. Frowning, Lao Li trained his flashlight on the dark corners of the exhibition hall unilluminated by the spotlights, all the while keeping one eye on the skeleton's shadow on the pillar. He had worked at the palace for over a decade and walked through this exhibition hall countless times every day. Shouldn't it be obvious if someone was hiding? He gave up fooling himself and walked back to face the black shadow, reaching out his hand to touch the pillar. The shadow changed form at his touch, then faded gradually until it disappeared.

He had heard stories from the older watchmen of strange images appearing in particular palaces within the Forbidden City, usually during thunderstorms. Experts speculated that the phenomenon was caused by the electrical stimulation of iron oxide in the palace walls, producing an effect akin to a video recording, replaying scenes from the past under the right conditions. Was this mysterious and unpredictable shadow caused by the same phenomenon?

Lao Li rubbed his eyes, wondering whether to report his encounter. Gradually, his taut nerves relaxed, and he turned to leave the exhibition hall when something made him look back. The skeleton reappeared on the wall behind him, clearer now than before. His flashlight dropped to the floor with a thud. Without picking it up, Lao Li stumbled out of the exhibition hall, not looking back.

I

Returning to the police department after his honeymoon, Zhou Ning immediately took over the peculiar case. No case was trivial so far as the Forbidden City was concerned, where the merest rustle of leaves was cause for concern. On the other hand, nothing was damaged, no one was hurt, and even the report's veracity was in question. The only witness to the incident was an elderly caretaker on the cusp of retirement. Although his colleagues were unanimous in their assessment of the old man as an honest and reliable employee, Zhou Ning was still inclined to think he had made a mistake. Still, to be sure, he decided to visit the scene and find out.

Zhou Ning arranged to visit on a Monday when the Forbidden City was closed to the public. After coordinating things with the palace security staff, he stepped into the world's largest and best-preserved palace complex just as the sun was setting. Since there were no tourists on closing days, he anticipated little disturbance at the scene. Moreover, the night staff were just beginning their shifts, allowing for a more relaxed and familiar environment to recreate the scene from that night as accurately as possible.

Zhou Ning hadn't waited long before one of the security staff approached him with an older man following behind. The older man was in his early fifties, thin but not tall, and though his hair was already graying, he carried himself upright. His eyes were sharp and alert, and he looked very spirited.

"Hello, Officer Zhou," said the security officer. "This is Lao Li from our security department. He is a veteran employee who transferred to our institute from the army. Lao Li, this is Officer Zhou. He'll be handling the incident from the other night. Please cooperate with him."

The security guard departed after making the introductions. Zhou Ning recalled the bureau's attitude regarding this matter. Perhaps the staff at the palace museum were similarly skeptical.

With the departure of his familiar colleague, Lao Li looked a little embarrassed. He kept his head down, occasionally stealing glances at Zhou Ning, seemingly hesitant to speak. Seeing this, Zhou Ning took the initiative to open the conversation.

"So, you're a retired soldier? No wonder your colleagues speak so highly of you."

"Officer, you've spoken with my colleagues and superiors?" Lao Li asked with a wry smile, no longer hiding his feelings.

"Yes." Zhou Ning nodded.

"Do they think I'm lying?" Lao Li's voice was low but firm, and his tone hinted at his stubbornness.

"Lao Li, rest assured, no one here doubts your sincerity. Only, what you saw that night was too bizarre to have been a natural phenomenon. But if it was man-made, you know better than I do the layers of security our man would have to get past. The chances of pulling off such a trick within the Forbidden City are close to zero. Besides, what would be the point?"

After exchanging a few words, Zhou Ning felt that Lao Li was as dependable as his colleagues described. The man expressed his doubts simply and without reservation.

"Yeah, I can't figure it out." Lao Li shook his head in confusion.

The two men fell into silence as Zhou Ning followed Lao Li through several palaces and exhibition halls. Although the sky was already dark, Lao Li moved with ease, navigating the chambers and corridors without hesitation. Their footsteps echoed in the empty palace, steady and deliberate, until they reached a hall at the end of the path. Here, the rhythm of their steps was disrupted. Lao Li paused for a moment as if he wanted to make a detour.

"What's the matter, Lao Li?" Zhou Ning's years of experience as a criminal investigator had given him extremely keen observational skills, and even the most inconspicuous changes hardly escaped his notice.

"This is where I saw the ghost that night," Lao Li said faintly, with the unique tone of someone awakening from a nightmare.

Zhou Ning gently patted Lao Li's shoulder. "Let's go in and take a look," he said.

Infected by the young policeman's calm demeanor, Lao Li felt more at ease. He nodded his assent, and he and Zhou Ning stepped into the palace together.

Following the incident, the decoration work in the exhibition hall was temporarily put on hold, and the scene remained unchanged from that night. Zhou Ning immediately noticed that, due to its layout and location, this palace was darker than the previous halls, with poorer lighting and ventilation. The exhibition hall where the shadow appeared was located in the innermost part of the palace. Standing in the center of the hall, Zhou Ning felt vaguely cramped. He touched the pillars and walls, but they didn't seem coated with chemical pigments. Carefully examining his palm, he found nothing abnormal.

The spotlight magnified the shadow of his palm, reflecting it upon the wall in a distorted and twisted manner. As he slowly moved his fingers, the shadow trembled. The effect was eerie.

Zhou Ning pondered for a moment, then chuckled softly. Perhaps the truth was that simple—on a dark and stormy night within the dimly lit and secluded palace, the mind played tricks; the lonely watchman mistook his shadow for the skeleton. It wasn't such a difficult thing to understand.

Not wishing to upset Lao Li, Zhou Ning did not state his inference directly. He circled the palace silently a couple of times before withdrawing with the watchman.

Outside the palace, the bright moon hung high in the sky, and the gentle breeze immediately swept away the oppressive feeling. Zhou Ning accompanied Lao Li to the palace gate, where he exchanged a few words with the officer assigned to him, thus concluding the investigation. Before he left, Zhou Ning glanced back, sensing there was something behind him.

Beijing was exceptionally quiet that night—one of those rare times without traffic—and Zhou Ning opted to walk instead of driving. He strolled into a narrow alleyway, then stopped abruptly as he rounded a corner, sensing someone behind him. He turned sharply, assuming a grappling posture, ready to face whoever was following him.

"Who's there?" he shouted, ready to pounce. Caught off guard, his opponent shrank against the wall, trembling with fear, not daring to move. Only then did Zhou Ning discover that his pursuer was a pretty young woman dressed in a white coat and black trousers.

Zhou Ning looked this strange stalker up and down. Her short hair cropped at the ears, and the thick lenses in her eyeglasses made her appear older than she was, a far cry from most young girls who dressed up to show off their youth. Zhou Ning had an excellent memory for faces, and he felt sure he had seen her earlier that evening when he entered the Forbidden City. Since there were no visitors around on closing days, she was probably a staff member of the Palace Museum.

If Lao Li's ghost was not a hallucination, could it have been a prank orchestrated by someone on the inside? Zhou Ning's mind was spinning out possibilities, and he immediately connected the girl's furtive behavior with the case.

Zhou Ning relaxed his guard, and the girl gradually calmed down. As it turned out, she wanted to speak to him regarding Lao Li's case, but what she said next took Zhou Ning entirely by surprise.

She introduced herself as Chen Wen, a conservator working in the calligraphy and painting group of the Palace Museum's Department of Conservation Science. Founded in 1953, the Palace Museum's restoration center relied on the traditional master-student relationship to pass down restoration skills from generation to generation. Today, most of the collection's best paintings and calligraphy scrolls had already been restored, and those of Chen Wen's generation are unlikely to have the opportunity to work on these national treasures. Instead, their daily work consisted mainly of repairing the lower-grade calligraphy scrolls and paintings that were once widely displayed throughout the palace, affixed to the lintels and interior walls, most of which were now in deplorable condition. Spending day after day in a working environment almost entirely disconnected from modern society, their youthful years slipped by as they diligently practiced their ancient craft, quietly awaiting some future day when this essential skill might be required again.

Chen Wen entered the Palace Museum after graduating from the Academy of Fine Arts, and had been studying under her master for more than five years. Unlike most of her colleagues, who found the work tiresome, she had fallen in love with her work from the very first day. But a few months back, she was restoring a decorative painting that had originally been affixed to a door panel. Long exposure to the weather had left the painting severely damaged and it required delicate handling. After moistening the paper with warm water, Chen Wen began carefully unmounting the painting, using tweezers to remove it from the frame. As the old mounting was slowly peeled away, a strange symbol was gradually revealed.

She described it as a symbol because even with her professional eyes, she couldn't recognize it as any Chinese character—it looked like a little running man. At the time, she assumed it was some mark or graffiti left behind by the painter. She didn't take it too seriously and went home after finishing her work.

Yet, to her disbelief, when she looked at the painting again the following day, something incredible had happened: the little man had moved from the upper left corner to the middle. Not only had he changed position, he had also grown much larger.

Initially, Chen Wen thought this might have been caused by an ink smudge or mildew brought on by oxidation, but she was sure she had followed protective measures before leaving the day before. She inspected the painting under a magnifying glass, hardly able to believe her eyes—the little man was no longer a mere outline painted in broad strokes; the magnifying glass clearly revealed the bones, joints, and other human structures. It was absurd enough that human-shaped symbols should suddenly appear on ancient paintings, let alone begin to move and grow and slowly develop!

Within a few days, the figure had reached a level of detail comparable to surgical anatomy diagrams, and Chen Wen was on the brink of a nervous breakdown. She made up her mind to tell the master, yet as soon as he arrived, the little man on the back of the painting vanished without a trace. Faced with her master's criticism, Chen Wen was at a loss; she began to suspect that the little man was a figment of her imagination caused by spending too many long hours at her desk. Yet, just as she was beginning to forget the incident, the figure suddenly reappeared, this time on a sheet of drafting paper, covering the entire page. Chen Wen was so frightened that she tore the paper to shreds.

After that, Chen Wen's work and life returned to normal, and the little man never appeared again. Yet, no matter how she tried, she could not shake this strange incident from her mind. And so, when news spread about the night watchman having encountered a ghost in the palace not far from where she worked, she felt sure that the ghost and the little man were one and the same. It was under her encouragement that Lao Li finally reported the incident to the authorities.

Chen Wen knew that no one at the palace believed Lao Li's story, and she couldn't blame them. When she caught sight of Zhou Ning as she was leaving work, she felt a glimmer of hope. However, because she hesitated to approach him at the palace, she had ended up looking like some stalker with ulterior motives.

II

Zhou Ning had thought the case was closed, but now he was perplexed. He was forced to admit that the ghostly apparitions were not an illusion but a real phenomenon. There were three things worthy of attention in the witness records: Firstly, those areas where Lao Li and Chen Wen had seen the ghost were in a relatively remote corner of the Forbidden City, close to each other and far away from the main building. Secondly, according to their recollections, the ghost appeared each time during a thunderstorm. Thirdly, although the ghost appeared without warning, it was always attached to particular objects, such as ancient paintings, paper scrolls, or the palace walls.

Zhou Ning resolved to follow this lead. He vaguely felt that this was not a "case" in the usual sense; there were no victims, no suspects, and no losses incurred. If he continued to rely on traditional investigative methods, he feared he would never uncover the mystery behind the shadow's apparitions. He needed to leverage outside forces, the most crucial being experts in history and physics. But, prerequisite to all that, he needed to gather enough evidence to convince both the Forbidden City and the police department that the ghost, in fact, existed.

After careful consideration, Zhou Ning disclosed his plans to his immediate supervisor, Director Liu. The director thought Zhou Ning was making a fuss out of nothing. The most he would agree to was to help facilitate things with the security department at the palace museum so that Zhou Ning could continue his investigations without restriction.

Meanwhile, Lao Li had been absent from work for several days. It turned out that his supervisors at the museum, concerned about his mental health, had explicitly arranged for him to take time off. It seemed that Chen Wen's concerns were not unfounded. Until the situation was more apparent, it was better not to involve her further. Zhou Ning understood that from here on, he would be fighting the battle alone.

He gathered the weather forecasts for the coming weeks, pinpointing the days when thunderstorms were most likely to occur. On those days, he resolved to return to the scene and keep watch, hoping to catch a glimpse of the mysterious ghost.

To find a suitable surveillance point, Zhou Ning consulted the architectural drawings of the palace. He discovered that another building was marked on the map between the space where Chen Wen worked and the palace where the ghost appeared. However, in his memory, the location was only an empty field. The staff member who provided the drawings explained that the building depicted was an underground storage facility used to store paintings and calligraphy from the Song Dynasty. Due to the number of priceless cultural relics stored within, the basement was rarely opened to the public, and it was impossible to discern anything from the outside.

Since the vault was locked all year round, Zhou Ning thought it unlikely anyone could sneak inside. He was still inclined to believe that the ghostly phenomena was the work of man. After surveying the surrounding environment, he decided to begin his stakeout as planned.

Several days passed, but the predicted thunderstorms never arrived. The turning point came one afternoon when, according to the forecast, it was supposed to be a fine, clear day. The weather remained fine throughout the morning, but the sky suddenly darkened in the afternoon. When Zhou Ning opened the window, a strong wind rushed into the office, whistling in his ears, and he knew it was about to rain. Zhou Ning collected the documents blown about on his desk, rushed out of the police station, and hurried to the Forbidden City as fast as he could.

It was completely dark as Zhou Ning took up position under the eaves of the palace where the ghost had appeared. He had carefully chosen this point for its unobstructed view across the open space above the vault. In the distance, it was also possible to see the outer wall of the small compound where Chen Wen and the rest of the painting and calligraphy restoration team worked.

With the help of his police-issue thermal imaging goggles, anything emerging from that compound or the palace halls would immediately draw his attention. Zhou Ning slipped into his optical camouflage and lurked quietly, almost blending in with the palace behind him as the lightning flashed above. The rain was getting heavier now, and as the workday came to an end, people emerged from the palace carrying umbrellas. At this moment, there was a call incoming through the police headset.

"Officer Zhou, I saw your police car parked outside!" Chen Wen said on the phone. She probably hadn't expected Zhou Ning to come back; her voice was tinged with excitement. "Where are you? Did you discover something?"

"Calm down. Seeing is believing, so they say, and I still need to confirm," Zhou Ning replied cautiously. He paused. Guessing that no one else was on the line, he asked again, "By the way, have you seen the little man on the paper recently? Have any of your colleagues been acting out of the ordinary?"

"Everyone is fine, but I've been nervous. The weather is just like it was when I saw the ghost for the first time. I was on edge all day, but nothing happened." Chen Wen chuckled bitterly.

"Well, it's raining hard now; you had better hurry back. I'm going to get to the bottom of this." Zhou Ning gave Chen Wen a few words of comfort and then hung up the phone.

He waited until late in the night. The rain had ceased now, and he examined every corner of the hall, then walked out to the courtyard and patrolled the walls. The hall's furnishings were unchanged; apart from the night staff, there was no sign of anyone else having been in there. The only door to the palace remained locked, and he found no suspicious traces or footprints outside the walls. He sensed that his efforts today were going to be fruitless.

Zhou Ning wasn't discouraged nor impatient, except he couldn't help but wonder whether his presence had somehow disturbed the ghost. Although his optical camouflage provided excellent concealment, it did not render him invisible.

Just at that moment, he sensed a sudden change.

The rainwater that had not yet drained away, forming puddles in the open courtyard, reflecting the waning moon like the compound eyes of insects. A dark figure emerged from the water, swallowing the moonlight as it leaped between the puddles. With each movement, its outline gradually became more defined until it took on the definite form of a skeleton.

Lao Li and Chen Wen were not lying!

Zhou Ning's blood surged as he chased after the ghost, attempting to capture it with the camera function in his goggles, but he could hardly keep up with it. Not until the shadow crashed into one of the spirit walls erected outside the palace to ward off troubled spirits, did it finally stop. Then it detached itself from the puddle and slithered up the wall like ivy, slowly, as though waiting for Zhou Ning to catch up.

But as Zhou Ning approached, the ghost's lower body all but disappeared, and the rest sank into the ground along the base of the wall, soon vanishing without a trace.

Although the goggles had captured only a few blurry after-images, Zhou Ning was greatly encouraged. He immediately expanded the scope of the surveillance, hoping to identify a pattern in the ghost's appearances.

Over the next few months, Zhou Ning encountered the ghost many more times. The ghost materialized for longer or shorter durations and reacted differently each time, but the appearances were obviously centered around the open courtyard above the vault and clearly diminished as one moved away from there. Based on his observations, Zhou Ning deduced that the ghost demonstrated a certain level of intelligence. He speculated that it was likely being manipulated by an unknown person, probably hiding nearby. The truth was almost out, and there was only one place that had escaped Zhou Ning's search: the basement vault containing the calligraphy scrolls and paintings from the Song Dynasty.

Zhou Ning immediately appealed to his superiors, requesting access to the surveillance footage from the underground repository, but he received no response. How did the perpetrator sneak into the vault? How did they come and go without being detected? Zhou Ning speculated that his counterpart possessed some kind of advanced technology, and that the ghostly manifestations were only a smokescreen used to deceive others and cover the villain's tracks.

If whoever controlled the ghost could enter and exit the basement at leisure, they were more than capable of removing the treasures inside. Once accomplished, the theft could be blamed on supernatural events, thereby distracting the police while the villain made good his escape. Zhou Ning could not sit back and watch while his country's national treasures were being stolen away. He felt he had no choice but to force his way into Director Liu's office and demand an answer.

"Director Liu, haven't you obtained the surveillance footage for the vault at the palace museum? The situation is urgent!"

"Enough, Zhou Ning! You have no idea how I stuck my neck out for you. Look where it got us. I've completely lost face over this, and it's your fault."

Zhou Ning hadn't expected to snag on a nail right as he entered the door. Faced with his superior's stern glare, he saw no way to defend himself. He caught the memory card thrown by Director Liu and, feeling disheartened, left the office.

Zhou Ning knew how complex inter-departmental coordination was at the bureau, and he understood why the usually amiable Director Liu was furious at the lack of progress. But as long as he could find a solution to the problem, he thought to himself, suffering a few scoldings was no big deal.

He inserted the memory card into his computer, replaying back the footage. But after watching for a time, his brow furrowed. The surveillance footage was different from what he had imagined. Had he missed something? He stopped fast-forwarding and spent several days carefully reviewing the footage captured before and after each apparition.

Nothing happened. No living thing or other object appeared.

Zhou Ning had the impression that time had stopped in the basement vault, frozen ever since those paintings and calligraphy scrolls were stored inside. Had his opponent's technology advanced to the point that it surpassed even the very latest in optical camouflage? Zhou Ning found it hard to believe, but how else to explain a ghost that came and went without a trace?

III

After the trouble he had caused, the bureau was increasingly distrustful of Zhou Ning's words. Fortunately, Zhou Ning was of a temperament that grew stronger with every setback. That night, he returned to the Palace Museum to continue his surveillance. He resolved not to give up until the truth behind the ghost incident was brought to light.

His hard work soon paid off, and Zhou Ning saw the shadow ghost several more times. Yet the cause of the phenomena remained shrouded in mystery. The manifestations appeared randomly but always near the underground vault, indicating that his previous speculations were not unfounded. But alone and without help, it was difficult for Zhou Ning to discover the truth. Though he had grasped its outline, he could not go further and was getting increasingly desperate.

When one night he encountered the shadow ghost again, after playing cat-and-mouse for a while, Zhou Ning finally snapped. When he saw the ghost about to sink into the wall again, he rushed to try and prevent it from escaping. It was a conditioned reflex borne of a moment of desperation, and naturally, it had no effect. The shadow ghost swiftly disappeared.

The terrible events unfolded only after Zhou Ning returned home. To avoid waking his soundly sleeping wife, he tiptoed into the bathroom and changed out of his sweaty police uniform. While unbuttoning his shirt, he noticed a dark patch on his left shoulder.

Probably just rubbed against something dirty on the wall, he thought, paying little mind to it. However, when he took a shower, he found that no matter how hard he scrubbed, he couldn't wash it off. In the mirror, the surrounding skin was rubbed red from the scrubbing, yet the dark patch remained as stubbornly as a birthmark. A feeling of foreboding arose in Zhou Ning's heart.

Could it be some kind of skin disease or melanoma?

Lying in bed, Zhou Ning tossed and turned. An Ran grasped his hand as she slept, smiling contentedly. *Let's not scare her,* he thought, *better to let her sleep.* Zhou Ning abandoned the idea of asking An Ran, a surgical oncologist, to examine the dark spot. He closed his eyes uneasily.

Early the next morning, the last trace of hope left in Zhou Ning's heart was shattered. The dark spot had moved from the left shoulder to the right, and the familiar outline of a skeleton was becoming increasingly prominent. There was no need to show it to An Ran— no skin disease or melanoma could metastasize overnight. He had no choice but to face an unthinkable truth: he was possessed by the shadow ghost.

"What's the matter? Are you feeling unwell?" An Ran asked with concern, seeing Zhou Ning's pale face as he emerged from the bathroom.

"It's nothing, I just didn't sleep well last night," Zhou Ning replied, not knowing where to begin. Not wishing to worry her, he tried to brush it off, but he felt uneasy as she fussed over him. After a few bites of his breakfast, he hurried out the door. One way or another, he had to sort out his own problems first.

Zhou Ning's mind was made up, and he went directly to the hospital and made an appointment with a specialist in the dermatology department. While waiting, he touched his shoulder again, felt no discomfort, and wondered whether he should have come. But now that he was here, he could only take one step at a time.

The attending physician patiently listened to Zhou Ning's description of his condition, showing no signs of surprise. Perhaps he had seen so many complicated cases that nothing fazed him anymore. Zhou Ning followed the doctor's instructions and removed his shirt. The doctor's gaze lingered on his shoulders and back for a long time, and he asked if he had any symptoms, such as pain or itching. When Zhou Ning answered in the negative, the doctor circled around him and inquired, "You said that you're a police officer and often on active duty. Is that right?"

"That's right. Zhou Ning nodded, not understanding what the doctor meant in asking this.

"Go home and have a good rest. Try not to stay up so late." The doctor signaled to Zhou Ning that the consultation was over without even prescribing any medicine.

"You mean there's nothing wrong with my body?" Zhou Ning asked incredulously.

"See for yourself. There are no black marks or skeletons, nothing at all." The doctor brought a mirror and showed Zhou Ning his back.

"But it was there when I woke up this morning!" Zhou Ning couldn't help but argue, except before he even finished speaking, a wave of dizziness overtook him, leaving him unsteady on his feet. The doctor held him up and said carefully, "If things don't improve, I suggest you see a psychiatrist."

"No, there's nothing wrong with my mind!" Zhou Ning vigorously rubbed his temples, trying to wake himself up, but what he saw next left him dumbstruck. The doctor before him had transformed into a 3D anatomical model of a human being. His skin was a layer of transparent plastic wrapped around his muscles and bones, while the internal organs were faintly discernible, slowly contracting and pulsating. With a slight adjustment of focus, Zhou Ning saw the muscles in the doctor's chest peel away as in an animation, gradually revealing the beating heart on the upper left side. The atria, ventricles, arteries, veins, and even the blood that rushes endlessly within them—everything was so vivid, precise, and real. Although Zhou Ning had dealt with criminal cases for many years and seen plenty of human bodies, nothing had ever shocked him quite like this.

"My God," Zhou Ning murmured, pushing away the monster he saw moving toward him. He fought his way out of the hospital under the doctor's bewildered gaze and struggled on, though he felt like he was treading on cotton, suppressing the churning feeling in his stomach, until finally he emerged outside. Amidst the hustle and bustle of traffic and pedestrians, the mundane world continued as normal.

Zhou Ning clasped his sweating forehead, breathing deeply, slowly recovering his strength. He felt steady for the first time in a long time. His headache faded. He was not crazy; the world was not crazy. He didn't care to know why or how; for the moment, he only felt grateful to be alive. However, what appeared like a castle of solid rock was a reality built on quicksand. When Zhou Ning altered his focus for a moment, the fragile balance was shattered. All of a sudden, people and objects were drained of their color and three-dimensional forms, flattened like insects dried and pressed under glass.

The ghost had not left him. It lurked within his body, the cause of these inexplicable changes!

Struggling to hold onto reality, Zhou Ning walked into the road in a trance, staring blankly at the precisely structured cuboids passing by. *Oh, that, it's a flattened car!* For a moment, Zhou Ning wondered what might happen if one hit him.

"Are you blind? Trying to get yourself killed?!"

Out burst an angry curse, and one of the rectangular bodies close at hand hurriedly changed its direction. Zhou Ning felt helpless. Feeling like he was walking through a photo, he gradually relaxed his vigilance. It wasn't until some tremendous force struck him suddenly from behind and he felt his body floating weightlessly that he realized the real world was still running in an orderly manner, and the only one who was changing was himself ...

IU

It was a scorching summer day in the fourth year of the Daguan era in the reign of Emperor Huizong.[1] A group of students gathered at the painting school beside the Tongjin Bridge in Kaifeng. Excited and apprehensive, they pushed and shoved at each other, trying to find their names on the imperial list. Now and again, bursts of cheers or sorrow erupted from the crowd as people discovered their fates and went in different directions.

He watched from afar, remembering when he had first entered the painting school three years ago. As the youngest and weakest student at the school, he was often bullied, and he felt no desire to join in the fun now.

A long time had passed since he received word from the imperial tutor, and he worried the old man might have forgotten him. Although

---

1 Prior to the Ming dynasty, it was common for Chinese sovereigns to change the era name multiple times during their reigns. Daguan was the third era of Huizong's reign and lasted from 1107–1110 CE.

he was still young, his experience of living under other people's roofs since childhood had made him particularly sensitive. He knew in his heart why the imperial tutor had taken him from the woodshed at Brother Ling Rang's[2] house and arranged for him to enter the painting school early. What better pawn to please the emperor than this humble, sickly, young relative with a great talent for painting?

According to the plan, once his apprenticeship was over, he would enter the Hanlin Academy of Calligraphy and Painting and become a full-time painter in the emperor's employment. But unexpectedly, since last year, as though they had conspired in advance, the court officials had come forward one after another to denounce the imperial tutor. The storm gathered quickly. First came a report from a student of the Academy listing the imperial tutor's fourteen major offenses, which sent shockwaves through the court and the commons. Scholars scrambled to transcribe the accusations as if they were factual records. Later, one of the royal censors accused the Imperial Tutor of being greedy, untrustworthy and disloyal. When the emperor heard this, he became suspicious of the imperial tutor and immediately demoted him to the rank of Shao Bao[3] and exiled him to Hangzhou.

Unlike his elder brother, who was born into the royal bloodline, he was the son of a maidservant. Moreover, partly due to the soul-leaving sickness[4] he'd suffered from as a child, his father abandoned them. Fortunately, he displayed an exceptional talent for painting and could perceive color, light, shade, and perspective in a way that ordinary people simply could not see. He listened in secretly while his brother studied the art of landscape painting, and imitating the styles of General Li senior and junior,[5] he soon became a widely renowned

---

2 Zhao Lingrang (active ca. 1070–1100) was a Chinese painter and a scion of the Song imperial family.

3 In Song Dynasty China, the Shaobao was mainly responsible for handling government affairs, while the Taibao held a more important role, directly responsible for protecting and managing the safety of the emperor.

4 *lí hún zhèng* ("soul-leaving syndrome") is an old Chinese medical term that refers to a condition where individuals feel as though their souls have separated from their physical bodies, often resulting in sensations of floating or being detached from reality.

5 Li Sixun (651-716) was a Chinese painter and general. His son, Li Zhaodao was also a famous painter, and the two are often referred to together.

child prodigy. Three years of formal study at the painting academy broadened his understanding of the three perspectives of mountains: the high, the deep, and the level perspective.[6] Even without the master's tutelage, he felt confident in his talent and proud of his work. But the way things were, he feared he would be deprived of the opportunity to demonstrate his abilities.

When the crowd finally dispersed, he discovered what he had expected—his name was not on the list. In the great city of Kaifeng, once deprived of the protection of power, it was difficult to move forward. Although he had anticipated this outcome for some time, now that the result was really before his eyes, he couldn't help but feel despondent. He just wanted to jump off the bridge and be done with it.

After his father died, his elder brother had taken charge of the family. Thinking of his mother, who worked herself blind to feed him, and even his elder brother who regarded him as the God of Pestilence, [7] he hesitated. Reluctance and resentment tore his heart to pieces, leaving only this mortal bag of skin. The river flowed quietly under the bridge, and he didn't know where to go.

It was already late when Chen Wen heard the news and rushed to the hospital. The operation was not yet finished, and the family members waited anxiously outside the theater. Just as she was about to go over and inquire about the patient's condition, the doctor burst out of the operating room, and the family gathered around him.

"Severe traumatic brain injury," he said, "especially to the frontal lobe. I originally hoped to drill a hole and drain the swelling that way, which would be less invasive, but the swelling is already too extensive— there is now no choice but to perform a craniectomy. Additionally, a portion of the brain tissue must be removed."

---

6 The master Song painter, Guo Xi (1023-1085) introduced the concept of "three perspectives" in landscape painting in his essay, Advice on Landscape Painting. The Level Perspective emphasizes depth through foreground, middle ground, and background relations; the Deep Perspective depicts vertical views, showcasing height and depth in landscapes, and the High Perspective offers a bird's-eye view, capturing vast natural expanses.

7 Wen Shen is a deity or group of deities responsible for illness, plague, and disease in Chinese folk religion.

The hospital was particularly quiet in the early morning, and though she was far away, Chen Wen sensed the doctor's frustration and fatigue.

"Doctor, please help my son! He is still so young!" Upon hearing the news, the old woman staggered and almost collapsed. Fortunately, the young woman at her side was quick to notice and held her up.

"Mom, please calm down. The doctor is doing everything he can, and we must believe that Zhou Ning will pull through."

After helping the old lady into a chair, the young woman tugged the doctor away towards Chen Wen, whispering to him in a low voice. "Doctor, you said that the damage to the frontal lobe was severe. I understand that this area has much to do with memory, emotions, and personality." The doctor looked dumbly at the woman, surprised by her words. "I'm also a doctor," she said, "and I trust you to tell me the truth. What are his chances?" Pain and strength mingled in the woman's eyes; she seemed prepared for the worst.

"As it stands, saving the man's life should not be an issue, but even if he is revived, he won't be the same as before. Your family needs to be mentally prepared for that."

"As long as you can save him, that's all that matters. Please do everything you can." The woman took a deep breath and squeezed the doctor's hand firmly.

Storms arise out of clear skies, and blessings or misfortunes may appear at any moment. For those who love each other deeply, no matter if the other has lost their memories or even become a different person, there is still hope as long as he remains alive.

After speaking with the family, the doctor turned and entered the operating theater. The young woman talked to the older relatives, who were frightened out of their wits. She spoke for a long time before convincing them to go home together and wait for news.

Once things were settled, the young woman, always the backbone of the family, let fall her tough disguise and squatted against the wall. She hugged her knees and buried her face in her arms, leaving only a section of her fair neck exposed. Tears ran continually down her arms and dripped to the floor as her body trembled slightly.

Chen Wen felt terrible about what happened. She felt sure the truth behind Zhou Ning's accident was not so simple. After meeting Zhou Ning several times, his courage and carefulness left a deep impression on her. He didn't seem the type of person to cross the road recklessly. She even suspected that the bizarre car accident might have something to do with the case Zhou Ning was investigating. If that was true, then it was her fault he was involved. With this on her conscience, Chen Wen pulled out a tissue, stepped forward and gently patted the young woman's shoulder.

"Sorry, do I know you?" The woman raised her head. Her eyes were red, and her face was wan and sallow.

"My name is Chen Wen. I've been involved with the case Zhou Ning is investigating. He is a good, dependable policeman. I came to see him."

"Oh, hello. I'm Zhou Ning's wife, An Ran. He's always been like this, putting work before anything else. I always complained and then something like this goes and happens. I just hope he gets better. I dare not show it in front of his parents, but I'm more afraid than anyone. I can't live without him ..."

Maybe Chen Wen appeared at the right time. In front of this stranger, An Ran no longer had to conceal her helplessness and fragility. She stood up and hugged Chen Wen, then burst into tears.

Feeling guilty, Chen Wen could only mutter a few comforting words to console her. The minutes ticked by slowly; it was almost dawn when the door of the operating theater swung open. Though exhausted, An Ran stood up and rushed to the doctor, with Chen Wen following closely behind.

"Doctor, how is my husband?" An Ran tugged at the doctor's sleeve, her voice hoarse and trembling.

"The initial operation was successful. Intracranial pressure has been temporarily reduced, but he'll need to be transferred to the ICU for intubation. We'll continue to monitor the EEG response and body temperature to prevent postoperative seizures and strive to revive the patient as soon as possible."

"Thank you, doctor, thank you!" Hearing the doctor's words, An Ran and Chen Wen repeatedly bowed in gratitude, feeling relief in their hearts.

For the past two years he had been employed as a scribe in the archives outside the city's Jinyao Gate. This remote government office was primarily responsible for storing more than five years' worth of financial records, and even the supervisor was no more than a minor official. By now, the young man had long since resigned himself to a fate of organizing and transcribing, his talents buried under this dull and insipid life. Even when he heard that the imperial tutor had been recalled into the emperor's service, the news failed to stir up any waves in his stagnant mind.

First his brother, and now the master—he was fed up with relying on others, fed up with always being a puppet without dignity, fed up with feeling like he was not in control. What's more, he had heard what the master had done. Although he was no gentleman, he still had his pride; he wouldn't resort to flattery and treachery for the sake of his future career. Besides, it wasn't for people like himself to have such extravagant dreams.

The trees long for peace, but the winds do not cease. When the imperial tutor returned to Beijing, he immediately summoned him to court.

"Master."

Arriving at the tutor's mansion, he felt like he was entering another world and was struck again by the feeling of helplessness in the face of destiny.

"Rise," the old man said slowly, without raising his head. He was seated in a chair, drinking tea.

He got up slowly and stood quietly with his head bowed. Before he came, he had resolved to no longer allow himself to be manipulated by this old schemer, but under the master's influence and prestige, he could not help but feel apprehensive.

"Prepare yourself. In a few days, you'll be leaving the archives. From here on, you'll be in the emperor's service. You have a fine future ahead of you." The master finally turned his attention upon him, gently blowing away the steam from his teacup.

Upon hearing this, he could not keep the astonishment from his face. He reflected for a moment before replying. "I appreciate master's kindness, but I fear I can no longer shoulder such a heavy responsibility. For too long, I have neglected my painting. I request that master ask someone else."

"Oh?" The old man raised his white eyebrows, and the stern look on his face softened. He sighed. "No matter. If you are not willing, no one will force you. Only—I already informed your elder brother and made him promise to take care of your mother. He'll be very disappointed if things don't work out."

Two years in seclusion had calmed the old fox's blustering but only made him more cunning. With those few words, he felt the life crushed out of him. Cold sweat dripped down his back, his knees weakened, and his voice whined like a mosquito.

"As you command, master. I will do as you ask. Please don't make things difficult for my mother."

"Where is this coming from?" the old man asked as he helped him up. The scorn in his eyes had faded completely, and he spoke with regret, his face full of compassion. "I know the past two years have been discouraging, but my judgment has never been wrong. The emperor values Ling Rang for his talents, but naturally, being from the same lineage, he always got a little more attention than others. But he relies too much on his noble background; he carries himself with arrogance and self-righteousness and opposes me secretly. From what I see, your art is in no way inferior to Ling Rang's. I'm sure the emperor would look upon you favorably. When an opportunity like this falls from the skies before your eyes, it's up to you to seize it!"

Years in officialdom had sharpened the old man's skills in wearing down a man's defenses.

Seeing that he had aroused his pupil's interest, the old man was secretly pleased, yet he spoke resignedly. "Since I entered the civil service in the third year of Xining,[8] my official career has moved smoothly along. In the first year of Chongning,[9] I found favor with the emperor and entered the imperial service. Though I was later disgraced and exiled, I never lost faith, even when things seemed hopeless. Do you know why?"

"I don't know," he replied. He had lived with his mother in his brother's house ever since he was a child. Until he embarked upon his

---

8 Xining was the first era of the Emperor Shenzong's reign, and lasted from 1068–1077.

9 Chongning was the name given to the second era of the Emperor Huizong's reign, lasting from 1102–1106.

studies, the woodshed and garden were his entire world. What could he know of the unfathomable intricacies of politics?

"Haha!" the old man laughed triumphantly, stroking his beard. When he first took the boy under his wing, he thought he was simple-minded and easy to manipulate. Even after two years, he had not changed a bit. But now that the pawn was to be put to use, he would need a little guidance.

"It's unimportant, really. My standing in the court relies on the emperor's imperial favor. The world has been at peace for a long time; the emperor is rich, and if not for the criticism of his courtiers, he might have led a life of pleasure. I always governed in his interests, in accordance with the principles of prosperity and abundance. While I act as his hand, he enjoys peace without criticism. How could he sincerely dismiss me? It's only a ploy to appease public opinion, to keep everyone quiet. In this way, my life, wealth, and honor are all tied to the emperor's decisions, and I must do whatever he asks." Seeing him nodding in understanding, the old man took a sip of tea before continuing.

"The emperor has been on the throne for over ten years. He seeks to surpass the legacy of his father and brother, and I am his minister again. If at this time, I present a grand painting depicting the great rivers and mountains of our Song Dynasty with the people living and working in peace and contentment, surely the old dragon's heart will be pleased!"

"I am at your command. I will go and prepare." After going around in circles for a long time, the master finally made himself clear and found himself unable to refuse.

"From now on, you don't have to worry about the archives. I've instructed the warden to arrange a spare room for you to use as a studio. The pens and inks are ready, and the silks sent by the emperor will be delivered soon. Keep in mind, you must finish as soon as possible."

"I understand."

U

"Has Zhou Ning's condition improved?" Chen Wen asked softly as she strolled into the ward carrying a lunch box. Ever since the accident, she had brooded over whether to tell An Ran about her part in it. But when she had finally confessed, not only did An Ran not blame her, she tried to comfort her, saying that it wasn't yet known whether Zhou Ning's injuries had anything to do with the case he was investigating; besides, it wasn't in Zhou Ning's nature to back down from a case just because it was dangerous.

Touched by An Ran's kindness and strength, Chen Wen started visiting the hospital now and then; the two soon became close friends and talked about everything.

"He seems stable now, but his brain activity is still very weak, and we don't know when he will wake up." An Ran fussed distractedly at the tubes and the EEG cap on Zhou Ning's thin, shrunken face.

After eating the takeout, they exchanged a few words, with An Ran reminiscing about how she and Zhou Ning met and fell in love. Chen Wen didn't mind; she just sat quietly with her, letting the time go by. The setting sun shining through the window reflected the tiny wrinkles on An Ran's forehead and in the corners of her eyes. Her best years had slipped quietly behind her, but Chen Wen saw clearly her face radiant with love and humanity—she was as beautiful as an angel.

Night fell without their noticing. An Ran, immersed in past happiness, was startled to find Chen Wen still sitting silently by her side.

"Look at me. I've been so busy talking on that I'd almost forgotten you were here. I'm afraid I've wasted half your day."

"It's okay. I'm on leave today, and I have nowhere else to go. To tell you the truth, I envy you both. Because of you, I'm beginning to believe in love again." Chen Wen smiled knowingly.

"Oh, don't make fun of me. If the doctor hadn't said that talking to Zhou Ning would help him recover, I wouldn't have thought of all these old things." With Chen Wen at her side, An Ran felt much better.

"It must be hard on you," Chen Wen sighed.

"As long it helps Zhou Ning to recover, I'm not worried about how hard or tiring it is. But Zhou Ning is still in a deep coma. Can he even hear a word I'm saying? I'm not sure it's really any use …" An Ran was a little dispirited but then seemed to think of something. "You know, the doctor said they will try a newly developed brain imaging device on Zhou Ning. This machine can project pictures and simple sounds to his visual and auditory nerves through electrical signals. At least it has to be more effective on the auditory nerves than my clumsy attempts."

"That's wonderful! Is there anything I can do to help?" When she heard this, Chen Wen felt happy for An Ran.

"Well …. The doctor asked me to prepare some materials over the next few days. This new method is much more direct and intense than traditional means and uses different information. It's best to choose something that Zhou Ning is interested in but not too familiar with; that way, we can best tap the potential of his brain and arouse his dormant consciousness to promote his recovery." An Ran looked into Chen Wen's eyes, speaking solemnly. "I think the one who tied the bell should be the one to take it off."[10]

"Leave it to me," Chen Wen agreed. An Ran's meaning couldn't be clearer. She also suspected that Zhou Ning's accident was related to the Forbidden City case. So, wouldn't more information about the case be precisely what Zhou Ning needed?

After getting off work the next day, Chen Wen began aggressively searching for information. Both at the police station and within the Forbidden City, the case was treated as a farce. Few believed the witnesses, and almost no one took it seriously. Fortunately, this meant that Chen Wen wasted little time determining the progress of Zhou Ning's recent investigation. She disapproved of his conclusion, which pointed to the basement vault, because she was simply too familiar with the room. Although she had been inside only a handful of times, she thought of it as a sacred place that held the best efforts of generations of painting and calligraphy restorers, including one cultural treasure restored by her master's own teacher when he was young.

Her master had lived in the Forbidden City all his life, and his temperament was tempered by his time there. He was calm as an ancient well. But whenever he recalled those past years, he always looked cheerful—only then did her stern and old-fashioned master become kind and affectionate. Immersed in his memories and proud of his past, he talked endlessly about his own good fortune and sighed distractedly when remembering the rare splendor and melancholy of one particular painting. Chen Wen would always draw up a small stool and sit beside her master like a little girl listening to her grandfather's stories, her feelings a mix of longing and admiration. The ancient craft

---

10 *Let he who tied the bell on the tiger take it off*, is a Chinese proverb which can be traced back to a Song dynasty poet, Huì Hóng

was passed down from generation to generation, and while faces grew old, the culture and spirit would endure forever, echoing in every corner of the palace.

Chen Wen knew how difficult it would be to hide something in this place. Besides the several security checkpoints in the entrance and exit channels, the vault employed an extremely sensitive monitoring system due to the need to maintain constant temperature and humidity in the environment. An insect flying in would cause disturbance enough to trigger an alarm, let alone an unauthorized person. Zhou Ning's ignorance of the specificities of cultural relic protection led him to make the wrong inferences. But now, if she wanted to untie the knot in his mind, there was no avoiding the basement.

Chen Wen couldn't enter the basement on Zhou Ning's behalf, but with her knowledge of the interior, it was easy for her to create an immersive video with text and graphics. In the real world, the vault had never been opened to the public, but Chen Wen intended to guide this special visitor, operating in the deepest recesses of Zhou Ning's consciousness.

Impatient to help, Chen Wen worked hard and produced a video lasting several hours. She began by explaining the purpose and structure of the underground vault, then introduced in detail the cultural relics stored inside, telling everything she knew. When she returned to the hospital with the material, even An Ran was surprised by her efficiency.

"There are still no leads about the ghost, but Zhou Ning's treatment cannot be delayed any longer," Chen Wen said apologetically. "Let's try this first."

"It doesn't matter, you already did so much." An Ran looked exhausted, but her manner remained gentle and appropriate.

Not long later, the doctors converted the video footage into electrical signals. An Ran and Chen Wen waited nervously, holding hands, supporting each other, conveying confidence and courage. At the doctor's signal, An Ran pressed a bold green button on the machine, which emitted a low humming sound and began what the doctor described as "uploading."

In the boundless chaos, a vast and magnificent landscape unfurled. The scattered fragments of his consciousness, on the verge of drifting away completely, suddenly came together.

The painting is a large scroll, 51.5cm by 1191.5cm, painted in subdued greens. The whole is roughly divided into five sections and uses the tradi- tional scattered perspective to depict the mountains and rivers so that the composition and scenery shift with every step. Each section is interconnected, with the water surfaces, the people, fishing boats, and bridges arranged in picturesque disorder, creating a harmonious blend of varying perspectives. In terms of coloring and technique, the use of dense blues and greens as the primary tones, rendered on a base of ochre, vermilion and other shades, express the play of light and shadow upon the mountains. A combination of impasto and axe strokes is used to outline the texture of the mountains and rocks. Splashed ink techniques bring a vivid style to the sky and water surfaces, colored in shades of deep green and indigo. The entire composition is magnificent and imposing, yet remains lucid and lively. Its dazzling beauty may be attributed to its naturalness ...

Barely discernible, faint as an invocation, the ethereal female voice sounded familiar, but he was unable to recall who it belonged to.

The distant painting faded and gradually disappeared. But Zhou Ning's sense of self slowly became clearer. He was still very weak and had no idea where he was, but at least he wasn't about to sink uncon- trollably into another state of consciousness.

"At last, you're awake."

"Where am I? Who are you?"

"I am the shadow you've been chasing."

"The skeleton? The ghost shadow?"

"That is merely my projection in your world."

Surely, this was a dream. In this realm of reality and illusion, Zhou Ning felt like he was floating through clouds. There were no secrets in the universal consciousness. The voice penetrated directly into his soul.

"Do not doubt it. On your time scale, I last appeared hundreds of years ago. I am interested in you, but time is endless, after all. Even under the right natural conditions, projecting into this world requires using some familiar objects as anchors. Fortunately, I still have friends in this palace, and my paintings are well cared for among the other antiquities. Until I met you, I always used them to find my way back. But my attempts to connect with you almost cost you your life. You might blame me for acting in haste, but it took me over a decade to reach this point."

"Is it really you?" As Zhou Ning recovered from the shock, he remembered how, at his most vulnerable, he had clung to the other's consciousness like a parasite, as though the memories were his own.

"He is me, but I am not entirely him. To be precise, he is what I was before I surrendered my physical form."

"Whatever you are, someone is waiting for me outside. Can you help me get out?" A Ran must be waiting; she had never left his side. For her sake, he had to get back, no matter what.

"I've been lonely for so long. Come with me through my memories for a while, then you'll understand why I came and where you must go."

Before Zhou Ning could object, he was swept up by a great force and drawn into a river of memories reaching back nearly a thousand years ...

UI

Ever since he returned from the imperial tutor's house, his formerly lazy and indifferent supervisor was acting like an entirely different person. He busied himself in his work, and though he spoke little, his manner was highly attentive. The largest warehouse in the building had been emptied out overnight and cleaned like new. While he had suggested many times that the old files accumulated over a decade be sorted into categories and moved elsewhere, his supervisor had never paid him any mind until now.

He stepped into the warehouse uneasily. He saw a painting table made up of several long tables placed together in the center of the room, covered with a layer of palace cloth, white as silk and light to the touch. Arranged in one corner of the table was every kind of paint and pigment you could ever ask for—emerald, malachite, powdered gold, lacquer, azurite, gold leaf—all the expensive painting materials he never dreamed could be his. It was clear that the master had spared no expense this time and that the emperor attached great importance to him.

He hadn't picked up a brush in a long time and felt a little at a loss, afraid of wasting the palace's precious silks and paints. The warehouse supervisor, who was always following him, noticed his frowning and the sweat on his forehead. Thinking he couldn't stand the heat, he went out of his way to bring ice to cool him down. Hardly knowing whether to laugh or cry, he told his former boss not to disturb him for the time being and asked for some ordinary paper and ink to practice with. Embarrassed by his mistake, the warehouse supervisor hurriedly apologized before withdrawing in trepidation.

The initial panic passed quickly—after all, painting was his natural gift. Within a few days, his rough sketches were sufficiently impressive to be shown. The imperial tutor selected a few paintings and presented them to the emperor. But to his surprise, the emperor's reaction to the paintings was rather flat. He appeared more interested in the painter himself. The imperial tutor, experienced and astute, soon figured this out.

Emperor Huizong was highly accomplished in painting and calligraphy, but his eyes were higher than his head, and he claimed to be the best in the world. How could he easily express his appreciation of an unknown painter's work? However, he must have seen the great talent revealed in the painter's immature brushwork. As a mentor, he naturally wanted to meet the young man in person.

All that was fine. If the person he recommended became the emperor's student, his goals were already halfway there.

As expected, the imperial edict arrived a few days later, right on schedule. Watching the young man's thin back gradually disappearing behind the imposing palace walls, the imperial tutor sighed, a rare expression of compassion and solitude crossing his old, inscrutable face. In the end, the greatest talent is sacrificed to power. The old man hoped that by feeding the monster, he could bring peace to the realm, not realizing that everything is fleeting and living beings are the puppets of fate.

"You're that sickly child? There's no need for formalities. Many years ago, I heard of your talents from my servants at Ling Rang's mansion." The middle-aged man, ruler over the five mountains, had the aura of a king, but his face was sickly pale. Perhaps the rumors of his indulgences were more than just wind blowing through a cave.

"I am your humble servant." The young artist, prostrated upon the ground, tremblingly raised his head. He had long heard that when the emperor was still a prince, he had become friendly with his elder brother and often visited the house. Ashamed of his humble status,

410

his brother had kept him from meeting the distinguished guest. He had not expected the emperor to remember him.

However, the man's following words quickly shattered any hopeful illusions.

"The imperial tutor has shown me your sketches, and I understand his intentions. But he is always so eager to please that I hardly know what he means." The emperor seemed almost to be talking to himself. He unfurled a long scroll, one of his mountain paintings, and studied it with interest. The young artist felt too intimidated to speak.

After a long pause, the emperor addressed him again. "This painting lacks refinement. Do you know what is lacking?"

"Master once said that I was still light of years, that I had a surplus of technique but an absence of vigor, that I could paint a pretty scene but left no space for interpretation," he answered matter-of-factly.

"Haha, the imperial tutor has his opinions and believes himself to be an expert, but his vision here may be a little short-sighted. Firstly, when painting landscapes, we must make them practical, hopeful, navigable, and habitable, yet there are no signs of human habitation in your painting of mountains. How does this depict the peace and prosperity under my rule, the people living and working in harmony and contentment?

"Secondly, this painting places the peaks on an equal footing—the ruler is indistinguishable from his subjects, and the hierarchy is unclear. Such a serious violation of the rites must be punished!" The emperor's voice was mocking, but his eyes were dense with scorn.

"Forgive me, Your Majesty!"

While the first of the emperor's criticisms might be regarded as a remark on the theory and art of painting, the second comment manifested his true meaning. Every word was a stab in his heart.

"This painting was but a copy of the dry hills on the city's outskirts," he hurriedly explained. "The scenery is natural and unrefined. Your servant meant no offence!"

"*Humph!* Since the offense was unintentional, I'll spare you this once. When you go back, be sure to convey this to the imperial tutor." With a wave of his sleeve, the emperor departed.

By now, his back was soaked in cold sweat, and a feeling of desolation arose in his heart. The master used him to try and curry favor with the emperor, and the emperor used him to chastise the master.

He was like a puppet, manipulated by the ill-intentioned emperor and his minister, forced to act against his will. But he had loftier ambitions and was tired of being treated like a tool.

"Things weren't easy for you then." Zhou Ning traveled in the river of the man's memories; the ghost's youthful secrets unfolded without any barrier before his eyes, and he couldn't help but share the same feelings. He quickly hit upon a crucial question: "Did you ever paint anything to the emperor's satisfaction?"

He had wondered whether the ghost was doomed to haunt the palace because of his failure to fulfill the emperor's order. But the ghost replied calmly: "Of course, I completed the painting."

Meanwhile, the lonely youth in his memories returned despondently to the archives. The imperial tutor had waited a long time for him, but after listening to the boy, his face was uncertain, indignant, and a little afraid. Observing the young man staring at him blankly, the imperial tutor felt sure he was being mocked.

"Do as the emperor says," he growled. "If you displease him again, I'll hold you solely responsible!" Having absolved himself of any blame, the imperial tutor left hurriedly.

He never thought he'd see the emperor's most powerful courtier so driven to distraction. His heart was glad, feeling for the first time that his fate was in his own hands.

Once he had extricated himself from the complex political maneuvers of the emperor and the imperial tutor's uneasy alliance, the emperor's demands were not especially difficult. The main challenge lay in the fact that he had never painted anything of this scale before. The work would be more demanding of his abilities than anything he had previously attempted. Sometimes, he feared he would be forever trapped inside the painting, unable to escape.

He shook his head to drive away the thought. At this point, there was no longer anything to fear.

Having made up his mind, the young painter burned incense, bathed, drank plenty of water, then nailed shut the doors and windows of his studio and, seated upon the low couch, entered into a state of deep meditation. In the long river of memory, time was a vague and uncertain concept. When the ghost wanted it to move faster, it moved faster; when he wanted it to move slower, it moved slower. Zhou Ning could only infer the alternation of day and night based on the changes in light and shade penetrating the walls. But he was shocked to see that a whole three days had passed, and the young man remained motionless as if dead. Not until the fifth day did he finally awaken, his face thin and sunken but his eyes shining brightly.

He leaped up, burning with energy, wielding his brush and splashing ink, burning his entire life onto the snow-white silk. When he was done, he collapsed to the ground. He struggled to drink a little water and swallow some of the dry food he had prepared in advance, then fell back into his trance. This time, it was seven days before he awoke again.

The cycle repeated, with the young man spending increasingly longer periods in meditation. Each time he awoke, he painted unrestrainedly, expressing himself passionately on the white silk. Finally, waking from a prolonged trance that lasted twelve days, the young man put the final touches on his masterpiece.

Looking closer, Zhou Ning saw that it was the same landscape painting that had called him back. But it was no longer murky and indistinct—the mountains, the water, the people and buildings, everything in the painting was all-embracing, agile, and extraordinary.

Following Zhou Ning's train of thought, the ghost introduced the scenes in the painting one by one: "This mountain is Mount Lu. Here is a bird's eye view of Pengze Lake[11] and the marshes.

The waterfall is taken from Xianyou, and that long bridge is the Chuihong Bridge in Suzhou …"

"You were so young then. I didn't expect that you had traveled across the country." Zhou Ning sighed.

"I was a frail and sickly child. Until I entered the painting academy, I had never set foot outside my brother's house. But I have seen these things with my own eyes."

"Could it be that your soul-separation syndrome …" Zhou Ning quickly grasped the point. The ghost's self-contradictory statements pointed towards a possibility long foreshadowed but still absurd.

"Yes, my soul separation is the secret to my understanding of colors, light and shadow, even my ability to travel through space. It's not a

---

11 Pengze is the ancient name of Poyang Lake in Jiangxi province, the largest freshwater lake in China.

sickness but a power bestowed upon me by the heavens. Speaking in the words of your time, consciousness and the soul are invisible precisely because they are not confined to the three-dimensional world. Leaving one's body is akin to consciousness stepping into a higher-dimensional space. Even if the real world is thousands of miles across, in my eyes it appears in miniature, like a bonsai garden." Seeing that Zhou Ning remained skeptical, the ghost went on. "You were in this place before the accident. You felt this beauty and subtlety. You just couldn't adapt to it immediately."

Recalling his vision before the car accident, Zhou Ning finally understood. He posed one final question: "Since you can travel freely between the higher and lower dimensional worlds, why do you stay here now?"

"That is a long story," the ghost said ruefully. "Just follow me."

VII

Before half the year was gone, he completed the long scroll painting. When the emperor saw the results, he praised it endlessly. He summoned his courtiers to share in its appreciation, and everyone was astonished to learn that the painting was the work of an unknown commoner. All admired and praised the emperor for his wisdom and guidance, attributing the divine work to his enlightened rule.

The emperor drank several cups harmoniously with his subjects and then presented the painting to the imperial tutor. At the same time, he said meaningfully, "Talents are best expressed in action."

The master immediately discerned the emperor's praise and felt encouraged to serve faithfully, like a dog or horse. A weight had been lifted from his heart, and he bowed down in gratitude.

At the emperor's golden word, he became the emperor's favored student, under the guidance of the imperial brush. Pushing the boat along with the current, the imperial tutor arranged for him to be the emperor's personal attendant.

Contrary to his expectations, he found the emperor very amiable towards his attendants despite his arrogance and extravagancies. And being of the same clan, albeit not of direct royal lineage, his exceptional painting skills soon gained him the emperor's favor. For a time, he received special treatment, and his fame was unrivaled. But a sense of unreality crept in when the nights grew deep and quiet. After years of study and diligent practice, he found himself reliant on the emperor's whims. In this way, was he any different from the master and his ilk?

During his trances, when his soul wandered from his body, he traversed the great mountains and rivers and witnessed the myriad hardships endured by the common people. This led him to forge a path of awakening the world through his art, his heart connected to all under heaven. At every opportunity, he would advise the emperor to empathize with the sufferings of the common people and to refrain from monumental construction projects that exhausted the people and drained the treasury. Unfortunately, the emperor was too engrossed in his indulgences and pleasures and did not heed his words.

One day, utterly bored with his indulgences and distractions, the emperor suddenly ordered him to paint another picture. This time, he was to depict the current panorama of the world within the four seas and envisage a peaceful and prosperous era extending thousands of years into the future.

The task did not trouble him. He had long since discovered that when his soul left his body, he not only broke free of the bondage of space, but shattered the boundaries of time. With his current abilities, it was difficult to see events thousands of years in the future, but envisaging the next hundred years or so was well within his capabilities.

Up until now, he had rarely jumped through time. Firstly, it was not helpful for painting, and secondly, delving into what was divinely ordained would inevitably affect his present actions. Personal gains and losses aside, time could always counter whatever little adjustments he made. It was like throwing a stone into a river—it stirred up ripples for a moment, and then everything was calm again. Since it was futile, why bother striving?

However, he could not disobey the emperor's orders and had no choice but to comply. Most likely, the emperor wouldn't take what he painted seriously, and nothing would happen.

"Wait a minute, surely that is impossible!" Zhou Ning had followed the ghost until now, but he could no longer contain his doubts.

"Why not? Looking down from the higher-dimensional world, the mundane world appears like a ribbon of silk spiraling outwards. Vertical movements represent transformations in space, while horizontal movements signify temporal shifts. To me, there is no distinction."

"But even in my own era, when science is already so advanced, there is no evidence that the future can be predicted."

"Who says there isn't? After entering the higher-dimensional world, except under particular natural conditions, I rarely leave a shadow in the mundane world, yet I have patiently observed you. Think about it, haven't you already discovered the principle of shortest duration?"

"You mean that light travels on a zigzag line through different media but always on the path of the shortest duration in time?" Zhou Ning had already begun to piece things together, but the explanation was so mysterious that he didn't dare confirm it just yet.

"Be bold. You've seen enough bizarre things, after all," the ghost said with a smile.

"You're saying that light, even before it is emitted, somehow foresees the future and acts upon that information."

"Exactly."

All this conflicted greatly with Zhou Ning's long-held beliefs and understanding. He instinctively wanted to refute it but found himself unable to find any flaws in the theory.

"Don't let yourself be confined by low-dimensional experience. The world is more complex than you can imagine, but if you can only step away from it, you will find it extremely simple," the ghost shadow went on with a sigh. "If you still don't believe me, let me show you what I saw that time. Since it is already verified, it is the best proof."

What did he see?

The darkest future.

He had thought that everything was settled; although there were injustices in the world, things would eventually get better and get better. Who would have known that only a decade from now, the flowers would blossom into such a hell on earth? Knowing full well the fate of those who dared disobey the emperor, he depicted the horrifying scenes without concealing anything. This time, he didn't rest for a moment; the despair, resilience, and courage transformed into a raging fire, driving him to use his art to remonstrate even unto death.

Entering the inner chambers, the guards recognized him as one favored by both the emperor and the imperial tutor, and though their

416

faces were hesitant, they did not obstruct him. Unexpectedly, he happened upon a confidential conversation. Three people were in the room: the emperor sat upright with a hesitant expression, the imperial tutor stood beside him, eloquent as ever, and a foreigner clad in mink furs sat below, his face stubborn and unyielding.

Thinking of events that would unfold only ten years later, he immediately recognized the man for who he was. Disregarding etiquette, he rushed forward, exclaiming, "Your Majesty, do not believe the imperial tutor! The Liao dynasty is already weak and exhausted; it is the Jin that poses the greatest threat to our kingdom. If we form an alliance with them, when the Liao falls, we will be next!"

Their countenances changed upon hearing his words. How did this young man learn of the clandestine alliance between the two states?

The imperial tutor was the first to react. As the one who arranged this audience with the Jin envoy, he feared that the commotion caused by his student's outburst would lead both the envoy and the emperor to suspect he had leaked the information. He rushed forward and slapped the young man across the head and the face, cursing him. "Ignorant youth! How dare you meddle in politics? Get out of here!"

"You old traitor! You'll bring disaster upon the country and its people. I hope you die a painful death!" The youth glared defiantly, showing no fear. The guards hesitated, not daring to come forward.

"Wait a moment, tutor. Let him speak. I'm curious about what he has to say." The emperor dismissed the guards, turning to the master with eyes full of suspicion.

"Your Majesty, allow me to show you this painting, painted to your orders by your humble servant. If Your Majesty does not eradicate the treacherous elements and govern the realm diligently, the tragic events depicted in this painting will unfold in Kaifeng within the decade!" Seeing that the emperor's suspicion had been aroused, he abruptly unfurled the scroll, feeling that this was his chance.

The emperor, the imperial tutor, and the emissary of the Jin state all gasped simultaneously. They saw the corpses and hungry ghosts scattered throughout the painting, each grotesque and terrifying.

"I stake my life on this painting. What is shown in 'One Thousand Miles of Corpses and Skeletons' contains not the slightest falsehood. I implore Your Majesty to change course to avoid this fate!" The young

417

painter shouted himself hoarse and knocked his head on the ground until it was dripping with blood.

"You …. How dare you! The thousand miles of mountains and rivers …. How dare you curse the empire! Guards! Throw this madman in the royal prison! Cut off his head!"

Unpleasant truth grates upon the ear. The emperor turned pale with rage, and his voice trembled. The guards rushed forward and dragged the young man away. Having cast aside concerns for his own life, he laughed uproariously amidst the flurry of fists and kicks, but his laughter was tinged with immense despair.

"Retribution is coming! The unprincipled ruler dies in the northern lands, and the treacherous official is buried in the southern wilds. And all the common people of the world will be buried along with you!"

"The Jingkang Incident.[12] He didn't deceive me," Zhou Ning murmured to himself.

"Since that time, I have forsaken my physical body and entered the supreme land, knowing the mysteries of heaven and earth. I have no regrets, but I am alone here and lonely. Why don't you stay and keep me company?" suggested the ghost shadow.

"No way!" Zhou Ning opposed without hesitation. But as he calmed down, he felt a chill in his heart. Here, the ghost was all-knowing and all-powerful. What if the countless years of solitude had turned it into a paranoid, tyrannical monster?"

"Death is rest, and life is toil. In death, there is no ruler above, no subjects below, no seasonal changes; it follows the natural order of things. In the mundane world, humans live like ants, entangled in countless threads and burdened with many ties. Why should they suffer so?" The ghost spoke unhurriedly, gently persuading, guiding with skill and patience.

"If you never lived, how could you experience death? As it says in 'On the Skeleton':[13] Why do I toil when I might be at ease? I

---

12 The Jingkang Incident refers to the capture of the Northern Song capital by the Jurchen Jin Dynasty in 1127, leading to the downfall of the Northern Song Dynasty and the eventual establishment of the Southern Song Dynasty.

13 Cao Zhi's poem "On the Skeleton" reflects on the transient nature of life and the inevitability of death, using a dialogue between the poet and the skeleton to symbolize the impermanence of human existence.

firmly believe that suffering does not prevent the world from becoming a better place." After pondering for a moment, Zhou Ning
replied confidently.

"I appeared before you this time simply because I thought you
bold and curious. I never expected your thoughts to be so insightful,
so much like someone I knew ..." The ghost did not insist but spoke
with a hint of loneliness.

"Like who?" Zhou Ning asked, puzzled.

"He was also a painter. Like you, I also tried to draw him into
this world. But he rejected me for the same reasons. You are both
open-minded and optimistic people. In your eyes, the mundane world
has its own beauty, doesn't it?"

"Is that so?" Zhou Ning laughed dumbly, becoming ever more
curious about the man.

"He was born after the Southern Dynasties, quite distant from
your era. He only partially understood my words, and the painting he
made led to much speculation."[14]

By now, Zhou Ning had already guessed the identity of the ghost
and the man who preceded him, but before leaving this world, he
wanted confirmation.

"Can you tell me your name?"

"My surname is Zhao, and my given name is Ximeng."[15]

Epilogue

An Ran supported Zhou Ning as they walked together before heading
to the hospital ward. Although the CT scans showed that a small piece
of Zhou Ning's frontal lobe was missing, current research on the brain
was still limited, and its compensatory function sometimes exceeded
what was imagined to be possible. After enduring rounds of awakening

---

14 The person referred to is Li Song, a painter of the Southern Song Dynasty. His "Skeleton Fantasy"
is a surreal and imaginative artwork that combines elements of mythology and fantasy to depict a
whimsical scene featuring skeletons engaged in various playful activities.

15 Wang Ximeng (1096–1119), also known as Zhao Ximeng, was a renowned Chinese painter from
the Northern Song Dynasty, taught personally by the Emperor Huizong. At the age of 18, he created
his only surviving work, a long scroll known as "A Thousand Li of Rivers and Mountains." He died
at the age of 23.

and confusion, moments of blurred consciousness, sedation, and the removal of the ventilator, Zhou Ning finally pulled through.

Was he still the same person as before? An Ran often asked herself that. On the surface, he was as gentle, meticulous, optimistic and forward-looking as before, and even retained his past memories. However, deep down, An Ran always felt something was a little different.

"Don't worry, I'm still me," Zhou Ning joked, as though he could see into An Ran's mind. "After what I went through, aren't I allowed to be slightly more serious?" Zhou Ning put his arm around her shoulders, and they stared into each other's eyes. "There may be challenges and obstacles in the days ahead, but nothing will defeat us. Trust me, my dear."

"I believe you," she said, her heart suddenly at ease. She always felt safe at his side.

Two old acquaintances had been waiting for a while in the hospital room. Chen Wen and Director Liu were both here to see Zhou Ning. In the six months since they last met, Chen Wen had changed her hairstyle, swapped out her glasses for contact lenses, and dressed more fashionably; she looked like a freshly graduated college student.

Through An Ran's efforts and connections, Hu Yan,[16] the eccentric historian who had once helped Zhou Ning crack the "Blood Drop" case, intervened in the investigation. The case of the ghostly shadow finally caught the attention of the relevant authorities.

Perhaps because it was the first time she had witnessed such a close brush with death, during this period, Chen Wen began to have doubts about the path of her own future.

"Do you still remember why you originally chose to work in the Forbidden City?" Zhou Ning asked Chen Wen.

"I enjoyed the quiet time in the ancient palaces. As my master used to say, I can endure solitude." Zhou Ning's question brought her confusion back 'round to her original intention. Perhaps, after all, the palace museum was the best place for her.

"I'm sure that in the near future, you'll have the opportunity to restore top-tier paintings and calligraphy. These skills will be passed

---

16 Hu Yan is the protagonist's best friend, first appearing in the story "Blood Disaster," published in issue 4 of the Chinese edition of *Galaxy's Edge*.

down to you and flourish under your hands." After comforting Chen Wen, Zhou Ning turned to greet his former leader. Director Liu appeared a little embarrassed. After all, he hadn't initially given much attention to the case, and now he had to deliver some news to Zhou Ning, but was unsure how to broach the subject.

"Director Liu, I'll soon be leaving the police. I want to thank you for taking care of me all this time. Even though I won't be working there anymore, my heart will always be with my brothers in the bureau," Zhou Ning said sincerely.

"But …" Director Liu was somewhat taken aback. He hadn't even mentioned the news yet—how did Zhou Ning already know? For a moment, he wasn't sure how to respond.

"An old friend is arriving soon, and I'll be busy again," Zhou Ning said with a smile, speaking almost to himself.

Before he finished speaking, the hospital room door was pushed open, and a chubby man rushed in. It was Hu Yan.

"Can you move?" Hu Yan asked jokingly.

"Brother, I'm perfectly fine," Zhou Ning replied.

"Good, then you're joining our Abnormal Incident Bureau team."

The two exchanged a smile, then high-fived in tacit understanding.

Editor Biography

Lezli Robyn is an Australian author, developmental editor, and assistant publisher, who lives in Myrtle Beach, South Carolina, with her blue-eyed chiweenie, Bindi. Since her first short story sale to *Clarkesworld*, Lezli has sold short fiction to over a dozen countries, to professional markets like *Asimov's* and *Analog*. She is the Associate Publisher at Arc Manor, the current editor of the *Galaxy's Edge* science fiction/fantasy anthology series, and the developmental editor for the Caezik SF & Fantasy and Caezik Romance imprints.

Lezli Robyn has been an Aurealis Award finalist for Best SF Story, a finalist for the Spanish Premio Ignotus Award for Best Foreign Short Story, and a finalist for the prestigious Astounding Award for Best New Writer. She has also won the Catalan Premi Ictineu Award for Best Translated Story twice. Her first solo short story collection, *Bittersuite*, and her first urban fantasy novel, *In Her Wake*, is forthcoming.

Printed in the USA
CPSIA information can be obtained
at www.ICGtesting.com
JSHW082359151024
71761JS00006B/166